Praise for

"Uncommonly good storytelling."
—Beth Kery, *New York Times* bestselling author

"Scintillating sexual chemistry."
—Lauren Dane, *New York Times* bestselling author

"Anne Calhoun . . . tugs at your heart."
—Jill Shalvis, *New York Times* bestselling author

Also by Anne Calhoun

GOING DEEP

Anne Calhoun

St. Martin's Paperbacks

This is a work of fiction. All of the characters, organizations, and events portrayed in this novel are either products of the author's imagination or are used fictitiously.

GOING DEEP

For information address St. Martin's Press, 175 Fifth Avenue, New York, NY 10010.

ISBN: 978-1-250-08462-0

Our books may be purchased in bulk for promotional, educational, or business use. Please contact your local bookseller or the Macmillan Corporate and Premium Sales Department at 1-800-221-7945, ext. 5442, or by e-mail at MacmillanSpecialMarkets@macmillan.com.

Printed in the United States of America

St. Martin's Paperbacks edition / November 2016

St. Martin's Paperbacks are published by St. Martin's Press, 175 Fifth Avenue, New York, NY 10010.

10 9 8 7 6 5 4 3 2 1

For Jeffe Kennedy.
Thanks for the brainstorming session.
Sorry about the lemon drop martini!

For Robin Rotham,
who read the early draft and knew exactly how to fix it.

And for Eileen Rothschild,
who polished out the rough spots.

As always, for Mark.

CHAPTER ONE

It was good to be home.

Cady Ward stood under the spotlight, the crowd's manic, vibrant energy rolling at her in waves, all but lifting her off her feet with the surging roar and applause. She smiled, lifted a hand in acknowledgment. The clapping and whistles tick up again. Sweat trickled down her ribs and spine. Her silk tank top clung to her skin as she shifted her guitar to her back, put her hands together, and bowed her appreciation to the crowd. Some of them were still singing the refrain to "Love-Crossed Stars," her biggest hit, the final song of her encore set.

"Thank you," she murmured, not sure if the sound engineer had cut her mic feed or not. Though they echoed back into her earpiece, the spoken words were lost in the din inside Lancaster's Field Energy Center.

Hometown crowds were always generous. By this time in the show, after two encores and several minutes of applause, people started to trickle out, maybe making one last stop at the merchandise table for a T-shirt or a magnet or a CD. But these folks showed no signs of dispersing. Just as reluctant to leave the high behind, Cady bent over and made her way along the edge of the stage, high-fiving and clasping hands with the people in the front rows. Her Nana's bracelet, a cherished keepsake she always wore when she performed, nearly clonked a girl on the forehead as Cady swept by. "We love you, Maud!" she cried out, borderline hysterical as she waved her homemade poster.

Maud was Cady's stage name, borrowed from her grandmother back when she needed a persona to work up the courage to put her voice out there, back when all she wanted was to be Beyoncé, Sia, Adele, a one-name wonder with multiple hits, Grammys, platinum albums. But after eight months of touring as Maud, she was back in her hometown, able to spend a few weeks being herself. Ordinary Cady Ward.

"I love you too!" she called back, vaguely aware that lurking behind the adrenaline rush of performing was the knowledge that tomorrow she'd feel like someone had taken a stick to her legs and back. Out of the corner of her eye she saw her manager, Chris Wellendorf, standing in the wings, tight shoulders and unsmiling face telegraphing his nervous tension. He didn't like it when she got too close to the fans without security personnel at hand. All it took was one crazy person to break a finger or stab her with something, one interaction gone wrong to spread all over social media.

She straightened and stepped back, automatically adjusting both bracelet and guitar, then held up her hands. "Thanks for coming, everyone. Happy holidays. Drive safely, and good night!"

The wave of applause carried her offstage, and continued until the lighting engineer cut the stage lights and turned up the house lights. Breathing hard, Cady washed up against the wall. Around her, the band was efficiently packing away their instruments. Next, the road crew would take down the set, then the stage. By the end of the night, the auditorium would be empty, waiting silently for the next event. Given the time of year—early December—probably a Lancaster College basketball game.

"I can't sing it again." She turned to look at Chris. "I can't. If I have to sing 'Love-Crossed Stars' one more time, I will go out of my mind."

"That's the end of the tour talking. 'Love-Crossed Stars' will be your cash cow for the rest of your life. Besides, you think Paul Simon doesn't roll out 'Sounds of Silence' or 'Graceland' or 'Mrs. Robinson' at every show?"

"Paul Simon has dozens of songs he can use for a final encore," Cady said. "Dozens. All of them brilliant. All of them telling profound stories about the human condition. Are any of them love songs? No."

"Paul Simon is Paul Simon, with fifty years of singing and songwriting behind him. You are just starting out. Be happy. It was a good show," Chris said.

"You always say that," Cady replied, looking around for her water bottle.

"And I always mean it," Chris said smoothly, producing a bottle from his jacket pocket and restoring the normally impeccable lines of his suit. In concession to the casual concert venue, he'd stuffed his tie into his pocket and opened the top two buttons of his shirt. A single strand of his dishwater blond hair escaped from the gel slicking it back, giving him a vaguely rumpled look. "This time was different. Normally you're dialed up to eleven on the scale. Tonight you were around fifteen."

"These are my peeps," Cady said after she swallowed half the water. She hooked her thumb in her guitar strap and hoisted it over her head. "I'm home. I've been playing for them since I was fifteen, busking in SoMa."

"Usually without a permit," came a familiar voice next to her.

"Eve, hi!" She backed away a step when Eve reached for her. "No, you really don't want to hug me. I've sweated through my jeans."

"Don't be ridiculous," Eve said, and swept her up. "That was amazing! I loved the new take on "Summer Nights." Where do you get your energy? You've been on the road for weeks now!"

Cady hugged her back, just as hard, so grateful for her friend's early and vocal support. Chris was checking Eve out, not all that covertly, either. Eve had that kind of impact on men, even in jeans, ankle boots, and a crisp white button-down. "I've been on the road for *months*. We did the state fair circuit over the summer, where I ate every kind of food on a stick you can eat."

"Including fried candy bars?" Eve asked.

"*All* the fried candy bars," Cady said. Performing burned so many calories, she could eat whatever she wanted and stay in shape. "I drew the line at a Twinkie log on a stick, though," she added before finishing the rest of the water.

"You've got standards," Eve said, still smiling. "Oh, it's so good to see you!"

"You too." Absently, Cady introduced Chris and Eve, peering around the rapidly dismantling backstage, looking for her sister and mother. She heard Emily before she saw her, high-pitched voice, the clatter of heels as she rounded the corner and made straight for Cady.

"You're home!" Emily shrieked and launched herself at Cady.

"You're taller!" Cady laughed into Emily's hair as she wrapped her arms around Cady and pulled her close. "Great outfit," she said when Emily let go long enough for her to lean back and get a closer look.

"She tried on everything she owned," her mother said, coming in for a hug.

"Hi, Mom. Thanks for coming," Cady said.

"Ah, good to see you again, Mrs. Ward," Chris said.

Her mother smiled at him and reached for Cady to give her a quick hug and kiss. "We need to get home soon. It's a school night."

"It's Cady's homecoming concert! We talked about this. I'm going to drive Cady back to—" Chris shot her a warning glance. Emily transitioned smoothly. "—home."

"You said you were going to do that, and I said I don't want you driving late at night."

"Mom," Emily started mulishly.

"It's fine," Cady said, snagging her guitar case from the roadie who'd appeared beside her. Best to head off a fight at the pass. "I'm coming home tonight, so Emily will get a good night's sleep. Right, Em?"

Emily had the good sense to be gracious in victory, giving their mother a big hug and standing demurely by Cady's side to hold the guitar case for her. "You really like the outfit?"

At sixteen, her sister was five ten without the three-inch heels, slender as a wire coat hanger. She wore a black skirt with car wash pleats, a slim gray turtleneck, and gray suede over-the-knee boots that left a good four inches of bare thigh. The outfit would have been sleek New York professional except Emily had gone for broke with her makeup, layering in smoky eyes, a hint of blush, and dark lips. She looked far older and more sophisticated than the gawky girl Cady remembered from her last visit in February, before Emily's birthday. Emily had been trying on styles for a couple of years now, trying to find who she was as a growing woman. "You look amazing," Cady said.

"I made the skirt," Emily started. "The sweater's from—"

A mic stand tipped into an equalizer before crashing to the floor just before a man stumbled out from behind a wall of boxed equipment. He untangled his feet, then tripped again as the mic stand rolled back in his direction. He got himself upright and looked around with the fierce concentration of the stupidly drunk. He caught sight of Cady, and everyone stopped talking.

"Maud!" he yelled. Man-bun drooping at his nape, he stretched a hand toward her. "Maud, I need to talk to you!"

"Who's that?" Emily asked.

"No idea." Cady quickly scanned the backstage area for an exit strategy. The last thing she wanted to do was bolt onto the stage, where a crowd still lingered, with their phones and cameras. Her back was literally to the wall, and her little sister stood beside her in heels Cady would bet her Fender Emily couldn't run in. As unobtrusively as she could, she stepped in front of her not-so-little sister.

"You said we didn't need security in Lancaster," Chris said, his voice low and calm, not taking his eyes off the man.

"We don't. . . . Hey, big guy," she said easily. "What's up?"

"Maud, I love you. I love you, and I want to be with you, and I've written some songs for us to sing together."

Once, just once, I want a man to confess his love for me using my real name. Not Maud. "Really? I could use some new material," she said, because keeping him talking was obviously the right thing to do, and because behind the drunk, two men in police polos with badges and guns clipped to their belts had materialized. One had reddish brown hair and a lean build that would be easy to underestimate. The other man had a good six inches and fifty pounds of muscle on the drunk guy and shoulders as broad as a steer's that tapered to a narrow waist. His dark brown hair swooped back from his forehead, emphasizing a square face dominated by cheekbones and a fighter's chin.

"Hi, Matt," Eve said, lifting a hand in a casual wave. Her tone was totally relaxed, but Cady knew that "Matt" was a detective with the Lancaster Police Department. Her attention switched from the admirer, stumbling into boxes and amplifiers and lighting rigs, to the two men stalking him from behind and back again. Cady was pretty sure "Matt" wasn't Shoulders, the one who'd drawn up silent as smoke just behind the drunk guy. She got a flash of slate blue eyes when he flicked a glance her way. *Distract him.*

"Um . . . what kind of songs?" she asked.

"A sequel to 'Love-Crossed Stars.' It's about our love. Because I love you."

Beside her, Chris snorted. Trust him to find this amusing. "Uh-huh," she said. Shoulders was inches from the guy's back, so she flashed her brightest smile, gave him a bobblehead nod, and lied through her teeth. "That's my favorite song. I'd love to sing a sequel."

When Shoulders' badge and gun registered in her admirer's alcohol-soaked brain, he swung out wildly. Shoulders ducked an ineptly aimed backhand and stepped right into the drunk's body, shoving him off-balance then catching his arm on the forward swing.

"Hey," the drunk guy said, indignant, struggling. "Get the fuck off me, man. I just want to talk to her."

The taller cop got the guy's other arm in a firm grip, then locked eyes with Shoulders over the flailing drunk's head. "One . . . two . . . three."

Shoulders thrust his leg behind the drunk's knee. A neat twist of hips, and they took the drunk down, facefirst on the floor. A grunt, then a high-pitched yelp. "Ow! Maud!"

"Hey, Romeo," Shoulders said, snapping a cuff around the man's wrist. "You think this is your best move? Coming backstage where you don't belong, smelling like a frat party?"

"I just wanted to talk to her," the drunk slurred. "I love her. We're going to make music together."

Shoulders clicked the cuff around the second wrist, then

nodded at the other cop. Together they hoisted the guy up and set him on his feet. It was an impressive display of strength, given that the drunk guy's man-bun balanced out a significant beer-and-wings gut. Cady found herself staring at the band around the sleeve of Shoulders' polo choking his biceps, the way the muscles in his forearms shifted as he easily controlled his prisoner.

"How about you write her a nice letter from jail?" Shoulders said. "No, I've got this," he said to the other cop. "You stay with Eve. Come on, Romeo. You can serenade the rest of the drunk and disorderlies in the van."

Everyone watched him guide the drunk guy through the maze of equipment, including Cady's suitcases. She cast them a loathing look. Tonight was the last night she'd live out of her suitcase. Tomorrow she would unpack in her own house, eat food from her own fridge, sleep in her own bed.

"Cady, darling, the only reason we let Evan go was you saying Lancaster was safe. That nothing ever happened here. That you were no big deal here," Chris muttered.

Evan had been her bodyguard on the tour. An obsessive workout that required two hours a day in the gym meant he had the strong half of "strong silent type" down, but he talked almost incessantly, a running commentary mostly on his workout and diet that, over the course of the tour, drove Cady nuts. "It is. It was," Cady replied, fingering the bracelet in a habitual nervous gesture before she caught herself. "And you know Evan had to go. I was ready to kill him in Topeka."

"Barbecued beef tongue is delicious," Chris said, back on his phone.

"It's tongue. It's gross. I didn't care that he ate it. I cared that he wouldn't freaking shut up about it."

The chestnut-haired cop strode over to the small, frozen group. "You all right, Ms. Ward?" he asked, his gaze skimming the group before settling on Eve.

"I'm fine," Cady said. Her voice sounded almost giddy. She wasn't sure if she was relieved the guy was gone, or that this was obviously Eve's Matt. "Thank you for handling that so quickly. Please tell the other officer . . ."

"McCormick."

"Please give Officer McCormick my thanks."

"I will," he said.

"Cady, this is Matt," Eve said, as if the smile on her face and the delight in her eyes didn't give it away. "Matt, meet Cady."

"Nice to officially meet you," Matt said with a nod. "I'm a big fan."

"Thank you. I've heard so much about you from Eve."

"That's not good," Matt said easily.

"It wasn't all bad," Cady said, to laughter.

"He's been a fan almost as long as I have," Eve said. "Your first Maud concert was when?"

"The Slowdown, five, no six years ago," Matt said.

"Wow, that is a long time," Cady agreed. She'd been nineteen, on her father's shit list for refusing to go to college, singing wherever she could get a gig and eating ramen noodles out of Styrofoam cups. "I was still singing covers at that point."

"Yeah, but you had something," Eve said. "We all knew it."

"Thanks," Cady said again. She was too tired to think of something more creative to say, but with Eve she didn't have to. "I really need to get going. Emily has school tomorrow."

"Of course," Eve said. "Get some rest, then come see me. I'd love to have you at Eye Candy when you're ready."

"Ms. Ward won't be taking any engagements for the next few weeks," Chris said smoothly.

"It's not an engagement," Cady said. "It's a favor for a friend. A very dear friend."

Chris gave her a look reminding her that she needed to rest her voice. Only a few people knew about the upcoming album for which the label planned a surprise Beyoncé-style drop around Valentine's Day, less than three months away. The thought made her stomach turn a slow loop. Chris chalked it up to nerves, to exhaustion, to creative fatigue, to anything but Cady's growing uncertainty that the album was the right thing to release now.

Chris broke the silence. "We can talk about it tomorrow, when you've had a chance to rest up. I've booked a car for you."

"Hello, remember me? I'm taking her home," Emily said.

"Even better." Chris slid his phone back into his jacket pocket. "With you she's totally anonymous."

Emily's eyes darkened behind the mask of makeup. "Our time together starts now," Cady said cheerfully. "Let's grab my suitcases and we can head out."

Cady, Eve, Matt, and Chris scuffled over who would carry the two enormous suitcases she'd lugged all over North America on tour buses and the occasional plane for the last eight months. Matt and Chris finally won, and followed Emily's runway catwalk stride through the backstage area to the arena door. Eve and Cady trailed behind them.

The cold air instantly froze the sweat still drying in her clothes. Cady shivered, and Chris immediately pulled her back inside. "No way are you going out there without a coat and a scarf," he said. "Em, pull the car around for her."

He unzipped one suitcase and flung the lid back. The thick, spiral-bound notebook Cady used as a diary and scratch pad for songwriting slid out of the unzipped mesh pocket, onto the floor. Cady crouched down and gathered it up, tucking it back into the pocket along with an assortment of cocktail napkins and scraps of paper.

"Working on anything new?" Eve asked, helping her gather the loose paper. She'd been around Cady long enough to know that her process was firmly twentieth century.

"I am," she said, shooting a defiant glare at Chris across her suitcase. With a total disregard for her privacy, he rummaged through a stack of underwear and her nightie, shifting heels and Converse, and two of her favorite T-shirts, in search of her scarf and coat.

"She's always writing," Chris said, extracting the thick green scarf and her down jacket from the bottom of the bag. "Put these on. Hot water with honey. Bed."

"I know the routine," she said. She shoved her arms into the coat sleeves and wound the scarf around her face and throat.

"Part of the routine is me reminding you to take care of yourself," Chris said.

"I know," she said, this time softly, in apology. Snapping at Chris was a sign of her exhaustion. He'd been her manager and agent, her advocate and supporter, since the day he saw her singing on a street corner outside a Harry Linton concert, tracked down her YouTube channel, and signed her.

He smiled back and zipped up the suitcase. Properly mummified, Eve opened the door again. Em's Corolla was idling by the arena's loading dock. Matt and Chris stored the suitcases in the trunk while Cady slid into the passenger seat. Heat blasted from the vents, almost making up for the cold air billowing in the open door.

"I'll call you," Chris said, leaning over the frame. "We need to talk about your security."

"No, we don't," Cady replied.

"My flight's at four," he said implacably. "I'll call around ten."

"Fine," she said absently. She wanted to ask Eve's Matt about Shoulders, but couldn't think of a way to do it that wouldn't set a bad example for Emily, so she called, "I'll see you soon!" to Eve and Matt, and closed the door on Chris's yelp about not raising her voice.

Emily zipped out of the parking lot and turned onto Tenth Street, then braked hard at the red light. Cady's shoulder harness jerked. She shot Emily a glance, but her sister stared straight ahead. In the streetlight her eye makeup was starting to smear. Cady couldn't even imagine what her face and hair looked like. After a show, her face could resemble melting plastic as the lights and sweat worked away at enough makeup to animate her facial features.

"What's wrong?"

"Nothing."

In that tone of voice, something was obviously wrong. "Em," Cady said.

No response. The light changed and Emily accelerated into traffic. Her sister's expression, shrouded in darkness broken only by the dashboard lights, was still a little lost, a little mad. She reached across the console and hugged her sister. "I've missed you."

The car swerved in the lane before Emily corrected. "Knock it off, teen driver here," she said through giggles as she lifted one hand and hugged Cady back. "Mom just started letting me drive with other people in the car. If I get in an accident now, I'll be in so much trouble."

"When you move to New York, you won't need to drive," Cady said. "Have you sent in your application?"

A junior in high school, Emily was applying to Parsons School of Design. It was all she could talk about, and based on the state of her fingernails, all she'd been worrying about while Cady was on the road. "Not yet." She drove a little more smoothly out of the downtown neighborhood. "I'm still working on my portfolio. Maybe I can show it to you tomorrow, before you abandon me for your new big fancy house?"

"Sure," Cady said. "Thanks for getting the house ready for me. I'm so excited to see it. How about we plan on having you sleep over this weekend? You can help me decorate."

Emily's face lit up. "Ugh, I've got homework, stupid finals coming up, the application, but we can hang out when I'm off."

"I remember what December's like when you're in high school," Cady said with a laugh. "It'll be fun. Like old times."

The drive through the back streets into one of Lancaster's older neighborhoods took Cady back in time. Her mother still lived in the house she'd bought after their dad left. It was small, but refurbished inside and out. The house was from the fifties but recently renovated top to bottom, three bedrooms, a full bathroom she'd shared with Emily, a three-quarters bath off her mom's bedroom, a kitchen with an eating area that overlooked the backyard and a den. Lights burned brightly over the front and side doors, but her mother's bedroom window was dark.

Her sister grabbed the bigger, heavier suitcase and started lugging it toward the door. "What's up with you and Harry?"

"Nothing," Cady said as they hauled the bags through the front door. Thank goodness. In hindsight, starting a relationship with an international superstar just before her first album dropped was great for her visibility and pretty disastrous for her heart.

"That's too bad," Emily said. "He got you a ton of publicity when you were dating."

"We weren't dating."

"I know that's the official line, but still. He was cute, too. Want some Maud juice before bed?"

"I can make it," Cady said. Exhaustion seemed to seep from her pores, but she needed to take care of her throat or Chris would worry.

"I'll do it. You unpack." Emily strode into the kitchen.

Cady got her bags into what had been her room until Emily converted it into a studio after she left, using a big piece of plywood to transform the single bed into a cutting board. Emily had moved the wood to the sewing station that took up most of the floor space. The wall above the sewing table was plastered with images torn from magazines: *Vogue,* the *New York Times* Style inserts, some that were obviously printed from the social media feeds of up-and-coming designers. Mixed in with the high fashion photo shoots were images of a teen star Cady recognized from a show featuring teenage werewolves in Manhattan. Her current crush. Which made her think of Harry, and try to figure out how long that had been over. Months and months. Which meant it had been a very long time since she'd gone to bed with anyone, superstar or not. Adrift on a sea of exhaustion, she found herself staring at the narrow bed, wondering if there was any way she could fit herself and Shoulders, aka McCormick, into that bed.

That wasn't going to happen. It was a random encounter with a man doing his job, nothing more. She left the bags where they were and walked back down the hall to the kitchen, where Emily was drizzling honey into steaming water. A cup of hot cocoa sat on the counter.

"Does that happen often?" Em asked.

"What?" she asked, still distracted by the memory of Shoulders' muscles flexing.

"Crazy drunk guys coming out of the shadows." Emily held out the mug.

Usually security prevented them from doing much more

than shouting from the public areas. To avoid worrying her mother and Emily, she'd kept the details of her security from them.

"Meh." Cady shrugged in what she hoped was a casual way and held out her cup for Emily to clink in a toast. She sipped the drink that was as much honey as water, and let out a sigh. She'd shed Chris, her stylist, her bodyguard, the band, the roadies, the fans, and was finally alone and home, the place she'd been longing for. Everyone thought she was home for the holidays, catching up on sleep and Netflix.

Emily was watching her over the rim of her mug. "I'm serious, Cade."

Cady gave her a tired smile and sipped her honey water. "Forget about him. I have, because it's so good to be home."

CHAPTER TWO

Connor McCormick drove through the gate in the six-foot chain-link fence topped with razor wire encircling McCool's Garage and pulled into an empty parking space. When he opened his door, the November wind bit through his denim jacket, so he flipped up the sheepskin collar, shoved his hands in his jeans pockets, and trotted around the corner of the building, ignoring the door labeled OF-FICE in favor of the unmarked one next to the bays. The sound of an air-powered socket tightening a bolt covered his footsteps.

His closest friend, Shane McCool, stood under Conn's '69 Camaro ZL1, cursing steadily as he cranked away at the car's undercarriage.

"Hey."

Shane jumped about a mile, barking his knuckles on the transmission housing when his grip slipped. "Jesus Christ," he said, his smile softening the words. "A little warning?"

"What's wrong?"

"Your fuel pump, that's what's wrong. You need another

new one, and you need to race this beauty more than once a month."

"I've been busy," Conn said. "Work."

"Then let me put on an aftermarket fuel pump."

"You know the rules," Conn said. "Nothing on this car changes. The weight needs to stay exactly the same."

"Yeah, except when something else falls off," Shane quipped. He reached into the backseat and hauled out an alternator. "If I'm making another trip to U-Pull-It, want me to find one of these, too? For when this one breaks."

"Yeah. At least my Dad drove a Camaro. He could have raced a Model T."

"You know," Shane said, "you probably did more damage to your times by gaining twenty pounds of muscle than I would by putting on an aftermarket fuel pump," Shane said.

"I weigh what Dad weighed," Conn said as he ducked under the Camaro and peered up into the undercarriage. "She's leaking oil, too," he observed.

"I can see that," Shane said testily. He was shorter than Conn's six foot five by three inches, and carrying more fat, but enough muscle to threaten. "You're a couple of races away from blowing the head gasket. I've had a couple of offers to buy her . . ."

Conn ignored the suggestion. "Not yet," he said. "We're coming on the best part of the season. I'll beat his time."

His father's dial-in time was 9.99 seconds. The closest Conn had come to his father's best time in the ZL1 was ten even. Less time than it took to blink. He was racing the car his father raced, with the same components, at the same weight. At this point the only difference was driver reflexes. Conn could live with the car being the reason he couldn't beat his dad's time, but it wasn't. Every time his time flashed on the scoreboard felt like a backhand to the face. A reminder he couldn't get out of his head.

Quick reflexes aside, in the rest of his life his dad had been a small-time loser more invested in his own ego than in his family. He'd skipped town more times than Conn could count, chasing the next scheme, the next big thing, until finally he stayed gone for good, leaving Conn to bounce among his extended relatives, none of them all that excited about raising a deadbeat's kid, all of them relieved when he joined the army straight out of high school. Conn had enough psychology classes under his belt to know why he wanted to beat his dad's time. He just couldn't figure out how to do it.

Shane tucked the socket wrench back into its slot on his massive toolbox. "Fine. I'll go to U-Pull-It and freeze my balls off finding you a part that will blow in two races, max."

"You need a self-confidence course." Conn grinned as he turned a shoulder into Shane's halfhearted punch. "This one lasted three."

McCormick and McCool. In every elementary school classroom they'd been seated in the same row, Shane with his shock of white-blond hair, angelic face, and burning desire to repair cars like his dad. He sat in front of Conn, with his dark hair, motor mouth, and burning desire to race cars like *his* dad. After a while all they knew was that if they came up with the idea together, it was a bad one, but they'd sure as hell have fun until the shit hit the fan. Until he left the army and joined the LPD, Shane was the only person Conn trusted, the only person Conn counted as family.

"I'm off today. We'll freeze our balls off together."

"They're your balls," Shane said. "I'm out for lunch," he called to the two mechanics who worked for him, the words barely audible over the air compressors. Thumbs-up from both of them, then Shane pulled on a Carhartt jacket, grabbed a travel toolbox, and clomped after Conn.

They drove out to the junkyard and spent an hour searching for the part, then another hour getting it out. By the time they finished, Conn had grease all over his hands and clothes, and Shane's face was as white as his hair.

They drove to an East Side dive diner known for giving customers heart attacks and ordered chicken fried steak lunches, warming their hands around cups of coffee while they waited for the food.

"Have you ever considered that you just might not be able to do it?" Shane said finally.

He knew exactly what Shane meant. "All the time," Conn answered. "Can you get the fuel pump in by the race this weekend? "

"Yeah, only because you're buying lunch. And because I like your sorry ass, for reasons that still aren't clear to me."

"Thanks."

Shane wiped his mouth with his napkin and stretched one arm along the back of the booth. "What's new?"

"I worked security at some concert over the weekend."

"The Maud Ward concert?" His eyebrows popped toward his hairline. "You worked that?"

"Yeah."

"How was it?"

Conn shrugged and shook pepper all over his fries. "It was a girl singing pop songs. I was working."

"You do know who she is, don't you? She's from Lancaster. Spent years going from club to club, singing for anyone who would listen, posting videos online. Some famous manager saw her performing on the street one night and got her a recording deal."

Conn swallowed his mouthful of fries and signaled the waitress for more coffee. "I just work security."

"You work security at concerts all the time—"

"It's an off-duty job that pays good," Conn interjected.

"And you never pay attention to the concert."

"I'm working," Conn repeated patiently. "Surveilling the crowd for threats. Making sure people are safe. You know. Being a cop. A drunk guy somehow got through security and headed for her backstage. He was halfway into his declaration of undying love and devotion, but we took him down before he could, you know, show her his songs."

Shane laughed. "You stood in the way of true love?"

Conn snorted.

"I bet she probably hears that all the time," Shane said. "What's she like up close? Pretty?"

Conn considered this. Sleek, poker-straight hair. Wide brown eyes rimmed with enough eyeliner to make her look like a manga character. Skin and bones. "She looked like every other celebrity you see," he said. "Hair, makeup, clothes, they all look like they ordered from the same shiny catalog. She handled herself pretty well, though. Kept him focused so me and Dorchester could sneak up on him."

"You have all the fun," Shane said.

"You want to do this job?"

"No way," Shane said with a chuckle. "I'm happy where I am."

Shane didn't need the police department like Conn did. Shane had four brothers and extended family spread out all over Lancaster. His mother had been including Conn in family holidays and big celebrations since junior high school, but while Conn always went, his real family was the police department. All the dynamics were right: brothers and sisters doing the job every day, father figures in his training officers, stern maternal ones in the women who'd fought the first battles for equality, the offbeat ones you avoided. The McCools included him, but the department was like the McCools on crack, and steroids. Most cops felt the same way. Family was family, but the department was blood. It's why working the job tended to run in families, sons and daughters following in their fathers' footsteps. It drew you in, formed your thinking, your feelings. Once you were in, you stayed in. Very few cops quit for other jobs, because very few jobs provided the same high, or the same connection.

It was the only family Conn counted as his own.

As if he could read minds, Shane said, "Mom's expecting you for Christmas."

Conn's phone, silent through the meal, buzzed. He picked it up and read a text from the duty sergeant. *The Block. Now.*

Something big must be going down for him to call Conn into the East Side Precinct on his day off. He wasn't detailed to the undercover unit, but had gotten a reputation as a useful officer for street work. Clean-shaven with his hair slicked back, he looked like a cop. Tousled, unshaven, in a stretched-out, grimy wife-beater, he looked like a guy fresh out of prison looking to score a hit. Hawthorn didn't hesitate to use him when he needed him.

"Work calls," Conn said.

"Me too," Shane said. "I'll have that fuel pump in by the weekend."

"Thanks." Conn paid the bill, then drove Shane back to his shop. After a couple of years on the job and a few run-ins with sergeants, he lost the jitters that appeared any time he got called on the carpet. But something about this had his stomach kicking around the chicken fried steak.

Underneath the layer of Christmas cheer—garland, lights, a decorated tree sheltering toys for the boys and girls club—the precinct was business as usual with civilians filing reports, uniformed officers catching up on paperwork, detectives making calls. Even in the age of email and texts, the phones still rang constantly, doubling up on each other. It was a familiar sound, one Conn walked through without thinking much about it. He was in a place where he didn't have to listen for the unexpected, where he could turn down the preternatural alertness he'd learned early in life.

He rapped his knuckles on the duty sergeant's office door, waited until the guy looked up. "Hey, how's it going?"

"Hawthorn wants to see you," he said, his face blank.

Conn felt his eyebrows pull together slightly. The sergeant was easygoing, and had a reputation for backing his officers in questionable situations. Conn had given him no grief, or less than he usually gave a sergeant. "Where is he?" he asked.

"Briefing room," the sergeant said, and went back to his paperwork.

Conn made a right at the bullpen and turned into the briefing room to find Hawthorn waiting for him, a couple of manila folders in his hand. "Close the door," he said.

Conn closed it, shoved his fists into his jeans pockets. Lieutenant Hawthorn gestured for Conn to sit down, so he did, shifting his hands to his jacket pockets.

"What can you tell me about arrest of Jordy Bettis?"

Conn frowned, and stared straight at his LT. Other cops managed to look at people without coming across like they were two seconds away from hitting something. Hawthorn was capably demonstrating that exact technique: cool, collected stare, unwavering but also not challenging. Conn still hadn't mastered it. "Not much to tell. It was a noise disturbance call. He got in my face. I arrested him. It's in my report."

"I want to hear it from you. What was Bettis's condition when you booked him?"

Conn felt his shoulders hitching up toward his ears, and consciously lowered them. "I had to take him down to get him cuffed, so he's probably got a few bruises."

Without a word Hawthorn flipped open the manila folder to reveal pictures of a battered, beaten face. Two black eyes. Split lip. A gash on his cheekbone fastened together with surgical tape.

"He's got multiple bruises on his torso consistent with a beatdown, and no defensive wounds other than deep abrasions on his wrists."

Incredulous, Conn flashed a look at Hawthorn. "You suggesting I handcuffed this guy then beat the crap out of him?"

"That's what his lawyer's suggesting," Hawthorn said.

Conn's brain danced sideways, like a deer on black ice. Hawthorn opened another folder and slid it across the table. "Look that over. If you have anything to add, or change, now's the time to do it."

Conn kept his hands in his pockets. He didn't even look down at the report. "I stand by my initial report, sir. Whatever happened to him did not happen in my custody."

The open file remained on the table between them. Conn had spent enough time in offices to know the furniture was pretty much the same—gray tables, chairs and cubicle walls in matching fabric. The difference here was the guns, the uniforms, the handcuffs, and the fact that this was the only world had Conn ever wanted to be in.

"It's not your first time having this conversation," Hawthorn said.

That's what was in the other file. Conn's personnel record. He felt the tips of his ears heat, but he didn't respond. Hawthorn could read, and he was third-generation LPD, the son of the former chief of police, now the mayor. He had knowledge and connections in the department Conn couldn't begin to imagine, much less understand. Connor didn't make the mistake of assuming Hawthorn didn't know every single detail of Conn's history from the moment he reported to the academy.

"No, sir," he said finally.

"Four months ago you drove your cruiser through a chain-link fence."

"In pursuit of a suspected rapist," Conn said. "I caught him, too."

"Six months before that you used the butt of your service weapon to threaten a suspect who was driving away from a scene."

"I was on the running board of the guy's Flex while he accelerated up the Thirteenth Street on-ramp to the interstate," Conn said. "He was endangering my life."

"The individual, when apprehended, also suffered abrasions and bruises."

"He fucking tripped over his own fucking feet when he was running away!" Conn took a deep breath and reached deep for some self-control. "How is it my fault he faceplanted in the gravel by the side of the road?"

Hawthorn's gaze was bland and level, his voice perfectly modulated. "It's your fault, Officer McCormick, because part of the job is keeping control of situations, not escalating them."

Conn remembered how surprised he'd been when Hawthorn pulled him off patrol to work undercover. Conn knew where he was going to spend his days as a LPD officer: on patrol, in a cruiser. He didn't have the temperament to make detective. He sat back, breathing slow and deep, trying to keep his temper under control, knowing he was walking a very fine line between angry and insubordinate. "What's going on here, LT?"

"I'm reassigning you," Hawthorn said.

Conn was on his feet, leaving his stomach around his knees. "LT, I didn't do that!"

Hawthorn's gaze flashed over Conn's fists, planted on the table, and the breadth of his shoulders. It was a subtle, Hawthornesque reminder of the very temper Conn tried so hard to control. "Until we can ascertain who did, I need you out of sight."

Conn's mind stumbled over the implications, emotion warring in his gut. "To desk duty?" He hated desk duty. Being inside all day made him want to crawl out of his skin.

"Not exactly."

"I didn't beat up Bettis. Things get out of control when I'm around. I know that. But I've never"—he shoved his fists against the sheepskin-lined pockets of his jacket for emphasis—"ever, so much as pulled a dog in the road with someone who's in my custody."

"The problem," Hawthorn said, "is that you act like someone who could. Would. What you do before a suspect is in custody always bleeds over."

Rocked to his very core, Conn sat back down. A black hole yawned inside him, sucking at all his carefully constructed defenses. It wasn't the first time he'd been falsely accused. He'd been six feet tall by the eighth grade, with a temper, which made him an easy target for finger pointing and had gotten him sent to anger management classes. Name the emotions. *I'm afraid of being abandoned by my family. Again.*

He shook it off. He was thirty years old, not nine. Thirty-year-old men didn't fear being abandoned. If the department thought they could take his gun and badge, they'd better think twice. "Reassigned."

"Temporarily," Hawthorn said, the threat of "permanent" implicit in his tone of voice. "Someone assaulted him while he was our responsibility. We'll start digging and find out exactly what happened."

A knock at the door.

"Yes," Hawthorn said, looking up.

"Someone here to see you, LT," the duty sergeant said, not making eye contact with Conn.

"Send them in."

"Am I dismissed?" Conn asked, getting to his feet.

"No. You need to be here, too."

Out of the corner of his eye, Conn saw a flash of suit. He turned to look at the newcomers. He was prepared for Internal Affairs. He was prepared for Captain Swarthmore. He wasn't prepared for the guy in the suit from the concert last night, courteously opening the door wider for a tiny slip of a girl with wild brown hair shot through with streaks of gold and big green eyes, dressed in an oversized down parka, jeans, and fur-trimmed boots.

"Chris Wellendorf," the guy said, holding out his hand to Hawthorn. Conn barely heard him over the thrumming in his ears as the girl made eye contact with him. His heart kicked hard against his ribs, signaling recognition on multiple levels, but it was the green scarf around her throat and the mug in her hand that made him do a double take.

Queen Maud was standing beside the conference table, shaking her head to Hawthorn's offer of water or a soda. Was there some problem with last night's arrest? He'd filed his report before going home, so it was fresh in his memory.

"I've got my own brew," she said, holding up one of those thirty-dollar insulated mugs.

"Hot water and honey," Chris said quickly. "Not *brew* brew."

"I didn't think she was drinking beer at one in the afternoon," Hawthorn said mildly as they took seats at the end of the table. "Have a seat, Officer McCormick."

Feeling clueless, and not liking it, Conn sat back down, but this time next to Hawthorn rather than across the table from him. The choice of seat presented a unified LPD and gave him the opportunity to get a good look at this new iteration of Queen Maud.

"Thank you for meeting with us so quickly," Chris said.

"I'm on a flight back to New York in a couple of hours and want this squared away before I leave."

"You feel you need police protection, Ms. Ward?" Hawthorn asked.

"Not really," Maud said with a stubborn lift of her chin. "But Chris does. And what Chris wants, Chris gets."

Chris smiled blandly, apparently unfazed by being thrown under the bus. "The incident at the concert last night only confirms—"

"That once in a blue moon a crazy guy will get through security. It hasn't happened before. Not on this tour. Not on the last two," Maud said.

"But it could happen again," Chris said.

Maud sipped from her tumbler, then slid a glare at Chris.

"You want peace and quiet," Chris said. The words held a significance Conn didn't understand. "You've got a few weeks. You'll work better if everything's taken care of, and you don't have to worry."

"I don't worry," Maud said. "You do that for me."

"I do, and that's why we're here, having this lovely conversation with these gentlemen who carry guns for a living. If I'm not worried about your safety and security, I can worry about other things, like the conversation I need to have with Eric."

Maud leaned over to say something to Chris. Conn seized the moment. "What the hell is going on, LT?"

"Ms. Ward's representatives have asked us to provide twenty-four hour protection for the duration of her stay in Lancaster," Hawthorn explained in an undertone. "You're it."

Conn's jaw dropped. "What?"

"He asked for you specifically." Hawthorn flicked a glance at Chris, unruffled despite Maud's furious glare. Her next words got Conn's full attention.

"You're blackmailing me!"

Conn and Hawthorn both looked up.

"Not that kind of blackmail, gentlemen," Chris said, looking entirely at ease with being accused of committing a Class A felony. "Decide which option you prefer."

"Fine," Maud said. She sat back in her chair and folded her arms in a way that indicated she was anything but fine.

Conn had no doubt in his mind that the not-quite-blackmail involved accepting police protection. The only thing worse than doing close protection work was doing close protection work for someone who didn't want it. "Why me?" he said to Chris.

"Based on your performance last night, you're eminently suited to the job," Chris said.

Conn bit back his automatic *hell, no.* He flicked a quick glance at Hawthorn. Was this an order? Defying a direct order would get him in immediate trouble. Insubordination. Hawthorn's face wasn't giving anything away.

"I'm not trained as a body man," Conn said.

Chris waved away the objection. "Our devoted fan last night got past two others cops, but not you. Why?"

"He tripped my crazy wire," Conn said dismissively.

Chris nodded encouragingly, like Conn was a slightly slow child reciting his letters. "Can you be more specific?"

That's where the preternatural alertness came in handy. Like most kids with a temperamental father and who'd bounced in and out of homes and schools, Conn was an expert in reading people. It wasn't until he joined the force that he realized that between his childhood and his time in the army, he had an advantage over clean-cut suburban kids. Conn knew from liars, from cheats, from crazy. He sat back, folded his arms over his chest, and let him have it.

"He looked like the rest of the band. Flannel over jeans, Converse, beard. No big deal. But he was casing the place like it was new to him. Like he didn't know what all the equipment was. And he wasn't doing anything useful.

Everyone else was breaking stuff down at Mach 2, all systems go, like they just wanted to get out of there. He seemed aimless, out of place, intoxicated, and a little wild around the eyes. Like I said. He tripped my crazy wire."

Silence around the table. Chris's eyes had gone from amused kindergarten teacher to assessing. Conn doubted the change meant anything good for him. Hawthorn was still blank. Maud was focused on the table, but she slid him a sidelong glance that sent his heart rate up again when he met her gaze.

Hawthorn opened a file folder. "Is there a specific threat we need to be aware of?"

Chris said nothing, just pulled a manila folder of his own from his briefcase. But rather than handing it to Hawthorn, he pushed it down the table to Conn. After a long moment, Conn leaned forward and opened it. Inside were dozens of pages printed from websites, some emails, a few actual letters typed on typewriters. He read the first two, both containing lurid descriptions of how the anonymous writer wanted to torture Maud before raping her.

It made his stomach turn. He looked up. "Jesus Christ," he said before he could filter his words. "This is above my pay grade. You guys must know of security firms that specialize in close protection."

"We do," Chris said. "Cady prefers to have someone local."

Conn blinked. "Who?"

"My name is actually Cady," Maud said. "Maud is my stage name."

Great. A stage name. Like this wasn't ridiculous enough. "Why someone local?" he asked, trying to get a handle on the insanity.

"I'm home," she said simply. "I want someone who knows this town like I do, who's going to be comfortable here."

"What kind of hours are we talking about?" Conn asked.

"All of the hours," Chris replied cheerfully.

"Twenty-four seven?" Conn said with a lift of his eyebrows.

"I realize the situation is unusual compared to other off-duty jobs," Hawthorn said. "Your cooperation in this matter is noted."

In other words, *take the batshit crazy assignment as a body man to the bubble gum pop star, and I'll back you when you need it.* Conn huffed and sat back again. "The lady gets a say," he said, because arresting people was one thing but he was done forcing his company on someone who didn't want it. He spent enough of his life with people who didn't want him around.

Cady looked at him, sizing him up. It took a split second, maybe two, and everyone did it, because he was six foot six and solid muscle. Gang members did it to search for weaknesses, knowing they'd likely have a long-term relationship with him. Women in bars did it, gauging whether or not they'd have any luck approaching him. Hell, he did it himself, with women, with other men, but mostly with himself in the mirror every morning, wondering if this was the day he'd beat his dad.

But Cady's look was mostly business. She was hiring him for a job. It was the heat glimmering behind those green eyes as, for just a moment, she looked at his shoulders that made his blood feel like syrup in his veins, his nerve endings glow.

"What do you know about the music business?" she asked. The lift to her chin was back.

"I don't see how that's—" Chris started. He subsided when she lifted her hand without looking at him. The dynamic was interesting. Chris was in charge, but she held a fair amount of sway. Sensible, not throwing a tantrum, determined to hold her ground.

And maybe there was a way out of this. Maybe ignorance was bliss. "Not a damn thing," he said, truthfully.

"Ed Sheeran?"

He free-associated, knowing his motor mouth was his last chance of getting him out of this. "Overexposed."

"Why did Zayn break up with Perrie Edwards?"

"Zayn? Is that a name or an alien invasion force?"

"What kind of music do you listen to?"

He shrugged. "Country, mostly. It's just background noise."

"Go to concerts?"

"Only when I'm getting paid to work them."

"Any aspirations to work in Hollywood?"

"Hell, no."

Cady turned back to Chris and Hawthorn. "He's hired."

Goddammit. He had real problems to deal with. Someone was railroading him for a brutal assault he didn't commit, which meant someone in the only family he had had turned on him. His dad's best time came in December, with the cool dry weather making for perfect track conditions. Now wasn't a good time to switch careers and babysit a pop star who wanted him around about as much as he wanted to be with her.

Exactly how much was that? In the cold light of day after the concert, he thought he'd imagined the connection humming between them. Now he wasn't sure. But with Hawthorn staring at him and Cady giving her reluctant consent, he really had no other choice. "When do I start?"

"Now," Chris said.

Everyone stood, Cady zipping her coat to her chin and pulling up the hood, thanking Hawthorn for his help.

"I'll keep the file," Conn said to Chris, like a good little Boy Scout. "Unless you need a copy."

"I have an electronic version of every threat we've received against Cady. The internet chatter is too voluminous to archive, but we screen cap the worst ones."

Voluminous? "Okay," Conn said. He brazenly tucked the file with the pictures of the assault he allegedly committed under the psychos file.

Cady was already out the door, peering around the bullpen with interest. Conn stopped Hawthorn on his way out. "The county runs the jail," he said, under his breath.

"I'm aware of that, McCormick. I'm looking into the matter," Hawthorn said testily. "You need to stay out of trouble. You need to stay busy. You need a rock-solid alibi for your movements from here on out, which, thanks to Ms. Ward, you now have. And for once in your fucking life, you need to stay out of everyone's grill while we work this case."

CHAPTER THREE

Did Shoulders know how he looked at people?

Feeling shorter than usual, Cady followed her little entourage down the hall. Chris and Lieutenant Hawthorn were of a height, around six feet tall, but Shoulders, aka Officer McCormick, towered over all of them. Especially her. He was easily twelve and maybe fourteen inches taller than she was, and up close, he blocked out one of the overhead lights.

"Excuse me, Ms. Ward. Could I get your autograph? It's for my daughter."

The middle-aged officer's request for her autograph turned into posing for a picture. Once someone broke the ice, other, less adventurous folks always followed, and it was a good ten minutes before they were able to leave the precinct. She was aware of Chris waiting somewhat patiently behind her, and hyperaware of Conn looming just to her left in jeans, a hoodie, a sheepskin-lined denim jacket, and running shoes. She'd never seen him in uniform. Now surrounded by them, she found herself wondering how he'd look in dark blue. Did the uniform transform his face from pugilistic to authoritative the way her stage makeup and costumes transformed her from plain Cady Ward of Lancaster to the Queen of the Maud Squad?

Maybe. Out of uniform he looked like a boxer, maybe an MMA fighter. Okay, realistically he looked like a thug. The muscles in his shoulders pulled taut the fabric of his jacket, and his thighs bulged in the soft material of his jeans. His hands were balled into fists and straining at the pockets of his denim jacket. His dark brown hair fell forward over his forehead, but whereas that softened some men's faces, all it did to Conn was draw attention to his blue-gray eyes, the fistlike jut of his cheekbones, the full contours of his mouth.

She handed back the paper, gave the Sharpie to Chris, who held out a hand without even looking up from his phone, then reached for the door.

"I've got that," Conn said, and reached past her to push it open, his chest and arm pushing heat and strength at her like a punch. Her body responded, sending a sharp zing along her nerves. Her nipples peaked in the warmth of her down coat. No way could she blame that on the cold November wind. That was pure physical response to Conn.

"Go ahead," he said, his gaze searching hers, then the parking lot. "Everything okay?"

"Yes," she said. Did he have any idea *at all* how he looked at people? He threw looks like most people threw punches—hard, fast, aiming for a TKO with every look—but all she could see was the vulnerability, the need, the plea underneath the look, the gray in his eyes.

Then he blinked. When his eyes opened again, the vulnerability was gone.

"Can we please walk through this door?" Chris said from behind Cady. "At the risk of sounding like a cliché, I've got a plane to catch."

"Over here," she said to Conn, leading the way to her

car. He looked it over appreciatively. She'd bought an Audi
RS5 just before returning home, splurging on a car that hit
sixty faster than a Porsche 911 but with all-wheel drive to
get her around in Lancaster's winters. Conn held out his
hand for the keys.

"I drive myself," she said.

"That's going to be a problem," he said.

"Why?"

"It's a control thing."

"It's *my car.*"

"I can't protect you if I'm not in the driver's seat," Conn-
the-thug said, causing serious cognitive dissonance in
Cady's brain. He looked like he was two seconds away
from starting a bar fight, but he sounded like a highly
trained professional. Up close his voice was like a low curl
of sand, not a bass or a baritone but a dry, husky tenor rasp.
She found herself wondering how it would sound murmuring in her ear as he took off her clothes.

"Cady, at least unlock the car so I can get inside before
I freeze to death," Chris said. "You two have ninety seconds to hash this out."

Cady clicked open the doors. Chris, thank God, jammed
his lanky limbs into the backseat and slammed the door.
Conn unzipped his jacket and reached into the inner
pocket.

"Oh my *God,*" she said. "Do you *smoke*?"

Her appalled tone got through the glass to Chris, because the door swung open and he clambered out, glaring
at Conn as he straightened his jacket. He pointed at Conn
with one finger, the remaining digits wrapped around his
phone. "Smoking around Cady is expressly forbidden."

"It's a deal-breaker," Cady added. "You can't be jone-
sing for a ciggy every twenty minutes. It makes you anxious, which makes me anxious."

Conn flicked her a glance, then pulled a black watch cap

from his jacket and yanked it over his head to cover his ears. "I don't smoke," he said, reaching back into the pocket for a pair of fingerless gloves. "Now give me the keys and we'll be on our way."

Chris got back in the car and slammed the door again. Cady took a couple of steps closer to Conn and found herself looking way, way up into his face. Good thing she knew how to project.

"I drive around this city all the time when I'm on a break. It's one of the things I look forward to when I'm not on tour. I drive myself places, I buy my own groceries, I shop without an entourage. I understand we've hired you to do a job. But the thing is, no one is going to try and run me off the road in Lancaster. They're not going to tail me or whatever."

He stared down at her, but this time the mask was firmly in place. She refused to budge, looking right back at him despite knowing she was losing this battle without him saying a word. "This matters to me. Please."

The car door opened behind her. "Cady, you can't stand around in this dry air, and if I miss this flight I swear to God I'll spend the night at your house. Give him the goddamn keys and get in the goddamn car."

Ignoring Chris, she said, "It's a stick. Can you drive a stick?"

Conn's brows lowered, the portrait of a Neanderthal thug's amused disbelief. He held out his hand.

"Fine," she said ungraciously, and slapped the keys into Conn's palm. She walked around the trunk trying to ignore the heated surge inside her when her fingertips brushed his. They were warm, his body like a big, hardworking engine, pumping out heat.

"Which airline?" Conn said when he strapped himself in and adjusted the mirrors.

"United," Chris said from the backseat. He fastened his

seat belt, then reached into his carry-on bag on the seat beside him. "Hold on a second, Officer McCormick."

"Conn," Conn said, the car already in reverse, his foot on the brake. "Call me Conn. Officer McCormick is about five syllables too long for regular conversation."

"Fine. Conn. Two things. First, as Cady's body man, you do whatever she needs. Driving, protection, errands, whatever."

Cady saw a muscle pop in Conn's jaw and resolved to deal with that the moment Chris was in the terminal. "Yes, sir," Conn said tightly.

"Second, sign this," Chris said.

He extended a sheaf of papers between the seats. Conn shifted back into PARK and slung around to look at the stapled papers, taking up even more of the room on Cady's side of the car. She could smell him, his skin, a faint overlay of grease and oil, industrial soap, and a gravy she'd bet her gold album came from The Coop, a dive diner on the East Side. Her mouth watered. "What is it?" Conn asked, not taking it.

"It's a confidentiality agreement. The short version is that you agree to never speak to anyone from now until the end of recorded time about anything you see, hear, or do while in our employment or we will sue you and your entire family for every collective last penny you've all made or ever will make."

"Chris, for the love of God," Cady said.

Conn seemed almost amused by this. "And if I refuse?"

"Then you can go back into the police station and explain to your lieutenant why you're here and not on the road to the airport. We'll come with you and start this whole process again with a different cop, which will mean I'll miss my flight and spend the night at *your* house."

Conn took the paperwork. "Pen?"

Chris handed one through the gap. Conn flattened the

pages against the Audi's steering wheel and scrawled his signature on the last page, then handed it and the pen back to Chris.

"Thank you," Chris said, satisfied. "Now that you've given in to my entirely unreasonable demands to ensure your safety . . . I've set up a meeting with Eric next week. Right now he's dead set on dropping the new album right before Valentine's Day, like we've planned."

Cady took a sip of her honey water, marveling at the insulated cup. The water was still hot enough to send steam drifting into the air. Everything was perfect. She had a couple of months to rest her voice after months of touring, and a big uptick in hype and brand awareness from the tour. The calendar of new releases was light early in the year, so she'd have less competition from other artists' new albums. She had a solid album ready to go.

The only problem was that it was an entire album of love songs, relationship songs, sexy hookup songs, all written by a team of songwriters. Not her. The longer she'd been on tour the more convinced she'd become that this wasn't the album she wanted to release.

"It's a good time," Chris said, cajoling. "All the stars are in alignment. You can work on different material for the next album while you're touring. You'll be at a different stage in your life, and so will your fans. Right now they want to hear you sing about heartbreak and romance and making up and hooking up."

Cady huffed. As if she'd have time to write after the promo appearances, the North American tour with more appearances, the awards shows and social appearances, all carefully managed to keep her in the public eye. She could do some work on material for a new album on the road, but not the deep work needed to write, sing, and produce the kind of album she wanted.

"That's at least eighteen months away, Chris," she said firmly.

"And here you are, with weeks and weeks of time off," Chris said. "How fortuitous!"

Eight weeks, half of which would be taken up with the holidays and family time, wasn't enough to write an album that would convince a major record label to take her career in a new direction. She looked at Conn, trying to gauge his interest in what could be considered fairly important music industry gossip. But Conn's gaze was entirely focused on the road, taking the side streets to Thirteenth Street, the quickest route to the airport. He knew all the shortcuts, drove the car like he knew his way around a gearshift and a performance engine.

"Cady? It's not like you to give up on an argument with me."

She wasn't giving up on the argument. She was just paying attention to her body, which was reminding her that eight months of touring and no sex made Cady a dull, dull girl.

"This album is the safe choice," she started.

"Safe sells records. Ask Justin Bieber."

Which was the heart of the problem. Industry execs didn't care if the critics blasted the album if fans bought it in droves. Only Cady cared. It was a huge risk for her; if the label dropped the wrong album, they'd just find another Cady with an active following on YouTube or wherever, and sign her. Throw more spaghetti at the wall, relegating Cady to third-rate venues suitable for one-hit wonders. She needed to make them wait, and to do that, she needed good material. Really good material.

"Yes, but creative and adventurous sells even more records. Just ask Beyoncé."

"We're ready to go with this one, Cady. We've got bookings on all the major talk shows. Jimmy Fallon wants to do the classroom instruments thing with you. The tour schedule will capitalize on the summer concert season. After this album's a hit and the public knows exactly who you are, you can branch out."

After I've sold out, I can buy my soul back?

"I'm tired of being safe," Cady said, then stopped. Chris was playing the devil's advocate, part of his job as her manager. She trusted him to guide her career, and in just over two years he'd gotten her from busking on street corners for pocket change to her own tour. "It's my vacation, Chris. If I want to spend it writing songs, I will."

"I'd be delighted to take something groundbreaking into Eric's office," Chris said.

Conn turned onto the drive leading to Lancaster's small but busy airport. When he braked in front of the United sign, Chris flung open the passenger rear door, shoved his suitcase onto the sidewalk, and followed it.

Cady got out herself. "Thanks for everything," she said. "Have a good trip."

"I really do have your best interests at heart," he said, all the brash confrontation gone from his voice. "Both for your safety and for your career. Trust me."

Cady looked over her shoulder at Conn's big, bulky body hulking in the driver's seat. "You owe me," she said, resigned. "This is totally unnecessary."

"He looks like the strong, silent type," Chris said. "Probably you won't even notice he's there."

Their running joke. Chris always promised the bodyguards were the strong, silent type, and he was always wrong. But Conn fit the bill, with his big, pushy muscled arms and his Neanderthal forehead and his thousand-yard stare. So far he had the silent part down pat. She pressed her lips together and nodded. Chris hoisted his bag and strode through the big revolving doors, into the terminal, leaving Cady with no other option but to get back in the car with Conn.

Strong, yes. Silent, yes. She'd met people who talked all the time about nothing, people she could easily tune out. Conn fell into the other camp, barely saying a word but his body talking all the time. Right now, his gaze alternating between the mirrors and the traffic, both car and pedestrian, he smoldered with a banked fury.

"Where am I going?"

"Forty-third and Hanscomb," she said. "My mom's house."

Without a word, he signaled, then merged into the slow-moving traffic along the airport's main drive. Cady wrapped her hands around the insulated mug, held it up to her nose, and inhaled the sweet scent of hot honey water. "Ignore everything he said, by the way. Except the confidentiality agreement stuff. He loves litigation. He'll happily sue you for the rest of your life, just for the fun of it."

"I don't doubt it," Conn said. "What can I forget? The bodyguard part is non-negotiable, and if you go out, I'm driving."

"Yes to all of that," Cady said. She waved her hand, dismissing it. "The rest of it, the anything-else-she-needs part. That mostly applied to tours, getting meals and running errands. There won't be any of that. Because I'm going to cook my own food and run my own errands."

"Which I'll drive you to," he said.

"Fine. But I'm not happy about it."

"I get why," he said. "This is a sweet, sweet car."

Pleased, she let her shoulders relax. "I love driving. I love speed and power and handling."

"So letting me drive is a big concession," he said.

"Huge. The hugest. What do you drive?"

"A squad car, most of the time."

"What do you drive that you own?"

"I've got a pickup," he said. "Getting to work isn't optional for me, and in these winters you need four-wheel drive."

"Well. Feel free to let her run."

"There's at least fifteen stop lights between here and your mother's house."

He was driving faster and more assuredly than she would, his big hands with the oil in the creases handling the manual transmission, feeling out the best places to shift, listening to the engine. "Where were you today?" she asked. Without thinking, she reached out to touch the grease in his pinky's nail bed.

An electric shock coursed through the pad of her finger, straight to her throat and chest. He looked at her, but behind the blade shades his face was inscrutable. She jerked her hand back. "Sorry."

She felt like an idiot. Ever since "Love-Crossed Stars" went big, she'd moved in circles where bodyguards were common occurrences. They all had the same hands-off vibe Conn did. She'd never cared. Life on tour was already busy and full of drama; adding an illicit affair with a bodyguard might tip the controlled chaos into disaster.

But this wasn't tour. It was home. And Conn was . . . making her skin ache for his touch.

"I was at U-Pull-It taking an alternator off a '71 Camaro," he said.

"Oh. You said you drove a truck."

"I do. I race the Camaro."

She thought about it for a second. "They still run drag races at the old airfield?"

"Every weekend it's dry," he confirmed. He downshifted and took the left onto Hanscomb Street just a little faster than legal. The car held tight and growled as the RPMs wound down. "You know about those?"

"I grew up here," she reminded him. "I spent my share of Saturday nights watching guys race souped-up junkers."

"But never wanted to race yourself?"

"I'm pretty sure I've got some kind of clause in my contract that forbids any dangerous activities. Drag racing. Sky diving. Swimming with sharks. That kind of thing."

Thinking of the forbidden wasn't helping. She could feel the post-tour crash welling up from deep inside her, longing for the two things she never got enough of on tour: sleep and sex. He parked the car and switched the shades from the bridge of his nose to the back of his neck. His eyes reminded her of the blue-gray hue of the winter sky.

"Guess it's a good thing I'm driving."

He wasn't conventionally handsome, like a pretty boy movie star or singer, although she'd been around long enough to know that acne scars were airbrushed away, hair thickened and extended, personal trainers and chefs hired to get those rock-hard abs. But there was something about Conn. Women would look twice. "Speaking of contracts, thanks for not giving Chris a hard time about the confidentiality agreement."

He shrugged as he shut off the engine. "I'm not worried about it. The police union's lawyers can handle him, and I've got no family to sue."

They got out of the car and headed up the walk. On the surface, the words came out in the same light-hearted tone he'd used with the drunk guy, but still, she paused while climbing up the front steps. "Oh."

He held the screen door for her while she unlocked the front door, her mother's Thanksgiving wreath scratching against the wood when the door swung open. The house was quiet, dark, the curtains drawn.

"Come on in," she said. "Mom's at work and Emily's at school."

"I don't have much to take over to my new house," she said.

He followed her down the hallway to what used to be her bedroom. She saw him take a quick look in Emily's room, which looked like a tornado tore through a Kardashian's closet, then another in her mother's bedroom before coming to a halt in her doorway. A seasoned traveler accustomed to short-notice trips, she'd packed her toiletries and pajamas as soon as she got dressed. Her suitcases were jammed between the single bed and the sewing table. Bolts of fabric occupied the rest of the available floor space, and pencil drawings with swatches and trim tacked to them covered the walls.

"Your mom sews?"

"Emily," Cady clarified. "She wants to be a designer. She's applying early decision to Parsons. I used to stay here but Em's taken over my room. I don't want to mess with her process."

He nodded, recording the details, no more interested in it than he was in the music business.

She hoisted her suitcases. Without a word he reached out to take them from her.

"I've got them," she said, her heart picking up speed as his big, warm hands wrapped around hers. "I said body guarding and driving, and I meant it."

"Then consider this something a man does for a woman," he said.

He was close enough for her to feel heat radiating from his bared throat to her cheek. She wondered what the rest of his body felt like, if his skin was hot to the touch everywhere, if it was as soft as the spot where his stubble ended.

"They're heavy," she warned.

He didn't even pop a muscle as the weight shifted from

her arms to his, just turned sideways to get the big bags through the bedroom door and walked down the hall. "Anything else?"

"Mom and Emily moved my boxes over after I closed on the house," she said. "That should be it."

The front door handle started to turn. Conn dropped the suitcases with a thud, his right hand moving automatically to his hip to close on air. He muttered a curse under his breath.

"It's just Emily," she said, pointing at the blonde head visible in the half-circle window at the top of the wooden door. "See?"

Emily was through the door by the time this exchange ended. Her eyes widened as she looked first at Cady, then at Conn, then back at Cady. "What's he doing—?"

"Emily, this is Officer Connor McCormick from the Lancaster PD. He's going to be my bodyguard while I'm home. My sister, Emily Ward."

Emily held out her hand. "Nice to meet you, Officer McCormick."

"Just Conn." He gave her hand a brisk shake, then dropped it to fold his arms across his chest.

"We're moving my stuff out to the house," Cady said.

"Did you remember your steamer?"

"No," Cady said. "I'll get it."

"I'll help you." Emily sidled between Conn and Cady's red hard-sided suitcase. "Mom's moved things around in the kitchen. Why do you have a cop with you?" she whispered as soon as they were in the kitchen.

Cady unplugged the steamer. "Chris insisted on a bodyguard. We'd fired Evan, so I needed someone new, and local."

"I thought you didn't need a bodyguard when you were home."

"I thought I didn't, either. After the drunk guy go so close at the concert, Chris thought differently. It was easier to give in than fight him on this. I need all of my ammo for convincing the label not to drop the new album."

Emily's shoulders dropped. "I thought . . . you were going to help me work on my designs while you worked on some songs."

Cady wrapped her arm around Emily. "I'll still do that. It's no different than Evan," she started.

"*He'll* be around," she said, jerking her thumb in Conn's direction. "Also, are you blind? He's way different than Evan! He's, like, mountainous, for starters."

"Shh!" Cady threw a fast glance at the entrance to the front room. "I promise we'll spend time together every day. This doesn't change anything. You'll still come over for the weekend, I'll still come here to work on designs with you. Okay?"

"It's not going to be the same." Her face brightened. "I'll come over now and show you where things are."

Cady looked at the clock on the microwave and tried to remember the high school's schedule. "Aren't you due back for fifth period in twenty minutes?"

"I can cut class."

"No way. Finals are in less than three weeks. You need to stay on top of your grades."

"Why?" Emily said mutinously.

"College, that's why. You're applying to Parsons. That's the plan, right?"

"It's a stupid plan."

Cady set the steamer back on the counter, and tried to ignore the headache building in her temples. "Why is it a stupid plan?"

"It just is."

"Honey. Why?"

"I'm a failure. None of the regional fashion shows

picked up my designs, and my social media channels are going nowhere. There's no point."

"Emily. Sweetie," Cady said. She pulled her younger, taller sister into a hug. "Becoming an internet sensation isn't the only way to make it these days."

"Ella Bergstrom got a write-up in the paper and an invite to the show in Philadelphia," Emily said. "I'm your sister and I've only got a couple thousand followers on Instagram. She's nobody and she's got fifteen thousand!"

"Good for Ella," Cady said. She leaned back and looked into Emily's mutinous face. "Right? Good for Ella. You can be happy for someone else's success and still work your butt off for your own. Lots and lots of people make it in fashion the old-fashioned way, by going to college, learning their stuff, interning at small houses, and getting jobs at bigger houses. And you're going to one of the best."

"That's not how it happened for you."

Her sister's face reflected all of Cady's fears, but she wasn't about to burden a seventeen-year-old with them. "That's exactly how it happened for me. I played two hundred small shows a year, until Chris heard me in Chicago and signed me. I look like I came out of nowhere, but you know how much I was on the road before anyone noticed me. And I should have gone to college. You're as good as your last project. If my next album bombs, how much attention do you think I'll get? None. Right now all I'm qualified to do is ask people if they want fries with that."

Emily shoved her hands into her hair. "Maybe Dad's right. He said if I went to a school with a pre-law major, he'd fund my business the whole time I was in college."

Parsons School of Design trained generations of creative thinkers, but decidedly did not have a pre-law major. No matter what he promised about funding her business, taking their dad's deal would effectively derail Emily's dream, and how like him to take Em's dream and hold it out like a carrot. "You don't need to do that. You can go to law school later if you decide you don't like design. You've got ambition, and talent, and drive. You're going to get into Parsons. So go back to fifth period and ace your finals."

"I really just want to hang out with you," Emily said quietly.

"This weekend. I promise."

"Conn will be there?"

"Yes," Cady sighed. "Conn will be there."

"Fine. Have it your way," Emily said. She opened the fridge, snagged a Greek yogurt container and a spoon from the drying rack beside the sink, and stalked back through the dining room to the foyer. Cady grabbed the steamer, tucked it between her arm and her hip and followed her, watching as she snagged her tote, flashed Conn a fake smile, and whirled back out through the front door.

When it slammed shut, Cady looked at Conn. His face betrayed nothing, so maybe he heard the whole conversation and maybe he heard none of it. "It's a difficult age," she said.

He just nodded. "Ready to go?"

"I think I've got everything."

"Wait here."

"Okay," she said. She pulled out her phone to run through the latest social media while Conn trotted down the steps, popped the trunk on the Audi, and tucked the suitcases inside. She answered a few fans, retweeted pictures from the concert, added a couple of her own from backstage at the homecoming concert. The label's publicity team handled the glossy official images, but she liked to do the more intimate shots from her own social media handles to stay in touch with fans.

Conn came back for her, hovering behind her as she

locked the door, then escorting her to the car. She was used to having a big guy by her side most of the time, used to tuning out Evan's stream of chatter, but Conn was a looming, silent presence she couldn't shut out.

"Where to now?"

"Do you know the Whispering Pines community?" she asked.

"The gated community just the other side of the county line?"

"That's the one," she confirmed.

He started the car and wound their way north, out of the city and into rolling hills. He turned up the drive to the imposing brick and wrought-iron gates, then used the remote clipped to the visor to open them.

"All the way down to the bottom of the hill, then turn right," she said.

Trees bare of their leaves stood among thick, tall pines; in the summer it was impossible to see even a hint of the houses widely spaced on wooded lots, giving her ample privacy. The location had the added advantage of being a short drive from Lancaster's prime entertainment district, SoMa, and the airport.

"Turn here," she said.

He was already making the turn up the long driveway to the house. It was dark, not even the exterior lights on, and the sun had all but set, so the trees cast deep shadows across the driveway as he pulled into the garage at the north end of the house.

"The real estate agent who sold me the house turned the water back on and made sure everything still worked." Her voice echoed in the garage, as did the closing doors.

Steamer under one arm and her purse over her other shoulder, she opened the door leading to the mudroom. Other than three built-in cubbies for hanging coats and storing shoes, the white-painted room was empty. Cady toed out of her boots and carried the steamer through the door into the kitchen and looked around.

The house was beautiful, rich with dark hardwood floors, white cabinets, and dark granite surfaces in the kitchen. The open floor plan flowed from the kitchen, in the center of the house, to a dining room and living area next to floor-to-ceiling windows. The last of the setting sun gilded the tops of the trees sloping gently up the hill. She had no one behind her, or visible to either side; the nearest neighbor's lot was two acres away.

As she watched, Conn walked around the main living space, opening doors, peering behind curtains. "You're good at this," she said.

"Making myself at home in other people's houses?" He gave her a quick grin, but it didn't quite reach his eyes. "I've got some experience with that."

"I suppose you do," she replied.

"Where should I put these?" Conn asked, back by the suitcases. Even with rugs under the dining area table and anchoring a leather section facing the fireplace in the living area, his voice echoed in the big space, a suitcase dangling haplessly from either fist as he looked around.

"In my bedroom," she said.

She looked at him as she spoke. The moment they made eye contact, a bolt of sweet electric heat shot up her spine, lifting the hair on her nape. Her nipples tingled and hardened. His eyes darkened in response, going from all business to a heavy-lidded possessiveness she couldn't ignore.

They were alone, in her house, and he was looking at her like if she said the word, he'd have her right there on the hardwood floor.

CHAPTER FOUR

"Through there?" Conn said. He tipped his head toward a wide doorway just off the family room. Anything to break the tension thrumming between them, because no way was this happening. She was Cady Ward, pop star, and he was Connor McCormick, a cop on the verge of being suspended for an assault he didn't commit, which would likely earn him jail time. Nothing good would come from acting on a desire that twenty-four hours earlier hadn't existed.

But he wanted to. He really, really wanted to.

She blinked, then cleared her throat. "Yes. My . . . um . . . bedroom is the one on the left. The spare room is across the hall."

She turned on lights as she showed him the rooms. He brushed past her to set her suitcases down by the king-sized bed. They weighed a freaking ton, and he mentally revised his estimate of her strength. The room was decorated as if being photographed for a magazine. Pictures sat on the dresser, with larger ones on the walls. Cady and her sister, her mother, her friends. The surfaces were dust free, the comforter and mounded pillows giving off an expensive sheen.

It was the biggest bed he'd ever seen in his life. In a split second his mind betrayed him, sending up a vivid image of Cady's slender body under the sage green down comforter, nothing visible but her wild mass of brown and gold hair.

Two people could have some crazy hot sex in that bed and not even mess up half of it.

Not happening. He turned around. Through an open door he saw an enormous tiled shower with jets set into the walls. His brain spun, heating like racing slick tires doing a burnout, then shot off in the direction of sex in the shower.

Not. Happening.

"First things first," he said, then cleared his throat and said the words again, this time in a voice that sounded professional, not like he'd said *Your place or mine?* "I need to do a security sweep. Get familiar with the layout, exits. I'll start with the yard, because the sun's about to set, then do the interior."

"Of course," she said. "This way."

She led him down a set of stairs between the living room and the bedrooms to a finished walkout basement. "Thanks," he said, and slipped out the door and into the yard.

Where he drew in several deep, cooling breaths as he used the rapidly fading light to make a quick circuit of the perimeter. The air was cold and sharp enough to sting his skin, signaling snow was on its way. For a singer who wanted privacy, the house was perfect, set well back from the road, barely within shouting distance of either neighbor. The front of the house was an imposing stone-and-brick facade with a few unobtrusive windows. From a security standpoint, it was a nightmare. The pines were dense enough to hide anyone from paparazzi with a zoom lens to a crazy guy with a sniper rifle and loomed up from the edge of the lawn. She must have the latest in security cameras because he couldn't see any at all around the house's doors or windows.

He skirted the brick patio with built-in fire pit and edged around the side of the house, ears tuned to the stillness of a winter night. The air was cold and sharp, and all he heard was something scuttling near the neighbor's woodpile. The shape resolved into a raccoon when it came close enough.

"Gun. Badge. Taser. Mag light," he said to himself as he crossed the driveway, heading for the front door. He'd sleep a lot better if he had the contents of his utility belt, because he was a cop. Hawthorn told him to stay out of everyone's grill. In other words, be someone he wasn't. Forget that. He wasn't about to get shoved out of the department and into jail. He wasn't going to back down from this.

He rang the doorbell. Cady opened it without confirming his identity.

"You need to ask who it is," he said.

"I saw you coming up the stairs," she said reasonably. She'd taken off her coat while he scouted the grounds, and now had her hoodie pulled up over her hair. In jeans with the hoodie up, she looked both young and worldly wise, the dark circumference of her hood accenting her flushed cheeks, her lips, her big, bright hazel eyes.

"Where can I view the security camera footage?"

"Nowhere," she said. "I don't have any."

Are you insane? "Why not?"

"It's another level of security but it's also another level of exposure. Feeds can be hacked. Images stolen. Right now I'm relying on the house being in a LLC's name, and my car not being that well known."

"My first recommendation is that you get security

cameras installed. And motion detectors. We need to know who's around the house while you're gone. I'm only one person and I have to sleep."

"No."

Point blank. No room for argument. This was his first glimpse into Cady when she wasn't willing to negotiate. He set it aside. Maybe, just maybe, if he kept moving, his body would forget its visceral, immediate reaction to Cady.

"Here's what's happening next. You're going to give me a complete tour of the interior. Then we're going to drive over to my place so I can pick up a few things. Then we're going to take a look at the emails from the psychos folder and go over your schedule for the next few days so I can do any preliminary planning before we leave the house. Do you need to do any grocery shopping?"

"Mom and Emily picked up a few things for me before I arrived," Cady said. On closer examination, her face was dark pink, her lips full and red, as if she'd bitten them, or better, as if he'd bitten them.

"Look," he said suddenly, because the signs couldn't be clearer that she was responding to the close quarters and instant attraction, "this can't happen. We're going to be in each other's pockets for the foreseeable future, and getting physical won't make it better. It will only make it worse."

Those impossible green-gold eyes widened. "Excuse me?" she said.

He sketched a vague circle in front of his face while looking right at her.

Her brows drew down, then she laughed. "It's not lust," she said. "It's the steamer."

It was his turn to frown, confused. She pointed at the black granite countertops in the kitchen, where the steamer was hissing and popping gently next to a towel. "Dry air is hell on vocal cords. Cold, dry air is even worse. I have to keep my sinuses moist, because that warms the air before it reaches my throat. I use it a few times a day, depending on my schedule, how dry the air is."

He flushed, shoved his hands in his pockets, and felt his shoulders crawl up to his ears. "Sorry," he said. "I was out of line."

"No, you were observant," she said.

He looked at her, feeling a little of the heat drain from his cheeks.

"And you're right. It's not a good idea. I appreciate you stopping it now, before I really made a fool of myself."

Her smile was a little forced, not quite reaching her eyes, and the color on her cheeks was now the dull red of embarrassment, not the bright flush of attraction. He reached out and snared her wrist, stopping her in the act of turning away from him.

"That's on me," he said, too rough, then moderated his tone. "I feel it, too. That's why I said something. If it was just you, I would have ignored it. You're savvy enough to read the signs. But this way . . ."

His voice trailed off, because he could feel her pulse skipping and thunking under his thumb, even through the thin fabric of her hoodie. A split second later he saw it in her throat. He wanted to back her into the wall, span her throat with his hand, and kiss her, measuring the strength of her response in her blood rising heated to her face under his fingertips.

She drew in a swift breath. He dropped her wrist, knowing he was over the line. No touching the star.

He wasn't prepared for her fingertips to close around his. His gaze flashed to hers, and he could feel it happen, all the defenses drop, the stupid, dangerous, wide-eyed vulnerability he showed every single time someone wanted him.

"But this way," she said, "we acknowledge it. It's out in the open. We both know how we feel, where we stand. We're both responsible for . . . managing it."

"Managing it," he repeated. Her touch had short-circuited his brain.

"Coming off tour is like coming off an eight-month adrenaline high," she said. She didn't drop his hand. "There's a pretty predictable pattern. I sleep. A lot. Binge on TV shows. Eat all the junk food I couldn't eat when I had to fit into a skin-tight costume. Stare into space. And I have all the sex I didn't have when I was on tour."

His heart stopped. Literally stopped. Like, he'd give himself CPR if he could move. His throat wasn't working either.

"That's probably a couple of days away," she said. "I'm still in the sleep-and-take-hot-showers stage. Is it going to be a problem if I bring someone home?"

Hell, yes, it was going to be a problem. Voyeurism didn't even make the bottom of his kinks list, and the thought of watching some hipster roam around in his boxers after a night with Cady made him see red. The thought of listening to it in this quiet, secluded house shut his brain right off.

He inhaled deep, and forced himself to pull his hand free from hers. "We'll cross that bridge when we come to it."

"Fine," she said. Her chin was still lifted, but she was cucumber cool about the whole thing. Except for her pink cheeks, no longer the steam-tomato or embarrassment-brick. No, the color in her face was the deep rose of desire.

He cleared his throat, stepped to the side. "Complete tour of the house. Please."

There wasn't much to see he hadn't already seen. The upstairs consisted of a huge living space. A big area rug and long table sectioned off the dining area, while the island with stools sectioned off the kitchen. A leather sofa and chairs clustered around a fireplace with a stone chimney stretching up to the top of the vaulted ceilings. A screen hid the television above the mantel. Shelves stretched from the floor by the hearth to the ceiling and held an astonishing array of items: a taxidermied armadillo, a turtle's shell, a deflated football, a complete, articulated skeleton of some animal he couldn't identify without the fur to help him along. Books held together by two rearing-horse bookends. Pictures in mismatched frames, some of people he recognized, some of people he didn't, and lots of landscapes and city streets.

"I take a lot of pictures," Cady said, following his gaze. "Some of them are even good."

He recognized the clutter of someone who lived her life from her deepest soul to the most unimportant possession. None of this was junk. It all held a story Cady could tell about somewhere she'd been, someone she'd met, something she'd done. It was the kind of decorating that put a magazine's spread to shame, and the kind of thing he'd never been able to pull off on his own. Not because he lacked some decorating gene, but because he'd never been able to get past the idea that at any moment he might have to pack up his stuff and move.

"Interesting," he said. "Let's move on."

Two bedrooms with a big landing/sitting area in between finished the main level. Downstairs there was an empty basement with a wet bar running along one wall, finished and ready to be turned into a movie or game room. A treadmill, elliptical, rower, and TRX setup were behind one door opposite the bar. A small recording studio was behind the other. He peered into the utility room, but no one was lurking behind the water heater and furnace.

He nodded at the boxes stacked neatly along the far wall. "What's in the boxes?"

"Stuff from my childhood, mostly. The Christmas

decorations we'll put up in a couple of weeks. The usual crap you'd find in someone's basement."

"Who knows your address?" he asked, moving on.

She shrugged as she led him up the stairs to the main floor. "Theoretically, only my family, a few really close friends, my lawyers, and my management team. I bought the house with an LLC—limited liability company—that's tucked under a couple of layers."

"Where do your fans think you live when you're not touring?"

"Everyone knows I come home to Lancaster. I guess they think I'm still living with my mom." She perched on the arm of the big leather sofa facing the fireplace.

"I thought you told your fans everything."

"I give them the impression I've told them everything, but this is totally under the radar. Not sure how long I can keep it that way. Chris was kind of pissed when I bought the house, because I wouldn't let *People* do an "artist at home" feature on me in my new house. I need somewhere to go to ground. Somewhere I can just be."

Her feet swayed gently, and she tugged the cuffs of her hoodie over her hands as she spoke. In the warm spotlights the shadows under her eyes became even more vivid. She looked exhausted, like she was sliding down the slope to a very long night of sleep.

"I need to go home," he said. "When I went to the precinct today I wasn't packed for an extended vacation. I can't leave you here alone."

"Okay," she replied gamely. She slid off the sofa's arm, grabbed her jacket from the hook in the mudroom, and preceded him out the door, into the garage, where she paused to look very, very longingly at her car.

"I'm really harshing your buzz," he observed.

"You are," she said, but slid into the passenger's seat without further complaint. She buckled up, then leaned back and closed her eyes. "About the only thing I can do on my own, without worrying about pictures showing up somewhere, is get in my car and drive."

He reversed down the driveway at a speed that made her eyes pop open. "Yikes," she said.

"Sorry," he said. "It's the car. And the driving course at the academy."

"Go ahead," she said. "One of us should have a good time . . . in this car."

But she was a little more awake now, looking out the window as they drove through Lancaster to his apartment complex in midtown, close enough to the precinct to make his commute negligible, but far enough away that he didn't run into people he'd arrested. He parked at the farthest entrance. "Stay close," he said.

She obeyed, pulling the fur-trimmed hood of her down jacket around her face, so her distinctive hair and eyes disappeared into the shadows. His apartment was on the top floor in the corner, and when he unlocked the door he tried to remember whether the place was a total disaster, or merely messy.

Messy. Really messy.

"I wasn't expecting company," he said. He gathered a stinky exercise T-shirt from the arm of the sofa, and dirty dinner plates from the dining set under the pass-through to the kitchen, then dumped everything on the kitchen counter.

"No worries," she said, standing just inside the door, looking around. "I spent most of the last year on a tour bus with a bunch of dudes. I'm pretty hard to faze. I see you're not an early Christmas decorator."

He had no Christmas decorations. Shane's family went to town with Christmas, and in the past, he'd gone along for the ride. Lately he'd been getting his Christmas fix at the Block. The holidays were a great chance for overtime, picking up shifts for cops with families. "Yeah, no. Not really. Make yourself at home. Grab something from the fridge if you're thirsty."

The fridge door opened, bottles clinking, as he ducked into his bedroom and snagged his gym duffle from the floor. He dumped his workout clothes on the bed, then replaced them with underwear, socks, shirts. A second pair of jeans, and a pair of khakis. Would he need a jacket and tie? She might go out to dinner somewhere nice, with the unnamed hipster hookup. He'd have to go along, sit at another table, or maybe hang out in the bar, and watch him seduce Cady, or worse, Cady seduce him. What was the protocol for going out? The department provided extra training to the officers assigned to the mayor's security detail, but the mayor was the former chief of police and Lieutenant Hawthorn's dad. It was a cushy assignment, made easier by the mayor's close relationship with the department. Either way, Conn hadn't been through it.

He added a button-down shirt, and a tie, then folded his blue blazer and laid it on top of the clothes. He peered out of the bedroom doorway to find Cady standing beside his dining table, an open bottle of beer in her hand.

"Do you mind if I use your workout equipment?" he asked.

"One of us should," she said, grinning. "I'm taking December off."

He added shorts and running shoes to the bag, set his laptop and power cord on top of the stack of clothes, then lifted it in one hand and his utility belt in the other. In the dining room he dropped the bag on the floor, then sat down to work his gear off his belt and check it. Badge. He still had that, and he was going to carry it until someone made him give it up. Handcuffs in the case went at the small of his back. Taser on his right hip, just to the front of where his gun would sit.

The equipment made various clicks and thuds as he checked it, then snapped it onto his belt. When he looked up, Cady was staring at him, her bottle of beer halfway to her mouth.

"Didn't Evan carry?"

She shook her head. "He was a bodyguard, not law enforcement. He had training in martial arts, that kind of thing, but the general idea was he'd get me away from a threat, not neutralize it. I'm not a head of state or something."

"I'm law enforcement on duty," Conn said. He pulled his Glock from its holster, checked the safety, ejected the clip, checked the rounds, then shoved it back in. "I'm carrying my service weapon. But between you and me, there's a ton of paperwork that comes after you fire your service weapon, even more if I shoot someone."

"With lawyers bearing the paperwork. Let's make sure that doesn't happen." An amused glint in her eyes, she lifted the bottle and swallowed the last of the beer.

He stood up and clipped his gun to his belt. The badge and gun, the Taser and cuffs, grounded him, counteracting that drifting feeling he'd had since he walked into the conference room and Hawthorn showed him the pictures of his arrestee, brutally assaulted, and said the word "reassigned." "All right," he said.

"That's it?" she asked.

He looked at his duffle. He'd moved so often, bouncing from house to house. Sometimes he had a room of his own, more often he slept on a sofa or in a sleeping bag on the floor. Only after he became a cop was he able to appreciate the fact that he'd stayed out of foster care. "I'm used to packing light," he said. "Let's go."

He was also getting used to keeping her close, one hand on her shoulder to guide her down the stairs in front of him. He dropped his hand when they reached the sidewalk, but she stayed on his left hip all the way to the car. He got her inside first, then dropped his bag on the backseat and slid in to the driver's side.

"You're good at this," he said.

"I know the protocol. I may not be happy about it, but I'll make the right moves."

"I appreciate it," he said. "I'm not trained for close protection work."

"I've got your back," she said seriously. A smile tugged at the corners of her mouth. "All I ask is that if I do something outside that protocol, you do your best to roll with it."

"You handled yourself okay at the concert," he said. "Let's get some dinner and go through the psychos email file. I'll feel better when I know exactly what I'm dealing with."

"Eat in or take out?" she said around a yawn.

"We'll get something to go," he said. "I don't want to have this conversation in a restaurant, and you look like you're on your last leg."

"The clock's definitely ticking," she said. "All I want is a hot shower, then about twelve hours of sleep."

The air crackled for a moment as he remembered exactly what happened after the sleep-and-shower portion of the post-tour crash. "What kind of food do you want?"

"Barbecue," she said. "Fat Shack. I'll call them now and we won't have to wait long for carryout."

She made the call while he drove out of his apartment complex. The server knew her voice, because there was a short conversation before Cady could order. "Brisket or pulled pork? Sides?" she asked.

"Brisket sandwich, and fries are fine."

"For you, maybe," she said, and added corn bread, baked beans, and a brownie to the order.

"Billy will call me when it's ready," she said. "Normally

I'd just wait inside like a normal human being, but right now I'm not up to a conversation."

When they pulled up, the parking lot was jammed. Cady slouched down in her seat and watched the door. When her phone rang, she answered it, then dug two twenties out of the slot behind her phone and opened the door.

"Stay here. I'll go," he said.

"I said body guarding and driving only."

"I have to go either way," he pointed out.

"Okay, but we won't make this a habit," she said and handed him the money. "Billy won't take it. Put it in the tip jar when he's not looking."

"Got it," he said.

The restaurant was crowded, people waiting for take-out orders occupying every available inch of the benches on either side of the picnic table by the front window. The rest of the tables were full. The guy behind the counter handled Conn a white plastic bag. "She called and said you were coming. On the house. Say hi for me."

"Thanks," Conn said, and took the bag. When Billy looked at the next customer behind Conn, he tucked the twenties into the tip jar and made his escape.

He handed off the bag when he got in the car. She opened the tin foil and stuffed two fries in her mouth. "Want some?"

He got a handful from the bag and multitasked like a mad man, shifting and steering and claiming fries all the way down Tenth Street, cutting through the Cherokee Hill neighborhood to get to her house.

"I should have asked. Are you vegetarian? Vegan?"

"I don't eat a ton of red meat," he said.

She scanned him in a way that shouldn't have been as crazy hot as it was, then lifted her eyebrows. "Really."

"Chasing down bad guys is hard enough without stopping to puke. They laugh at you if you stop to puke."

She had to open all the drawers to find the silverware, then started in on the search for the plates. "I'm still learning where everything is. Emily and Mom set up the house for me. I'll get to know the setup when I decorate for Christmas. We're having the holidays here so I'll have to find the plates by . . . there they are."

"I'd just eat it right out of the foil," he admitted, ignoring the holiday talk in favor of the psychos email folder. "How strong is your stomach?"

One eyebrow lifted. "The hate mail and death threats? I can eat and read at the same time."

He opened the file on the table between them, and started leafing through the pages. The language was horrific, the threats violent and specific and gruesome. Cady dipped her sandwich in the barbecue sauce and tapped one page with her index finger. "This guy's been around a while. He hates me because I'm part of the soulless machine that's destroying music. He threatens most of us equally, although the guys don't get as many rape threats as the female singers."

"Rape is not a joke," Conn said.

"It's the internet," Cady said. "You're familiar with the internet, right? Post even the most bland essay or article and the trolls come out from under a bridge."

"Who goes on the internet and threatens to rape someone?"

"People without lives? People with axes to grind? People who want to throw rocks at shiny things?" She shrugged. "They're entitled to opinions. I stopped engaging. I post, interact with fans, and let the label and Chris handle the rest via a press release or a social media post."

He stared at the pages and pages of fury, loathing, and aggression, then looked up at her, letting his disbelief show on his face. "You walk away from a fight like this."

"All day every day and twice on Sunday," she said. She

met his gaze with an even expression. "Sometimes walking away is the only thing I can do that makes sense. I can't win. I can absolutely lose. So I walk. Do you want something else to drink? I've got wine, soda, or water."

"Water," he said.

She got up and collected the trash in the plastic food sack, and stacked their plates. "By the way, I don't drink caffeinated coffee, so if you have to have it, we'll need to go out in the morning."

He blew out his breath. He could handle a run-in with Hawthorn and Chris, administrative leave, getting assigned to guard a pop star he was insanely attracted to, but not having caffeinated coffee in the morning might kill him. "I'll get some when we go out," he said. "What's the schedule for tomorrow?"

"I'm doing an interview with Hannah Rafferty at Eye Candy at four, then singing."

"Security shouldn't be too bad," he said, not bothering to tell her about Eye Candy's role in a major drug bust earlier in the summer. She knew Eve, so she'd be familiar with the details. Every cop attached to the Block knew about it, and kept an eye on the bar, especially because Eve was now one of their own. Eye Candy was one place she could go, and he wouldn't need to be on full alert the entire time.

"Glad to hear it. I'm going to bed. Make yourself at home," she said. She waved vaguely at the entire house, then padded through the living room, down the short hallway leading to her bedroom.

And his. God, this was going to be awkward. He heard the door close, then water rushing through the pipes. For a long, heated moment he let himself imagine her taking off the hoodie, jeans, those striped socks she was wearing with the boots. He let himself imagine her stepping into the big shower, tiled in a pale gray shot through with darker veins. He let himself imagine the steam rising around her body, her hair darkening as the water soaked it.

Mind on the job. Cady may have hired him because he knew nothing about the music industry, but no way was he doing LPD work without knowing her story. He could, and would, ask her, but wanted the basics so he felt like less of a fool.

Wikipedia had his back. Queen Maud (birth name Cady Marie Ward), was twenty-five, raised mostly by her mother, an accountant, after the family split up. Dad was a lawyer for an online brokerage. One sister, eight years younger, named Emily, who had a Wikipedia page of her own. The stage name came from a grandmother who was a singer in her own right in the sixties.

Chris was going to a Harry Linton concert with a friend in the music business when he spotted Cady, who had taken the initiative to make a few bucks singing for people walking from the elevated train in Chicago to the concert. He managed Cady's meteoric rise, getting her songs in front of other artists, even flying her to L.A. to fill in for Harry's opening act when the singer came down with the stomach flu. That led to appearances on a couple of Harry's more popular songs, then to a record deal with Harry's label. "She could sing," Chris was quoted as saying, "but it wasn't just her voice. It was her presence. Maud was meant to be a star."

Her first album had come out over a year ago, and featured songs cowritten by some of the industry's biggest names, none of which Conn recognized. The Personal Life section mentioned rumors of a relationship with Harry, never confirmed, and now over. Conn scrolled back and forth through the entry, committing sections of it to memory.

Then he shut it off and reached for the *other* folder, the one he'd swiped from Hawthorn on his way out of the conference room. He opened it and stared at the pictures.

Someone had given Jordy Bettis a thorough beatdown. Two black eyes, broken nose, split lip. Missing teeth. Stitches on his forehead and cheekbone closing gashes. Bruising down his ribs and stomach, again on his back. Avoided the kidneys, though. They were going for maximum pain without permanent damage.

Conn flipped through the pictures, then focused on the arrest reports and information behind the pictures. Jordy was a known, repeat offender, his arrest reports escalating from petty theft to possession to possession with intent to distribute to assault as he aged. He was making his way up in the Strykers, a gang that controlled a significant amount of territory on the East Side. There were a dozen reasons why someone would beat the hell out of him, but why blame it on Conn? He looked at Jordy's various mug shots. He looked familiar, but for the life of him, Conn couldn't remember an incident out of the ordinary.

A quick scan of the arrest reports confirmed this. He'd arrested Jordy once before when he pulled over an SUV, ran the licenses of everyone inside, and found Jordy was wanted on outstanding warrants.

Conn frowned and pulled his phone out of his pocket. Normally he'd handle something like this on the job, ask around, both at the Block and on the street. But no way was he taking the Queen of the Maud Squad to the East Side, no matter how familiar she was with the neighborhood. His next best option was Kenny Wilcox, his training officer and mentor.

The shower shut off. He looked up, but her door remained closed. She was so strong, so human when stripped of the sleek hair and clothes, the contoured makeup that made her almost alien. He'd thought she was an airheaded twink.

He was wrong.

Hawthorn told him to stay out of it, but his family had literally written the police department's rules and regs. He had a reputation for thinking of the department first, his officers second. Kenny had also been with the department for twenty years, which meant he knew his way through all the hidden power channels and secret societies. Either way, Conn had to be careful. He had legitimate reasons for contacting Kenny, but his phone could be confiscated any time. All contacts would be examined, and he wouldn't drag Kenny into this. Not yet.

He got to his feet and swung his arms, pacing the length of the house from the mudroom to the bedrooms, using breathing techniques he'd learned in anger management classes to siphon off some of the emotion seething inside him.

Someone had set him up to take a big, big fall. He'd left guys in that kind of shape before, after a fight, but never on the job, and never handcuffed. That was a coward's way out, or worse, torture. Someone thought he was the kind of person they could pin that on and get away with it.

The pressure in his chest tightened. Cady was asleep, or getting there. He needed to get some sleep himself, but no way was that happening without some kind of workout first. He spun on his heel, heading for his bedroom, where his duffle sat beside the impersonal bed. He came up short at the sight of it, yanked into a past where he'd packed in a hurry or had an aunt or his grandma pack his bag for him, shoving things in randomly, eager to get him out of her life for a few months. He was always leaving things behind, kind of like his dad. In the beginning his dad would forget clothes, shoes, sometimes an entire bag of worthless salesman junk, but he always came back for it, reclaiming his car and his son. Eventually, he left everything behind, including his Camaro. Including his son.

Cady's bedroom door opened. Startled, he whirled

around, dropping the duffle from his hand, reaching for his gun. Backlit by the lamp from her bedroom, she was just an outline, all vulnerable shoulder joints and the soft scent of her soap rising from her skin. She folded her arms and leaned against the doorframe.

"Are you sure we can't?"

CHAPTER FIVE

Cady's gaze flicked to the open duffle, then back to Conn's alert face. She spent a solid six to nine months a year on the road. She knew how much a person's packing could tell about his personality. Most people didn't travel like she did; a few days away from home hardly warranted homey touches like pictures or mementos. She had a picture of herself, Emily, and her mom, a casual pose taken in SoMa the last time she was home, just as winter was surrendering its grip on the city. Tulips and crocuses bloomed in big circular planters. Chris had taken the picture with his phone, surprising them in the middle of a cheerful argument about the best ice cream flavor. No matter how cramped the tour bus, how dingy the hotel room, she put that picture on her nightstand. And she always wore her Nana's bracelet.

Conn had no pictures in his apartment. Not a single one. The only thing on the walls was a gigantic television. What was in that bag?

"What?"

His tone was brusque, making her question her decision.

By rights she should be blissfully dreaming by now. She'd sat on the tiled bench in the steam shower until her throat felt liquid and the last of the stage makeup and crap road food seeped from her pores. She'd slathered her face in moisturizer, her body in lotion. She'd braided her hair, gotten into the big bed, arranged the pillows into a down-filled burrow. She was past bone-tired, into a profound exhaustion that was more mental than physical.

But she couldn't sleep. Not with her mind replaying Conn's every glance, his eyes guarded under the black watch cap, his every movement. She wanted to know what the planes of his chest looked like under the soft gray T-shirt, wanted to smooth her palms over his thighs and buttocks.

She should have been able to sleep. She couldn't. And yes, she could take matters into her own hands, but that was for the tour bus, a quiet release to burn off enough energy for her to sleep.

She was home. In her own house. With a man she wanted as badly as she'd ever wanted a man before. "I've changed my mind. I don't feel like managing it," she said. "There's no reason to manage it. I want you. You want me. We're both adults who understand the situation."

"You don't hook up on tour."

A statement, a question, or a deflection? "Tour doesn't work for me like that. Guys on the road, a groupie is just a release."

"Keeps them from getting SRS?"

"What's that?"

"Sperm Retention Syndrome."

"If the main symptoms are a bad temper and a total inability to think straight, then yes."

"But not you."

"It's a risk that isn't worth the reward. It's too complicated."

He huffed a laugh, private, darkly amused.

"What?"

He took two slow steps across the floor, closing the gap between them. "I packed a dress shirt and jacket because I thought I might have to wait in the bar of a really nice restaurant while you seduced some hipster into your bed."

He was close enough to touch, close enough to smell, and he smelled like all the best things: hot male skin and barbecue, with a hint of sweat.

"I can do that," she said. She reached out and rested her fingertips against his hipbone, jutting above his belt. "If it turns you on. And if you find me a hipster. At the moment I'm fresh out of bearded guys in skinny jeans and black-rimmed glasses."

His eyes were stormy blue now, dark with an intent desire that sent sparks crackling along her nerves to pool in her core. "Over my dead body," he said.

Her gaze locked with his, she tugged his shirt up and settled her palm over the bare skin of his hip, stroking the hard bulge of muscle above it. "Let's add that to the list," she murmured. "No lawyers. No dead bodies. Just live ones. Very, very live ones."

She slid her hand from his hip to his back, fingers dipping into the groove of his spine before flattening at the base. Moving him was impossible; pulling only brought her body up against his. She inhaled quickly. He smiled, a wolfish, predatory smile that was mostly about his lips and not at all about his eyes, and she mentally revised her theory of what he'd be like in bed to include words like "implacable" and "hard" and "domineering."

Oh, yes, please.

She went up on tiptoe and pressed her mouth to his, feeling the plush of his lips, the way he parted them obligingly enough. Heat trickled through her, lit up her entire skin. But other than a quick inhale when her tongue touched his, a tensing of muscles, Conn didn't respond. His eyes were still stormy blue, waves churning on the surface but there was movement in the depths. Something else was going on inside him, something long buried and deeply emotional. Her gaze searched his while she waited, leaving space for him to respond.

Or not.

"Message received," she said, remembering his comment that she could read the signs if he didn't want her. "My mistake."

Another kaleidoscope spin of emotion in his eyes, then they went dark, pupils blowing wide as he gripped her upper arms and bore her back against the wall. The impact drove the air from her lungs. A gasp followed as her senses kicked into overdrive, recording impressions, volatile emotion held in check by strength and power harnessed in service of control. For a second she wondered if the promise of a walk on the edgy, barely restrained side was more than she could handle. But she felt alive, more alive than she had in weeks, maybe months. Performing plugged her into the vast, creative energy swirling around her, but she'd been slowly withering away in the downtime.

She wasn't withering now. Her body swelled with hot, saturating desire. She stretched into his grip, rolling her shoulders back, shifting against the power in his hands, all that he was using to hold her against the wall. She came up against the edge of what her body could do, felt his thumb press down into her shoulder joints. She lifted her hands, felt the constriction of movement, flattened them against his torso, and pushed.

It wasn't "no," or "stop," or "don't." It was an exploration of how this could be between them, and a quick glance at his face confirmed this. Desire had won, the mask firmly in place. Heat infused his cheeks, and his abdomen rose and fell under her hands. He slowly took all control from her, leaning in with hips, then chest, then his mouth, his lips hot and demanding against hers until he'd stolen her ability to breathe.

She took her air from his lungs, a lingering taste of barbecue on his tongue, spicy-sweet until it faded into the pure heat of his kiss. She arched under him, straining against his hands until he released her shoulders and slid his hands down her arms to twine his fingers through hers and press her palms against the wall by her head. Bracing his forearms along hers, he leaned down, impossibly closer, his muscles shifting until all her curves melded into the angles and planes of his body.

It was gently brutal, or brutally gentle, the way his body caged her, restrained her. She wasn't sure which, only knew that his mouth was soft, almost tender while he used his body, hands and hips and chest and thighs, to hold her exactly where he wanted her. He wanted her pinned, helpless, and completely at his mercy.

She gave a hitching little sigh that could have been a sob if he'd let her breathe, then surrendered.

"There you go," he murmured. "There you go."

He kissed her for far longer than she thought he would. On so many levels, she'd been wrong about Connor McCormick, mistaking size and an obviously tightly reined temper for lack of feeling, mistaking his hard body for a typical muscle-bound player, someone who'd be easy to sleep with, and easy to leave.

She'd been wrong. He kissed like he loved it, like he luxuriated in the competing sensation of teeth against slick lip, tongue on a long day's rough stubble, the undeniable intimacy of sharing breath, noses rubbing. He didn't move, just kissed her and let her feel his cock hardening between their bodies, shifted his hips in a subtle parody of sex, let her delve into him and get a little breathless from the weight of his body against hers, get a little panicky from the futile effort before pulling back. He was reading her reaction like . . . well, like a trained observer who routinely used his body to manage situations and control people.

Heat pulsed through her, liquid and thick and stinging her nerves, pooling in her nipples, between her legs, rising in her belly each time his abdomen brushed hers. Needing more, she wrapped one leg around his thigh, then hitched it to hip height and brought her other leg up to cross her ankles.

He didn't even grunt, or shift his weight. She laughed at the realization she could climb him like a tree and not even faze him. He was that strong. That immovable.

The bulk of his solid weight rested on his elbows and forearms, she discovered, because she was able to wriggle her hands in his until he let go, very reluctantly. "I'm not going anywhere," she said, and suited her actions to her words by looping her arms around his neck. She pulled his T-shirt to the side, mouthed at his neck, his ear, his jaw, luxuriating in the edge where soft skin met stubble and the hard angles of his jaw. Teeth on his earlobe made him shiver. Tongue against his pulse made him wrap one arm under her hips and hold her still so he could thrust forward.

"Really?" she asked. Such simple kisses never spurred that kind of reaction from a man before, like a barely tamed animal discovering it was okay to arch into a touch. Delighted, she did it again.

He growled, a rough sound she felt as much as heard, and tipped his head to the side, the male lion demanding more from his lioness. She clasped the back of his head, digging her fingertips into his scalp, making even more of a mess of his hair, and applied herself to her task, stopping just short of sucking a mark into skin visible to anyone. But it wasn't easy, because the way he was breathing, each exhale vibrating through his vocal cords, and the way his grip tightened on her bottom made her want to respond in kind. She bit down on the straining tendon on his neck, and felt him wince.

"Sorry, sorry," she whispered, and soothed the spot with a lick.

"No, damn, I like it, but . . . ow, Jesus, *yes, there* . . . but not tonight."

She almost asked him if there was an agenda for this, a schedule she hadn't gotten for this thing they both agreed was a bad idea and shouldn't do, but settled for yanking on the back of his T-shirt until he got the message, lifting his arm so she could pull it over his head, then shifting his weight from hips to his other arm so she could drop it to the floor.

And stare.

"Oh my God," she said, getting the words out before she got lost running greedy hands over planes of muscle. He was put together like a rough sketch of a superhero, maybe the Hulk, sloping rectangles of all sizes overlapping each other to form pectorals, abdominal ridges, shoulders. Dark ink swirled in interesting patterns over his shoulders and down his side, and wiry hair covered his chest. She combed her fingers through it to find his nipples, drawn in to tight, hard buds. The hair tapered at his navel to a single line dead center between his hipbones, disappearing into the elastic band of his underwear, visible above the looser waist of his jeans.

"I think I just regressed through thirty thousand years to the caveman days."

He huffed out a laugh that made his abdominals flex in interesting ways. "If you're still talking, I can do better."

She looked up at him, saw his stark lines, all anger and tattoos. His hair had been molded to his forehead by the watch cap. He looked brutal. He looked wounded.

But his thick, scarred fingers were gentle when he reached for her old T-shirt doing duty as a pajama top.

He pulled it up, again swamping her with that arousing sense of vulnerability as she lifted her arms to facilitate drawing it over her head. His hands swept up from her ribs, going not, as she expected, to her breasts but rather to curve around her shoulders. He lifted her, again gently but implacably, and settled her back down so his cock nestled into her sex. The thin layers of jersey sleep pants and panties were little defense against his button fly, or the thick weight of his shaft, pulsing as he cupped the curves of her breasts. His fingers were so close to where she wanted them, close but not touching, just holding, letting her feel his rough palms against her tender skin. A single rocking move rubbed her clit against all that hardness, sending sparks along her nerves to her nipples. They peaked, pleading for his touch.

His mouth hovered over hers, swift, flickering licks that did nothing to stifle her soft gasps as his hands scudded down to her breasts. He alternated pinches and sweeps of his thumbs over her nipples as his hips rhythmically ground into her sex. She clung to him, letting it wash through her and drive her responses, holding nothing back as slick heat gathered between her legs.

"I want more than this," she said, and bit his shoulder.

"You sure?" he said. "I can make you come like this."

"I need more." She nipped her way up to his ear, then bit down on the lobe hard enough to make him inhale and close his fingers tight around her nipples. "I need you inside me."

He gave a soft growl, then wrapped one arm around her hips and pushed away from the wall with the other. Her bedroom was dark, the covers twisted awkwardly where she'd tossed and turned before giving in to her body's basic need. He stopped to set her down on the bed.

"Do you have condoms?"

So the duffle didn't hold condoms. That was rather

sweet of him. Wordlessly she reached into the top drawer of her nightstand. She'd unpacked them from her tour bags, where they stayed in an inside pocket, ready for action that never came. Still looking up at him, she reached for his belt and plucked apart leather and metal.

"That's the hottest thing ever," he said.

"What? This?" She popped the top button on his fly, revealing dark cotton underwear distended by the heavy thrust of his shaft. She glanced quickly at the mirror over the dresser opposite the bed and saw exactly what she'd expected to see. "Oh. Topless girl kneeling while she opens your jeans."

His big hand clasped her chin, calluses scraping rough over her jaw as he lifted her face to his. "You showing me how much you want me."

It was a confession, offered up in darkness, too tender to be exposed to the light. Still looking up at his face but unable to see his expression, she opened the next button. His shaft flexed in response. With the next button, his thumb stroked her lips, and with the next, dipped inside. By the time she had his fly open she was sucking on his thumb, letting him see her face, her eyes as she did.

She eased his jeans and underwear over the tight curve of his buttocks. Denim and cotton thudded to the floor under the weight of his gun and handcuffs. His cock bobbed free, and he wrapped his hand around the shaft, stroking. She bent forward and opened her mouth, but he stopped her.

"That's going to have to wait," he said, and reached for her sleep pants.

Everything came off at once, pants, panties, and the thick socks she wore to bed. He opened the condom and rolled it down his shaft, then studied her for a second, his face unreadable.

She was small, blessed with a frankly skinny build and

the ability to eat pretty much whatever she wanted as long as she stuck to some kind of workout routine. She'd lost weight on tour, too active to stomach junk food, and bored with hotel food. She was built like a tween girl, and she knew it.

Conn seemed to come to some kind of conclusion. "Okay if we try it like this?" he asked, guiding her to face the headboard.

"Um, okay," she said, trying to get with his program, shifting gears from a fairly intense desire to get pounded into the mattress to whatever he had in mind.

"Give it a minute, and if you don't like it, we'll change it up."

The rough, sandy swirl of his voice in her ear, sending goose bumps down her nape, loosened her spine. She let him position her on her knees with her arms against the wall. He swept her hair over her shoulder, kissed her nape, and slid his fingers into her folds.

She was ready, really ready, swollen and slick, but he didn't rush, gently circling her clit until she quivered and gasped. Then he knee-walked closer to her, aligned his hips with hers, and nudged the tip of his cock into place, sliding in an inch. She went rigid. What had been a very nice handful only a minute before now stretched her sharply.

"Easy," he murmured, and stopped moving. "Take it when you're ready."

He waited patiently, teasingly stroking her clit while his other hand brushed over her jaw, stroking her lips, then wound into her hair. She closed her eyes and focused on her pounding heart, the stinging sensation just inside her sex, the way it was fading into a more generalized ache. Experimentally she wriggled her hips, taking another inch or two of his length. His abdomen was hot and bare against her bottom, his rough thighs holding hers open, and she was well on her way to losing her vocabulary, just as he'd promised.

The slow, light circles around her clit made her want to move. The thick pressure of his cock inside her made her want to open to him, to take as much as she could. Freed from the restraining pressure of his chest she could now breathe, except she couldn't. Finally she had the full length of him inside her. She lifted her body so only the tip held her open, then slid back down and cried out as he seated even more deeply inside her.

Again. With this stroke his fingers tightened in her hair; he was breathing short and sharp, forcing it to even out while his fingers relaxed a bit and the arm around her waist loosened its grip just a little.

"It's fine, it's fine." She adjusted her arms on the wall and did it again, beyond desperate. "You," she gasped. "You move, too."

The first stroke made her head drop back. Involuntarily she spread her knees and tipped her hips back, her body's demanding plea for more, more, *more*. He set a slow rhythm, once again surprising her. She'd figured him for a hard and fast man, but he held back, the muscles in his forearms quivering with the restraint, and matched every thrust with attention to her clit, sweet, secret circles that sent her into whiteout overload. She let her head drop between her forearms and stopped caring what kinds of sounds she was making because it was good, so incredibly good. Soles-of-her-feet-on-fire good. His hips slapped against her bottom with every thrust, the sound sharp and lurid in the darkness.

Between one moment and the next her orgasm went from possible to certain, her entire body quivering as she flattened her palm on the wall and pushed back into his thrusts. Then she was there, there, buried under collapsing panes of white noise as the spasms wracked her body.

He thrust through it, still slow, still measured, drawing out her pleasure until she shuddered in his arms.

"Oh, God," she said in a voice completely unlike her own.

"Hold on," he said.

The arm around her waist tightened. The other slid under her arm to grip her opposite shoulder. He thrust deep and hard and steady, setting satiated nerves alight once again. She reached back blindly and clasped the sweat-damp hair at his nape, gasping from the impact of his body into hers. When he came she cried out, his pleasure eddying from his muscles, through her skin, into her bones.

They panted together for a few moments, then he pulled out, steadying her until her leg muscles stopped quivering. "You okay?"

"Great," she said. "Never been better." She was halfway down the long silk slide into sleep. All she'd wanted was release, something to wear down her edginess. Instead she got something surprising. Hotter. Mind blowing.

Complicated. Not what she expected.

The last thing she remembered was the bed dipping when he got out of it, and the covers drawing up to her chin as if by magic. Then, nothing.

CHAPTER SIX

Well, *that* was confusing.

Conn had assumed no-strings-attached sex with a hot celebrity would be fantastic. He didn't think he was all that unusual—being used and left by a Hollywood star was supposed to fulfill every red-blooded American male's wildest fantasy. The sex fit the bill—hot enough to turn his bones to ash, obviously just a thing she did to come down off the high of touring. She wasn't looking for a relationship, and neither was he. No strings; no harm, no foul. He should have been cool with it. Thrilled.

He was, and he wasn't.

Thinking about that while lying beside a sleeping Cady seemed dangerous, even more so when, beside him, Cady made a soft, throaty sound and snuggled into the pillows. He pulled the comforter up to her chin, scooted out from under the covers, snagged his jeans from the floor, and backed quietly out of her room, snagging his T-shirt from the hallway floor once he'd closed the bedroom door. Jeans on and buttoned, he put his hands on his hips and blew out a breath.

Out of the corner of his eye he saw movement in the front windows, a change in the way the light lay over the porch's railing, nothing more. His heart rate spiked. His room overlooked the porch, while Cady's faced the more private backyard. He ducked into his bedroom, pulling on his T-shirt as he did, and crept along the wall to the window. Parting the slats with his index finger, he scanned the front yard, thankful he'd spent the last thirty minutes in the dark with Cady since his eyes were already adjusted to the near total blackness. He found himself wishing for a few good, old-fashioned streetlights, because he couldn't see anything beyond the ornamental evergreen pots lining the porch.

A car door slammed down the street, then an engine turned over.

"Fuck." He sprinted for the front door, clearing the steps to the slate sidewalk in a single drop. By the time he reached the end of the curving driveway, the car was gone, red taillights visible rounding the bend.

He almost, *almost* sprinted up the hill in his jeans and T-shirt, but the thought of leaving Cady alone in the house stopped him. This could have been a distraction. He trotted back up the driveway, steam rising from his skin into the cold air. He'd left the front door wide open. He closed it and went into full cop mode.

The first room he checked was Cady's. No difference there. Only her hair was visible above the comforter. He checked the closets, bathroom, and under the goddamn bed, all the while listening to her steady, deep breathing. Trustingly out for the count.

The rest of the house was empty. A quick search of the likely hiding places in the backyard turned up a possum who scared Conn almost as badly as Conn scared him before scuttling into the safety of the woods. Conn sent up a silent prayer of gratitude that he wouldn't have to write a report explaining why he'd shot a really ridiculous animal, holstered his gun, and tried to bring his heart rate under two hundred.

Two things were now clear. One, whoever had been in the car acted alone. Two, this gave him a valid reason to talk to Hawthorn. Back in the house, he called Hawthorn's cell. The LT answered with his last name, as usual.

"I need to talk to you."

"Can't it wait?"

"No. I'm at Cady's house. Do you have the address?

"Yes," Hawthorn said. "I'll be there in twenty minutes."

Conn gave him the gate code. "Don't ring the doorbell when you get here."

Hawthorn disconnected without even asking why. Conn took advantage of the delay to take a fast shower, with all the doors between him and Cady open and his gun on the sink. He was dressed in his game face and all his gear when Hawthorn tapped one knuckle on the window. Conn unlocked the front door and opened it.

"Why can't I ring the bell?" Hawthorn said from the porch.

"Cady's asleep. She finally crashed a couple of hours ago," Conn said, truthfully. After Hawthorn walked in, Conn peered into the darkness. Hawthorn's SUV was parked behind a stand of evergreen trees, out of sight from the road. Conn shut the door behind him, then explained what happened, leaving out the sex-with-the-star part.

"No one's here?" Hawthorn leaned against the kitchen island, looking at Conn like he knew all his secrets.

"I checked the house and the property. Nearly shot a possum in the process."

That got him one of Hawthorn's rare quick grins. "How many people know where she lives?"

"I don't know exactly. I'll get a list tomorrow. Not many. She said she just bought the house, through a holding company or something. Her family. Her manager. Maybe a few friends?"

"People talk. 'I know where Queen Maud lives' is big-time social currency. Get that list and we'll start running it down. Chances are it was a friend of a friend after a peek into the lifestyles of the rich and famous."

Conn looked around the house. Hawthorn had grown up on the Hill, so he doubted the house was all that different from what Hawthorn was accustomed to. "What if it's not?"

"That's what you're here for." Hawthorn studied him. "You kept my file on Jordy Bettis."

Conn shot him a look that stopped just short of insubordination. "You knew I would."

Hawthorn folded his arms. "Any ideas?"

"I've been thinking about Jordy's known associates."

"The Strykers."

"They're in a turf war with the Demons."

"Go on."

Conn tried not to feel like he was back in college, giving a presentation to his classmates. This wasn't his comfort zone. This kind of thinking was one step above the typical patrol cop's response to calls, normally reserved for detectives and officers well above his pay grade "Someone from the Demons would have access to him in jail."

"Go on," Hawthorn said.

"What's strange is that I'm named in the complaint. When gang violence spills back into the prison system, usually no one saw nothing, including the guy who took a beating. Even when cops or COs do give a beatdown, nobody saw nothing. "

Hawthorn quirked an eyebrow.

"So," Conn said slowly, working it out in his head, "either someone in the Strykers has it out for me, or one of the guys at the jail does."

Hawthorn nodded. "Exactly. Start thinking about all the people you've pissed off, McCormick. Make that list. Then we'll talk."

"It's going to be a long list, LT."

"You got another idea?"

"Were there any cameras in the vicinity of where the beating went down?"

Hawthorn shook his head. "This was pretty carefully planned."

After a long pause, Conn said, "Looks like I'm making that list."

Except he did have another idea, one he'd keep to himself for the time being. His LT was still thinking by the book, like he always did. But Conn had other channels for information, and tomorrow, he'd follow up with Kenny.

He slept fully clothed and lightly, waking at the slightest scratching on the roof or a sharp crack of wood outside. When the sky turned gray, he got up, searched for coffee until he remembered she didn't drink anything high octane, and settled for a diet soda, grimacing at the chemical aftertaste. The woods seemed less threatening this morning: bare trunks and branches stark against the thin winter sky. Mounds of leaves and fallen logs gave the hillside a rustic look, if you were into that sort of thing. He had a long time to stare at them while he ran on her treadmill and worked his way through a TRX routine, his attention split between listening for any signs of life upstairs and looking for movement outside.

Turning the TV on gave him something to do. Alternating between texting Shane to check on the fuel pump repair and starting the list of people who could carry a grudge against him filled the commercials. Around eleven Cady's bedroom door opened. He looked up and did a double take. Her hair was a wild rat's nest around her head, and not in a good, sexy-angel-just-out-of-bed way.

"Yeah, yeah," she said through a huge yawn. "Welcome to reality."

He watched her shuffle over to the counter and run water into the steamer, then drape a towel over her head and hunch over the machine. A few minutes later she emerged, red-faced and with some hair clinging to her damp face. She rummaged in the fridge and came up with two hard-boiled eggs, already peeled, and an English muffin.

"We're due at Eye Candy at four," he said as she shuffled back toward her bedroom, chewing a big bite of egg. "Yeah," she said again, giving him a distracted wave of her hand. The door closed, the bedsprings creaked, and then silence.

This was more boring than the days he spent doing surveillance on Matt Dorchester's house last summer. He channel-surfed until he found one of the Bourne movies, and settled down to pass the time.

Just after two he heard the shower turn on. Forty-five minutes later the blow dryer shut off and Cady Ward, singer-songwriter, celebrity, walked out of her bedroom, slipping the wide green bracelet she always wore onto her left arm. She wore skinny jeans, knee-high boots, and a soft V-neck gray sweater that exposed her sternum and throat. Her hair had been tamed and curled into thick waves, and she wore enough makeup to look slightly mysterious. He caught himself before he did a double take, because her boobs were noticeably bigger. She carried a guitar case she set down beside the door, then turned for the kitchen. A minute later she had a thick paste of honey in the bottom of the travel mug and water boiling in an electric kettle. A quick stir, then she was back in the foyer, digging in a huge, fancy-looking leather bag.

"I'm starving," she said without looking up. "Lunch?"

"Whatever you feel like," he said.

"I feel like Sunny Side Up." She cursed, then set the bag on the bench beside the door, went to her heels, and started taking things out of it. Wallet, keys, tablet, bottles of over-the-counter pain relievers, an e-reader, gum, lipsticks, a pair of leather gloves. He stared, fascinated. "But you ate there yesterday."

He frowned. "How do you know that?"

She looked up at him and smiled. "I could smell the gravy."

"I can eat there again," he said.

"Good, because it's close to Eye Candy and we're running late. Aha!"

She pulled a pair of starlet sunglasses from the bottom of the bag and started jamming the contents back in while he shrugged into his jacket. She unwound a thick, soft, purple scarf from the old-fashioned hat rack and wrapped it around her throat, then added a denim jacket to the ensemble before finishing with her puffy down coat. With the sunglasses she looked remote, untouchable.

Not at all like Queen Maud, or the woman who'd propositioned him the night before, yet somehow exactly like the kind of woman who'd proposition her body man.

"What?" she said as she led him through the house to the garage.

He'd thought he was keeping this pretty under control, but maybe not. The conversation at the Block hadn't covered who to tell about incidents. Was Cady on the need-to-know list? Was Chris?

He'd told Hawthorn. Good enough for now. He jabbed the button to open the garage door and said the first thing that came to mind. "Why do your breasts look bigger?"

She laughed. She unzipped her jacket and reached into her bra, holding up what looked like a really flexible gel pad. He gaped at it, then overcorrected to avoid hitting one of the big evergreens lining the driveway. "There are my boobs, the very small ones God gave me. These are my backup boobs. They give me the cleavage God didn't."

Fascinated, he handled one. It was warm to the touch and had the consistency of a thin piece of raw chicken. "Why do you wear them?"

"It's part of my image. My label believes boobs, as well as my voice, sell albums, songs, concert tickets, and merch."

"And you're wearing them today because . . . ?"

"Interviews where photographs will be taken require the backup boobs."

"Okay," he said, as if it made sense.

"Come on," she said, tucking the gel pad back into her bra. "That can't be the weirdest thing you've heard in your line of work."

He turned right out of the community's pompous gates and headed back into Lancaster. "Are we including un-medicated paranoid schizophrenics? Then no. It's top five on the list of weirdest things I've heard from people who don't talk to their toasters."

"Well," she said lightly, and turned to stare out the window at the barren fields. "Sorry for the false advertising."

He processed that, remembering the reality comment when she stumbled out of bed a few hours earlier. Did men go to bed with Queen Maud and gripe about waking up with Cady? "I wasn't complaining," he said after a couple of miles.

She turned to look at him, all big sunglasses and red lips, still swollen from his kiss.

"I wasn't. We were . . ." He paused, not sure what to say to someone so clearly out of his league. "It was really good."

Her lips curved into a smile, one he could tell reached her eyes. "Yeah," she said. "Me too."

At the diner she got the chicken fried steak and fries, and ate two thirds of the platter. Aside from a couple of glances, and every cook in the kitchen peering through the window at her, no one approached her. He stopped her when she pulled out her wallet at the end of the meal.

"I've got it this time."

"Are you getting reimbursed for your expenses?"

He laughed as he thumbed through his cash and dropped a couple of bills on the table.

"Apparently not," she said. At least she could find her own naiveté amusing.

"I have no idea how this works," he said. He zipped up his jacket and shrugged to release the tail from his gun. "Maybe I'm supposed to submit expenses? Hawthorn didn't say one way or the other."

"It's easier for me to just pay," she said. She picked up the money and offered it back to him. "It's a tax deduction for me. I think."

He looked at her. This wasn't a date, but something about her buying his meals raised his hackles. "It's business."

Her cheeks turned a shade of pink that went nicely with the thick purple scarf. "Mostly business."

Keeping his emotions locked down, not getting attached to people who might leave, which was everyone except his fellow cops, was his specialty. But the sore twinge in his chest when she said it was an old, familiar hurt. *Don't get your hopes up. There's nothing to hope for here.*

He took the money back, folded the bills, and tucked them away. She left the same amount on the table. "Ready?"

"Let's go."

A smooth transition to the car, then they were back on the road, headed for Eye Candy. "You're going to be late."

"It's expected," she said, her attention focused on the street. "Things are looking good."

He didn't say anything. He saw too much of the East Side's underbelly to appreciate a few planters and a couple of new businesses.

Eye Candy was located on the next street over from the construction zone for Mobile Media's new data division and call center. The front of the bar faced Thirteenth Street while the back patio's wrought-iron fence opened to what would be Mobile Media's nicely landscaped headquarters. Right now bulldozers, cement trucks, and a huge crane dominated a big hole in the ground, girders and concrete rising from the poured foundation.

The door opened and Matt Dorchester's girlfriend Eve braced it open. The skirt of her gray dress swirled in the wind as she called, "Hi! Get in here before you freeze to death!"

More hugging while he stood off to the side and did his job. No one had followed them from the restaurant, but he couldn't shake the memory of the car's taillights, bloodred and ominous as they disappeared over the hill. He'd been in the bar before, when Eve had worked as an informant for the department. He was never quite sure what to say around her, for two reasons. A few months earlier in the heat of the summer, he'd killed someone in front of her. Heroics aside, in the aftermath, it was awkward. The other reason was that he'd never seen two people look at each other like Eve and Matt did: as long as they had each other, they could handle anything.

"Is Matt coming later?" Cady asked, shrugging out of her coat.

"He thinks so. It depends on calls. Give me your purse, too. I'll put them both upstairs in my office. Get whatever you want from the bar," she called as she climbed the stairs. Eve navigated the spiral staircase pretty well for a tall woman in spike heels.

Cady walked behind the bar and surveyed the worktop like she knew what she was doing. "What can I get you?"

"Coke," Conn said.

She scooped ice then aimed the nozzle into one of those tall slender glasses that holds far less than it looks like it does, then ran water for herself. He raised an eyebrow.

"I've spent more than my fair share of time in bars," she said. "Singing, waitressing, bartending. For a while I thought that's as far as I'd go. Thanks for letting me do the interview here," Cady said when Eve crossed the dance floor.

"Are you serious? You're doing me a favor," Eve said, settling onto one of the bar stools. Both women had their cell phones out for a selfie. There was a moment of silence when he assumed they were posting to various social media sites. Eve set her phone facedown on the bar. "I can't buy publicity like this, and it's good to be in the paper for my actual business plan—entertaining people—not for taking down a drug ring."

"Did business fall off after what happened?"

"Immediately after, no," Eve said. "Lots of gawkers and first-time customers. We had a couple of slow months in the fall, but after I opened the patio for a Halloween party it picked back up again."

Cady nodded. "You've got to keep things fresh."

A brisk round of knocks ended the conversation. Cady unwrapped her scarf while Eve let in a woman carrying a big purse and a man with camera equipment around his neck. Conn sized them up. The photographer wore credentials for the *Star Trib*, and had been around a few crime scenes. He recognized the reporter, Hannah Rafferty, from her picture next to the columns she wrote. Human interest stuff, mostly. Features seemed to be her specialty. He turned his attention back to Cady, to find that she'd changed once again, holding herself straighter, cocking her head to the side just a bit, a big smile that didn't quite reach her eyes on her face. Even her laughter and voice were different, a little higher, a little younger.

So there was concert Cady, sleepy Cady, at-home Cady, and now this Cady, who seemed to be a dialed-down iteration of concert Cady, wearing a version of the same smiling mask.

He understood why. He did the same thing himself. The man who appeared in photos with Shane didn't look much like the cop he glimpsed in the rearview mirror during a traffic stop or in plate glass windows at crime scenes. But this, with the makeup and hair and clothes, was almost a disappearing act.

He faded into the background while the reporter, photographer, and Cady determined the best location for the interview. They settled on the bar, Cady directly under one of the canister lights.

"Mind if I record this?"

"Not at all," Cady said.

Hannah set her phone on the bar, then flipped open a notebook. "It's nice to see you again. I think the last time we talked was about this time last year, when your first hit went big. How does it feel to be back in Lancaster?"

"Good. Really good. I noticed the new planters on Thirteenth Street, and there's a building going up in the big hole in the ground behind Eye Candy."

"No grass growing here," Eve said, to polite laughter.

Hannah's pen moved swiftly across the page but her eyes never left Cady's. "You were on the road for six months?"

"Eight. Not that I'm counting," Cady said. More polite laughter. "The opportunities just kept coming, each too good to pass up, a regional tour, then a national tour. I was fortunate enough to sing in new venues, in front of different audiences. I couldn't ask for more."

"Beats the state fair circuit?"

"Oh, I like the state fairs. The midways and the crowds, they're just this fabulous cross section of humanity, and the smell of machine oil and sweat and funnel cakes. I like wandering through the barns, too."

"Really? I've covered my share of state fairs. You must have been seeing something I wasn't."

"I liked watching people get their animals ready to show. The girls grooming horses, or fluffing the cow's hide so it shows better. Bathing sheep. It's so different from anything I know."

Conn all but gaped at her. The woman swaying on her feet from exhaustion after eight months on the road was gone, replaced by the smiling shell who was always ready to give her fans more of what they wanted.

"Speaking of the music business, what's next for you?"

"I'm taking some time off around the holidays," she said smoothly. "Christmas is an important time for my family, and I'm happy to be home for longer than a couple of days."

"You missed all of the excitement that happened here last summer," the reporter said.

"Eve told me what happened. I was so afraid for her, but also really proud. We have to take a stand if we're going to transform the East Side and ensure all of Lancaster continues to grow. Eve's done the hard work for us. Now it's up to the rest of the community to build on the momentum."

"Is that the reason for the concert tonight?"

"We are taking a free-will donation to support the community center, but the main reason for the concert is to give back to the people who've supported me and my music from the beginning."

"How do you keep your voice fresh?"

"I've got a comprehensive regime designed specifically to take care of it."

Cady launched into a description of steam, hot sooth-
ing drinks, no caffeine or alcohol or soft drinks, enforced
rest periods between shows, which lead to the question
everyone seemed to want answered. . . .

"When is your next album coming out?"

"We've been working on material for a while now, and
I'm pretty hopeful it will be ready to go soon."

Nice. All true, nothing specific. Which occurred to
Hannah too. "Come on. Throw me a bone here," she said,
like they were besties.

Cady shook her head, smiling that big smile all the
while. "I understand people are excited for new material,
and I'm so grateful for their enthusiasm. We're just making sure what we release is worthy of their excitement."

Hannah looked at her list of questions. "And what about
Harry Linton?"

The big smile never faded. Conn was absolutely amazed
how she handled such personal questions, asked as if
people had every right to know all the details of her personal life. "He's a friend, that's all."

"So you're not planning to fly over to see him? That was
on Twitter earlier today."

"Was it? I can assure you the last thing I want to do right
now is get on another bus, or plane, or train." She and Hannah both laughed. "No, I'm spending the holidays with
my family."

"So you're broken up?"

"I don't believe either of us confirmed we were together,
so I can't say we're broken up." A response worthy of a defense attorney. "I'm fortunate to call Harry a good friend."

The interview wound down as Eve's staff started to set
up seating for the show, carrying chairs from a storeroom
out the back door to the patio, now enclosed in a big white
tent. Cady posed for a few official pictures, then with Hannah, the photographer, and a couple of Eve's staff.

"I'll take care of the mic and amp myself," Cady said.

Eve flashed her a thumbs-up and stepped out of the path of an employee wheeling out another stack of chairs. Conn's eyes narrowed. Most of the back-office staff had gang ink he recognized.

"Eve certainly puts her money where her mouth is," Hannah said. Her observant gaze followed Conn's and connected the dots. "Even after what happened. It's commendable."

"She doesn't back down," Cady said. "That's why I'm happy to be here, supporting her work. Thanks for the interview. I need to get ready to sing."

Hannah's gaze flashed over to Conn. "Officer McCormick, you were part of the team that rescued Eve when Hector Santiago kidnapped her."

"I was," he said. No use in denying it. His role was a matter of public record.

Hannah stayed by his side while her photographer reviewed shots. "Why does she have police protection?"

Conn said nothing. Even without the confidentiality agreement, he wouldn't give a reporter a single detail about Cady.

"Is this an official presence, or part of the off-duty work officers can do?"

"Any questions about the LPD's role in Ms. Ward's security detail can be directed to Lieutenant Hawthorn, East Side Precinct."

"You're just the muscle?"

"I'm just the muscle."

Hannah all but rolled her eyes. "What's she like when she's not performing?"

"You just talked to her for thirty minutes," Conn pointed out, keeping one eye on Cady.

"And she was performing every single second of those thirty minutes." Hannah looked at him. Conn just stared back, expressionless. He was beginning to understand why Chris had him sign the confidentiality agreement. Twenty-four hours into this gig and he could blow Cady's privacy all to hell, putting Cady in danger and making the department look like a bunch of unprofessional amateurs.

"Maybe none of us know," Hannah said. She collected her photographer and left. Outside the door a line had already formed. He made a mental note to check in with the bouncer before he opened up, and see if Eve could spare another big guy in case the crowd got out of hand. Getting Cady to safety would be easy; the big gates on the far side of the patio were unlocked, simply barred with a bolt.

He walked through the double doors leading to the patio, where a crew was setting up a temporary bar and three big heaters were blasting away. Cady was unpacking equipment when he approached. "Don't you have someone to do that for you?"

"It's a single amp," she said, uncoiling a cord. A glass of ice water and her mug of hot water and honey sat next to a stool. "I've done it myself literally thousands of times."

"Are all interviews like that one?"

"That was pretty standard. Why?"

She was so small. So vulnerable. A powerful, protective urge swept through him, to keep her safe, bundle her away so she could get the quiet and privacy she obviously wanted. "Never mind," he said.

That kind of tenderness was unfamiliar, a little scary. He needed space, so he fell back on what he knew, crossing the dance floor to talk to the big bouncer waiting by the door. The guy was Conn's height and wider, but he shifted his weight and forced himself to make eye contact as Conn approached. He was a big, open-hearted puppy. This guy wouldn't have lasted five minutes on the streets.

"What's your name?" Conn asked. His mental database was coming up blank for a name or an arrest history, but gang ink doesn't lie. If he was inked and didn't have a record, he was the first in history.

"Cesar."

"Worked here long?"

He straightened his shoulders and met Conn's gaze, like he'd remembered a lesson in interpersonal communication skills. "Ever since Miss Eve opened."

"You a friend of hers?"

Cesar nodded.

"I'm Ms. Ward's security detail."

Matt Dorchester strode in from the parking lot and nodded a greeting to Conn. Conn threw a quick glance at Cesar. Matt gave an almost imperceptible nod to indicate Cesar was okay.

"I've got the entrance to the patio," Matt said. "See you in a few."

"You tight with Dorchester?"

"Yeah," Conn said, then remembered he wasn't in uniform or wearing his name tag. If it would get him Cesar's focus on the line now stretching down the block to see Cady sing, he'd play up the connection. "I was there when he took down Santiago," he said, aligning himself with Eve, Matt, and everything they were doing to clean up the East Side's drug and gang problem.

Recognition flickered in Cesar's eyes. Good.

"You've got a handle on that line?" Conn said.

"Yessir," Cesar said firmly. "I've got this."

"Good." He pulled out his phone and took Cesar's number, then texted him. "That's me. Text or call if you see any trouble."

CHAPTER SEVEN

"I brought you fresh ice water, and refilled your Cady juice," Eve said with a smile.

Eye Candy was a little island of Eve in the middle of the East Side, upscale, sassy, determined. She admired how thoroughly Eve had held on to her sense of self, how she could transform the space around her, own it. Cady knew how to do that on stage, the moments to approach the audience, when to hold back and linger behind the mic. Doing the same thing in her regular life wasn't as easy. "Thanks," she said, and sipped the Cady juice.

"How are things going with Conn?"

"He's all cop, still. Just doing a job. Is he former military?"

"Yes. Army, I think, like Matt. He shot Hector's accomplice." At Cady's astonished glance, Eve added, "He did the only thing he could do. From what Matt says, that's pretty much Conn's reputation. Whatever it takes, he'll do it. He's blue, through and through."

Loyal. That's what Eve meant. A man like that wouldn't

play by the shifting, shallow rules of celebrity "relationships." "I need to make a phone call. Where can I get a little
privacy?"

"My office, upstairs," Eve said immediately. "Thick
walls on three sides, and no one goes up there except me
and Natalie."

She followed Eve up the stairs, and tapped Chris's name
in her most-recent-calls list. He was always on the first
screen, and always picked up on the first ring.

"I was just about to call you. What's this I see on Instagram? Pictures of my favorite pop star getting ready to
do a charity show we agreed she wouldn't do?"

"Don't talk about me in the third person, Chris. I told
you I was doing this show as a favor to Eve, and I'm doing
it. Period. Also, what the hell? I just got blindsided by Hannah Rafferty with rumors about Harry!"

"Who is Hannah Rafferty and how would she know
anything about Harry?"

"She's the features reporter for the *Star Trib*, which has
been extremely supportive of me and my career."

"Ah, yes, Lancaster's *Star Trib,* the pinnacle of jour-
nalism."

Cady was scrolling through search engine hits on her
and Harry. "Oh my God, these rumors are all over the gossip sites."

"Cady, stop reading the gossip sites. There is a good
reason why I don't round up every single trail of bullshit
on the internet and send you a daily summary, and that's
because the rumors are like the demons in those pigs in
the Bible. They're legion and will only drive you over a
cliff. There are also rumors you're half alien, rumors that
you've joined some wacko cult in Oregon, and my favorite, that you're having John Travolta's love child."

"John Travolta is something out of the *Enquirer.* The
rumors about me and Harry are on every celebrity gossip

site!" She walked over to the floor-to-ceiling windows overlooking the club and parted the curtains. Conn was talking to Eve, who was pointing at her office. He looked up, saw her, and his expression went even more blank.

"I know. Forget about it. I'm on it. In the meantime, stay inside, and be lazy." Chris sounded distracted. Cady could hear a keyboard in the background.

"I can't just switch from one to the other. I'm not a machine you turn off," she said as she watched Conn's long strides cover the distance between the dance floor and the spiral staircase to the office. "It takes time."

"What's going on, Cady?" Chris asked, his voice gentle.

It was the gentleness that did her in, every single time. Most of the time he was cutthroat and mercenary and absolutely ruthless, shoving and chivvying her up the career ladder, but when she needed it, he was there for her. But the one thing that had become clear in the last day or two was that the album they'd started a year ago wasn't the one she wanted to release now. She was different, changing from day to day.

Just the thought of the chaos she'd cause at the label if she stopped the process now made her light-headed.

"I need time to think," she said, unexpectedly choking up. "I'm just not sure about this album."

A double rap at the door.

"Come in," she called, clearing her throat to cover the thickness in it.

Conn walked in, his gaze sharpening when he saw her face. He took up position against the cinderblock wall, shoulders and one foot braced, jacket open to reveal gun, badge, cuffs all on his worn brown leather belt. Neanderthal thug does insouciant combativeness. For a split second she wondered if he'd agree to a quickie before she went on stage.

"Cady."

Chris's voice in her ear made her jump.

"You're saying you don't want to drop it?"

"I'm saying I'm not sure."

A long silence. "Honey, you're just tired. A couple of months off, a nice Christmas turkey dinner, a happy New Year's, and you'll be so bored you'll be begging me to drop the album."

She tucked the phone between her ear and shoulder and fiddled with the clasp on Nana's bracelet. "I don't know, Chris. I really don't know. It's not me. It's not my sound. It's not the music I want to make."

"What are you talking about? You were there for all the songwriting sessions. You recorded multiple versions of all of these songs, fine-tuning the right sound."

"I know," she said. "I know I was, but it's . . ." She searched for the right words. "They're fine songs. They're fine. I worked on them, and I can sing them. But I think I want more than *fine*."

She could practically hear the wheels spinning in Chris's head, all of the logistics around dropping the album, the appearances already planned, the timing. The money involved in recording the album, the musicians paid. If they junked the album, they lost all of that. She wasn't a big enough star to pull that kind of stunt and hope to have any kind of career afterward.

"You wanted this," Chris said. His voice was wary as he backpedaled in search of his footing. Cady knew how he felt. "Two years ago when you asked me to represent you, we sat down and planned out what we wanted. I got you exactly what you wanted."

And when did this become about him? "I know," she said. "But . . . I don't know anymore. That was a long time ago."

"Cady, sweetie, talk to me after Christmas, okay? Just

take the next few weeks and rest up. If you still feel the same way after the holidays, we'll talk."

"Okay," she said, knowing it was a concession she didn't want to make. "But it's not going to get any easier to pull the album."

"Let's cross that bridge when we come to it. Spend some time with your sister. Get some rest," he said again.

"Rest might not fix this," she warned.

"And it might fix this," he shot back. "Look, you hired me to give you advice. I'm giving you advice. You think you're the first singer to get cold feet about a sophomore album? Please. It happens all the time."

Maybe it did. Maybe she was wrong, maybe all she needed was to mainline gingerbread lattes and shortbread, do some Christmas decorating, watch a Netflix marathon. "Okay," she said again. "I'll give you until Christmas."

"That's my girl," he said, expansive and obviously relieved. "Enjoy the show. Don't sing too long. It's inside, right?"

"Goodbye, Chris," she said, and disconnected the call.

"The building's already at capacity and the line to get in is around the block," Conn said. "I called for backup."

"Is that really necessary?"

"There's a crowd forming on the Mobile Media property, which is trespassing, and also dangerous given that there's a big open pit over there. Big companies don't like bad publicity any more than you do."

"Got it. Do you want me to talk to them?"

"No. I want you to stay inside. I warned the bouncers about your drunken admirer from the last concert. He won't get in. When you're ready to go onstage, I get you there. Clear?"

"Clear." Chris was pissed enough at her. If she got injured at a benefit concert to which she'd donated her services, he'd probably fly back to Lancaster just to kill her himself. She shook out her arms and legs, rolled her head on her neck, blew a few lip trills. Business never, ever entered her performing headspace. The day she couldn't give a great show to a live audience, she'd hang up her guitar. "I'm ready."

He didn't move. "You don't look ready."

"This is my ready face," she said, and smiled at him, the smile that was all teeth and no eyes, the one she'd practiced. His expression didn't change. "Seriously," she said. "This is it. I'm ready."

He pushed away from the wall, shifting planes of muscle and God, the shoulders on him. She expected him to open the door for her. Instead, he walked right up to her, cupped her jaw in both hands, and kissed her.

It wasn't soft and sweet, or reassuring in the slightest. His hands were rough with weight-lifting calluses and the male attitude that skin-care regimes were pointless wastes of time. What sent heat zinging through her was the rough texture of his lips, chapped from days in the cold and wind. For a split second she imagined Conn behind the wheel of a dragster, winter air pouring into the car's interior as he warmed up the tires. Rough, intense.

Then his tongue touched hers, his breath heating her mouth as he tilted his head and parted her lips with his own. Her hands gripped first his jacket, then slid inside and around to his shoulder blades, where his body heat seared through his T-shirt. She went up on tiptoes and kissed him back, answered his demand with a call of her own. More.

Then he stepped back, breathing hard, hands on his hips.

"What the hell was that?" she said.

"Don't know," he replied. He swiped the back of his

hand across his mouth, then stared at the color smeared there. "But now you look ready."

She felt it, the jumpy dance of her stomach, electric ripples along her nerves. She was excited, not nervous, anticipating something good, the chance to connect with the audience, connect them with each other, connect everyone in the building with the basic rhythms of life. Breath and voice and song all coming together to make meaning. To show people what it meant to be alive.

The gray-blue glint of his eyes flashed in Eve's brightly lit office. She laughed, feeling witchy, bewitched, slipping into her stage persona. He didn't back away as she took one step forward, closing the distance between them.

"Again," she breathed.

Then she kissed him. Her breath hiccupped in her throat as she fisted her hand in the front of his jacket and pulled. She had as much chance of moving him as she did of moving one of the trees in her backyard; all she did was yank herself full length against his body but it was worth it to feel his size and strength, how immovable he was. She didn't even rock him on his feet when their bodies made contact from thighs to chest. It wasn't the most sophisticated kiss she'd ever given, mashing their lips together just long enough for blood to bloom in her mouth. Conn stood rigid just long enough for her to get a hint of his erection against her belly. She looped her free arm around his neck, knowing this was spiraling out of control, unable to help herself.

His hair bristled against her palm when she cupped his nape. Conn let out a rough growl, hoisted her right off her feet, and walked her backward, into the wall. Head, shoulders, and hips hit at the same time, knocking the wind from her. His kiss left her no chance to get it back, deep and thorough and definitely, definitely caring about something. Wanting something.

"What is it with you and walls?" she gasped when he came up for air.

"Gotta make sure you're not going anywhere," he replied. He tugged down the collar on her V-neck sweater, and sucked at the thin skin over her collarbone.

She wriggled and tried to climb his body to notch his cock where she wanted it, needed it. "Trust me, I'm not going anywhere."

His hand was on his belt when a sharp knock came at the door. "Cady? Eve says we're pretty well ready to go down here."

Natalie, Eve's manager and friend. This wasn't her house, her wall. She had a show to give.

Conn looked at her, his eyes sharp and glinting with the unwanted return to reality. "You're going somewhere, Queen Maud. You're definitely going somewhere."

He leaned away from the wall, easing up the pressure so she could lower her feet to the floor. "Thanks," she called. "I'll be out in a minute."

Conn clasped his hand to the back of his head, and turned his back to her. Cady inhaled deeply, then ran a couple of scales, just in case Natalie was still listening. Conn was staring at her, expression dialed back to blank.

She picked up her guitar case. "Let's do this."

A cheer went up when she stepped through the office door. Cady smiled, waved both hands, took a quick picture for her social media accounts, then set off down the spiral staircase leading from Eve's office. Conn stayed one step in front of her, surprisingly deft on his feet for a man built like a solid wall of muscle. Eve was waiting at the base of the stairs, guiding Cady through to the patio. Conn's thick, outstretched arm gave her a few inches of breathing room. She needed it. When she'd fisted her hand in his shirt she'd revealed the ink hiding under the soft cotton. Just a hint of the sharp geometric design gave her flashbacks to the night before.

Before she quite knew what was happening, she was seating herself on the stool on the little stage, adjusting the microphone and her guitar. She looked up but the fairy lights strung from the tent's center pole didn't do much to dispel the winter darkness.

"Hi," she said. "I'm Maud."

Then she launched into the acoustic version of "Street (of) Dreams," a song she wrote years before, after visiting a showcase of homes with her mom and Emily. It was about looking into the windows of enormous homes her mom would never own, in neighborhoods where she didn't belong, after her divorce became final. Even at the age of twelve she could see her mother wondering if her decision to divorce was the wrong one.

She didn't sing the song often; it wasn't popular enough to make it into a concert set list, so only her truest fans who'd listened to every song on every album multiple times knew the words. But these were her truest fans, clapping along, and it felt right now, a way for her to work through the questions troubling her.

"I don't know what just happened there, but that was good." She strummed a few chords, smiled at someone's shouted *Yeah!*

But she did know what happened. Conn happened. Conn and his rough mouth and muscled shoulders, his tight fists and iron control. That thought turned at the back of her mind as she spoke. "Songs always surprise me. I think I know them. I mean, I wrote that song, I should know it, right? But sometimes they surprise me. Maybe it's not the song. Maybe I'm different."

Where did we get the idea that dreams would pay us? The question lingered at the back of her mind as she scanned the crowd.

"I remember you," she said to one man in the third row. He froze, then gestured to himself. "Me?"

"You used to work in SoMa, at Il Cortile, right? You'd come outside and listen during your breaks, or before the dinner rush started."

"Yeah," he said. "I did."

"What do you want to hear?"

"'Painted Walls,'" he said immediately.

"Wow. That's an oldie. I love that you guys want to hear songs I wrote," she said. She'd written the song while dating an artist moonlighting as a tagger, one of the graffiti artists Conn probably arrested. The waiter she'd pegged as one of those shy types, because he'd never worked up the courage to approach her. "On slow days, I'd sing for you. It helps sometimes, makes you less nervous to imagine you're singing to just one person. Even after I started playing bigger shows in indoor venues, like clubs. That was a big step up for me, singing indoors. Thanks, my friend," she said when the laughter died down. The former waiter had flushed with delight. Then she sang it for him.

After that she changed up to her more recent songs, the ones written by committee, slowing a tempo, trying a different key, trying to make them her own. In between songs she mentioned success stories for the East Side Community Center Eve's father ran, reminding people that the cover charge and anything else they cared to contribute went entirely to the ESCC.

"Any chance of something new?" Eve called as the set drew to a close.

"Ah," she said. "That I cannot do. I'm working on some new material, but it's not ready yet."

She finished with a Lancaster favorite, one that described a girl's reaction to her first night cruising the strip, the streetlights, the fast cars, the boys racing each other off the red lights. The end of the show devolved into the usual blur, applause, thank-yous, calls for an encore, which she provided, though not a second one, then a crush of people at the edge of the low stage, clamoring for pictures or autographs or to tell her a story. Conn stepped forward and stuck two fingers between his teeth. The sharp whistle, and his gun, badge, and shoulders, cut off all conversation.

Firmly in control of the situation, he held up a hand and leaned close. "How long do you want to stay?" he murmured in her ear.

A shiver of delight raced across her nape. "Until they're done," she said simply.

"Form a line against the wall," he said, and gestured for Eve. She trotted over, then nodded her head and gestured for Natalie to open the gate to the sidewalk, ensuring that Cady would sign for the people who came to see her, not the crowd now forming for Eye Candy's usual Friday night. It took over an hour, but she chatted with everyone who wanted face time. She put her guitar away, wrapped her scarf around her throat.

Eve walked out the back door, crossing the brick-paved patio and rattling the big jar crammed full of cash, checks, and change. "Cady, Dad's going to be so thrilled. Thank you so much!"

"My pleasure," Cady said.

Eve's forehead wrinkled. "The sound system could use some work. You sounded amazing, as always. You had a richer, deeper tone," she said. "I like it. Also, your sister left a message with Cesar. She'll meet you at your house. She tried to get into the bar, but we've got a no-exceptions policy for minors. She left. I think she's kind of upset."

"I forgot about her," Cady said. "She's spending the night tonight. Thanks for everything, Eve. I'll call you later."

"Why are you thanking me?" Eve said from the stage.

"This way," Conn said. He held open the gate leading

to the sidewalk. Across the street, lights illuminated Mobile Media's construction site. The sidewalk hugged Eye Candy's back wall, ending where the parking lot began. He clicked open the locks on the car, parked close to the building's corner, and hustled her inside. Feeling like an idiot, she pulled her hood up over her hair and let Conn pull into traffic without incident.

Once inside the Audi she sank into the post-concert lassitude. The only way she felt whole was in the act of singing. A long time ago, when she first started writing her own material and before other people started "helping," her songs told the truth of how she saw the world. The material she'd just spent eight months singing and promoting felt hard and flat, like a granite countertop, impenetrable and flecked with fool's gold. Pretty, but giving nothing back.

Was she writing music a generation would remember? Would they look back at important times in their lives and connect with a song they heard on the oldies station? She wanted to write the songs that snuck into their mental chatter, not an earworm but songs that changed them, that gave them something every time they heard it, not just nostalgia.

Or maybe that was just her, wanting to sing songs that changed as she changed.

Except she couldn't change. Her entire career was resting on this next album, a logical if somewhat careful transition from aspiring pop star to pop star. People's livelihoods depended on her success, backup singers and road crew, tour manager and designer, everyone at the label. More and more, financial success depended on a few huge megastars, and the up-and-comers came with their own base of support in social media followers, all primed to buy albums and concert tickets and memorabilia and tie-in materials. More and more, the music was about sounding just enough like another popular song, to entice people to buy it.

More and more, all she wanted was to go back to writing her own songs. But she was as much of an airhead as most people thought pop stars were if she believed the label would discard a complete album custom tailored for her voice, the moment, just waiting to drop and launch her to the next level.

What if she made the wrong choice? She'd come so far. A slip now, so close to the top, could lead to irrecoverable fall.

"You okay?" Conn asked.

She clutched her cup a little closer, sipped the hot, sweet water. "I'm great," she said. "Everything's just great."

CHAPTER EIGHT

He might not be the most experienced guy with relationships, but even he knew when a woman was faking a reaction. Cady was no more "great" than he was.

That said, Conn knew exactly what his strengths and weaknesses were. His strength was his body, not his brains. He'd been a mediocre student all the way through school, less interested in the theory behind anything than in the reality of life. He'd always traded the intellectual for the physical, book learning for street smarts. He was capable of quick reads on people, easily discerning when someone offered harm or danger. It made him great at patrol and the first stage of undercover work, simple buy-and-busts, because his radar went off before a situation went to shit.

This was always his weakness, too.

He knew as well as anyone, even before Hawthorn pointed it out, that he missed nuances right, left, and center. That was fine by him. He'd never wanted to be anything more than muscle. The big shots could have the months of planning, the strategizing over a large-scale operation, the press conferences and citations when it was over. Bring him in for the takedown and he was happy.

Working Cady's security used his strengths, yes, but also called his weaknesses front and center. He needed to focus on her immediate security, but also keep in mind the internet threats, the eerie woods at the back of her house, the disappearing tail lights. Being a body man challenged him unlike any other role he'd played as a cop.

Until Cady kissed him in the privacy of Eye Candy's office, the beat of whatever was playing on the house system thumping up through the soles of his boots had set his body vibrating.

Kissing her was an impulse move, based on motives he shied away from exploring. Her kissing him back was Cady to the core. Unpredictable and irresistible. He was still vibrating with all that focused energy as the Audi purred from streetlight to streetlight.

"The concert was really good," he said, playing it cool.

She looked at him and smiled. "You liked it?"

"Yeah," he said. "I've never been to a show like that before. You had a different connection with the audience than you did at the Field Energy Center."

"Hearing fifteen thousand people sing the refrain to one of my songs is pretty cool. But being five feet from a long-time fan, looking into her eyes, knowing what I created affected her is the best thing ever," she said. "That's the high I keep chasing."

"Natalie made you more hot water with honey," Conn said.

She picked up the hot cup and sipped, then gave a little sigh with pleasure as she cradled the cup between her palms. Only her slender fingers protruded from the cuffs of her puffy jacket. He glanced at them, remembering the way they shifted on the guitar's neck as she sang. The calluses on her fingertips made sense now, the slight edge and rough texture lighting up his nerves when she touched him.

He liked her hands a little rough, because her touch registered more than smooth manicured fingers did. All his life he'd reveled in the soft hands of a woman. Until now. Until Cady, fierce and tender at the same time, grabbed him and kissed him back, like she needed what he'd wanted to give her.

He shifted in the seat as his cock hardened. The car's interior crackled with tension humming between them, like a taut wire struck and vibrating, like a guitar string. She'd tightened them between songs, plucking at them until she got the sound she wanted, carrying on a conversation with the audience the whole while.

"You okay?"

She was slouched down in her seat a little, the hood and scarf hiding her eyes, but he knew exactly what she meant. He had only the vaguest idea who Harry Linton was, but a quick Google search revealed he'd been profiled in *People, US Weekly,* and the *New York Times,* which meant he was Someone. And so was Cady. She stood in a bright spotlight, one that relentlessly picked out the details of her life: her hair, her clothes, her relationships, the meanings behind her songs. Conn was just LPD. Nothing more, nothing less. As her security, no one would care who he was, what he'd come from. But as her lover?

Good thing you don't have to worry about that. This is temporary, and we both know it.

But Cady wasn't angry or upset or pouting. She just sounded curious, and in that calmer response he found the space to tell her the truth. "I'm fine."

Those full, pink lips pursed thoughtfully, making him wish he could see her eyes rather than the fur trim on the hood caressing her cheek. "So we're both fine. Or we're both pretending."

"You want me to tell you you're special?" he asked roughly, uncomfortable and turned on at the same time. Like she didn't already know it. He'd seen red-carpet pictures too, Cady in some sexy, slinky gown, turned to face the cameras.

She turned to face him, giving him the full blast of those wide hazel eyes. "People tell me I'm special all day, every day. I want you to tell me the truth. That's all."

The truth was he'd never felt this way before with a woman. But he wasn't about to tell her that. "It's good between us," he conceded. "Chemistry."

"Oh, yes," she said. A little smile quirked the corners of her mouth. "I believe in chemistry. Only the most successful collaborations have good chemistry. You can create a technical masterpiece of an album, but something raw and heartfelt, created between a singer and her producer, or members of a band, will always catch a bigger wave than virtuosity."

He braked for the turn to Cady's gated community, and used the pause while the gates opened to look at her again. "How's your chemistry with Chris?" he asked, remembering the phone call in Eve's office.

She shrugged. "I trusted him with my career. Deer."

He followed her gaze and caught the glint of eyes, standing off to the side of the big gates. Two of them, stock-still at the edge of the tree line, then a flash of white tails and rumps, and they were gone.

"Deer," he repeated. He let up on the brake and the car rolled through the gates and down the hill. Something was niggling at his brain, something about the car. It was the instinct that served him well on those dangerous middle-of-the-night calls. Something about Chris set off his radar, not at full whoop-whoop blare, but he couldn't ignore the tingle at the back of his neck. "What motivates him?"

"Money. Fame. Respect in the music business. Pretty standard stuff."

"Is that what motivates you?"

She waited a long moment. "I'm not sure anymore. Right now I'm thinking about something more basic."

Then her hand was in his lap, cupping his cock through his jeans. He inhaled sharply, then lifted his hips to grind against the heel of her hand. She made a soft little humming noise as they turned the corner to climb the driveway.

"Cady. There's someone on your front porch."

Just a glimpse of yellow in the burning porch light, and he'd never gone from turned on to alert so fast in his life. Adrenaline and sex made for a sizzling cocktail in his veins. Cady sat upright in her seat, so by the time they were visible it looked like nothing was going on. No conversation, no flirting, no heavy petting.

"It's Emily," she said. "I thought she'd be waiting for us at Eye Candy. She's spending the night."

Emily ran to the wooden railing and leaned over to wave at them as Conn pulled into the garage and parked the Audi. He looked at Cady, she looked at him. "Probably for the best," he said over the heavy thumps of Emily's boots down the front steps. His voice sounded normal, totally at odds with his hard-on straining against his zipper.

"You have a very odd definition of 'best,'" Cady said.

With a high-pitched squeal, Emily flew into Cady's arms. "I'm so excited! I have to work tomorrow night but I can stay until three or so. I brought fabric and sketches and movies. Oh! And we can make cookies. I bought the ingredients for chocolate chip cookies, because we'll make Christmas cookies with Mom, right? You're planning on that. Hi, Conn."

The rhythmic bumping sounds weren't Emily's boots but rather a suitcase the size of a recliner that had fallen to the garage floor in Emily's wake. Conn grabbed Cady's guitar from the backseat.

"I'll take that," Cady said.

"It's no trouble," Conn replied.

"She doesn't like anyone else handling her guitars," Emily said, chin lifted, arm firmly tucked through Cady's.

Conn handed over Cady's guitar without comment. For a brief moment their eyes met, hers filled with rueful amusement. *Later,* she mouthed.

He hesitated for only a second. Why not? Why not be her holiday fling? What did he have to lose?

Everything, a small voice at the back of his brain whispered. *You could lose everything.*

He gave her a small nod, then hoisted Emily's suitcase and followed the sisters up the stairs. Emily was still chattering away. "Can you believe Eve wouldn't let me in?"

"Yes," Cady said bluntly. "It's illegal for minors to be in a bar, and you're not even eighteen yet."

"I'm your sister, and it was just the patio. It was embarrassing."

"Because you put yourself in that position," Cady said as she unzipped her jacket. "Being my sister doesn't change the law."

Conn watched this byplay without seeming to watch it. "Where should I put this?"

"In my bedroom," Cady said. She'd toed out of her boots and now stood in the kitchen in her stocking feet, running water into the steamer. "You're in the spare room and I don't have any furniture in the spare spare room."

"He's sleeping here?"

The whisper reached Conn's ears in Cady's bedroom, where he set the enormous suitcase on the floor nearest the window.

"He's sleeping here," Cady said, in a normal tone of voice. "He's no different than Evan."

"Evan didn't sleep in your room!"

"No, he had the room next to mine, just like Conn does."

"It's different," Emily said, still in that stage whisper. "It's your house. It's, like, intimate."

Cady's next reply was muffled, probably by the towel over her head as she breathed in steam, but Conn got the gist of it, the same calm, rational tone.

"Whatever," Emily said. "Let's order pizza! . . . Fine, I'll ask him, but who doesn't like pizza?"

Emily appeared in the doorway. She'd taken off her bright yellow wool coat and was dressed in jeans, ankle boots, and a hoodie that slipped off one shoulder. She had the long legs and slender bone structure of a model, but lacked her sister's poise. She was a kid, trying on different brands of adult for size. "Is it all right with you if we order a pizza?"

"Sure. I'll order it," Conn said. That way he could keep Cady's name off the order.

Emily didn't seem interested in logistics of Cady's privacy or safety, just bounded back into the main living area. She opened her laptop, then said, "Hey, Cady, is your website down for maintenance?"

"Maybe," Cady said. "It would make sense for Bryan to take it down now but he usually tells me when he does it. I'll call him and see."

She pulled up the phone, then set it on the counter on speakerphone. It rang once. "I know. I'm on it."

Apparently Bryan's people skills weren't all that great. "On what?" Cady asked. Emily was in the living room, surfing through social media faster than Conn could track.

"Your website's been hacked," Bryan said. Conn could just imagine him, beard stretching to his plaid shirt, jeans sagging on his narrow hips, surrounded by wrappers and bottles from the new age energy bars and high-octane drinks. "At first I thought the server was down, but the firewall state table has locked up. It's a DDoS attack—."

"A what?"

"Distributed denial of service. It's when someone floods the site with requests, more than the server can handle, and it crashes. Give me a couple of hours and I'll have it back up."

"Em, can you bring me my laptop?"

Em hurried over, her open laptop in one hand and Cady's MacBook Air in the other. For good measure Conn went into his room and grabbed his own laptop. A minute later they stood around the island, Cady's cell on speakerphone in a cluster of laptops. Conn typed in Cady's website. The screen came up with a white screen and a 404 error. Reading it was the extent of his ability to handle cyber crime. "You fucking motherfucker," Bryan said. "You think you're anonymous?"

"We've got backups, right?" Cady said. "You can restore it?"

"This doesn't affect the site or the data. It's just a way of taking your online presence offline."

"Just great," Cady said, scrolling over to her social media apps. "I'll post something so fans know what's going on. When will it be back up?"

"When it's back up," Bryan said, obviously distracted. Conn could hear keyboard clicks in the background.

"How did this happen?" Cady asked. Worry pinched the corners of her eyes.

"I don't know, but I will," Bryan said, grim. "I'm going to crawl so far up this guy's ass I'll be able to inspect his brain stem and figure out exactly where he and his deviant relatives branched off the tree."

Emily's eyes widened.

"How soon?" Cady asked.

"I'm on my way to the colo." Conn heard the sound of

a coat being pulled on, then a door slamming and feet on the stairs. "Once I'm there I can bridge a hub in-line and analyze the traffic. I've got a ticket escalating with the ISP, and I've switched to a secondary ISP and set up a quick page to let your fans know the site is down. That should be up in a couple of minutes."

"What's a colo?" Conn asked.

She gave him a bewildered shrug. "Bryan, you know I don't understand a word you're saying."

"I'm on it. That's all you need to know, until I find the little fuckers who did this," Bryan said. The call disappeared from Cady's phone. Cady looked at Emily, then at Conn. It was the first time he'd seen her looking even a little lost.

"Sounds like he's got that under control," Emily said brightly. "Don't worry about the website. Bryan will fix it. I'm going to put on comfy clothes. We can still watch the movie, then I'll show you my designs. Okay, Cady?"

"Okay," Cady said. Her smile was forced, something Emily didn't seem to notice. She trotted into the bedroom and closed the door.

First the drunk guy, then the car, and now this. "I don't like the timing," Conn said.

Cady scrubbed her fingers through her hair. "Me, either. It's the main hub for my connection with my fans. The database stores all their email addresses for newsletters, their birthdays, all the boards where people talk about concerts and songs and the things I'm doing. I've got other social media accounts, of course, but they all feed back to the website . . ."

She trailed off, and he put two and two together. "If you drop the record they want you to drop, they don't need it. But if you go out on your own . . ."

"I need it. It's my only consistent connection to my fans. I set up my first website before I left home."

He folded his arms across his chest and tried to think about the big picture. "How likely is it they won't drop this album?"

"Extremely unlikely, unless I write new material to convince them to hold it, something to show that if we go in a different direction, it's going to pay off."

"You don't get any say in this?"

"You have to be huge before you get much control over your career," she said. "You've got control when you're nobody, or when you're Beyoncé or Taylor Swift. Or totally independent, like Amanda Palmer."

"Where do you fall in that scale?

She huffed out a laugh. "I'm somebody, with a small *s*. If the album drops and goes big, I could be somebody with a capital *S*."

"Mostly what I'm worried about is you. This feels like a purposeful effort at sabotage."

"It's probably kids messing around, seeing what they can do." Her eyes went blank for a moment. "Wait, do you think the drunk guy from the concert is behind this? Because you arrested him?"

"I've been at this less than forty-eight hours," he said. "My gut reaction is no. This is different than beer-fueled courage. I'm wondering if it's one of the psychopaths from the file."

"Why?"

"It's a logical next step from anonymous threats in the comments section," he said. He stepped closer, the better to keep this away from Emily's listening ears. "The drunk guy was a crime of opportunity. This is a calculated psychological attack. It's a direct hit on your business, and on you."

He wasn't sure how it happened, if she decided to do it or if he did, or if they both did, but her hand turned in his, then his fingers slid along hers, then they wove together.

Looking deep into her eyes, he squeezed gently, hyper-aware of her slender bones, her wide hazel eyes.

"I didn't think about it that way," she said quietly.

"That's my job. I've got this. You think about your new music." He covered her fidgeting fingers with his own, debating whether to tell her about the mysterious car. In the end, he decided not to worry her further.

The bedroom door opened. Cady picked up her phone and tapped in her lock code. A moment later a new text appeared on his phone with Bryan's contact card attached. "I'll let him know to keep you up to date. Let's get this party started, Em," she said.

There was a lot of bouncing and squealing to this sleepover thing, Conn reflected as they sat down in the living area. He hauled in a couple of armloads of wood from the pile and built a fire while Emily popped popcorn and opened bags of snacks. The wood popped and crackled in the background as the opening credits for *Love and Basketball* flashed on the screen.

"Do you have sisters?" she asked Conn when Emily got up to make hot cocoa.

"No," he said. "No brothers or sisters. A good friend has sisters, though. I get the basics of a sleepover."

Her face cleared. The microwave timer dinged. Emily brought in two mugs of cocoa and set them on the coffee table, then squirmed under the covers like Shane's mutt did when he got invited up on the sofa during a marathon video game session. Emily and Cady claimed the sofa, leaning against piled pillows at either end, sharing a big blanket between them.

The movie was pretty good, actually, enough sports to keep his interest. The pizza delivery guy arrived twenty-five minutes in. Conn paid the guy, who showed absolutely no interest in the house, the property, or the address, then closed and locked the door.

"How much?" Cady said as she set three plates on the granite-topped island.

"Fifty-five with tip."

She nodded, handed him two beers and a bottle opener, then returned with the cash. He traded her the open beers for the money, which he shoved in his back pocket, then helped himself to breadsticks and two big slices of pizza. Emily was still on the sofa, using her knees as a table, ostentatiously ignoring him.

Conn relaxed back into the armchair, which let him see into the backyard, although with the reflection from the TV, the fire, and the lights in the kitchen, he couldn't see much, and tuned out the movie. He still hadn't heard back from Kenny, or Hawthorn, for that matter. Watching Cady sing was a pretty good distraction, but sitting around watching a movie while she and her sister munched their way through a bowl of popcorn mixed with M&Ms was about to drive him crazy.

"I'm going to step out for a second," he said.

Even though they were snuggled under a blanket, watching the movie, Cady's energy danced at him, as subtle and playful as one of the songs she sang tonight. Emily's was like coal smoke, thick, dark, toxic as she obviously didn't look at him. He gave a mental shrug. As long as Cady was happy, Emily could resent his presence in her special girls' weekend to her heart's content.

The December wind hit him like a slap, cold, sharp enough to freeze his breath in his lungs. He peered into the woods beside the house, wary of the possum or deer or crazy internet stalkers who might jump out of the deep shadows stretching up the hill behind Cady's house. Shivering, he shoved his hands into his jacket pocket and jogged to the woodpile. Might as well get a few more logs, in case movie night turned into a double feature. He grabbed an armful of thick, rough-split logs and carried them up the steps to the deck, then rapped a knuckle against the glass.

The slats parted with a click. Cady peered out at him. "Let me in. I'm freezing."

She opened the door. "Thanks," she said. Her voice was low, her smile as promising as her singing.

"If you had security cameras and motion detectors I wouldn't even need to go outside."

"You look pretty tough to me," she said, soft and low.

That was still a no to the cameras. He added logs to the fire, settled back into his chair, and accepted a bowl of popcorn from Cady. Emily still wouldn't look at him, appearing to be transfixed by the ending of the movie. When it was over, Cady gave a jaw-cracking yawn.

"Sorry," she said through the end of it. "Between the fire and the blanket and all the heat you give off"—she nudged her sister under the blanket—"my day caught up with me. Turn on the lights and get your designs out."

"No," Emily said. "I'd rather talk about it when you're fresh. Tomorrow morning?"

"Don't you want to sleep in?"

"It's fine," Emily said in the tone of voice that meant it obviously wasn't fine. She got up and wandered over to the floor-to-vaulted-ceiling built-ins, and started examining the objects on them. As she passed, Conn got a big whiff of pissed off teenager. "No big deal."

"I'm sorry, honey," Cady said. "Tomorrow. I promise. What time do you work?"

"Not until three."

"Great. I'll make brunch, and take a look at everything then." She yawned again. "I'm going to take a steam shower, then go to bed."

Conn resolutely did not think about Cady's body slowly turning pink in the heat, steam drifting against the glass, her hair dark and wet against her cheeks and shoulders.

"I'll come with you. I brought my laptop. I can check out the chatter about the website, see if anyone's taking credit for it," Emily said.

"So it's a home day tomorrow?" He almost dreaded the answer. Doing nothing was going to drive him insane.

Cady smiled ruefully and nodded. "Good night."

"I'll shut everything down," he said, adding a look and a wave that meant he'd take one last look around inside, too. Cady smiled her thanks, but her eyes held a hint of regret.

Emily followed her sister into the master bedroom. The door closed, then a few seconds of low-voiced girl murmurs, then the water started running through the pipes. Conn checked every window latch, every door lock. He checked that the garage doors were closed. He turned off all the lights but the one over the stove. Then he looked around the dimly lit space. It seemed warm, homey, secure. But he couldn't shake the feeling that the threat Cady dismissed so easily was real, and close by.

CHAPTER NINE

The next morning Cady woke up alone in her bed.

Blinking against the bright sunshine streaming through the wood slats of the blinds like the world's worst wakeup call, she looked over at the other side of the bed, where Emily had fallen asleep last night. She'd washed her face while Cady leaned against the tiled wall and tried hard not to resent her sister's presence. Emily was such an important part of her life, and time with her was too limited. Once Emily started college it would be even more limited. They were close, but Cady didn't harbor any illusions that she could compete with New York City and the fashion career waiting for Emily there.

She leaned over and patted the fluffy down comforter, just in case Emily was facedown and dead to the world. No Emily. But she smelled coffee, so odds were good Em was in the kitchen, ready to talk fashion. She scooted to the edge of the bed and jammed her feet into her slippers. Hopefully Conn was a late sleeper. Odds were equally good he'd be bored into a stupor by the time Em finished. So far she'd seen him in the same off-duty uniform:

no-nonsense running shoes, jeans, river driver shirt with the sleeves pushed to the elbows, and his denim jacket. His only concession to the cold was to flip up the collar.

Keeping his hands in his pockets was about something else. She felt sure of it.

Her fleece robe was hanging on the back of the bathroom door. She pulled it on over her pajamas and belted it tightly at her waist. Her hair, she discovered, was somewhere between Medusa and electrocuted. Oh well.

She opened the bedroom door and shuffled into the hall, heading for the kitchen. "Whoever made coffee is my new favorite—"

The remaining part of that sentence was cut off when she saw Conn and Em together in the kitchen. Conn was standing on the opposite side of the island, a steaming cup of coffee on the granite surface, his attention firmly fixed on the phone in his hand. Em was leaning against the stove, wearing a pair of footed pajamas covered with bright red kisses. She held a cup of coffee between her hands and was studiously ignoring Conn.

"Good morning," Cady said.

"Morning," Conn said. He looked at her, gaze skimming from hair to monkey-slippered feet, then back at his phone.

"Hi," Emily said. "Sleep well?"

"Yes," Cady said, acting as if nothing were amiss. "Full strength?"

"I made it just the way you like it," Em said. "Half bold, half hazelnut, all decaf."

"How's the weather?"

"Warmer," Conn said. He looked right at her, his gaze never once flicking toward her sister. "A front came through last night. Highs in the forties today."

"Great. I'm going to sit outside and drink this," she said as she opened the fridge. Inside was a carton of her chocolate almond milk. She poured in a healthy dollop. "Care to join me, Em? I saw deer yesterday."

"Sure," her sister said.

"You mind if I make pancakes?" Conn asked.

"I would love it if you made pancakes," Cady said.

"None for me," Emily threw over her shoulder. "Thanks."

Whether the outdoors was warmer than the house's interior was debatable. Cady kept her mouth shut and unlocked the door leading to the deck. Sunshine pooled on the oversized wicker furniture, the dark red cushion covers trapping the heat. She tucked her feet underneath her robe, leaned her head against the chair's high back, and mentally rehearsed her approach to this.

The door opened and Emily came out, clutching the fleece throw from the sofa and a cup of coffee.

"Em," Cady started.

"What?" Emily replied, all innocence. Making Cady say it.

"You're being rude to Conn. Knock it off."

"Why? He's just a bodyguard."

"Exactly. He's my employee. I treat him with the respect and consideration due a professional doing his job."

Em settled into a petulant pout and examined her nails. Uncertain, impatient, and lacking the heavy layer of makeup she'd worn last night, Emily suddenly looked exactly her age. The footies weren't helping, reminding Cady of all the times she'd bathed Em and put her to bed when their mother was working late. "What's wrong?" she asked gently.

"I'm tired of waiting around for my brand to take off," Emily said finally. "It's been, like, forever."

Cady stifled a smile. "Be patient, sweetie. Good things are coming. They're all coming. They'll come a lot faster if you relax and enjoy what you have now."

"Ha," Emily said. "I remember what you were like when

you were my age. You and Mom fought all the time. You couldn't wait to get out of the house and start performing. You barely finished high school! Why do I even have to go to college?"

Cady felt a stab of sympathy for their mother. "Because everyone needs a backup plan."

"You don't have a backup plan. You don't think I'll be successful enough to not end up as a lawyer, like Dad."

"I do not!" Her voice was a little sharper than she intended. "Think about what that will mean if my career nose dives. I bet you can name me a dozen one-hit wonders, or one-album wonders, right off the top of your head. You're only as good as your latest release. Someone hacking my website won't help. I need to work over the next few weeks. Write some songs. Work on the ones I've written."

"You'll be fine," Emily said. "You've got a label. A plan. You're going to be a superstar when that album drops."

"It's not just about being a superstar," Cady said.

"That's easy for you to say when you've got that option. Try being a nobody."

"Em. I was a nobody. When I was your age, I was busking in SoMa for maybe ten bucks a night. And that was a *good* night! Just be patient, and do the work. The rest will come."

"You don't know that!"

"I don't," Cady said. "But I do know that something will come from doing the work. It may not be what you think it will be, but there's always a payoff."

"I don't want some vague new age crap about the work being the reward. I want the runway shows. I want New York Fashion Week. Milan. *Paris.* I want a million followers and people wearing my designs all over the world. Girls my age have that. I want it too!"

She'd forgotten what it was like to be sixteen, now remembering her epic fights with her mother and, less frequently, her father. "Do the work, Em. Do the work and don't get distracted by your emotions. That's the best advice I can give you."

Emily's eyes widened. "Deer," she whispered, pointing into the woods.

Through the trees Cady caught a glimpse of a doe trailed by leggy twin fawns, their spots only a memory. They watched the spindle-legged animals pick their way through the underbrush, then bound up the hill. Emily suddenly switched seats, snuggling next to Cady to lay her head on her shoulder. Cady smiled at her and flipped the end of the blanket over her legs.

Coffee finished, Cady said, "Okay, show me what you're working on."

Moving not all that differently from the deer, Em dashed for the bedroom and slammed the door. Cady strolled into the kitchen, set her cup in the dishwasher, ran water into her steamer for her morning treatment, then poured Emily another cup of coffee.

"No more coffee for you?" Conn said. He stood at the stove, four small pancakes bubbling in the cast iron pan.

"Smells delicious. I treat myself to one cup a day," she said. She walked around the island, as if taking advantage of the need to speak privately to get close to Conn again. Well, she liked being close to Conn, and she wasn't sixteen. Not by a long shot. "I'm sorry about her behavior. I talked to her. It won't happen again."

Conn looked toward the closed bedroom door, a little surprise showing on his face, then expertly flipped the four pancakes to show four golden brown sides. "That? That's nothing compared to what I get every day on the job."

"I know how she feels," she admitted. "We're sisters, down to the bone. She *wants*, you know? She wants out of Lancaster, she wants fame, respect, recognition. Love. She feels trapped, like if she doesn't take matters into her own hands, right now, nothing good will ever happen to her."

Conn peeked under the pancakes, then collected them in a stack and slid them onto a plate. "What did *you* do?"

"I took matters into my own hands. Moved out, started singing wherever I could. Taught myself how to stand out wherever I sang, built a fan base."

He poured four more circles of batter onto the pan, then glanced toward the shower in Cady's master bedroom suite. The water was still running. His gaze searched hers. He bent his head and brushed his mouth over hers.

"Are you listening to me?"

"Not anymore," he said.

She felt his lips quirk into a brief smile against hers. She smiled in response, then gently bit his lower lip, felt a growl rumble behind the planes of muscle in his chest. That was the thing about Conn. She had to be close enough to feel his emotions. Distance meant she got glimmers, flickers, a light in the distance. Up close, his emotions seeped from his skin to hers, big waves of energy transmitted by glancing touches, shared breath.

The shower shut off. "Later?" she murmured.

"Probably not a good idea," he said.

"Let's do it anyway." This time his tongue touched hers, slick, electric heat lighting her up.

"Almost ready!" Em called.

Conn straightened, muttered a curse, and flipped the four pancakes. Cady snatched up the towel, and had her face in the steam before Emily opened the door. She was no actress, but at least the heat would explain the flush on her face. "Wow," she said.

"Really?" Em spun in a circle, then strutted toward the island in a convincing runway walk before she snagged a heel, stumbled, and collapsed against the island in a fit of giggles.

"Yes, really." Cady draped the towel around her neck, boxer style. "Turn again."

The ensemble was a brown suede short skirt laced together along one hip, paired with a moto jacket in the same fabric.

"Nice choice with the suede. It's timeless but really on trend," Cady said. She rubbed the suede between her thumb and forefinger. Emily had taken her time with the stitching; the fit and finish was impeccable. "I love it. What else have you got?"

They ate while Emily modeled. It didn't escape her notice that under the attention her sister finished off six of the pancakes, snagging bites between striking poses.

"Do you need me for anything?" Conn asked. The conversation had turned to red-carpet wear. He was edging away from the kitchen, step-by-step, something she'd noticed only when the distance had accumulated.

"No," Cady said.

"I'm going to work out."

Emily had twenty pieces in progress and dozens of sketches: dresses, skirts, gowns, blouses, and tops. The conversation ranged over everything from the latest gala looks to social media, and included a lunch of sandwiches and fruit Cady made while Emily modeled. Cady did her best to stay engaged, but Emily could read her moods.

"What's wrong?" she asked, tossing her sketchbook on the coffee table.

"I'm just thinking."

"You want me to make you some Cady juice?"

"Actually, sweetie, this was really inspiring. I wouldn't mind doing some work of my own."

"Oh." Emily closed her sketchbook. "Okay. I'll head home and work on the things we've talked about."

"Or take a break. Hang out with your friends and don't think about fashion for a while."

"I could do that. Olivia and Grace were getting a group together to go to the movies tonight. I might go with them."

"That sounds like a great plan," Cady said. Emily seemed to be waiting for her to say something else. Cady struggled to come up with something. "When do you want to start decorating for Christmas?"

Emily shrugged. "I don't know. Will *he* be around?"

That was a very good question. Chris insisted on twenty-four-hour protection, but surely Conn had family to see, and things of his own to do. "He'll have the day off, of course."

"Okay. Good. I want it to be just the three of us, like old times. We need to pick out a tree, too."

"Over the weekend. Gotta stick to Mom's schedule," Cady said.

She waited while Emily packed up her overnight bag and her suitcase of designs, and waved from the garage as she backed the little sedan down the driveway. Then she closed the door and made her way to the exercise room.

To her surprise, Conn had his sneaker-clad feet tucked into the loops of the suspension straps. His weight was balanced on his left palm, his body rotated perpendicular to the floor with his right arm extended to the ceiling. Every muscle from his throat to his hipbones stood out as he held himself there to some mental count. "What's up?"

As she watched, a bead of sweat trickled along the first ridge of his abdominal muscles, then dripped to the floor underneath him. "I'm going into my studio," Cady said. "There's food in the fridge, sandwich fixings, eggs, some leftover Fat Shack."

"Thanks." He looked up at her, his blue-gray eyes translucent and unreadable in the winter sunlight streaming through the south-facing windows.

She watched for a moment longer as he transitioned to pushup position. Despite the potential for shifting off-balance and the tenuous resistance of the handgrips, not the floor, the suspension straps didn't move as he counted off pushups. She'd tried that, and knew exactly how much core strength and balance was necessary to make it look that easy.

He was the one working out, but she was the one with flushed cheeks. Heat trickled through her body to pool between her thighs. As she walked into her studios, reminders of Conn, his scent, his breathing, the soft grunts he made as he pushed his body to the limits of human endurance filled her mind.

"Stop being a cliché," she muttered, and turned on the soundboard. She settled in with her guitar and her notebook, paging through to find lines that caught her attention, images that spurred a response, searching for a subject to anchor a song, or even an album. Emily's enthusiasm and drive had inspired her, reminding her of the girl she used to be, living only for making music, trying to tell a story with words and harmony, but the problem was that somewhere along the way, she'd become a mouthpiece for someone else's lyrics, a tune composed in committee. Who was Cady Ward? What did she see? Believe? Hope for? Dream of? What did she want to share with the world? It was all colored by Maud's experiences, Christmas lights seen through a snow-smeared windshield. Who would she be after another album dropped, another year of performing songs she didn't write sung to tunes she tweaked, at best?

Two months. She had two months at home to ground

herself, to try to integrate the experiences she'd had since Harry discovered her with the young woman she'd been then. She could do it.

Resolutely she picked up her guitar, opened her notebook, and adjusted Nana's bracelet on her wrist. Positioned her tea just so. Strummed a few chords, hummed a few notes. But she couldn't shake the sense of unease sloshing inside.

CHAPTER TEN

Conn's phone rang the next afternoon. He felt a leap of relief that Kenny was finally calling him back. But the name displayed on the screen was Ian Hawthorn's.

"McCormick."

"It's Hawthorn. I'm checking in to see how things are going with Ms. Ward."

"Fine," Conn said. "She sleeps a lot. Her sister spent the night last night. We ate popcorn and watched a romcom."

"Sounds delightful," Hawthorn said drily.

"You want the job, it's yours," Conn replied.

"Bored?"

"Out of my skull." Except when Cady was awake, and not in her studio, as she was now. Just being in the same room with Cady made him feel more alive than he'd ever felt without gunfire involved.

"Anything suspicious?"

"Two things that may or may not be connected. One, someone hacked her website, which is a real problem for her right now. Two, I saw someone lurking at the end of her driveway," Conn said.

Conn heard him typing on the other end and knew he was making notes of his own. Nothing escaped the ice cool Ian Hawthorn. "Do you think the two are connected?"

"To each other, or to that file of psychos her manager compiled?" Conn said. "I'm treating them like they're all connected. Her website guy is working on tracing the hacker. I've stepped up my patrols of her perimeter. She once again refused to install security cameras. She doesn't have any appearances scheduled for the next few days. That will help."

"Do you need backup?"

He looked out the big windows into the bare trees climbing the slope behind the house, then crossed the floor to the smaller front windows overlooking the driveway and peered through the shades. "No," he said, surprising himself. A few days ago he would have given anything to get a break from this kind of work, to go back to the only family he had and find out who had set him up to take the fall for a brutal crime he didn't commit. But while he'd been assigned to protect "Maud," Cady was slowly slipping behind his defenses. She wasn't just a job anymore, an obstacle. She was his to protect. His.

Except nothing belonged to him, least of all Cady Ward.

"No," he said again. "I've got this."

"You know, McCormick, it's not a crime to ask for backup," Hawthorn said mildly. Conn could just imagine the LT leaning back in his chair, hands folded behind his head, staring at the ceiling. "Teamwork is considered an asset in most situations."

"I know, LT. But I really don't need it. She's used to one person. Another guy coming and going means more for the neighbors to notice, and handoffs mean more chances for something to slip by unnoticed."

"And a second set of eyes means it's more likely something *will* be noticed." More typing. "Fine. You're it, for the moment. Best to keep you out of sight."

"What's going on with the investigation?"

"We're investigating," Hawthorn said blandly. "And you are not. You're doing what I asked you to do and maintaining a low profile. Right?"

Calls to Kenny didn't count as getting in anyone's face. "Yes," Conn said.

"Good. Just stay out of sight. We want to keep this out of the media as long as possible."

The door to Cady's studio opened. "Got it. I have to go," Conn said, then disconnected.

"I'm going out of my mind," Cady said. She brushed past him, up the stairs to the main floor. Her voice floated down to him. "I've got to get out of here."

"Fine by me," he said.

She'd made her way to the kitchen, filling the steamer with automatic movements that went beyond habit and into the bone. "Like, now."

"Just say the word."

She contemplated him, her hot gaze flicking over his body. "You didn't have to hang up for me." Her hair looked like one of the clumps of brush out back, tangled golden brown thicket with a life of its own. "You really don't have any family, people you talk to on a regular basis? I don't expect you to give up your life entirely."

It had to be hard for someone like Cady to imagine, but the department was the only family he had. Maybe that was the other reason Hawthorn chose him for this gig. Most everyone else had a family to go home to, people who would miss them if they were assigned to a long-term close protection assignment. He had no one. "I'm good. My friends know I disappear, but I always turn up."

"What have you been up to?"

He shrugged. "Not much. Took a shower. Watched some NASCAR." Pored over the psychos file, then Jordy's file. Tried to figure out who in the Demons had the kind of access to beat up a Stryker in police custody and hang it on him. Both files were on the kitchen island, but he didn't reach for them. He'd learned that drawing attention to the scars over what you wanted to hide only made people that much more likely to poke at it.

But Cady wasn't looking at either file, just plugging in the steamer and reaching for her towel. He didn't understand that, either. If he was on the receiving end of a file like that, he'd track down each and every anonymous troll and make them pay. Cady seemed content to just do her thing. "Who won?"

He wrenched himself back to the moment. "Kyle Busch. He's first in points, too."

"I'm more of an Indy car fan myself," she said. Her voice was muffled by the towel. "But I'll take NASCAR when the Indy season is over."

"Want to watch some racing?"

"I thought the race was over."

"I meant at the airfield."

She flipped the towel back and stared at him. "You're still racing this late in the year?"

"As long as it's dry, we race."

"Yes." She gave a delighted little laugh. "God, yes. That's perfect. Let me get dressed."

He called Shane while she was changing her clothes. She came out of the bedroom wearing jeans and a turtleneck sweater, with her hair caught back in a braid and covered with a hat. She stomped her feet into fur-lined boots, and pulled on her down coat, gloves, and a scarf.

"Chris won't like this," he said.

"What Chris doesn't know won't hurt him," she replied as she pulled the scarf up over her nose and mouth.

"When did you hire Chris?" he asked, thinking about the website, and the sparring he'd seen at the precinct.

"The second he offered me representation. Agents weren't exactly beating down my door. Are you always this suspicious?"

"In this case, yes. So as long as you're acting in his best interests, he's got your back. What happens if you insist on taking a big risk at this stage of your career? Then your interests don't align with his anymore."

"Are you suggesting he's trying to ensure I do the financially lucrative thing for his own benefit?"

She could read him so easily he wondered if a news feed scrolled across his forehead. "I've seen people shot dead for the price of a cheap carryout pizza," he said. "I assume you're talking about a lot of pizzas."

"Many, many high-end pizzas, made with organic ingredients and the cheese from goats fed ground-up unicorn horns," she said. "I know Chris looks like a slick snake oil salesman. He pushes me, I push him. But in the end, I trust him completely."

He waited until they'd left her gated community and were heading south on Highway 75 before he brought up Emily. "Has your sister always been that . . . high strung?"

A smile flashed across her face at his diplomatic choice of words. "You really don't know any teenage girls, do you? Patience has never been Emily's strong point. She's impulsive, and emotional. She's ready to be done with high school but has to finish in order to get to college. She's trapped here, full of dreams and ambitions, but stuck. It's enough to make anyone irrational."

"You know how she feels."

Cady nodded. "Our mom wanted a house and a job and kids to look after. Our dad was the big dreamer, and when little Lancaster and our little family of little girls got too small for him, he moved on. We inherited his drive."

She spoke lightly, not bitterly, but he knew how much that kind of equanimity cost. "She's got plenty."

"It used to be cool to be my little sister. Now I think she wants to be known as Emily Ward, a person in her own right."

When they got to the airfield, he pulled up next to the guys taking admission fees in exchange for wristbands. "She's part of Team McCool," he said and got waved through. Inside the chain-link fence cars, trailers, and trucks were lined up in a staging area on one side of the runway. Big banks of lights illuminated the runway now serving as the drag strip. Tents covered the tire warm-up spot, while a couple of cars that just finished their run drove back along the other taxi strip. The big doors to the ancient corrugated metal hangar were open, and a steady stream of people made their way inside to get food and drinks or to warm up a little.

He parked the Audi in the grass, then got out to assess the temperature. Upper forties, he guessed, a little colder than his dad's best run. He wouldn't get weather like that again this year. The colder the air temperature, the better and faster the engines ran. He didn't want to beat his dad's time in more optimal conditions, but that wouldn't stop him from racing anyway.

She came around the Audi's trunk and met him in the weed-strewn gravel. "You going to be warm enough?"

"I'm wearing long underwear, and a down coat. I *do* live here," she said.

The fake fur around her hood wasn't moving. No breeze, which was a blessing and a rarity at this time of the year. Cold air could howl out of Canada at any time. He reached out and pulled her scarf up to cover her mouth and nose. "Got your Cady juice?"

She held up the thermos. "I made a fresh batch."

"Let's go."

She kept up with his stride as they crossed the tarmac, headed for a trailer parked in a prime spot close to the hanger. Shane was there, only his legs visible as he worked under Conn's car. "How's it going?"

"Fine. Just . . . fucking . . . fine," Shane said, between grunts as he tightened down the bolt on the fuel pump. He wormed his way out from under the car and took Conn's hand to get to his feet, then did a hilarious double take when he saw Cady. "Oh. Hello. Sorry about the language."

"Shane McCool, this is Cady Ward. Cady, meet Shane."

"Welcome to pit row," Shane said, doing an admirable job of putting the cool in McCool. "I'd shake your hand but mine's covered in grease."

Cady gave him a friendly little wave. "You're a friend of Conn's?"

"Since third grade. He wanted to race cars and I wanted to fix them."

"Sounds like a match made in heaven," Cady said.

"Shane's a pretty good driver," Conn said.

Shane jerked his thumb at Conn. "And he knows his way around an engine. But I'd rather fix them than drive them."

"I don't have time to do the repair work."

"She's a high-maintenance girl," Shane said, patting the roof of the car. "Good thing I'm patient."

"Good thing one of us is," Conn said.

Shane snorted. "You're more patient than I am. I would have given up on this a long time ago."

Conn shot Shane a look. He wasn't ready to tell Cady about his quest to beat his dad's time. Shane knew about it, had known almost as long as he'd known Conn. But he balked when it came to telling a stranger, an outsider, someone who might not understand.

But Cady was just smiling, looking around, then focusing on Shane. "McCool from McCool's Garage?"

"That's us."

"My mom takes her car there. She says she's found the real unicorn, an honest mechanic. She was married to a lawyer, so she knows unicorns when she meets them."

"Your mom's Patty Ward? She brings in cookies and cider every year at Christmas."

"That's my mom. "

Shane laughed. "You're basically family, then." He turned to Conn. "You driving, since you're here?"

His first priority was to Cady. "Finn can make a couple of runs," he said, nodding at Shane's nephew rummaging in the tool chest.

"It's all right if you want to," Cady said. "No one knows I'm here, and I'm all masked up like a bank robber. I'll sit on the bleachers and watch."

"You sure?" Conn asked.

"I'm sure," she said. Hazel eyes twinkling, she pulled her scarf up over her nose and mouth.

He got a folding chair from the trailer and set it up by the trailer's bumper, where he could easily see her. How could she go unrecognized? She was beautiful, vibrant, famous, and apparently, perfectly happy to sit on a sagging lawn chair in a drag race pit and watch him tinker with a forty-year-old muscle car.

"We're getting good times," Shane said. "The weather's damn near perfect."

"Who's running?"

Shane started rattling off teams and names. As Conn worked on the engine with Shane, he glanced around the airstrip. Lancaster's airport was basically for small planes, a skydiving school, and the occasional weekday commuter flight to Chicago or Pittsburgh. The weekend hobby pilots had an amicable relationship with the drag racing association. Occasionally they had to clear a taxi strip of cars finished with their runs so a private plane could land, but the announcer kept his ear tuned to the air traffic and just about anyone who flew in and out of the airstrip on a regular basis had the announcer's cell phone. On one memorable occasion they'd had an engine-failure emergency landing, but as there was always a fire engine and ambulance on standby; a good chunk of the racers were off-duty firefighters, cops, or EMTs; and the cars were all designed to go very fast, very quickly, the crisis went like a textbook training exercise.

Between making adjustments to the fuel pump, he looked around the airstrip, seeing it through Cady's eyes. A taxi strip flanked either side of the main runway; Conn, Shane, and Cady and the rest of Team McCool, along with the crews for the other cars were arrayed in a kind of pit row along the one closest to the airfield entrance while cars that had finished their runs cruised back to the pit along the other. Cars lined up to make their runs at the near end of the runway before rolling up the staging lanes to the burnout strip. Two cars revved their engines on the burnout strip, warming up their tires, sending the smell of hot rubber into the air.

He and Shane both stopped to watch the run. The cars roared down the track, engines revving into a high whine. Ten seconds, give or take—races won or lost in hundredths of a second. It was a sport of reflexes and speed, reputations solidified and legends made on less time than it took to blink. When they'd made the final adjustments, Conn rummaged through the trailer for his safety jacket and helmet.

"I've got that," Cady said.

He looked over at her and found his jacket draped over her legs. "I'll swap you," he said, and shrugged out of his jacket. "Sure you're not too cold?"

"Not at all."

He zipped up the jacket and plucked his helmet from

her outstretched hand. "Thanks. You don't have to watch or anything," he said. "Grab some tea. They've got portable heaters inside the hanger."

"I wouldn't miss this for anything," she said. "It's a dial-in night, right?"

"Yes," he said.

Some races were straight head-to-head competitions, but Conn wasn't here to race kids in their souped-up street cars. He was racing a time. 9.99 seconds. That was his dad's best time in the ZL1. In dial-in, the focus was on the driver's performance, the starts adjusted so that, theoretically, the cars would cross the finish line at the same time. It rewarded both the driver and the car's consistency, not who had the most cash to buy the newest, best equipment. It was all about driver skill.

"What did you dial-in?" she asked, peering at the slip of paper in his hand.

"Nine point nine-nine."

His dad's best time. Conn had never broken ten seconds. A 9.99 finish would tie him with his father. Nine point nine-eight or faster would mean he'd "broken out"; he'd be disqualified from the race, but would've beaten his dad's time.

Still carrying his jacket, Cady kept pace beside the ZL1 until he turned right to get in line for his run and she turned left to find a spot in the bleachers. They weren't crowded, only family members, girlfriends, and die-hard fans willing to sit on backless metal bleachers in this weather. Cady got a good seat on the first row and draped his jacket over her knees again. She was looking around with interest, taking in the Christmas-tree starting system, the interval timers, the speed traps used to calculate top speed.

Shit. This was a stupid idea, leaving her protected only by her anonymity while he raced down a demon he'd never beat.

He rolled forward a few feet to prestaging, as another pair of cars left the line. Burn the tires to warm them up, roll to the starting line, watch the amber lights on the Christmas tree flash down in half-second increments. At the last one, he floored the accelerator and shot down the track. The bleachers passed in a blur. All he heard was the engine and his own breathing as he focused on a fast, clean run. Shit. He mistimed the shift from third to fourth! The GT beat him to the line, but in handicap racing all that mattered was staying under your time.

The interval timer flashed 10.00 just ahead of the shutdown area. Fuck, *fuck*! As he drove sedately down the taxi strip at ten miles per hour, he caught a glimpse of Shane sitting by Cady. Keeping her company, keeping an eye on her. It didn't matter. Shane had his back.

It was open night at the track, so he did a few more runs. His times varied from 10.01 to 10.00 before he gave up and exited the track, rolling back to the trailer. Shane was already there.

"Driver error," Conn said.

"Don't be too sure about that," Shane said, hands on hips, listening to the engine. "I'll take a look at it tomorrow."

"Thanks for looking after Cady."

"I didn't do it for you," Shane said, then winked at him. "She seems down to earth. Normal. Not like your typical famous person."

"How many famous people do you know?"

"One, now," Shane said. "Mom loves all those entertainment shows. Batshit crazy, the whole pack of them. But not Cady."

Not Cady, who had dated Harry Linton and planned to drop a record that would make her a global superstar. "No," he said absently. "Not Cady."

Cady strolled up, wearing his jacket over hers. She looked absurd, her petite body disappearing into her puffy down coat and his denim jacket. She had her hands jammed into the pockets, and based on the bulge inside the coat, her insulated mug wedged inside.

"Nice runs," she said. "You were close. A hundredth of a second."

Not close enough. "Thanks," he said, slicing Shane a look to keep him from telling her why they weren't great runs at all. He had maybe a month left of weather closest to the dry, cold air in which his dad made his best run. If he couldn't do it by Christmas, his chances were shot for another year.

"I'm going to stop at the porta-potty," she said.

"You sure? We're not far from town."

"I could wait," she mused, "but I have to pee, there are porta-potties by the hanger, and I'm not that fastidious about them."

"I'll come with you."

He escorted her there, and stood discreetly to the side when she went inside. He was leaning against the hangar wall, examining the grease under his nails and wondering what the hell had happened in his life, when someone very big and very solid thudded back against the corrugated metal beside him.

Conn straightened, shoulders squaring, hand automatically going to his hip before his brain caught up with his body. He recognized this guy.

"Cesar, right? From Eye Candy? Why aren't you at work?"

"It's my birthday. Miss Eve gave me the night off."

Conn's eyes narrowed. Could be true. Could be total bullshit.

Cesar kept his gaze focused on the line of cars waiting to race. Outside Eye Candy he seemed harder, the years of street life coming to the surface. The gang tattoo on his neck was visible in the light before he hunched his shoulders. "You're looking in the wrong place."

Two seconds earlier Conn's brain had been coasting along in neutral. Now it jerked from second gear into overdrive. "For what?"

Cesar just looked at him. He was all but hidden in the dark shadow angling across the hanger's metal wall; a sharp line delineated the lights on the drag strip and the pitch-blackness leading into the grassy field behind the hanger the jump school used as a landing site.

"It ain't the county. Ain't the street. Look closer than that. Inside the Block," Cesar said.

The Block was street slang for the Eastern Precinct, based on the building's square shape and brick facade. The architecture was uninspired, as most city facilities were, and felt like a prison or the kind of place to make a last stand when the zombie apocalypse arrived. Cops were insiders. Everyone else wasn't.

Cesar was saying the answer to who beat up Jordy Jackson and framed Conn for it was inside the Block. He'd been betrayed by one of his own.

CHAPTER ELEVEN

Fury seared Conn's veins. Police departments were no different than any other segment of the population; they had good guys and bad guys, but Cesar was hinting at a level of corruption that included assaulting a prisoner and framing another cop for it. The possibility was zero. His muscles tightened as his temper flared. The only thing that stopped him from fisting his hands in Cesar's hoodie and slamming him into the wall was the fact that their combined weight might send the hangar crashing to the ground.

Reflexively he shoved his fists into his jacket pocket, and got a grip. He had to ask the questions. Even false leads had to be run down, to prove a case beyond a shadow of a doubt. "Not the county."

Cesar shook his head. In the distant part of his mind Conn had to laugh. Cesar's big bald head was protected from the cold by the same type of black wool watch cap Conn wore.

"Where should I look?"

"Somebody has to replace Hector." He stepped further into the hangar's long, cold shadow.

Bullshit. "You're saying someone inside the Block went after leadership of the Strykers?" he asked, incredulous. "Who?"

Cesar edged deeper into the shadows. "I got people depending on me. I got a future," he said, shaking his head.

All of Conn's options zipped through his head. He could arrest Cesar on some charge, get him into the Block, make him talk. Until a few days ago that was exactly the kind of in-your-face move he'd pull. But Hawthorn told him to stay out of everyone's grill. So he bit his tongue, shoved his fists deeper into his pockets, and let Cesar walk away.

Cesar was lying. Had to be. Except . . . he had a good thing going working for Eve, and everyone knew messing with Eve would bring down Matt Dorchester's wrath, with the power of the LPD behind it. Cesar had nothing to gain by lying, and everything to lose. Unless lying to Conn got Cesar some kind of street payoff.

He shook his head. Instinct told him Cesar wasn't wired for the streets. He was too soft, too kind, too willing to work an actual job and struggle his way to a GED. The streets weren't easier for him. Which meant he had nothing to gain by lying.

Which meant Conn had to take his statement seriously.

Which meant Conn was in deep, deep shit. The average street tough couldn't do a tenth of the damage to Conn a crooked cop could. Everything was on the line. His job, his identity, possibly his freedom.

Fuck Hawthorn. Time to do some detective work. He strode back into the light and found Cady helping Shane close and lock the trailer doors. "There you are," she said when Conn rounded the corner of the hangar. The crowd had dissipated, only a few lingering to talk to the racing teams as they drove cars onto trailers and closed up folding chairs.

"Watch your fingers," he said.

"We were very careful," she said solemnly, but the teasing in her eyes faded as she got a good look at his face.

"All set?" he said to Shane.

"We're good to go," Shane said, then turned to Cady. "You're officially on the pit crew for Team McCool."

"Wow," Cady said. "I'm honored."

"You're our good luck charm. Nothing broke on the old girl tonight."

Cady laughed. "I'll be your lucky rabbit's foot any day. Next weekend?"

"Every weekend it's dry, we race."

She collected her insulated mug from the ground beside the trailer and fell into step beside Conn. He was prepared for feminine inquisitiveness, but Cady didn't say anything as they climbed into the Audi, or when he gave it too much gas and kicked up gravel as they shot out of the lot and down the road to the highway.

"That was fun," she said with a longing look at the gauges. "Thanks for suggesting it. Makes me want to take her out for a run."

He struggled with an answer. She obviously wanted to burn off more energy, and it was her car. The odds of a stalker running them off the road were slim, but the odds of nailing a deer on some back county road were pretty good, this time of year. He wanted to get back to her house and sign into the department's system and start running down more information on Jordy's known accomplices, and the current situation on the street in Lancaster.

"Conn. At least let me drive home," she said as they neared the stop sign at the intersection of the airport road and the highway.

He shifted into park at the stop sign and got out of the car. In a flash she was out of her seat, darting around the hood. "Yes, yes, yes," she said.

He'd barely buckled up when she peered around him to

her left, then back down the highway toward Lancaster. Nothing coming in either direction. She turned right, away from town, then jammed the pedal to the floor.

The Audi hit sixty miles per hour in the time it took him to scrabble for the sissy bar above the passenger door. It hit a hundred before he could draw breath. The engine purred hard up to a hundred and ten, RPMs screaming into the red by the time he bellowed, "Slow down. Right fucking now!"

"Sorry, sorry," she said, already easing back to the speed limit. "God, I needed that."

"Do you think me being in the car with you means you won't get a ticket? Hell, I'll write you one myself!"

"Go for it," she said. Her right hand rested on the gearshift while she drove with her left, handling the sports car with ease. "But it would be worth it. Again? Just once more? Please?"

"No," he said, finally letting go of the sissy bar. "No way. If you really want to drive fast that badly, I'll bring you out for the next test-and-tune event."

"Fine, but I'm going home by the back roads. What's a test-and-tune?"

"It's a good time for beginners to take some practice runs and for the rest of us to see what tinkering over the week did to our times."

"Your times were extremely consistent," she said. She'd slowed down to the speed limit and turned on the high beams, the better to see the pinpoint reflections of deer's eyes in a ditch before they bounded up onto the road.

"I've been racing that car since I was eighteen," he said. "I know what it can do."

"The point of a dial-in is to get as close to the time you choose without going over, right?" At his nod, she added, "So you were really close. Very consistent."

He consistently failed to beat his dad's time. "Yeah."

The car purred up and down the wooded, rolling hills to the north of Lancaster, quiet, controlled but with a hint of menace to it. Or maybe that was just him, projecting. She pulled up to a second set of gates on the opposite side of the development and keyed in her code. She cruised through the streets. Conn studied the houses more closely: big, mostly brick but some modern architectural statement houses scattered throughout the lots. The big windows weren't covered, the homeowners' Saturday night on full display to anyone who drove by.

"Good thing you didn't pick a house like that," Conn said. "That be a nightmare to secure."

She glanced over. "That's a Maud house," Cady mused. "Maybe I'm not sophisticated enough, but that feels like a small museum to me, not a house. Where did you grow up?"

"Here."

"I meant, where, here? Which neighborhood?"

"The South Side."

"Oh. I don't know that neighborhood as well."

His monosyllabic approach worked, because Cady drove the rest of the way in silence. He waited while she parked the car then escorted her up the steps. Moving on autopilot, he left her in the kitchen filling her steamer, to hang up his jacket. When he came back, she was staring down at an open folder he'd left on the island. "I was thinking about some of these emails, and the website going down," she said. Then her voice slowed. "What's this?"

She'd opened the folder on Jordy, not the psychos folder. He wanted to leap across the table and tear it from her hand. *Don't show weakness. Don't flinch.* Instead, he shoved his fists in his jeans pockets, hunched his shoulders. She was reading it, flipping through the pages, the damning pictures.

Then she looked at him, her hazel eyes wide with disbelief. "You're accused of doing this."

It wasn't a question. "Yeah," he said. His voice sounded both rough and emotionless at the same time. He waited for the automatic question. *Did you do this?*

"You didn't do this."

He opened his mouth. Closed it. Obstinately chose the devil's advocate role. "You don't know that."

"Yes. I do."

"One trip to the drag races and a night in bed and you know me? You don't know me. I'm capable of that. When I was a kid, I got into fights for the fun of it. I've got all kinds of anger issues."

She looked at the close-up of Jordy's face. "We all are. Everyone's capable of violence if the right button's pushed. But I know you a little. You're not the kind of man who hurts someone else when he's angry or in pain."

He snorted to cover the hot rush inside him. "Sure I'm not."

She paged through the report. It was official police business pertaining to an open case. She was a civilian. He should have confiscated it. He didn't, although he couldn't say why. Maybe because she deserved to know who was living in her house, sleeping in her bed. Maybe it was because he wanted her to know. "Most people look at me and see brutal."

She looked up. Blinked. "Are they blind?"

"Why don't you?"

She shrugged. "I'm not blind. You didn't do this, so who did?"

"I don't know," he said, frustration surging again. His hands were jammed so far into his pockets he thought he might rip the seams at the bottom. "That's why I'm here, with you. Hawthorn needed to get me out of sight while he investigates." He pulled his hands out of his pockets, the denim scraping his knuckles before he shoved his hands over his head. "Fuck!"

"I can get someone else," Cady said. "You've got better things to do than babysit me."

"No way," he shot back. Not without cameras or motion detectors.

"At least take a couple of hours off. Investigate on your own. I'll be fine."

"I'm not leaving you. *No way*."

He stopped because he had no right to say that to her. No claim on her. She could fire him, demand a replacement. No one wanted to be around a guy with that kind of shit clinging to him, and no matter what Hawthorn said, that shit would stick to him for the rest of his career. His life. She would leave after the holidays and go on a world tour, meet up with Harry Linton again, marry a movie star or a music star or a tech mogul, and he'd be here. The only thing that made sense was to clear his name so he could keep the only life he'd ever wanted. The only family he'd ever truly belonged to.

She closed the folder, covering up the damning pictures, the allegations laid out in precise black and white letters on the page. Her movements were precise, straightening the edges so only the tab with BETTIS, JORDY showed. She did the same thing with the psychos email folder. The silence in the kitchen thrummed in his ears. No traffic noise, no television or radio, only the chirps and vibrations from her phone, cheerfully pinging notifications of new texts, tweets, posts, emails.

Then she tilted the phone and shut off the ringer, opened the drawer holding her hot pads and kitchen towels, and dropped it inside. Three steps and she'd closed half the distance between them. She looked up at him, but he couldn't identify the look in her eyes. Desire, yes. Check. That was totally familiar. But something softened the look, something he didn't recognize.

It was too much. Aware that his hands were tightly fisted, his shoulders rigid, he looked away.

Another step. Another infinitesimal tightening of his fists. His nails were all but embedded in his palms. He could smell the track on her hair, the cold air, hot rubber, grease, and underneath it, Cady's wild, warm scent. "Don't get too close," he said.

She took another step. Less than an arm's length between them now. Couldn't she feel him vibrating? If he let go, he'd blow apart like a bomb.

"I'm serious, Cady."

At that, she stopped. "You're not in the mood? You don't want me?"

The answer to both those questions was no. He wanted her more than anything he'd ever wanted in his life, all the basic things, like a permanent home. A family. A place he didn't have to earn, didn't doubt would always be there. He'd thought he had that in the department, but now even that was up in the air. Possibly, one of his brothers or sisters had betrayed him.

He stared at her. Never back down. Never walk away from a fight. This wasn't a fight, except it felt like one, had all the charged emotion and threat of bruises, blood, getting scraped raw, inside and out.

Holding his gaze, Cady stepped through the invisible barrier defining his personal space. The shock of it went through him like a sonic boom. As the wave passed, echoes fading, all his nerves jangling, she reached out her hand. Impossibly, he stiffened even more, tensed and ready for God only knew what. A kiss.

She laid her hand on his shoulder then trailed her fingers down the length of his arm to his wrist, nearly numbed by the edge of his pocket digging into his flesh. The contrast between her callused fingertips and her gentle touch confused him for a moment. Then the tug coalesced into a request, and he pulled his hand from his pocket.

She rubbed the tender skin of his knuckles, then turned his fist over, clenched fingers up. Without applying any pressure, she stroked the skin until his fingers relaxed, tightened reflexively, then eased a little more. Before he knew what was happening, his whole hand relaxed, opening space for her fingers to stroke from his wrist to his fingertips.

A quick glance at his hand, then back at his face. She smiled, then set his hand on her hip. "Give," she said, tapping his other hand.

She repeated the process, but this time his attention was torn between her touch and the heat of her body radiating through her jeans to his hand. Before he knew it, his left hand was open, vulnerable nerves set alight by her index finger tracing the creases in his palms.

This hand she lifted to her mouth and kissed. Training and experience prevented him from looking away, but the shock he got when he watched and felt her mouth against his skin nearly stopped his heart. She wasn't looking away, either. Her gaze held his without challenge. As she kissed each fingertip, then bit the base of his thumb, he felt himself softening from the inside out, his shoulders relaxing, all the tension in his body slipping down to harden his cock.

He'd taken the edge off with sex before, a quick, hard fuck to let off some steam, but this was different. He couldn't frame exactly how. The only way to know was to see it through.

The thought terrified and exhilarated him.

She lifted her chin and drew his hand down her throat

until the heel of his palm rested over the notch in her collarbones. He could feel her pulse thudding under his fingertips and thumb. For a split second he wondered if she was crazy. She'd just opened his hands and put them on her body in the most fundamentally vulnerable way possible.

His heart took off as fast as her car, skittering sideways in his chest, individual beats blending together into a frantic thrum. His cock was an iron rod in his jeans.

She wasn't looking away. Her pupils were blown wide, and a pink heat infused her face. She should be scared. She should be on the phone to Chris, or Hawthorn, demanding another bodyguard.

Not running.

He stood there like an idiot, her slender neck under his hand, until she spoke. "Do you want me?"

"Yeah," he said. No point in lying. Not with his cock pushing against his zipper.

She laced her fingers through his and led him to her bedroom. His heart kept doing crazy things, and he couldn't seem to stop fine tremors from running through his body. Cady didn't seem to notice, or if she did, his lack of control didn't frighten her. She left the bedside lamp off; the light from the kitchen lit up the door but the rest of the room was in darkness. He heard the rustle of fabric as she pulled back the comforter and the sheets.

"Come here."

He did. He couldn't do anything else. Any rational thoughts about department protocol, his future, even his past disappeared into dim, protective darkness of her bedroom.

"This is me being selfish," she said, then pulled his Henley over his head. "I've wanted to do this since I saw you."

"Do what?" he managed.

"Get my hands all over my body man."

Before he could laugh, her hands were on him, slow, sweeping movements from his neck to his fingertips. When he relaxed, involuntarily, with no more forethought than a dog easing into its owner's touch, she made a soft purring sound. He did it again, softened, almost leaned his big bulk into her tiny body before he caught himself.

"It's okay," she said. "I can take it."

So he relaxed, leaned into her, then got an electric shock when her thumbs swept over his nipples. Sensation speared through him, as if his relaxed state meant his nerves were more receptive. Crazy, and yet true, because when she did it again it lit him up from his jaw to his cock, stronger this time. Fiercer.

More dangerous.

He shifted his shoulders, rolled his head on his neck, trying to find his footing. A cute girl wanted to make him feel good. Go with it. But this wasn't just any cute girl he'd picked up in a bar or met through Shane's family's extended connections.

"Okay," she said, although he hadn't spoken. "Lie down."

It was kind of amusing, the way she used her body to maneuver him to the edge of the bed, and kind of arousing too. Each bump surprised him, her abdomen against his hip, the way their feet tangled so that he lost his balance and fell backward, wrapping one arm around her back to pull her down with him. It was, he realized, a fight move. If he was going down, he took the other guy down with him. Fists did less damage than feet.

But Cady wasn't using her fists, or her feet. Instead, she straddled his hips, swept her hair over one shoulder, and kissed him. This was better, because he had her body all along his, grounding him against her fine cotton sheets. He wrapped one arm around her torso and fisted the other into her wild hair and tightened his grip. When she gasped, he slid his tongue into her mouth, seeking the wild, the frenzy.

But she tore her mouth from his. "Slow down," she said, a smile in her voice. "I'm not missing this opportunity."

"To do what?"

She braced her weight on one elbow and smoothed her palm over his shoulder, then his chest. "This," she said. "Last time I didn't get to touch."

He gritted his teeth. Fine. If she wanted to touch, she could touch, but distant sirens were ringing. She stroked and smoothed and petted him, dropping him into a dark velvet moment outside space and time, coaxing his muscles to relax so she could shock him with a brush of her thumbs over his nipples, or, eventually, her fingers on his button fly.

His brain was buzzing, his breathing harsh in his ears, his skin sensitized to the point where her sweater was scratchy. "Take this off," he muttered.

Obediently she sat up and swept it over her head, transforming her hair into a witchy nimbus around her head. He looked at her smooth long underwear top and knew without touching it would also be too rough. "That too."

Another top discarded, another inch added to Cady's hair. "How about this?" she asked, her hands behind her back at her bra clasp.

Lace and silk, he guessed. "Yeah," he said.

Shoulders hunched, the bra dropped forward. His eyes had adjusted to the dim light, so he could see her dark pink nipples. He swept his hands up from her narrow waist to her breasts. She gasped, dropped her head back, arched into his touch, driving her sex against his erect cock.

"Get down here," he said. His voice was rough with demand as he flattened his hands against her shoulder blades. She dropped forward, catching herself on her elbows, her mouth a breath away from his, her soft skin pressed to his so he could feel her quick inhales and exhales as she resumed that maddening, arousing sweep of her hands. Each time her fingers circled his navel or traced the ridge of his hipbone, she toyed with his fly, opening a button then retreating to his chest.

A low groan of desperate desire rumbled through the room. Couldn't be Cady. Had to be him, and why not? Her skin against his soothed the ache she'd aroused and made it worse, because all he wanted was more, more, more. The tense energy he'd been holding inside for the last few days, maybe for his entire life, was being transformed, pulsing through him in big waves that made him lift his hips into hers, tighten his arms around her, loop one leg around her thigh. She kissed him back, hot and passionate and open, unafraid of the way his body trembled under hers.

She had his fly open now, her thigh draped over his, not pinning him but reminding him of her body, her sex, rubbing against his hip. The tease was maddening, the slowest of slow builds, so that when she worked his jeans and boxers down to free his cock, the shock of skin on skin sent a jolt through him.

He threw his head back and groaned again as she jacked him, her hands rough and sure, working him up until she slid down his body and licked a wet, hot strip from base to tip. The contrast between her hands and her mouth was startling. He kept making these hard lefts from what he expected to Cady's pace, from fight to purring, from desensitized to desperate for skin, from callused fingers to the hot, soft clasp of her lips and tongue around his shaft.

He shouldn't let her do this, but his fingers winding into her hair said otherwise. He braced himself on one elbow and watched her. His mind filled in the details in the darkness, Cady's sweet lips stretched around him, her hand gripping the base of his shaft while her mouth worked the tip. Pleasure speared through him and he lifted his hips, struggling against his jeans around his thighs.

He stopped caring about his jeans when she engulfed him with a greedy sound that knocked him flat on his back. Her tongue fluttered against the bundle of nerves, then her lips closed around the shaft for a long, sucking pull. She alternated those two moves until he thought he would lose his mind, his hips rolling to her rhythm.

"Stop, stop," he groaned.

She sat back and yanked his jeans down his legs and off. The cold air of her bedroom curled around his aching, wet shaft, hardening his nipples. She scrambled off the bed and stripped down her jeans, leaving them, long underwear, and socks in a pile on the floor before she darted into the bathroom for condoms. She came out with the box, tearing one packet off the strip then tossing the rest casually on the nightstand. She knelt between his thighs and sheathed him with a total lack of coyness or self-consciousness. Shrugging the comforter over her shoulders, she straddled his hips while he held his shaft upright.

When the tip of his cock nudged into her hot, wet folds, he both resented and appreciated the latex barrier between them. He wanted to feel her skin against his along every inch of their bodies, but without it he wouldn't last thirty seconds. Even the slow, measured way she took him all the way inside her made his heart pound. When her bottom came to rest against his thighs, she sighed and twisted her hips a little, seating him even more firmly.

"So good," she murmured, then leaned forward. Her hair and the comforter shrouded them in a cocoon of heated, electrified darkness slick with sweat and charged with a connection he couldn't begin to describe. Nothing else existed. The world outside Cady's soft sheets and silky skin disappeared, leaving only nerve endings tingling for more.

He couldn't respond. His heart had pounded its way up to the top of his throat and was firmly lodged there, thunking away. He ran his palms up the backs of her thighs until he could cup her hips and brush his thumbs over the trimmed curls at the top of her sex.

She writhed on him, sending a spike of desire up his spine. "Are you teasing me?" she asked.

"Yeah," he said. He was going to wring every single second of heated bliss from each moment he had with Cady. Because they wouldn't last. This wasn't real.

With each pass of his thumbs he opened the tender folds a little more, exposing her clit. Right now his touch was a faint promise, but with her first rise and fall on his cock he brushed the slick, swollen bud. She quivered, let out a trembling sigh.

She set a slow pace, giving him every opportunity to feel the hot, slick clutch of her walls around him, drawing up until his tip barely nestled inside her, pausing, then back down just as slowly. Pleasing herself, and him. He found a rhythm that matched hers, slow circles of his thumb at the top of her folds, dipping lower to rub her clit just as she took him inside her. His eyes had adjusted to the darkness, so he could see the shadowy outline of his hands on her, gripping something solid and real, not fighting to hold on to his temper. Unless he gripped her hips hard enough to leave bruises, fine tremors ran through his fingers. He gave up fighting it and started to guide her movements, bring her down hard and firm, the soft slap of her bottom against his thighs muffled by the fluffy comforter.

Then her mouth found his, blundering from his ear along his jaw to pause, her lips gently pressed against his in a not-quite kiss. Hot, soft, swollen lips parted over his, then her tongue flickered into his mouth. She drew out of him all of the darkness and pain, taking it into herself. It was enough to almost shut him down, send him into overload. Without seeming to, she was taking him apart, picking him apart at the seams, but gently, like she knew she'd have to put him back together afterward and wanted to make sure all the pieces would fit.

He slid one hand from her hip up her back to close in her hair and press her mouth to his. Their rhythm was disintegrating, flying apart as the pressure rose in his cock. His hips snapped up, thudding against her body. She gasped, braced her hands against his chest and pushed back into his thrusts. The comforter dropped to her waist, revealing her cheek, flushed with desire, and the fine bones of her shoulders and arms, muscles straining in greedy demand for all he could give her. The sight pushed him over the edge. Instinctively he sustained the deepest possible thrust as he tipped over the edge, grinding his hips against hers.

Her head dropped back. She gave a sharp cry of release and froze. Even through his own release he could feel the tight clench of her sex. Then the tension ebbed from her muscles and she languidly shimmied her hips.

"Oh, yes," she whispered.

Words were beyond him. Maybe when his heart settled back into his chest. After a long moment Cady lifted herself off him and collapsed to the side. "Yup. That's what I needed."

He grabbed onto the casual lifeline like a comedian getting no love, and huffed out a laugh. "Not drag racing?"

Her head lifted. She tried to shove her hair out of her face, but a thick tendril escaped her, hanging over one eye. "I didn't drive," she said, emphasis on I. "I sat on my ass on the bleachers and watched you drive."

He couldn't help himself. He smiled at her outraged

tone. "Based on what I saw when we left the track, I'm doing my civic duty keeping you from behind the wheel."

"It's a rural paved road through twenty-seven miles of farmland until you hit Pender. In winter the fields are stubble, so you can turn on the high beams and floor it. Or so I hear. From, you know, lawbreakers who do things like that."

"So you're saying we should run some speed traps out there?"

"Spoilsport." Giving up on controlling her hair, she dropped a kiss on his nose, of all places, then clambered over him, heading for the bathroom. "It was kind of fun to be an anonymous spectator."

He gave her a minute, and when he heard water running in the steam shower, he followed her in and dealt with the condom. Steam puffed from the jets in the walls, enshrouding Cady's figure. As he watched, her finger appeared, writing letters backward on the glass wall.

YOU COMING IN?

He couldn't help himself. Despite everything—his false allegations, suspension—he laughed. Maybe he was paranoid. Maybe the website thing was a coincidence, coming on the heels of the mysterious person lurking in the trees. Maybe this would all clear up.

Until then, he'd wring every last moment out of his time with Cady. He opened the door and stepped into the heat.

CHAPTER TWELVE

Sunday morning Cady woke up alone and with her troubles on her mind. The alone part wasn't a surprise, as Conn had wrapped a towel around his lean hips, gone to get dressed, and not returned before she fell asleep. She pawed back the comforter and her hair, and looked around the wreck of her bed. Her side, closest to the door, was a tumble of pillows smashed against the headboard and rumpled sheets. The other side was pristine—fluffy pillows protected by pillows in shams, little throw pillows neatly arranged in descending size.

Maud would have walked away. It was funny to think of it that way, but Maud, who had started as a way to psych herself up for a performance, had become all about doing the safe thing. Release the safe record, wear the safe clothes, appear on the safe talk shows, date the safe celebrities, all in a quest to keep her career safe. Maud would have been relieved to wake up alone.

Conn McCormick wasn't safe. But Cady wanted Conn, so she had him.

It was a tiny rebellion, or so she thought the first time,

like sneaking a second piece of chocolate when she had to fit into a red-carpet dress. But after last night, after he let down his guard and showed her the anger and fear that made him vulnerable, it wasn't just a rebellious choice to put Cady's desire before Maud's career. It wasn't just fun. Not anymore.

Nothing in her life was fun at the moment, except Christmas. She knew in her heart she didn't want to drop that album, but she had nothing else to replace it, and the scant hours she'd spent in her studio weren't much more useful than wandering through a furniture store's showroom. Her career was like the house they drove past the previous night. She had to fill the space somehow if she was going to have a career, not a hobby. The songs she'd written so far weren't a bright red leather ensemble for the family room, or an eye-catching wool rug to anchor the dining area. They weren't songs that anchored an entire album, much less a career. Details mattered when it came to making something look effortless: design, fashion, decorating. Music. All art.

Falling for Conn.

"Let's not go there just yet," she said.

She sat up, tamed her hair into a ponytail, then reached for her phone, wondering where Conn was and what he was doing. It wasn't her job to keep tabs on Conn. She was used to being the center of a whirlwind of people, Chris a near-constant presence, her stylist, her publicist, members of various bands or tour musicians coming and going as the bus trundled down highways from show to show. She moved, other people appeared, followed, disappeared. It was, she realized with a start, unusual to want to keep tabs on someone else.

Had her view of normal become that skewed? Everyone else—her mother, Eve, her friends—all texted her with little updates. But toward the end of the tour the frequency of Emily's texts had slowed down from twenty or thirty random thoughts, pictures, and updates a day to a handful. Mostly updates on her whereabouts. *Going to school.* That usually came with a picture of the day's outfit. *Headed to work. At the game.* All with pictures.

What was missing, she realized, was the insight into Emily's mind. Maybe it was normal for a teenage girl to withdraw from her older sister. Maybe it meant something else was wrong. She made a mental note to get some real time alone with Emily and ask her. She'd promised her sister-time during this break in her schedule, and so far she hadn't delivered.

It wouldn't be easy to do that today, with church and brunch and picking out a Christmas tree, all with Conn in tow. Emily didn't like Conn, and the ease with which he ignored her wouldn't make her like him any more.

As if subconsciously prompted, her phone lit up with a text and a picture from Emily. *SNOW!!!!!!!!!!!!!!!!!!!*

Cady scrambled out of bed and hauled open the blinds. Fluffy snow covered the driveway and the railings on the deck, and lay on the twigs and branches of the evergreen trees lining her driveway. She hurried back to her closet and grabbed her fleece robe, then shoved her feet into her monkey slippers and opened the bedroom door.

"It snowed!" she said to Conn.

"Yeah," he said. He had his hands braced on the edge of the kitchen island and was bent over his phone. "The roads are a mess. Everyone forgets how to drive when it snows."

An emotionless male voice crackled out of his phone. "Lights down at Ninety-First and McKinley. Female, white, driving a Chevy Tahoe, black, just drove through the intersection."

"What are you listening to?" Cady asked.

"The police scanner," he said as the dispatcher repeated the information.

"Aren't the lights down there?" said a different, female voice.

"Be advised, I think she's dragging them," came the male voice, clearly amused.

Cady looked up at Conn and burst out laughing. "Good thing the Audi's got four-wheel drive."

He turned down the volume on his phone, but Cady could tell he was listening, processing the information unconsciously. "What's the plan for today?" he asked.

"Very boring," she said. Her phone lit up. Emily again. *11 service you're coming right?* "Church, brunch, buy a Christmas tree."

He looked at her, then out the big windows overlooking the winter wonderland in her backyard. "You want to go out."

"The Audi has four-wheel drive," she repeated. "How are the roads?"

"Highways and main roads only are cleared," he said.

"That works. Mom's just off Decatur Street and everywhere else we want to go is on the main roads or a highway. The high is in the low forties. This won't stick around for long."

He looked at her, obviously thinking about arguing. "Okay," he said. "We'll need extra time to get there."

"Church is casual," she said as she ran water for tea. "The pastor wears jeans. No need to dress up."

No time for a cup of coffee on the deck today, just her steam routine, then taming her hair and getting dressed. She tucked jeans into a pair of knee-high boots, pulled a turtleneck fisherman's sweater over her head, then quickly plaited her hair into a loose French braid.

Conn appeared in the bedroom doorway. He'd shaved

the scruff from his chin, combed his hair, and put on a button-down shirt, tucked into his jeans. His shoulders strained against the seams, which tapered nicely to his narrow waist, where his gun, cuffs, and badge were clipped to his belt. Bright sunlight streamed through the uppermost windows, burnishing his hair with a gold light.

"You ready?"

"From the kitchen you looked like you had a halo, like one of the saints in a really old painting." She rummaged through her jewelry box, then through the top drawer of her dresser.

He snorted. "What are you looking for?"

"My grandmother's bracelet."

"The one you wear all the time?"

"Yes," she said, shifting aside a tangled pile of vintage necklaces and bangle bracelets for the third time. Her heart sank. "It was here when Emily slept over. I'm pretty sure it was on top of the dresser when she left. Now it's gone."

"Are you sure? Maybe she took it with her."

"Emily wouldn't take it without telling me. She knows how much it means to me."

Conn stepped into the room as she sank to her knees and flung open the dresser drawers, then went into the closet to ransack the shelves and drawers in the built-in storage unit. The green enamel and winking rhinestones should stand out against the white shelving units. No bracelet. She texted Eve to see if it had fallen off at Eye Candy. By the time an answer arrived, she'd looked through her purse, her coat pockets, the hallway, and the car.

No one turned it in, sweets. I'll keep an eye out.

"Maybe someone picked it up at the club that night," she said.

"Maybe. That's one option."

Cady glanced at him. His tone of voice was too even, the tone he used in cop mode when he was considering all

options and had his guard way, way up. "You think someone took it from my house."

Disbelief tinged her voice, because the possibility was
incomprehensible. She'd worn that bracelet on every tour
and gig since she was seventeen years old. It had been to
gigs all over Lancaster, and as far away as Munich and
Tokyo. Not once in eight years of touring via car, van, bus,
limo, and airplane had it gone missing. And now, in her
own home, the home only a few people knew she owned,
it was gone. Conn held out his hand. "We need to see if
anything else is missing," he said.

She didn't let go of his hand as they walked through the
house until she had to rifle through closets and drawers.
"You're shaking," Conn said quietly as they stood in the
basement, looking at the boxes of things she hadn't yet
unpacked.

"I'm a little freaked out," she admitted. "They don't
look like they've been moved or opened. There's no point
in going through them. I wouldn't know what was or wasn't
in them."

"Let's go upstairs."

Back in the kitchen Conn ran water into the electric
kettle. "What are you doing?"

"I'm making you Cady juice," he said without turning
around.

"Is that standard procedure after a . . . home invasion?
Burglary? What is this?"

"You always have some with you and it will help you
feel calmer." He added honey to her insulated mug, then
quirked an eyebrow at her.

"More," she said. "Right now you can't add too much
honey."

A thick stream ran from the bear's head into the mug
while he added water and stirred, then brought her the
mug. "Why is the honey in a bear?" she asked, hearing the

brittle tremor in her voice. "Bears don't make the honey. Bears steal the honey."

"Because bees' butts are too pointy to balance on the counter."

"You didn't answer my question."

He crossed his arms over his chest and his legs at the ankle. "A standard burglar is in and out fast. They hit the living room for electronics, the top drawers in the dresser and the closet for jewelry, and they're out again. Usually the biggest sign of a burglary is a sneaker tread mark on your door where they kicked it open. Only one item is missing from your house, an antique piece of jewelry with no value on the market other than its meaning to you."

"There were no signs of forced entry," she said, thinking back to their tour of the house. He'd kept his cool and her close while looking at the doors and windows.

"I checked the locks before we left last night. Whoever got in had a key. Did you have the locks changed after you bought the house?"

"Mom said she would, but to be honest, I don't know if she did or not."

"We'll ask her today. Either way, I'll call a locksmith and get him out today to change them."

"Quietly. I don't want her or Emily to worry. Ugh. Speaking of worry . . ." She let her head drop into her hands.

"You have to tell Chris about this."

"Yeah," she said to the countertop. "*Damn.*"

"Do you have to tell him?"

"Is there any chance this is just a prank?"

"Do you have friends that would fuck with you like this?" he countered.

"No. There's always at least one practical joker on tour. A realistic cockroach in bunks, Saran Wrap over the toilet, that kind of thing, but I don't think that would extend to my home after we went our separate ways."

"How many people know about your grandmother and what she meant to you?"

She squinted, trying to come up with a number. "Thousands? Tens of thousands?"

"What?" he said, obviously started.

"It's part of my story the label likes me to play up, so I've talked about it on stage, during interviews. My grandmother played electric guitar in an all-girl rock band in the 1960s. They were really good; I've heard recordings they made. This is a pretty conservative part of the country, and women weren't supposed to do things like that, but she told everyone to go to hell and did what she wanted. She and her friends traveled all over the Midwest in a VW van, playing in nightclubs and bars. Even after she got married she kept on doing it, until she got too pregnant to play. She's my inspiration, musically and professionally. It's common knowledge among my fans."

He blew out his breath. "So, the likelihood is that someone who knew how much that meant to you and how devastating it would be to lose it got into your house and stole it."

"Damn," she repeated, then reached for her jacket, pulling her gloves from the pockets. "I'll call Chris on the way to Mom's house."

Conn took them out of her hands. "We're not going anywhere. I need to call in Hawthorn."

"We are going to *church,* then to *brunch,* then to the *Christmas tree farm,*" she said precisely. "My sister's choir is singing today, I have brunch with my mom every Sunday, and we always pick out our tree three weekends before Christmas."

A muscle flexed in his cheek. "Why three weekends before Christmas?"

"It's the routine. Three weekends before we get the tree. The next weekend we decorate it and go see Santa. Then we make cookies and wrap our presents for each other the following weekend. Then it's Christmas. That's how we do things."

He stared at her.

"Christmas only comes once a year," she said. "In a couple of months I'll be out on the road again. I need normal. Church. Brunch. Christmas tree shopping."

She must have looked absolutely mutinous, because he handed over her down jacket and gloves, then shrugged into his jacket and pulled his watch cap over his hair. "Ready?"

"I'm ready." She looked at the manila folders in his left hand. "Is that my file?"

"Yes," he said. "I'm going to dig deeper. I need to be able to give Hawthorn some answers when he gets here."

Conn reversed down the driveway while she buckled her seat belt and swiped through her recent calls to Chris's number. "Hello, my dear," Chris said expansively when he answered. "How are you?"

Cady held the phone away from her ear and looked at the contact information on the screen. Chris Wellendorf. "Chris?"

"Yes. What? Don't you recognize me in a good mood? I just got spectacularly laid. I'm about to enjoy the Sunday paper, and some excellent coffee, and maybe round two."

"Chris, TMI. You're with someone and you answered my call?"

"Because I will always answer your call. What's up? Tired of the sticks and ready to be a superstar again?"

"Someone broke into my house and stole Nana Maud's bracelet."

Dead silence. Then, "I can't decide if that's scary or hilarious."

"Tell him I said it's scary," Conn growled. The Audi's back end hitched sideways like a spooked horse. He downshifted, corrected into the skid, and the car obediently straightened out.

"I heard him," Chris said. Cady heard a door close in the background. "What happened?"

Cady explained that they'd left the house for a while last night, purposefully vague about the circumstances, said nothing about the sex, and added that she'd noticed the bracelet was missing that morning.

"Where were you?" Chris asked absently.

"Out."

"Where out?"

"It doesn't matter where I was."

"You were at the drag races. How charmingly NASCAR of you. And the weather was . . . mid-thirties and dry as a bone. Cady. Jesus."

"I hate Instagram," she muttered. "I didn't sing. I had a scarf over my mouth the whole time."

"If they ask you do to the National Anthem, say no. Was this Conn's idea?"

"No! I used to go all the time when I was younger. It was fun then, I thought it would be fun now, and it was!" Her voice was rising, both in volume and pitch. "I'm relaxing! You told me to relax."

"Okay, okay," Chris soothed. "Keep your voice down."

"Look, I'm calling to let you know we have a situation here. Conn has it under control. Lieutenant Hawthorn's coming over later to discuss security protocols, or whatever. That's all. Go back to your lady love. I'll let you know what we decide."

"Do you want me to make an appearance?"

"No," Cady said. Conn turned the corner to her mother's street and was nearly sideswiped by a city plow. "Please, I'm begging you, do not come back to Lancaster. We just got twelve inches of snow and it's a wasteland here. They'll probably close the airport any second."

Conn snorted. Cady heard a bed squeak and rustle, then the clatter of blinds.

"Cady. Please. You got six inches of fluffy white powder."

"How do you know that?" she asked, suspicious.

"The weather app on my phone," he said. "I want to be in on the conversation later today. What time?"

"It might be tomorrow. I'll let you know. I'm going Christmas tree shopping with my mom and Emily today."

"From NASCAR to Norman Rockwell. You cover all the cultural bases. Text me the time."

The call disconnected in the middle of a soft exhalation. "He hung up on me," Cady said. She scrolled through her texts. A bunch from Emily she didn't read because the last one was *!!!!!!!!!!!!* and a new one from Bryan. *DDoS again. Working on tracking this motherfucker down and nailing his balls to a cement block.*

"Great," she muttered.

"What?"

"My site's down again."

"I don't think this is coincidental," Conn said. "Where does he live?"

"Bryan? Here. I've tried to stick with local businesses when I could. My personal lawyer's here, too."

"No, Chris."

"Brooklyn."

"Did he go home when he left?"

"I assume so," Cady said. "Why?"

The Audi slid to a stop by the curb. "I'm not crossing anyone off the list until I can conclusively clear them."

"It's Chris. You might as well suspect my mother of gaslighting me."

"She had a key."

"Which sits on a hook by the kitchen door, where

anyone from a neighbor to one of Mom's or Emily's friends could have snagged it."

"That's why we're getting the locks changed today."

His focus shifted from her face to over her shoulder. Cady turned to see Emily and her mother standing on the stairs while her mother locked the front door. Her mother, dressed in blinged-up jeans and fur-trimmed boots marched down the neatly shoveled steps, Emily mincing along behind her in four-inch-heeled black boots and a bright red wool coat. Her yellow-and-blue plaid skirt barely peeked out from under the coat's hem, and a big shopping bag dangled from one hand. A handsaw hung from the other, kept well away from her wool tights.

"What's with the saw?"

"We cut down the tree ourselves," Cady said. "If you gave my mother a hundred and sixty acres of open prairie and a mule, in a year she'd have cash crops ready to sell."

Conn hit the button to open the trunk. "You didn't buy your mom a house after you made it big?"

"I offered. She refused. This is her community. She looks in on elderly neighbors, organizes block parties, and this is what she can afford. I think my dad left a bad taste in her mouth. His thing is the best. The best house, car, clothes, watch, barbecue grill tools."

Conn shot her a look. "Grill tools?"

"You know. Spatulas and tongs?" she said, demonstrating with flips of her wrists and pincer motions. "You name it, he's got the best. Every time you talk to him it's about how he's getting the best of something. Mom loves what she has. It's a point of pride for her to take care of what she's got on her own. She couldn't give us much, but she gave us *family,* a sense of pride in the things we did and the way we did them. These are our rhythms. Mom, come sit up front." She introduced Conn to her mother, took the saw from Emily and set it in the Audi's empty trunk, then climbed into the backseat with Emily.

"Good morning, Cady. Good morning, Conn." Em folded her long legs and smoothed down her skirt.

Emily's voice was pure sweetness and light. Cady was too focused on figuring out how to ask her mother about the keys without giving away the latest development to parse this change in temper. "You look great," she said, twisting sideways to take in every detail of Emily's outfit, including the six-inch gap between her knees and her skirt. "Are you going to be warm enough at the Christmas tree farm?"

"I said the same thing," her mother said from the front seat.

"I thought maybe you and I could take some pictures out there," Emily said, pulling her cell phone from her pocket and getting a good look at Cady's casual outfit. "What are you wearing? Did you do your hair? Didn't you read my texts?"

"I was busy this morning," Cady said, keeping it vague so she wouldn't worry her family.

"With what? Never mind. I brought you a coat too," she said, opening the bag to reveal a pea coat with wood toggles in a woodland green that would complement Cady's hair and eyes. "We'll figure something out with your hair."

Cady examined the lining, the carefully stitched label. Emily had obviously spent hours designing, cutting, and sewing the coat. "I'm sorry, sweetie," Cady said. "Something came up and I was on the phone with Chris. We'll get the pictures, even with my crazy hair. Can I put it on now?"

"Sure," Emily said. She shoved the bag on the floorboard at her feet. "Whatever."

Despite the distraction of the sloppy roads and Cady changing her coat in the backseat, Conn got them to church with ten minutes to spare. Emily reverted to flailing teenage girl and dashed off with her friends to choir rehearsal while Cady and her mother snagged a cup of tea from the coffee bar in the gathering space and caught up with old friends. Conn stood quiet and still just off her left shoulder, fading into the background.

"Any chance you'd sing with us?" the choir director asked. "The jazz band would love to have you for a song or two."

"I'm supposed to be resting," she said, not wanting to upstage Emily. "But I'll be in the choirs on Christmas Eve." Anyone who wanted to sing on Christmas Eve could sing, a tradition that swelled the choir to three times its normal size. After they filed into the sanctuary, Cady closed her eyes for a moment, took a deep breath and exhaled slowly, and let herself be just part of the crowd again.

The youth choir sang twice, and on the second hymn, Emily had a solo. Her voice was clear and light, filling the room with a pure soprano beauty. Cady smiled at her and gave her a thumbs-up as she returned to her seat with the choir. Emily grinned back, then rolled her eyes as she caught a heel on a cord running from the jazz band's amplifier.

Sometimes her sister was her normal, goofy self—tall and gangly and awkward and a teenage girl—and sometimes she was distant, aloof, almost angry. For now, normal and goofy had control.

"Where to?" Conn asked when they were all back in the car.

"Jiro Sushi," Cady said.

Conn's brows drew down. "I thought we were getting brunch."

"We are getting brunch. Sushi brunch."

"Which location?"

"SoMa is better. The location out west smells like tannin and dyes," Emily said, thumbing away at her phone.

"That's because the leather shop is next door. SoMa is in the opposite direction from the Christmas tree farm and will be more crowded," Cady said, mindful of the conversation she had to have with Conn, Chris, Hawthorn, and who knew who else after they bought the tree and got it home.

When they reached the restaurant, the hostess led them to a booth. Emily slid into one side. "I want to sit next to Cady," she said.

Her mother paused in the act of lowering her bottom to the vinyl seat. "All right," she said.

Cady shot Conn an apologetic look, but he was wearing that expressionless mask Cady privately called his cop face. He held out his hand to indicate her mother should precede him into the booth, then sat across from Cady. Emily brought up Instagram and started scrolling through posts in her feed, enlarging to examine detail, all the while giving a running commentary on what she saw. Cady looked over her shoulder and made appropriate noises, while eavesdropping on her mother's attempts to start a conversation with Conn.

"That one's kind of a disaster," Emily said, pausing to tap and enlarge.

"Are you from Lancaster, Conn?"

Cady looked at the outfit. "Kind of a disaster" was an understatement, as the outfit involved a felt hat with a floppy brim, a cropped white T-shirt, and a pair of shorts in an unfortunate purple calico. "Yeah," she agreed.

"Yes, ma'am. Born and raised."

"No . . . no . . . no . . . oh, that's nice," Emily said, scrolling faster than Cady could keep up.

"Slow down," she said while her mother extracted the list of schools Conn attended. "That teal thing caught my eye."

"You must have family in town," her mother said.

A pause. Cady glanced up from Emily's phone screen. "Not really, ma'am."

"Where will you spend the holidays?" Emily asked.

"With friends," Conn answered.

The waitress showed up with glasses of water, then paused, pen poised expectantly over her pad. "The usual?"

"Please," Cady said, then added for Conn's benefit, "We always get the same thing. What do you like?"

"A California roll and a tempura roll," Conn said.

Everyone handed over their menus. "Mom, Conn's best friends with Shane McCool."

"Cady, look at this," Emily said.

Her mother lit up. "You know the McCools? Shane's a wonderful mechanic."

"We went to school together," Conn said.

Cady dutifully observed the details of the picture Emily showed her, then said, "Tell me about the coats."

"They're kind of a retro side project," Emily said. "I went through the racks in Nana's basement for inspiration and chose fabrics in these super vibrant greens and golds and oranges for a fresher feel . . ." Cady listened with half an ear, straining to catch Conn's answers as her mother politely but relentlessly pried details of his past from him. What she heard intrigued her, things like "left when I was a baby" and "bounced around a lot."

He said it without much inflection, no hint of what it meant to him to have had no permanent place to call home. She thought about how homesick she got on the road, then tried to imagine what it would be like to be rootless, at the whims of adults who couldn't handle the responsibility of a child. That explained Conn's reserve. He was good at fitting in, but somehow always at a distance. She'd thought it was a cop thing. Maybe it went deeper than that.

"This one's from a pattern Nana had made . . . Cady, are you even listening to me?"

"Of course, sweetie. Fresher feel with the colors. Am I wearing the green one?"

"Yes," Emily said, but she put her phone away.

The meal arrived. Emily automatically split the rolls between the three women. Cady made sure to offer Conn some of her share. They finished the meal on a tide of Emily's chatter. Cady and her mom scuffled over the check for a few moments before she let her mother win. They bundled back into the car and set off for the Christmas tree farm. The roads were plowed and drying, but snow lay on the ground and in the tree branches, glinting in the afternoon sun.

"Hey, Mom," Cady said, trying for Conn's level of nonchalance, "did you get the locks changed on my house before I moved in? I found a key I can't match."

"I did," her mother said. "Burt Gibbons at A1 Locksmith did it for us, same as always."

"Okay, it must be one of the old ones. I'll throw it out."

CHAPTER THIRTEEN

Conn parked the Audi at the far end of the gravel parking lot and reclaimed the handsaw from the trunk of the car. The snow lingered on the trees, and the air had turned crisp and cold. Cady had traded her puffy jacket with its hood for the coat Emily made, so she lacked the protection for her ears and throat. "Wear mine," Patty—because after the sushi brunch, Cady's mom insisted he call her Patty—said, and took off her own scarf. Cady wound it around the lower half of her face and grabbed her insulated mug.

Cady and her mother had no problem with the gravel made rough by the snowplow's blade, but Emily was having trouble in her heels and fell a little behind. At the entrance they got a sled and a map of the farm. They huddled around it at a table outside the canteen. Conn, positioned by Cady's shoulder, smelled hot cider, hot cocoa, and peppermint drifting through the window.

"Here." Patty jammed one French-manicured nail at the map. "That's where we got last year's tree."

"I want to go here," Emily said, pointing to a spot on

the opposite side of the map. "See the fence line? It's a split rail, with those big Colorado blue spruces on the other side. That's a great place for a photo shoot."

"Those trees are a little big for the living room," her mother said.

"We're having Christmas at Cady's, remember? You could fit a twenty-foot spruce under those ceilings."

"Sixteen, tops, including a stand and the star," Conn said. "They're eighteen feet by the fireplace."

"How do you know that?" Emily demanded.

"Magic," Conn replied, then relented. "I eyeballed it."

"I'm partial to the balsam firs," Cady said. "The twigs on the Colorado spruces are harder to hang ornaments on."

"So we go here for the photo shoot, then here for the tree," Emily said, jabbing at the map.

"You're going to be pretty cold before we get from one side of the farm to the other," Patty said patiently.

"I packed jeans. I'll put them on under my skirt."

Cady looked at Conn. "I'm good," he said.

They set off for the photo shoot location. The farm was busy, but the crowds thinned out as they walked further into the woods, most people choosing a tree closer to the gift shop and the canteen.

"How do we get the tree back?" Conn asked.

"That's what the sled's for," Emily said. Her tone supplied the "duh."

"I figured it was for the photo shoot," Conn said, keeping his tone neutral.

"Oh," Emily said. Up to her calves in snow, she eyed it judiciously. "That's a good idea. Are you some kind of design expert when you're not a cop?"

"Not even remotely. I don't decorate for the holidays," Conn said. He looked around. It was really pretty back here, the sun glinting off the snow, the slight breeze picking up fine swirls and sending diamonds into the air. Cady and her mother were a few feet ahead, but Conn figured the snow would slow down anyone who made it this deep into the back of beyond to come after Cady.

"Why not?"

"It's just me," he said. "Sometimes I turn on that television fire, you know, the one the CW network broadcasts all night."

She narrowed her eyes at him. "No girlfriend?"

"Emily," Cady said.

"Or boyfriend?"

"Emily!" Cady and Patty said in unison.

"Neither," Conn said.

"Cady used to have the most famous boyfriend in the world."

"I never dated George Clooney!" Cady protested.

"Which is a crying shame," Patty said, slogging through a drift. "That man is gor-geous."

"He's so old," Emily groaned. Her mother shot her a look Conn recognized, the if-you-weren't-my-daughter-I'd-kill-you look. "Harry Linton is a hand-me-down I'd happily take," Emily said.

"Emily." Conn recognized the warning in her mother's voice.

"You really don't want him," Cady said.

"Why not? *He's* close to my age. I'll be in New York next year, not in this hick town in the middle of nowhere."

"You'll be here if you keep skipping school," her mother said.

"Mom!" Emily wailed. "Cady, how could you?"

"I didn't say anything!"

"How about an online introduction?"

Cady jerked the scarf down from her face as she spun to face her sister. Conn caught her elbow to keep her from falling over backward on the uneven ground, then discreetly stepped back. "No. Do you want to know why?

Because," Cady said, clearly clinging to her temper with her fingernails, "I broke up with him when I caught him in bed with a singer I can't name but who is a far, far bigger draw than I am."

She started coughing, dry, rasping hacks that would have turned Chris white with fear.

"Oh my God," Emily said, her voice both disapproving and gleeful as she twisted open the top of Cady's insulated mug. "Drink this. Who was it? Have I met her?"

"Him."

Emily stopped so suddenly Conn nearly ran her over. "What?"

Cady cleared her throat, then sipped her honey water. "Him."

"But . . . Harry's not out!"

"He's always claimed sexuality is fluid." Cady shrugged.

"Is the other singer out?"

"No comment."

"That's why you haven't officially broken up?"

"We weren't officially together so we can't officially break up," Cady muttered, huffing through the snow. Conn caught a glimpse of the split rail fence between two huge blue spruces.

"You dated for, like, eight months."

"It was a Maud thing, not actual dating. Trust me, you don't want this kind of dating life."

"Red carpets and paparazzi taking pictures of your every outfit? Sounds pretty good to me."

"Do you actually want to date Harry Linton, or do you want to use him to get exposure for your designs?" Cady asked, uncharacteristically sharp.

Emily deflated a little. "You make it sound so sordid. I thought that's the way it worked."

Conn looked at the horizon, the snow dusting the trees, the dark gray slivered wood of the split rail fence. Anywhere other than Cady's face. "It is the way things work, and it is sordid," Cady said. "What started out as liking each other and wanting to get to know each other turned into him getting me bigger gigs than I could get on my own, which means he thought I owed him"—she glanced at Conn—"things I didn't want to owe him. Keep your professional life and your personal life as separate as you can, Em. Stay you. How's here?"

Emily cheered up quickly, fussing over Cady's coat, flipping the collar up, then back down. "We really should do something about your hair."

Conn looked at it. Emily's dark hair hung sleek and heavy in the sunshine, lifting in picture-perfect tendrils to get stuck in her lip gloss and mascara. Wispy curls escaped Cady's loose French braid, the dry breeze lifting in one big airy mass. "You want my hat?" Conn asked.

"No," Emily said quickly, then looked at him. "Well, maybe. I'm not wearing one, so it's a contrast, and it's basic black, and kind of goes with the green. Yes."

Conn pulled it off and handed it to Cady. She tugged it down. Emily reached over, pulled Cady's braid over her shoulder and adjusted the back a little, transforming Cady into a model from a photo shoot for Pottery Barn or J.Crew, the kind with guys in flannel and skinny jeans, and the girls with braids and ankle boots.

"That works," Emily said. "Thanks."

"No problem," Conn said.

"Here," Emily said, and handed Conn her oversized phone. "Take pictures. Please."

He watched Cady blow out her breath to rein in her temper. Patty also had her phone out. The sisters started out beside the fence, Emily's face model-serious, lips pouty, eyes focused in the middle distance, Cady a little more amused but obviously trying to match Emily's demeanor.

Then Cady threw down a rapper flip of the hands.

"Gangsta-style," she said. "Remember when we used to watch videos and copy the moves?"

Conn thought she looked adorable, prancing and posing, but Emily shook her head. "Be serious. This is important."

"What about up here?" Cady asked, patting the top rail of the fence.

"You go ahead," Emily said, looking like she regretted wearing her skirt. Her tights couldn't be that warm.

With a sweep of her mittened hand, Cady cleared the rail of snow, then climbed up and plunked herself down. Emily leaned back beside her, hands in her pockets, expressionless again. Conn took a few more pictures, then Cady stealthily gathered a fistful of snow and sifted it over Emily's head. Her face was the picture of mischievous teasing. Conn got several great shots before enough snow melted into Emily's hair for her to realize what was going on.

"Cady!" she shrieked, then grabbed two handfuls of snow and flung them at her sister.

Laughing, Cady threw up her hands, overbalanced, and had to grab the rail to prevent herself from tipping backward into the snow bank. Emily took full advantage, gathering as much powdery snow as she could and hurling it at Cady, who launched herself from the rail to the ground and swatted a glinting snowy curtain at Emily.

The snow was too dry to pack, and both girls were laughing too hard to do any serious damage to each other. By the time they ran out of breath, Cady's cheeks were glowing pink, and snow dusted Conn's hat, her braid, and the moss green coat. Emily had fared no better, her heavy bangs dotted with droplets of melted snow. She wrapped both of her arms around Cady, and turned to her mother.

"Take our picture, Mom," she commanded.

She bent her head to Cady's. Smiling, her mother held up her camera and tapped the screen. Conn took a couple himself, first of Cady and Emily, arms around each other, smiling genuine smiles, not the fake ones for the covers of magazines, then of the three women, the family held together by tradition and a mother's will.

He'd never aspired to Shane's family life, a big extended family full of loving people who had their moments but held strong. He could be with them and not feel a hint of regret, because it was so far outside his experience. But being with Cady's family, he got a firsthand look into the kind of family he could have had. Broken. Real.

"Can we please get a tree now?" Cady asked, swatting her hands together to clear the clumps of snow from her mittens.

"Sure," Emily said absently. She'd reclaimed her phone from Conn and was going through the photos. She gave him a surprised glance. "These are pretty good."

"Thanks," Conn said. "I take pictures for work."

"You do?"

"Sure. Crime scenes, stakeouts, evidence."

"Crime scenes. Ewww," she said.

"Say *thank you, Conn*," Patty said.

"Thank you, Conn," Emily repeated.

Emily pulled Cady behind a convenient large tree, presumably to help her balance while she pulled on her jeans. When they emerged, Emily looked both warmer and happier than Conn had ever seen her. They slogged through the snow to the other side of the lot where the balsam firs grew in clusters Conn knew were carefully plotted to seem random and attractive.

"This one," Emily said, pointing at a bristling monstrosity that had to be twenty-five feet tall.

"Unless it's going in front of city hall, it's too tall," Conn said.

"No, it's not," Emily said.

"This happens every year," Cady said. "They look so

small out here, under the sky, but then you get them home
and they take over your living room."

"You have a huge living room now," Emily pointed out.

"Not big enough for that one," Cady said. "We could
hide an entire family of deer in that tree."

"What about this one?" Patty asked, standing beside a
more modestly sized tree.

"He's a little thin," Cady said. "He needs another year
to fill out. That one."

"Conn?" Patty said.

His heart thrilled a little to be automatically included.
"It'll fit under the ceilings."

"Just barely or is it going to look stumpy? Give me the
Goldilocks fit."

"You might have to shift the furniture a little, but it's a
good size."

"All in favor?" Cady said, lifting her hand in the air.

"Fine," Emily said, but she raised her hand. "Think
small, all of you."

Patty raised hers, then all three women looked at Conn.

"What?"

"You get a vote."

"Me? Why me?"

"You're here," Cady said. Her voice was raspy, warm,
like a shot of whiskey. She still wore Conn's hat, and her
golden green eyes danced under the black brim.

His hands were jammed in his pockets. Unless he was
working, they always were. But Cady's family was looking at him, waiting for him to join in. Slowly, he lifted his
right hand.

"Excellent. Consensus," Cady said. "Hand over the saw."

"I'll do it," her mother said.

"I've got it, Mom," she said.

"I'm not doing it," Emily said. She was thumbing away
at her phone. "Last year it took me a week to get the sap

out of my hair and we found a dead fox carcass under the tree. It was gross."

"I'll do it," Conn said, tightening his grip on the saw's handle.

"Really, Mom and I can do this," Cady said.

"Is it tradition?"

"I'm happy to include someone else in this particular part of the tradition," Patty said.

"Hold back the branches for me," he said.

"Not in that coat!" Emily yelped, surfacing from the world of pixels and likes.

"I left my other coat in the car," Cady pointed out. "I have to wear something. It's freezing."

Conn unbuttoned his jacket. "Wear mine," he said grimly. Never in his life had he sat through so many costume changes. The only person still wearing her original outfit was Patty.

Cady gave the branches a good shake, sending snow sliding to the ground like shingles off a roof. Conn went to his knees in the dead needles carpeting the dry, hard soil under the tree, and started sawing away at the base. Cady's mom kept her tools in good order so it didn't take long, but by the time he finished and the tree tipped over into the snow, his hands, hair, and shirt were covered in evergreen sap. Cady didn't look much better. While her mittens took the worst of it, his coat and hat were also smeared with sticky residue.

"Yuck," Emily said.

"How do we get this off?" Cady said to her mother.

"Goo Gone," Patty said.

"Let's get the tree on the sled before we start thinking about getting sap off our clothes," Conn said.

The tree was awkward, but not heavy, so they had it secured to the sled in a couple of minutes, but Conn, who had the heavier trunk end ended up with more sap on his hands. Emily and Patty set off for the barn, leaving Cady and Conn to haul the tree along.

"This is so outside your job description it's not even funny. What's the bodyguard version of combat pay?"

"No idea," Conn said. His nose was running, his socks, shoes, and jeans were soaked, and the sweat was beginning to dry on his shirt. "It's fine. Kind of fun, even."

She gave him a wry smile. "Did you buy Christmas trees every year, or did you have fake ones?"

"Depended," he said curtly. His grandmother had a fake tree she hauled out and put together, a cigarette dangling from her lips as she straightened the branches and handed them to Conn to slot into the metal stand covered in brown paper to mimic a tree trunk. Most years his uncle didn't have one at all. Shane's family picked one up at one of the lots that sprang up around town, and strapped it to the top of whichever minivan his mother was driving at the time. He laughed.

"What?" Cady said.

"I remember going with Shane to get a tree once. His little sister had a stomach bug, so his mom couldn't go, and his dad was working. So his mom gives him forty bucks and sends Shane to get it. But Shane had gotten grounded for sneaking out of the house, and his dad revoked his driving privileges. His mom didn't know about the grounding, because he was already on thin ice for something, I forget what, but it was probably something he'd done with me. So he calls me up, we drive to the lot, get a tree and tie it to the roof of the car. But Shane's scoping out this girl working at the lot, so he's not paying really close attention to his knots. We're halfway home when I take the corner off Forty-third and Lake too fast, the twine snaps, and the tree flies into the intersection and takes out a row of metal trash cans."

"Oh my God," Cady said, laughing.

"It was an unholy noise. We were lucky we didn't cause an accident. The cans and the tree are rolling around in the street, we're stopping traffic in all four directions, and the lady who owned the cans comes out of her house in a flowered housecoat with her three Chihuahuas. She's giving us hell about the cans, the other drivers are honking, and the dogs yapping at us the whole time. So we back up to the tree, hustle the cans back to the lady's driveway, open the back doors, we jam the whole thing into my car, and drove the eight blocks home, me driving and reaching back to hold one door and him crammed in the backseat with the tree holding the other."

"What did his mom say?"

"Nothing. She was holding someone's throw-up bucket. His dad was just getting home from work when we pulled into the driveway. He looked at us and said 'I don't want to know.'"

Cady smiled, and got a firmer grip on her part of the sled's strap. "How do we get it home?" Conn asked.

"They deliver."

"Not a good idea right now," Conn said.

Emily and Patty both perked up. "Strap it to my car?" Cady said in a hurry.

"It's going to scratch the paint."

"And look like Chevy Chase getting the tree home in *Christmas Vacation,*" Emily added.

"I'll call Shane. He's got a truck and can bring it over."

"I don't want to trouble him," Cady said.

"It's no trouble," Conn said. "And it's safer."

They paid for the tree. Patty bought a round of hot chocolates, and they trooped back to Cady's Audi. "Do I have any Goo-Gone?" Cady asked when they were inside, the heat blasting.

"I don't think so," Patty said. "You can borrow mine. Em and I are wet but clean."

"It's so weird not knowing what's in my own house," Cady said. She had her hot chocolate in one hand and her phone in the other. "Speaking of which, who has keys to my house?"

"I've got the one in the kitchen," her mother said. "I loaned that one to the realtor to get the house set up for you. Oh, and Chris borrowed them last week."

"Why?" Cady said.

"He took some of your stuff over to the house before the concert. I wasn't able to go with him, because I had to work."

"Okay, thanks. Hey, Em, when do you want me to tweet those pictures?"

"Let me mess with them first, then send you the ones I want out there. Thank you, Cady!" Bag swinging wildly, she dashed up the front steps, opened the door, and disappeared into the house. Patty followed her, then returned with a bottle of Goo Gone.

"Thanks, Mom. I'll get the tree set up. We can decorate next weekend."

"Sounds good, honey. Thanks again, Conn."

"No problem."

The roads were dry, the snow lying in sculpted drifts along the shoulder on the way back to Cady's house.

"He could have had a copy made," Conn said, jumping back a few hours to the reality, not the fairy tale of winter wonderlands and Christmas trees.

"He's not here, remember?" Cady said. She'd tucked her phone into her pocket and closed her eyes.

"He could have given the copy to someone else."

"So he's got an accomplice in his new gaslighting business? This is so crazy I won't even consider it. A random psycho from the internet spending his Christmas breaking into my house in Lancaster is more likely than Chris trying to scare me into dropping a record I'm having second thoughts about."

"How much money are we talking about? Hundreds of thousands?"

"Yeah. Maybe more, if the record drop goes like the label hopes it does." She opened her eyes and looked at him. He read so many emotions in there, the satisfaction of a day with family, physical tiredness from slogging through the snow with Emily, and a deeper worry about her future underneath it all. "I know, I know. People shot over a sandwich."

"Or take in kids because they get money from the state. Or steal their neighbor's eight-hundred-dollar TV, or an iPhone. What seems to us to be a lot of work isn't to someone who stands to reap the rewards. What makes more sense to you? A person close to you who knows which buttons to push to throw you off your game and stands to benefit from your success, or a random stranger tracking you down and breaking into your house?"

She thought about that for a beat, then shifted her weight in the seat and refused to look at him.

"I'm here to protect you against a stalker. In my opinion, you don't have one. You have a manager who sees his meal ticket getting cold feet just as his investment's about to pay off."

"Chris comes across like a jerk, but he isn't one."

"So ask him. Flat out ask him if he's been breaking into your house."

"No way," Cady said, hard and fast. "I trust him, and I'm going to keep working with him. If I tell him I think he's behind this, I damage a professional relationship that's worked very well for me."

"Until now."

"Creative differences," she said. "It happens. You work it out."

"Like you work things out with Emily?"

"I was too hard on her. Half of the teenage girls in

America fantasize about dating Harry Linton, and she actually knows someone who has. It's just . . . she's a typical teenage girl sometimes and then this super-savvy, super-driven designer in the making the rest of the time."

Conn consciously relaxed his hands. The road conditions didn't warrant fists clenched around the steering wheel. "I want to track down Harry Linton and beat him to a pulp."

Cady smiled. "Because he cheated on me?"

"Because he expected you to pay him back for favors with sex."

Her smile disappeared, and her expression clouded over. "Oh. That."

It took him a moment to decipher her tone. "You're ashamed. Why are you ashamed?"

"Because I did pay him back with sex. But it didn't seem like it at the time, you know? It wasn't until later that it felt cheap. And ugly. I really didn't like myself afterward, or how long it took me to figure out that's what was going on."

"Does Chris know about this?"

"He's perfectly aware of how power affects relationships, yes. But it's not his job to protect me that way. My business relationships, contracts, that kind of thing, absolutely. My personal relationships? I want him as far away from those as possible. Always have."

"But he didn't discourage you from dating Linton like you're discouraging your sister from running after older, more powerful men."

"No. I wasn't sixteen, or an industry virgin. I know what lots and lots of guys in bands are like. Music is cool, sure, and a super way to get girls. All the girls you want. Or guys. I walked into that with my eyes wide open."

"You'd dated enough to know?"

"Not really," she said, matter-of-factly. "Normally I

never date musicians. We're flaky, and bad bets when it comes to relationships."

She stopped short, as if she'd remembered she was talking to the guy she was . . . dating? Sleeping with. Conn stepped in. "People say the same thing about cops. It takes the right kind of woman to put up with the hours, the stress, what it can do to your head."

"Yeah. Exactly." She cleared her throat. "I never wanted to date the guy in the band. I wanted to *be* the guy in the band."

Silence cloaked the car, matching the deepening shadows thrown by the forest around Cady's gated community. Out of the corner of his eye Conn looked at her, getting little glimpses of her expression, the way she nibbled at her chapped lower lip when she was deep in thought, the way his hat covered her forehead and made her eyes huge, moss green. She wasn't for him. No matter what happened, whether she dropped the album or spent months writing new material of her own, Cady Ward was a woman leaving Lancaster. She might call the city he protected and served "home," but he knew how meaningless that word was when home was really a tour bus, or an airplane, or a thousand bland hotel rooms all over the world. Home was her music, her fans, the audience that filled auditoriums and bleachers and maybe stadiums.

"You get used to it after a while," she said, seemingly out of nowhere.

"Get used to what?"

"Blurring the lines between favors, until everything feels like a transaction, like you're using and being used. It makes it hard to trust people. Evan, my previous bodyguard had a career plan," she said matter-of-factly. "I was just a stepping stone to the big money and visibility— Hollywood. He wanted to get into acting. That's why I quizzed you at the police station. For all I knew you wanted the job because you'd gotten a taste of being a big shot bodyguard at the concert. You knowing nothing about the business sealed the deal."

"I've got a job," Conn said. "It's the only job I've ever wanted. I'm LPD, and I'm sure as hell not going anywhere."

The words came out more roughly than he intended. What should have been a lighthearted, reassuring response that matched their casual connection now sounded defensive, like he was hurt, or worse, slapping her down for assuming he was like all the other men in her life. But it burned to think of another man protecting her, let alone taking his place in her bed. In her life. In a few weeks Cady would pack up and leave again, and he'd be here, with . . .

With what? Would he have a job after Hawthorn finished his methodical, by-the-book review of the situation? The person who set him up knew him well enough to use Conn's reckless reputation to his advantage; he'd be smart enough to cover their tracks. Conn could be here in Lancaster without a job, maybe without his freedom, and Cady would be gone.

An old, familiar fear sidled up from his gut. Rejection, losing the home and family he'd claimed for himself, a loneliness so pervasive he thought no more of it than breathing. The McCools claimed him as one of their own; the next generation of kids even called him Uncle Conn. Cady's mother and Emily were very friendly and welcoming. But he didn't fool himself into thinking friendly meant forever. Cady's mom took care of people in her neighborhood; it was probably just instinct to include whoever was hanging around from Cady's entourage. Anyway, it didn't satisfy the urge for a family of his own, the one formed in partnership with the woman he loved, the children they made together. It was the dream he'd always had and never thought he would fulfill.

Because he didn't deserve it, and if he had it, he'd fuck

it up. Deep down, he knew this to be true. His father left him, and what little remaining family he had passed him around when raising him overwhelmed them. They did their best, but asking older relatives to take in a rambunctious, difficult kid was a recipe for trouble.

He'd been plenty of trouble.

They pulled into the garage, and fell into their rhythm, Conn leading the way, Cady half a step behind. They'd left lights on in the main living space, the soft spotlights over the stove, a reading lamp by the chair with its back to the big windows, but their careful scan of the rooms for any further signs of a stranger's presence in the house revealed nothing out of the ordinary. Everything was as it had been when they left.

Cady shrugged out of her coat and tugged his hat from her head, leaving both on the kitchen island. "Take off your coat and gloves," she said. "I'll see what I can do about the tree sap after I take a shower."

He shouldered out of his coat and set them on the pile of outerwear, then walked over to the sink to clean his hands. He'd scraped off most of the tree sap when Cady's phone pealed out Madonna's "Vogue." He dried his hands and fished it from the pocket. Emily's name lit up the screen.

"Hi, Emily," he said.

"Oh. Conn. Where's Cady? I want to talk to her about the pictures."

"Hold on a second," he said, and walked through her bedroom to the master bathroom. He tapped on the door with one knuckle, heard her call, "Yeah?"

"Your sister's on the phone."

"What?" she said, louder. "Just come in. The water's running and I can't hear you."

He opened the door, mouth already forming the words *It's your sister* when a cloud of steam billowed out. His mouth stopped and no sound came out. Cady stood naked beside the open shower door, one foot raised to step into the glass enclosure. She was all slender, womanly curves, hips and breasts and shoulders, her sex hidden by neatly trimmed dark curls. Her breasts lifted as she reached into the shower and adjusted the temperature. His heart did a funny little skip as she looked back at him, her hair curling as moisture gathered on the strands, one eyebrow arched inquisitively.

He couldn't have her family life, but he could have her.

"She'll call you back," Conn said and hung up.

CHAPTER FOURTEEN

"You're letting the steam out," Cady said. With every beat of her heart her extremities regained sensation as steam-warmed blood pumped through her body to her fingers and toes. "Come in and shut the door."

Conn tossed her phone on the counter and walked into the room, kicking the door shut behind him.

"Who was it?" she said. "You didn't just hang up on Chris, did you?"

"Your sister," he said.

"That's not much better," she said like she wasn't stark naked, like he wasn't looking at her like . . . like she didn't know what. No man had ever looked at her like that before. He stood just inside the door, feet spread and braced, hands jammed in his pockets, glorious shoulders gloriously squared up. She had the feeling that if he were wearing his gun belt, his thumbs would have been tucked in the leather. But this was an older reaction to the cop she'd seen at her homecoming concert. He looked a little lost, like the steam was dissolving his foundations so they coiled over their heads and away. He'd been there in body all day, but wary, hanging on the perimeter, and outsider to the end.

Until now.

"What did she want?" Cady asked, Emily's recent issues still warring with her desire and her growing feelings for Conn for space in her brain.

"No idea," he said. His eyes darkened as he looked her over. "I opened the door, you were naked, and my brain stopped working."

She had to smile at that. Steam hissed from the jets lining the tiled rectangular shower stall. She opened a drawer for a hair elastic, then pulled her hair up into a messy knot on her head. It flopped to the side, but the mirror had fogged over so she couldn't see how ridiculous she looked.

Based on the expression on Conn's face, she didn't look ridiculous at all. His gaze flicked over her once, topknot to tiptoe, then lingered on the way back up, pausing at the curve of her belly, her breasts, her face. Long accustomed to being objectified by men, by fans, by music industry executives, it took her a moment to understand how different she felt under Conn's gaze. She felt seen. Admired. Wanted. Not as Queen Maud of the Maud Squad, but as crazy-haired, uncertain-about-her-future, likes-to-drive-fast-in-the-middle-of-the-night Cady.

She opened the door to the big glass enclosure, but thought before she spoke. They weren't at the stage where they could take anything for granted. They'd made no promises, never gone past casual and into intimate. She'd heard what he said about cops being bad bets; he wasn't just affirming her truth about touring musicians. He was telling her a truth of his own. Realistically, there was no chance this would last longer than her stay in Lancaster.

But until she left town, she'd take everything she could from her time with Conn McCormick. "You coming in?" she asked quietly.

The words dissipated into the steam now drifting through the master bathroom, obscuring Conn's face like thin clouds obscured the sky. He answered with his body, reaching behind his neck to pull his Henley over his head, then set his hands on his belt.

She never, ever got tired of watching a man unfasten his belt. There was something so incredibly sexy about the movements. "Slow down," she said.

Both of his eyebrows shot up, making his forehead wrinkle in a really interesting, adorable way. Even though she'd been wearing his hat for most of the Christmas tree shopping trip, his hair hung over his forehead, turning his face boyish despite the tough set of his jaw. Some distant, recording part of her mind noted the incongruities. It was the sheer size of him, bigger than anyone she regularly spent time with, but the man inside the muscles didn't feel like he'd pumped the iron to boost his ego or meet the expectations of an image-conscious public. Based on the flashes of vulnerability she saw in his eyes, the way he looked at her askance, like he expected her to disappear, his muscles were a front, a defensive wall as unforgiving as the walls he liked backing her into. He wasn't anything as simplistic as "hot." Instead, he was compelling, made you look twice, then keep on looking in an effort to know more, trying to figure him out, catch his attention, keep his interest.

Cady was now of the opinion that "hot" was what you settled for when you couldn't get "compelling." When he was dressed, she forgot about the sheer size of him. He'd mastered the art of not being seen, somehow using his demeanor to hide his bulk, so that when he stripped, it was a shock to her system. He was a walking wall of muscle.

"Keep going," she said, because Conn was clearly a we-better-both-be-on-the-same-page guy. "Just . . . slower."

His face cleared, relaxed into something amused and

sexy at the same time. Hands on his hips, he rolled his head on his shoulders as if he was knocking out tension, then focused on her again. "Want to watch a show rather than be a show?"

"Something like that," she said.

Their voices were barely audible over the running water. Conn tugged the end of his worn brown leather belt free from the loop, waited, then tugged it back to release the prong. Leather glided against leather, and then the belt hung loose.

Without touching herself she felt the little electric shocks of arousal intensify between her legs. Steamy heat gathered, droplets of moisture forming at her temples, slipped down her sternum, gathered in her sex.

"Too fast?"

"Just right," she said, and waved her hand to indicate he should get on with it.

He took his time with his zipper, letting her see the strength of his erection straining at the gray boxers he wore before popping open the last of the buttons of his fly. The jeans came off first, kicked next to the vanity. He palmed himself through the soft cotton of his boxers, then stuck his thumbs in his waistband and lifted the fabric over his erection to fall to his ankles. Hands back on his hips, his cock bobbed straight out in front of him, lifting ever so slightly with his heartbeat. A flush darkened his skin from his cheeks down to his chest, the dark lines and swirls of the tattoos black on pink skin. Whether this was from the steam or arousal, she didn't know, or care.

Condoms were in the second drawer. She tore one free from the strip and turned back to the open shower door. "Come here," she said.

He crowded her through the door, hot skin and hard muscles chivvying her through the zero-entry doorway until he could close the door behind them. Steam enveloped them when the door closed. She turned to face him, lifting one hand to his sternum and holding her ground.

"You're doing that thing again," she said. It was hard to think with this muscled expanse at eye level, tattoos swirling under the sheen of steam gathering on his bare skin, and even harder to think when his fingers curled around her hip.

"What thing?"

"That thing were you use your body to herd me where you want me to be," she said, making shooing gestures with her hands into what little space remained between their bodies. "It's kind of hot."

He chuckled, the sound blending into the water, and stopped moving. "Kind of hot and kind of wrong?"

"Maybe a little bit wrong," she said, and smoothed her hands over his pectorals. In response his cock bobbed against her hip. "That doesn't mean I want you to stop."

He leaned forward just enough to get his mouth by her ear. "Good. I don't want to stop."

His teeth closed on her ear lobe, sending lightning streaking along her nerves. It was hard to breathe after that. How did he do this to her, short-circuit her brain with so little effort? They were naked, yes, but barely touching, and it was growing more difficult to even see him as steam obscured her vision, droplets condensing on her eyelashes. Conn looked down at her, his eyes darkened to slate blue, his hair clinging to his forehead as he backed her up a step, then another, across the floor to the tiled bench running the short length of the rectangle. She bumped into it, then sat down, no longer wondering how he did what he did, slipping into the flow as easily as water slid down the glass panels.

The new position put his cock, hard and straining upward, at face level. Automatically she reached for it, looking forward to going down on him, but to her surprise he kept moving and got down on his knees on the tile, edging forward until he could plant his hands on either side of her hips. Conveniently, the move parted her legs. A ripple of sensation eddied through her sex as she stared into his eyes.

"Hi," he said.

"Hi," she replied.

He lowered his head. Expecting a kiss she parted her lips, but he surprised her again by stopping with his plush mouth just above hers, with each inhale giving her fleeting contact that disappeared with each exhale. The contact was brief, sweet, tantalizing. She pushed her head forward just enough to satisfy temptation, and felt his hand close in her hair, pulling her back.

"Not yet," he said.

To her trained ear, his smile came through in his voice, but she could feel it against her lips as his hand flattened against the tile again. Desperate for more, she licked her mouth, scraped her upper teeth over her lower lip, trying to draw the taste of him into her mouth. He licked her lip, fleeting, hot. She whimpered, wriggled a little, feeling her nakedness and emptiness deep inside her body.

"You like to tease," she said.

"I like to take my time. Enjoy it." He kissed her then, quick and soft, no tongue, just the pressure of lips against lips. "I like to *have*." Shaping the words moved his mouth against hers, a different form of contact. She inhaled his breath, the intimacy of the air drawing from his lungs into hers, an intimacy she'd not considered before.

Just like the intimacy of having. She caught his jaw in her hand and leaned back just enough to get a good look in his eyes. He was so close she couldn't look into both eyes at once, but had to flick back and forth between them. Her mind was racing at the same speed. "Having" mattered to Conn. It mattered to everyone, of course, but it went deep into Conn McCormick's soul. "Because so much of what you do is fast," she said. "Drag racing. Eating on the run in your car. Going from call to call."

His hand stilled on her hip. She peered into his eyes,

Tell me more, Conn. You can tell me. I swear I'll keep your heart safe.

For a moment he looked like he regretted speaking the words. "Guess so," he said, minimizing the implications of what he'd said.

She brushed her thumb over his impossible mouth, felt his tongue briefly touch the pad. "You can have me," she said.

Under normal circumstances the language was old-fashioned, a euphemism for sex, for casual, for fucking. But she meant it in a different way, offering herself to him the way she used to build rapport with an audience at a personal show, starting with something softer, slow tempo, drawing them in without the crutch of an upbeat, driving song, a top-ten hit, a recognizable number. Back when she put herself out there through her music rather than "performed."

For a flash of time Conn's eyes widened, just long enough for her to see the expression, then see it change, then wonder if she'd seen it at all. But her heart skittered in her chest. She'd seen it. Her body told her that, more truthfully than words.

She was still cupping his jaw, her body language holding him ever so slightly at bay. Suiting actions to words, she slid her hand down his throat, then drew her thumb over his collarbone to the hollow in his shoulder. It was her turn to nip his earlobe.

"You can have me, as slow as you want," she whispered, and watched him shiver.

It felt so right to surrender to what she was making with him. For a long, charged moment she stared at him, wondering if he felt the same thing she did, that storm surge inside that usually meant songs were coming. Right now she wasn't sure what it meant, but she trusted it, trusted her body. Trusted Conn.

Wondering if she'd broken the spell, she leaned back a little, resuming their original positions, making space for Conn to have what he wanted to have. Time paused while he hesitated. She darted forward and nipped his lower lip. He growled, low in his throat, and kissed her, hot, possessive, licking into her mouth, obviously determined to switch gears to fast and furious. Panting, she tore her mouth away and rested her forehead on his, then gently kissed the tender corner of his mouth, coaxing him to stay here, with her. The stubble scraped against her lips, now swollen and sensitive. Then she lifted her head, recreating the hair's breadth of space between their mouths, and waited.

A shuddering exhale, then tension ebbed from his muscles and he picked up where he'd left off the first time, brushing his mouth back and forth over hers, stimulating delicate nerves to hyperawareness. She breathed out, soft and slow, and consciously relaxed. Without the driving desire her body softened, allowing her to feel the heat building in her core, her nipples, tight and hot despite the steam, the growing ache in her belly.

She wrapped her arms around his neck and shifted her bottom on the seat. Intense vulnerability shifted, strengthened, transformed into intense need as her body made known how desperately it wanted contact with his. All that hard, hot strength was within reach and yet so far away. He put one hand on her hip and pressed into her abdomen with his thumb, making her clit pulse and emphasizing the ache in her core. She circled her hips under his hand, the pressure frustratingly unsatisfying, but more than she had before.

"Give me something," she demanded, so he gave her his

mouth, his kiss blatantly, possessively mimicking sex, doing nothing to assuage the ache inside her. When she moaned, then nipped at his lower lip, he gave a soft rumble of a laugh, tightened his hands on her hips, and pulled her forward.

Caught off guard, her eyes flew open to find him gazing at her, heavy-lidded. He leaned forward and braced his arms at the elbow under her back, flattened palms supporting her upper body weight. Her skin was heat-reddened, the color similar to the flush standing high on Conn's cheekbones. It wasn't from the steam, but from the heat simmering between them. Still looking at her, he bent to her nipple and licked off the moisture collected on each hard tip. Cady's eyes closed again.

"Too much?" he asked.

She trembled at the rough scrap of his stubble over her soft flesh, then said, "I don't want to miss anything. Looking is distracting."

She didn't need to see him worshipping her body, the sounds and sensations told her everything she needed to know about his body position, and how turned on he was. The flat of his tongue against her nipple, then pointed to circle it, then the sharp edge of his teeth, gentle pressure tightening until she gasped from the sharp, hot flare of desire in her sex. The whispering pulse of steam from the jets, the prickling sensation of sweat blooming on her skin, her soft noises, his rougher ones, music in the sultry air.

When his mouth trailed down her abdomen, she broke rhythm by whimpering bereftly, then felt his chuckle against her skin when she lifted her legs and braced them on his thighs to give him better access. His mouth paused at the top of her sex, then one hand slipped under her bottom. A moment of breathless anticipation, during which she quivered like a guitar string, then his tongue circled her clit at the same time two fingers circled her soft opening.

It was hot, sweet torture, waiting while he opened her by infinitesimal increments, teasing, pushing, retreating to circle again, then dipping deeper. Her hands clutched at his shoulder and nape. Unable to get a grip on sweaty skin stretched taut over hard muscles, she slid her fingers into his hair and pulled tight.

Her reward for this pushy move was his fingers, deep enough to graze the aching bundle of nerves inside her sheath. Sweet heat zinged through her body and she moaned again, not stopping while he ruthlessly, implacably used the pressure of his fingertips and tongue to draw her climax from her. The steam hardly muffled her short, sharp cries.

"I've never done that in here before," she said when she regained her words.

"Come on," he said, his eyes flashing blue-gray through his damp lashes. "Really?"

"Never with another person," she amended.

He swiped the back of his hand across his mouth. "You've owned the house how long?"

"Fair point," she conceded. She leaned forward so their foreheads touched. "Don't stop now."

He opened the condom package, now softened by the steamy heat, and rolled the latex down his shaft, their heads bent together so she could stroke his nape.

"Now you like watching?"

"Love your hands," she murmured, stroking his nape while she watched the complex play of tendons, ligaments, muscle, and bone as his fingers performed the delicate task. "Also, there's nothing better going on."

He lifted her off the bench and onto his lap seemingly without effort. His cock jutted away from his pelvis, making it easy to center her over the tip and let her weight do the work. "How about now? Something better going on now?"

Her eyes fluttered closed again. "Definitely," she hitched out. Seeking entrance, the tip stretched sensitive, vulnerable flesh, then parted the swollen folds and slid inside. He controlled her descent with his hands, pausing when she flinched. She waited until the single pang passed, then licked his throat. He tasted of water, sweat, and his skin.

"All the way," she said, and stopped breathing until he was seated inside her.

He gave her short, slow, shallow thrusts, working the tip of his cock over the most sensitive tissue at her entrance, reminding her body that more pleasure awaited. His mouth was open against hers, soft, panting grunts increasing in intensity as he moved. He was holding back, she realized, so she kissed him, flickering her tongue over his lips, into his mouth, tempting him into kissing back as she circled her hips in his hands.

"Stop helping," he groaned.

"I'm not helping," she replied. "I want you deep."

A tremor ran through him. He lifted himself a little higher on his knees, bracing her lower back against the tiled bench. Cady flattened her feet on the floor but even then she wasn't ready for a thrust driven by his powerful hips. The only thing keeping her in place was his equally powerful arms, one around her waist, the other curving over her shoulder to hold her in place. His tempo increased, a solid, slapping sound became the counterpoint to her hiccupping cries.

"Again?" he asked.

"Again," she said through her tight throat, tipping over the edge into that pulsing certainty before she came. "Oh yes, again."

The deep shudders wracking his body and his arms tight around her told her he'd followed her into the void. Tension eased from his body in stages, his fingers trembling against her shoulder and hip, then relaxing. When she thought her arms would take her weight, she braced her palms on the bench behind her and lifted herself up and off him, his hand supporting her the whole way.

"That was intense," she said.

"Probably crazy to do in that kind of heat," he agreed, flashing her a softer, sweeter smile.

Probably crazy to do at all, she thought as she got to her feet and tottered over to the controls. With the twist of a handle she shut off the steam and turned on the shower jets, adjusting the temperate to a more reasonable warmth. The dual rain heads turned on, and she stepped under the spray.

He joined her a moment later, taking the shampoo bottle from her hand and setting it back in the niche, then taking her jaw in his hands and holding her for a series of sweet kisses. "I should have done more of that," he said.

"Well," she murmured against his mouth. "There's always round two."

Round two didn't happen. They soaped and rinsed and dried off, but when Conn wrapped a towel around his hips and headed for his bedroom, she caught his hand and pulled him into bed with her. When she woke up the next morning, pushed her hair out of her face and rolled over to see who was asleep beside her, the first word out of her mouth was "Ow."

Conn didn't move. Buried in her enormous, fluffy comforter, he was snoring faintly, and dead to the world. Cady smiled fondly. His hair was as much of a wreck as hers, sticking straight up off the side of his head where he'd fallen asleep on his side. Hers, no doubt, was a Bride of Frankenstein mess. She eased herself out of the bed, wincing at the soreness in her low back. A quick glance in the bathroom mirror showed a line of bruises forming at the base of her spine.

She shook some anti-inflammatories into her palm, then continued into the kitchen to down them with a glass of water, then do her morning steam treatment while the coffee brewed in the French press. When she turned around, Conn was standing by the island, resting his weight on one palm. She snorted.

"Yeah, yeah," he said, rubbing his hand over his crazy hair. He slept naked but was dressed in a pair of sweatpants and a T-shirt. "What have you got there?" he asked with a nod at her little pharmacopeia.

"Painkillers and vitamins," she said.

"What are the painkillers for?"

Wordlessly, she lifted up her fleece pajama top, tugged down the bottoms, and showed him the line of bruises along her back. Equally silent, he pulled up the cuff of his sweatpants and showed her a purplish-black bruise on his knee.

"There's a matching bruise on the other knee. I'll take a couple of the painkillers," he said.

She laughed as she dumped pills into his outstretched hand, then handed him what was left of her glass of water. "Pro tip. You don't want to spend a lot of time on your knees on tile. Or hardwood. Or concrete."

"Or carpet," he said, pleasantly willing to laugh at himself. "Rug burn is for amateurs. So variety isn't the spice of life?"

She twitched her wrist to adjust her bracelet, an automatic move she'd done thousands of times. But this time there was no bracelet. The smile disappeared off her face so fast the muscles in her jaw twinged in protest. "My life is already a little too spicy at the moment. I want safe, comfortable spices. Gingerbread lattes. Spice cookies. Peppermint candy canes. Holiday spices that smell like home and family and love."

"I get that," he said.

She was beginning to put together the pieces, his conversation with her mother, his relationship with Shane. Conn knew how it felt to never feel safe, to never know if home was the place where people took you in, or threw you out.

"I got another text from Bryan. There was another attack. I'm starting to see frustration from fans—emails, tweets, that kind of thing."

"What did he say?"

She showed him her phone. *Anyone in Lancaster hate you? IP addresses there definitely involved.*

"I thought I was safe here," she said. To her shock, tears were welling up in her eyes. She turned away, busied herself with pushing down the French press, then pouring coffee into two cups.

Conn's voice, sandy and resonant, came from behind her. "We will find this guy, and make this stop."

"I don't doubt it," she said, pleased to hear her own voice was steady. "But a dozen more are waiting to take his place. A hundred. This is my life. I can't believe in fairy tales anymore."

"Okay," he said. "Plans for the day?"

"I've got some ideas running in my head," she said, hearing the notes for the phrasing patter through in her mind. It was insistent, not catchy, but demanding her attention. "Studio time. You?"

"We need to have a meeting," Conn said.

That brought her up short. "With who?"

"Hawthorn. Dorchester. Whoever else they think is a good idea to bring in. We need to do it here. I'd rather keep you at home than risk you going out."

"Fine by me," she said, reaching for her phone. "Chris is going to want in on that conference."

He had some thoughts about Chris. "Understood."

After a few minutes of texting with their respective

tribes, they'd set a time to conference at Cady's house later in the afternoon. "I'm going into my studio," she said, and gathered her notebook and her guitar in one hand, and the handles of her tea and coffee mugs in the other.

Conn stopped her with a not-so-subtle lean of his body, then dropped a quick kiss on her mouth. "Keep your cell with you at all times," he said, his slate eyes serious.

She waggled it at him, shifting her guitar in its case in the process. "You know where to find me," she said, and walked downstairs, into the studio.

CHAPTER FIFTEEN

Conn peered in the opaque reflective glass on Cady's microwave and winced. He was about two weeks past a regulation haircut, and after falling asleep in Cady's bed with wet hair, he looked like he did after he'd let Shane's nieces and nephews go to town with their craft paste. He solved that problem with his watch cap, which, after ten minutes of riffling through pockets of every coat hanging in Cady's mudroom, he found drying on top of the washing machine in the laundry room. She'd scrubbed all the sap off his jacket and hers; they hung side by side on hooks by the garage. *His and hers hooks,* he thought as he shouldered into his jacket. He backtracked into his bedroom for his gun, badge, and cuffs, then walked outside. He was due for a perimeter check.

As he strode down the driveway, scanning the snow for footprints, his boots crunched in the dusting that had fallen over night. It made it easier to track an intruder or a peeping creeper, but all he saw were deer tracks on the edge of the woods and rabbit prints leaping from a den sheltered under the pine trees. The driveway, slate path, and porch

were all neatly cleared of snow, making it difficult to tell
if anyone had poked around.

He shoved his hands in his pockets and set off around
the side of the house, testing doors and windows, scanning
the ground, the bare trees sloping up the hill at the edge
of Cady's property, the house itself. Someone was in her
house, in her goddamn house, without her consent. By all
rights she should have collapsed in hysterics, weeping and
freaking out and calling in the National Guard or the
SEALs or whoever it was famous people had on speed
dial. Instead she womaned up and went on. He could tell
she was freaked out by the way she bit at her lower lip,
and by the fact that she looked worried when she went
into the studio. The first day or two she was home, her studio was her retreat, a safe place where she could explore
the stories she wanted to tell through songs. But the bastard who'd come into her home took away that security.

Conn wanted to wring his neck with his bare hands. A
more useful tactic would be to convince Cady to install
security cameras. He kicked at the woodpile, expecting the
mama possum to skitter out and head for the hills again,
but all he did was draw his attention to a gigantic wolf spider's
web, strung among the logs at the far end of the pile.
"Jesus," he muttered. The spider was the size of his fist, a
hairy malevolent-looking fucker, to quote Hawthorn after
a gang sweep briefing.

Only the LT would use a word like "malevolent." Conn
knew he needed to call him and report what Cesar said.
But if Cesar was right and someone in the Block was
behind Jordy Bettis's assault, who could Conn trust?
No one.

He needed to think. He needed to burn off some energy
so he could think.

An axe next to the pile of logs, left there by the former
owner, who'd dealt with the trees felled to clear the prop-

erty by slowly turning them into firewood. Shane's dad
had taken them camping off and on as kids, so Conn knew
how to use the axe, and knew he needed the release. He
set a log on the stump scarred with indentations from
the axe head, hoisted the axe over his head, and swung it
at the log.

Thwack-crack.

The impact of the axe up his arm and the crack the log
made as it split into two nicely sized pieces of firewood
gave him something to do while he thought through the
current situation. He had two problems. He was starting
to think they were connected.

Cesar said he needed to look inside the Block to find
Jordy Bettis's attacker. Conn wished he could say that
made no sense, but everyone knew it happened. But framing another officer for it was a completely different situation, explained only by the fact that no one in the gang
community was taking credit for the assault. Someone had
to roll. Hawthorn would have that information when he arrived in an hour or so.

But his brain followed the logic. If someone inside the
Block had attacked Jordy in order to grease up Conn, then
that meant anyone connected to Conn was also fair game.
He wasn't worried about Shane. Shane could take care of
himself, and his family. But Cady was another story entirely. Cady was already under incredible pressure. The
website attacks and the missing heirloom bracelet weren't
helping.

Thwack-crack. Conn set the split logs at the end of the
pile and lifted another log onto the stump. He hefted the
axe and paused.

Sneaky. Very sneaky. A psychological attack could tar-
nish Conn, make him even more vulnerable. Gang members wouldn't have the resources to track down Cady, but
someone at the Block would. They'd know how to work

through the records, or, failing that, have a network of people to call on who would know contractors, electricians, plumbers, kitchen and bathroom guys.

The whole thing was starting to make more sense. The drunk guy aside, the attacks all started after Conn signed on as her body man. What if, rather than getting him out of the way, he'd inadvertently brought the woman he was falling for into harm's way?

Thwack-crack.

His body was warm and loose despite the mid-December air, but the thought sent a cold shiver down his spine. His money was still on Chris. He wore his suits like Conn wore his uniform, so Conn had no doubt in his mind that despite the flippant attitude, if Chris had to land on someone like a ton of fucking bricks, he would. Chris had the most to lose if Cady decided to go her own way, which put him at the top of Conn's list, by a mile. But having a top of the list meant he had to consider everyone else on that list too. Getting a solve meant nothing if it wasn't the right solve.

Who else wanted to hurt Cady? The internet crazies came in second. She was ruining music, she was dating Harry Linton, she'd broken up with Harry Linton. What it boiled down to was this: She existed. She existed and she did her own thing.

Thwack-crack. Conn had a massive fucking problem with assholes who terrorized other people simply because they shone bright.

He made a mental note to go through the psychos folder again, with a fresh perspective. The threat had changed from physical to psychological. Reading explicit descriptions of someone wanting to take a baseball bat wrapped in barbed wire to Cady was obvious. He needed to think of this in a different way, and he needed to set aside his emotions to do it.

Thwack-crack. He tossed the logs on the pile and set another piece on end to split. Which led to problem number two: Cady's threat to him.

He was falling for her. Hard. He'd stood at the Field Energy Center and watched Queen Maud deliver a two-hour set, and felt not the slightest interest in her. But Cady . . . Cady drove fast and ate barbecue. Teased, and took care of, her little sister. Asked him for what she wanted, something he found hot as hell. Truth was, she was amazing. Not just as a singer-songwriter, because to be honest, it wasn't his kind of music at all. But he appreciated people who did things from their heart, with all of their passion behind it. He raced that way, worked that way, had everyone fooled that he felt that way.

She'd see through him, find the fear inside. Which frightened him more than walking down one of the dark alleys in the warren of the East Side's abandoned warehouses, more than flipping open the folder and seeing Jordy's jacked-up face, more than seeing 10.00 come up on the clock at the drag races, more than watching the McCools at a holiday meal or a family function. The deepest fear he had was that he'd never truly belong.

Cady was making him face that fear. He'd been accepted into Shane's family for so long he didn't think about it. But Shane's family was basically picture perfect, a miracle. He'd never aspired to have something like that for himself. But Cady's family, with her salt-of-the-earth mother and her snotty-teenage-girl sister, was imperfect enough that he could dream about it. She'd cleaned his jacket, shared meals with him, taken him Christmas tree shopping with her family.

"Because you work for her," Conn said, swiping the back of his hand over his forehead. His Henley clung to his back and arms. He shrugged his shoulders to adjust the fabric, then hoisted the axe and brought it down. The log splintered into two pieces that all but flew to the sides. "That's all."

Except it wasn't. She'd made it abundantly clear that she didn't sleep with everyone who worked for, or with, her. He knew her well enough now to believe he'd done her a disservice assuming he was just a way for the celebrity to blow off steam.

He'd made a dent in the woodpile but gotten nowhere by letting his brain churn along while he worked. Breathing hard, he pulled his phone from his pocket and checked in on Cady the same way Chris checked in on Cady: social media. She'd sent out a bunch of pictures he'd taken of her and Emily at the Christmas tree farm. Scrolling through the list of reposts and comments took five swipes of his thumb, and she'd posted it less than an hour ago. Emily's coats had struck a chord with Cady's followers, something that was sure to make her happy. Finally she posted a shot of her guitar and her notebook in the studio. *Going in for some songwriting time! <3 <3 <3*

She was in the house, and safe. The first part of that sentence was temporary: Cady was leaving town again, sooner rather than later. He'd damn well make sure she was safe when she left.

The woodpile workout gave him an excuse to take another shower, so he did, then pulled on a Henley and fresh jeans. His laundry was piling up, so he took it downstairs, threw in the pile of towels sitting in the basket to round out his load, puzzled his way through the high-end washing machine's digital readout, and pressed START. Water started flowing into the drum, so he guessed it was working.

"Hey there," Cady said. "Thanks for throwing the towels in."

He turned to see her peering around the doorframe into the laundry room. "As long as I don't throw in the towel?"

"Something like that," she said with a smile. "But you didn't have to do that. In fact, I don't think I've ever lived with a guy who offered to do anyone else's laundry, much less did it without being asked."

It was hard to unlearn patterns you learned as a kid. Travel light. Do your own laundry, wash your own dishes, be helpful if you can. He remembered all the times he offered to do the dishes, or mop floors, or fold laundry, trying to make himself useful so when he fucked up, lost his temper, got into trouble, he wouldn't be passed along to the next relative. It hadn't worked; enlisting was basically his best bet after he turned eighteen. He shrugged. "They were there, needing to be washed. It didn't make any sense to do a half-full load of my own stuff. Unless you've got some special secret towel washing method I don't know."

"Open door, insert towels, dump in detergent, hit start."

"That's what I did."

"You're golden, then."

"How did the session go?"

"Meh," she said with a casual shrug that didn't match the haunted look in her eyes. "Some days it's easy peasy. Other days it's a painful grind. Doesn't matter. You show up and do the work."

He caught her arm. "Hey," he said, quiet, low. "How did it go?"

"Pretty fucking awful," she replied, just as quiet. Like if the universe heard her, it would be twice as bad next time. "Thanks for asking. Want some lunch?"

"Sure," he said.

They walked back into the kitchen. "I heard you going at the woodpile," Cady said as she opened the refrigerator door. "Thanks. You also didn't need to do that."

"I'm used to a lot more stimulation than this," he admitted.

"So am I," she said, setting containers of stew and

chopped-up veggies on the counter, then reaching for the pan to heat up the stew. "No, sit down, I've got this. Unless, if you need something to do, I wouldn't mind being uncivilized and eating off trays in front of the fire."

He used the leather carrier to haul in some of the logs from outside. By the time he had the fire going, she was carrying over a big tray laden with bowls of beef stew, sliced whole-grain bread, butter, and the fresh vegetables. After setting the tray on the tufted leather ottoman, she handed him a plate for bread and veggies, then a bowl of stew.

Her gaze was distant as she tucked her feet under her and settled in with her own bowl, eating with an absentmindedness that told him she was still far, far away. "You're not worried about what's going on?"

"One of the things I learned early on was that if I was going to hire someone to do a job, I either let that someone to do his or her job, or they were just a distraction. You seem extremely competent. I do neither of us any favors if I micromanage you. More importantly, I trust you."

Her words startled him. She had no reason to really trust him, not at a time when he didn't know who he could trust himself. The people he thought had his back might in fact be betraying him right now. Cady had family, friends, connections. He had nothing but himself.

He was hers, if she wanted him.

The thought flashed through his mind with the speed and searing impact of lightning. Where the hell did that come from?

"Good," he said. He went back to eating stew, but now too distracted to really appreciate the flavors. It was a relief when he heard a car pull into the driveway, followed by a second vehicle. "Hawthorn and Dorchester," he said with a quick glance at his watch.

Doors slammed. One, two . . . three . . . four. "Get out of sight," Conn said.

"I'll clean up," Cady replied, stacking dishes on the tray.

The kitchen put her out of the line of sight to the door. Hand on his holster, Conn walked to the window and peered through the slatted blinds. He saw Dorchester's Jeep, Hawthorn's Durango, and a Mercedes no one he knew could afford. They'd come in personal cars to avoid drawing attention to Cady's house, and parked in front of the big evergreens, so no one could see the cars from the street.

Heads appeared on the stairs, Detective Joanna Sorenson behind Hawthorn, which accounted for one door. But the head that appeared after Matt had smooth black hair glinting in the weak winter sunlight. Eve Webber. Matt had brought along emotional reinforcements.

The last person trotting up the stairs, in a suit and tie, was a lawyer Conn knew only by reputation. Caleb Webber.

Conn opened the door, and his mouth. "No, we weren't followed," Hawthorn said.

Eve patted him on the arm to say hello, then headed for the kitchen like she knew the place. "You sure it was a good idea to bring her along?" Conn said to Matt. "She's had enough excitement to last most people a lifetime."

"She's not most people," Matt said wryly as he unzipped his army jacket and shrugged out of it. "And she insisted."

"I didn't insist," Eve called from the kitchen. "I simply pointed out that Cady might like a friend at the table. I know what it's like to be in the middle of something like this. Conn, do you know my brother?"

Caleb Webber held out his hand, not bothering to smile. "Caleb Webber. I'm Cady's local attorney. Her agent asked me to be here."

"I'll call Chris," Cady added as she fiddled with her phone. "It's so sweet of you to take time away from Eye Candy."

"Natalie owes me, big time," Eve said. "She took a few days' vacation with no notice and just got back today."

"That's nice," Cady said. "Where did she go?"

"Nowhere with sun. She's as pale as she was before she left."

"It's a little early for me," Cady said. "February. That's when you want to get away, when it's been cold and cloudy and slushy for months and you can't take another second of it."

"But you've still got March to go," Eve added. "You were in Turks and Caicos last year, right?"

"Just before the tour started," Cady confirmed.

Keeping Cady safe, let alone getting her any privacy, was going to be an impossible job. Anyone with access to the internet knew where she was, who she was with, what she was doing.

She gave him a bright smile. "Coffee, anyone?"

Everyone respectfully declined. It was interesting to watch Hawthorn, who was one of the most stone cold operators Conn had ever met, and Sorenson, who didn't flinch for anyone, watch Cady out of the corners of their eyes.

"Really?" Cady said, "I'm making some for myself."

"No coffee, Cady," Chris said, the sharpness of his tone moderated by the fuzzy speakerphone sound quality.

"I'm sorry, Chris, I was driving under a bridge and didn't hear that last bit," she said, pouring beans into her fancy coffeemaker. "Come on, people. I don't like to drink alone."

"I'd love some," Sorenson said. After that, the dam broke and everyone wanted coffee. Conn could almost smell Chris fuming away in Brooklyn as Cady happily scooped beans into the coffee maker's reservoir.

"How's the weather out east?" Conn asked casually.

"Typical December in the big city," Chris said readily.

"Yesterday it was in the fifties. Today the high is nineteen, and it's going to get sloppy."

Nothing anyone with a weather app couldn't recite. Chris was no fool.

Coffees in hand, everyone clustered around the big island in the kitchen, Cady's phone on speaker so Chris could hear everything and add to the conversation. Conn stood by Cady, both because he could, and because he wanted to keep one ear tuned to the background noise when he spoke. The guy was muting his end when he didn't have something to say; there wasn't enough static for the line to be open all the time.

They ran through official introductions so Chris would know who was who, then Hawthorn nodded at Conn. He flipped open his notebook and started the basic rundown of what had happened since he became Cady's official bodyguard. It was embarrassingly short: threat level high, actual progress on said threat level low.

"Counselor, who knows Cady owns this house?"

Caleb didn't bother to flip open the leather portfolio he'd brought with him. "All work and payments were processed through the limited liability corporation my firm set up for Cady. I know. My partner knows. Our paralegal knows. That's it."

Conn added three more people to his list of possible leaks.

"What are our next steps?" Hawthorn asked.

"We should install security cameras," Conn said.

"No," Cady said.

"I'm with Cady on this one," Chris said from Brooklyn, or possibly from some hidey hole in the woods behind Cady's house.

Conn's gaze flickered to Hawthorn, who lifted one eyebrow ever so slightly. Cady missed this, because she was staring at the phone, coffee cup halfway to her lips. "Who are you and what have you done with my manager?"

"The best security you have right now is the fact that no one knows you bought this house," Chris said. "If we involve a security company, that's one more group of people who know someone important lives at that house. All we need is one curious tech starting to dig, ask questions, post pictures, and your privacy is gone. Then the security cameras are no longer optional."

"People know where my mom lives," Cady said to Conn. "That's basically an open secret, and she doesn't have security cameras."

"Not that your mom's not a lovely, lovely woman," Chris said, "but no one really cares about her. Or your sister."

"You're pretty casual with the two people who matter most to Cady," Conn said.

Silence from everyone around the kitchen island, and from Chris. Cady's eyes were wide, unblinking. "You think this is a real threat. You're not just being paranoid."

"I'm absolutely, one hundred percent paranoid," Conn said. "That's my job. Over the last two weeks someone has taken down your website more than once and come into your home and stolen one of your most meaningful mementos. The attacks are getting closer. More personal. I'm making a very strong recommendation. You can choose not to take it, but if you don't, you're making my job that much harder."

More silence.

"We can install the cameras," Sorenson said. She was looking at Cady when she said it, not talking to Chris, or to Conn.

"We? As in one of your officers, who might also talk?" Chris asked.

"I can do it," Sorenson said.

"Who are you? Have we met? How do I know you won't talk?" Chris demanded.

Sorenson gave the phone a look that would have curdled milk. Dorchester hid a grin behind a cough. Hawthorn, as the ranking officer present, spoke. "The expression on Detective Sorenson's face may not be translating well through the phone—"

"Actually, it is," Chris said. "Ice crystals are forming on my screen as I speak."

"I can assure you that you can trust the discretion of every officer in this room," Hawthorn said smoothly.

"Up to you, Cady my dear."

Cady worried at her lip again. "I really, really don't want to do this," she said. "Home is the only place I go where I don't have to think about cameras. Every time I set foot off my property, I'm aware that someone could be taking my picture, or recording me. I have to think about what I'm wearing, doing, saying. Even here in Lancaster. It's different than before."

"Because you're a bigger star now," Chris interjected. "All the work, the millions the label has invested, is paying off. Just something to keep in mind, in case you were thinking about momentum. That sort of thing. Carry on."

Conn glared at her. Millions? *Millions* invested in Cady's next album?

It was Cady's turn to look daggers at the phone. "But when I'm in my home, it's the only place I can really relax. If you put up cameras, that changes the dynamic."

"They'd be on the perimeter only," Conn said, striving for reassuring. This wasn't his forte, negotiating with people he cared about. "Entrances and exits. The woods."

Cady shook her head. "It closes me down even more, Conn. My world is getting smaller and smaller when I need it to be big. Wide open. I *need* somewhere I can just be me. Not Maud. This house was supposed to be that place. Cameras turn it into a Maud space."

He thought about what she said about needing lots of material, space, and time to write her songs. He thought about how small she was, how delicate, how easy it would be to hurt her. "Someone broke into your house. This is the safest thing we can do."

"No one broke into my house," she pointed out. "There were no signs of forced entry. Whoever it was had a key. We got the locks changed. I asked Mom to take the key off the hook by her back door. That's going to narrow our field considerably."

But not exclude Chris, who had now heard everything, and managed to talk Cady out of installing cameras.

"Trust me, Cady," Conn said. The words echoed in his head. *Trust me. Trust me. Trust me.*

Cady looked at him, looked away, then glanced around the table. He was making this too intimate. He knew it, but didn't care. If making her safe meant exposing how he felt, then he'd do it.

"No cameras. For now," she said.

Her eyes pleaded with him to understand. They stared at each other for a second, and in that instant, Conn knew what he was going to do. He was going to install security cameras without her consent. He wasn't trained in the technology, but he knew enough to figure out the basics. A couple of cameras transmitting on a secure wireless network to his laptop. No big deal. Cady didn't want it, but the thought of someone sneaking in and out of her house made his skin crawl. He knew he was doing exactly what Hawthorn counseled him not to do, going rogue, but there was too much at stake.

Cady was at stake. Her safety, her security, her happiness. He'd probably just made the choice that would cost him her confidence, but better to remain alone than to be with her and lose her. He was used to alone. He was used to not letting the door hit him on the ass on the way out.

"No cameras," he said, not at all surprised to hear how level his voice was.

"Great," Chris said. "If we're done, Cady, I need a few minutes."

She picked up the phone, switched off the speaker mode, and walked toward the windows, her voice too low for Conn to hear. He pulled out his own cell phone and sent a text to Shane.

Need you to pick up a few things for me. He followed it up with a list. *Cameras. Discreet, wireless, secured.*

Shane's reply was almost instantaneous. *Want me to get the same setup I got for the garage? Easy to use.*

Yes.

It'll be cheaper online.

I need it ASAP.

I'm on it.

He turned to Hawthorn. Now was the time to tell him about Cesar's accusation, something that had been circulating about the Block for a long time. But Conn wanted proof, something solid to take to his LT, something that protected his own hide. So he stuck to the subject at hand.

"I don't trust her manager as far as I can throw him."

"You don't really have grounds not to trust him," Hawthorn said, still focused on his spreadsheets or pie charts or tables.

"Besides the fact that Cady's thinking about changing her direction in a way that could cost him his percentage of whatever Cady makes when her next album comes out?"

Finger poised over the power button, Hawthorn looked up from his laptop. "Come again?"

"I signed a confidentiality agreement. I can't say anything more than this: Chris and Cady are butting heads over her future. He could lose big bucks in the coming year if Cady gets her way. You saw him, LT. Two weeks ago he was dead set on her having total protection, and now he talks her out of getting security cameras?"

"Understood," Hawthorn said. "But none of this is what we'd normally classify as serious intent to harm."

"Which is a flaw in the law, and in your way of thinking." Caleb Webber spoke up unexpectedly. "It's psychological. The most damaging thing you can do to a woman is make her think she's not safe. As long as she thinks she isn't, she's off-balance, easier to control. This could easily be an attack not on her person but on her creativity."

Sorenson's face changed ever so slightly from professional blankness to faintly assessing. She gave him a small nod. "McCormick's got a good point. Cady's managed to tune out the internet trolls, but this is personal. If her manager wants to control her, this would go a long way toward doing that."

"He's not here, though," Dorchester said. "You'd think he'd swoop in to save the day."

"Maybe that's the next step," Conn said. "Freak her out, then calm her down. Problem solved, especially if the threats end."

"Did anyone else hear the SoMa trolley in the background when Chris was talking?" Eve asked.

They all stared at her.

"You're right," Conn said. "That was the dinging during his call. I knew it was familiar, but I couldn't place it."

"The trolley quit running after Labor Day," Eve said. "The city shut it down until the holiday season. It's a great plan. They decorated the interior and exterior, and they're using it to shuttle people between the different business districts. It gets people used to using the trolley, and it boosts traffic to the local shops."

"If that's the SoMa trolley, that means he's still in Lancaster," Conn said. "He lied to Cady. To me. He said he was going home. But he's still in Lancaster."

"You don't know that," Sorenson said. Caleb Webber stood to her left, watching the conversation with an intensity Caleb knew meant he was filing away every word.

"The trolley's bells were modeled after the street cars that used to run in the fifties," Eve said.

"Lots of cities had street cars," Conn said, his brain working away furiously. "But not anymore."

"San Francisco does," Sorenson said. When Dorchester lifted an eyebrow at her, she added, "What? Vacation last year. They're quaint."

"He lives in Brooklyn," Conn said, keeping the conversation on track.

"Are there street cars still running in Brooklyn?"

"No idea," Conn said, and made a note to check.

Eve had tactfully wandered away to inspect the items on Cady's shelves while Cady carried on her conversation with Chris. "We can't do anything without her permission," Hawthorn said, keeping his voice low. "We need proof he's gaslighting her before we make an accusation like that."

"I'll get it," Conn said. He'd get it or go down in flames trying.

"Don't tell me anything else," Hawthorn said, like he was reading Conn's mind. "All I'll say is this: You don't need to make it stand up in court. You just need enough to make him stop."

"I'll get it, LT," Conn repeated. "Can I have a minute before you leave?"

Hawthorn looked at him, then at Sorenson and Dorchester. "Head back to the precinct," he said quietly.

"Call me if you need anything," Caleb said to Cady. "The firm can handle any transaction for you, and run interference if you need it."

"Thanks, Caleb."

Dorchester collected Eve, following Caleb and Sorenson out the front door. It closed with a quiet snick of the latch. Conn wondered if everything Matt Dorchester did sounded lethal.

"What the progress into Jordy's beatdown?"

"Nobody saw, heard, or did nothing, ever, in the history of the world," Hawthorn said.

"Someone always rolls, LT," Conn said.

"Not this time. This time, nobody's talking. I offered every incentive I could think of to everyone who would normally sell his mother down the river to get a cop on his side. Not a thing."

Conn shoved his fists into his pockets and blew out his breath, trying to get his emotions under control.

"I recognize that look on your face," Hawthorn said. "It's the look someone gets right before he does something he'll have to explain later."

"I have no idea what you're talking about, Lieutenant."

"Don't feed me that line of bullshit, Officer McCormick," Hawthorn said amiably. "You think this is the first time I've supervised a hotshot with a temper? I'll give you a clue. It's not. Whatever you're thinking about doing, don't."

"Sir," Conn said.

Hawthorn's stare could have bored through steel. Conn knew his answer wasn't an affirmative, but his time in the army taught him how and when to keep his mouth shut. When uncomfortable, most people talked to fill silences; it was one of a detective's main staples to get information. Just wait, because the witness or the suspect would crack and start talking first.

But Hawthorn wasn't a witness, or a suspect. He'd been a cop longer than Conn, and came from a family of cops. But Conn knew he didn't have to outlast his LT. He just had to last long enough for Cady to get off the phone with

Chris. But it was like being ground between two stones: the LPD and Cady's safety.

"What are you two doing over here?" she asked. "Having a staring contest?"

"We're coming to an agreement, Ms. Ward," Hawthorn said, his gaze still fixed on Conn. He waited for his LT to throw him under the bus and tell Cady everything. "Is there anything else the department can do to help you feel safe?"

"No, thanks," Cady said. "You've already done so much. I'm comfortable with where we've left things."

"Then we will proceed exactly as we have been," Hawthorn said, still looking at Conn.

Conn didn't flinch. He didn't so much as blink. It was easy enough for Hawthorn to make promises and walk away, back to his budget meetings and his statistics. He wasn't the one guarding Cady every hour of every day, watching her struggle to finish her album, worry about her future, handle her family and friends and fans with grace and aplomb with this threat hanging over her head.

He wasn't the one in love with her.

Oh, *shit.*

"Great," Cady said cheerfully.

Conn startled before he remembered that while Cady's songs made it seem like she could see into his soul, she couldn't. She was looking at him like she'd looked at him every other second they'd been together, wary and fascinated, like she wanted to touch but wasn't sure she could.

Hawthorn arched an eyebrow, clearly catching some nuance he'd missed before, one Conn didn't want his LT recording, analyzing, slotting into the statistics and bar charts he probably kept on all his officers. *Likes Indian food and country music. Drives a Bronco. Takes kids on ATV rides in the winter. Breeds angora rabbits because his daughter loves them. Divorced twice.*

Falling in love with Cady Ward.

For the life of him, Conn couldn't figure out how to get out of this one. Cady saved the day. She held out her hand to Hawthorn, gave him a wide smile, and said, "Thanks so much for coming all the way out here, Lieutenant Hawthorn. I really appreciate it. If you're interested, I can get you tickets and backstage passes to the kick-off concert for my next tour. I always start in Lancaster."

Hawthorn blushed. Conn got a grip on the counter, because the world was reeling on its moorings. Ian Hawthorn actually blushed like a little girl, the tips of his ears going as red as the tomatoes ripening on Cady's counter. "That's not necessary, Ms. Ward," he said. "We're just doing our jobs."

Conn tried hard not to think about how extremely unprofessional his interactions with Cady had been as he watched Cady arch an eyebrow at Hawthorn. "You came to my house on a Saturday afternoon before the holidays. I'm sure you have better things to be doing, and I appreciate you going above and beyond to keep me safe. I'd be honored to have you come to the concert as my guest."

Hawthorn struggled with professional ethics for maybe another five seconds, then gave in. "That would be great," he said. "I used to watch you sing in SoMa, when I was on patrol."

She smiled. "I'll be in touch when we have a date, so I know how many tickets you want."

She'd managed to totally disarm Hawthorn, something Conn had never seen in all his time working with the undercover unit. Hawthorn collected his folders and his laptop, pulled on his coat and said goodbye. When she closed the door behind him, she flipped the deadbolt and turned to Conn.

"What was that all about?"

CHAPTER SIXTEEN

"What do you mean?" Conn said, stalling for time. He'd been in love before. He wasn't that badly fucked up that he thought he'd never love again. This felt different. Trying to pinpoint exactly why while Cady glared at him with narrowed eyes was beyond him.

"We're coming to an agreement? He's not trying to push cameras on me, is he?"

"No," Conn said, totally truthfully. "He meant something else."

"The accusation that you beat up that prisoner?"

Damn, she was quick. Also, not self-centered. Unlike all the stories he'd heard of celebrities becoming self-absorbed divas, Cady thought about the people close to her. If anyone was acting like a self-absorbed diva, it was Emily, but maybe that was just teenage girl.

He had less than a second to decide whether or not to involve her even more deeply in that case. "Yes," he said.

"Well? What's happening?"

"Nothing," he said. He took her arm to guide her away from the windows at the front of the house, but ended up with her fingers woven through his as they headed to the sofa in front of the fireplace.

"Nothing," she repeated. "Really? Don't the police take these accusations very seriously?"

"We do. We are. But usually someone rolls, talks, gives up someone else in exchange for a deal. That's what we've got to offer, a reduced sentence, time served, charges dropped. None of the usual fish are biting."

"That seems odd," Cady said.

"It *is* odd." Conn stared at his hand, linked with hers, and thought, *Not as odd as knowing I'm falling in love with you.* Did he tell her about Cesar's comment? Did he worry her more? How did people manage this relationship stuff? It was insanely complicated, and totally outside his experience. "Very odd."

They sat in silence for a moment, Cady just being Cady, the firelight making her crazy hair gleam like old oak, turning the curve of her cheek rose red. Conn's brain tried to think about two things at once: the way his heart was skittering in his chest and the extremely unusual show of solidarity from the East Side's biggest gang. Why would they do that? Someone usually wanted out badly enough to give up a piece of information, or could be enticed into it. It took real leadership to enforce that kind of solidarity, and the Strykers hadn't had that kind of leadership since Matt Dorchester took out Lyle Jenkins last summer.

Or so they thought.

Conn's brain jerked into a gear he didn't know he had. Maybe they were going about this the wrong way. Maybe there wasn't an absence of leadership in the Strykers. Maybe an invisible hand was holding everything together more tightly than before. Maybe Lyle's unexpected death didn't cut off the snake's head. Maybe it made room for a King Cobra to take over for a garden snake.

"Okay," Cady said, a little smile on her face. "I recognize that expression of someone deep in thought. I'm going back to my studio."

Conn tightened his grip on her hand. "No, wait," he started. Then he stopped. What was he going to say? *I'm falling in love with you?* She heard that a dozen times a day from complete strangers. Even if he did say it, nothing changed the fact that she was Queen Maud, and he was a Lancaster cop who'd just made a decision that would end what was growing between them.

Her expression turned from amused to slightly quizzical, her brows drawing in slightly, the smile losing its gleam. "What?" she asked.

"Just keep your phone with you. I'll be up here."

"Sure thing," she said.

She withdrew her fingers from his. He didn't want to let her go, but he had to, so he held on to what he could, the sweet, electric slide of her skin against his, lighting his nerves on fire. The heat remained long after he heard the door to her studio close.

Finally he shook it off, got up and grabbed his laptop and his notebook from his duffle bag, and opened it. He signed in to the department's secure database, and tried to think through how a detective would approach this. His detractors joked that Ian Hawthorn, the son of a loved and well-respected former police chief, thought he was the second coming of Jesus. What would Hawthorn do?

He wouldn't start with Conn's usual tactic: going out on the street and tracking down people he knew could give him answers, then threatening them until they gave it up. Hawthorn would gather data, analytics, metrics. Information, both detailed and bird's eye. Conn started by cross-referencing the gang unit's list of current and former Strykers, even the dead ones, with a list of arrests going back three years. Then he started looking at the results, which cases got dismissed or pled down, and which ones never went to trial because a witness recanted or evidence disappeared. The results matched both the official line when the city government wanted answers on the state of the East Side and the chatter in the department: the Strykers were slippery as fuck. This wasn't news.

Frustrated, he got up and headed back outside to tackle the woodpile again. It wasn't running full tilt after a burglary suspect, but it would have to do. Fifteen minutes in, his phone buzzed. Shane.

Got what you wanted. I also picked up her Christmas tree. What next?

Conn looked at the back of the house. Cady would probably be in her studio for hours yet, Shane could be here in twenty minutes, and Conn had no time to waste. He texted Shane her address. *Park at the end of the driveway.*

He stayed at the woodpile while he waited, but the physical exertion didn't drive away the conflicted emotions swirling in a sick dance in the pit of his stomach. He had to do this. Had to keep her safe. She'd asked him not to. But in a short span of time she'd gone from a face in the glossy magazine rack at the end of the supermarket checkout counter to the woman he couldn't bear to lose.

His phone buzzed again. *I'm here.*

He sank the axe into the stump and trotted along the shoveled path around the side of the house, skirting the big evergreens. A dark blue junker pickup with in-transit plates idled roughly at the end of the driveway. A watch cap similar to the one Cady had confiscated at the Christmas tree lot covered Shane's white-blond hair.

Shane rolled the window down with an actual hand crank. "I figured I should do this incognito, yo," he said with a quick grin. He handed a white plastic Radio Shack bag through the window. "It's pretty easy to set up. Took me and Finn a couple of hours while the software installed on our computers. You have wifi?"

"Yeah," Conn said.

Shane looked at the house. "Nice. Not what I expected a superstar to own, but it's nice. Homey. I'm kind of surprised it didn't come with a full security system and a trained guard dog."

"She doesn't want cameras," Conn said, because he'd never lied to Shane and wasn't about to start now.

Shane's brows lifted. "So what are you doing?"

"The threat is getting too close. Too personal. I don't want to lose her."

His friend was too smart not to follow the chain of repercussions all the way to the bitter end. He shook his head. "You always had to do the right thing. Where do you want the tree?"

Even when he knew another fight to protect a smaller kid would mean getting shuffled to the next family member in the contact list. It didn't matter if he was on the right side. All that mattered was that he was a pain in the ass. Not easy. He was big, loud, argumentative, stubborn, and in everyone's face. Bag clenched in one hand, he said, "Got a minute to help me get it into the house?"

"Let me check with my boss," Shane said. "Oh, wait. I am the boss. Yeah, I've got a minute."

Together they wrestled the fir into the house via the sliding glass doors. It was considerably longer than a minute before they had the tree straight in the stand. "The branches will settle in a day or two," Shane said. "It's a nice one."

Conn remembered tagging along with the Ward women to pick it out, the way Patty and Cady included him in their decision. The plastic bag with the cameras tugged at his conscience. "Does doing the wrong thing for the right reasons make it right?"

"Who the fuck knows?" Shane said philosophically. "Do what you have to so you can look yourself in the mirror, and pray. Mind if I wash my hands before I go? I left Mickey in charge of the shop. I just hope it's still standing when I get back."

He interpreted silence on the social media front to mean Cady was deeply entrenched in her songwriting session. The cameras were small, and simple, the batteries already installed. They were triggered by motion, the footage stored in the cloud. He borrowed a sturdy deck chair. Using the screwdriver attachment on his pocketknife, he had them installed and turned on in less than half an hour.

Observation was on his mind as he worked, surveillance, recording details, actions, which led him to Hawthorn's meticulously compiled reports, the ones he barely glanced at during briefings. But between one turn of a screw, a thought occurred to him: How did the Strykers stack up compared to other gangs in Lancaster? Surely the units compiled the same metrics on other gangs. Hawthorn was a metrics freak. But Conn couldn't remember the same chatter about the Twentieth Street Bloods, or the Murder Angels.

He folded up his pocketknife, put the deck chair back, and hurried inside. Behind Cady's studio door the same fragment of the same song was now on some kind of loop. He didn't stop, just took the stairs two at a time to the main room and opened his computer again.

Knowing what he was looking for and how to compile it meant the second round didn't take him as long. The numbers were so interesting he did the same thing for the Solo Angeles. Then he sat back and blew out his breath.

Strykers were arrested as frequently as members of the Twentieth Street Bloods or the Murder Angels crew. Those statistics matched. What didn't match was the rate of dismissals. Three years ago, the department's ability to make a good case against the Strykers started to drop. Not off a cliff, but over the course of about eighteen months, something very interesting happened. The Strykers were the baddest guys in town, based on his experience on the streets. He'd assumed that the higher-ups were accumulating trends that contradicted his lone perspective.

The number of arrests started to drop just after a specific group of cops moved over to the gang unit. Conn knew these guys. They were the guys he met for a beer a couple of times a month, guys who got him through his rookie probationary period, who'd watched his back ever since.

The official story was that the Strykers were in disarray, weakened, no longer a threat. The Twentieth Street Bloods and the Murder Angels were smaller, more deadly gangs with connections to out-of-state groups that made them a higher priority than the homegrown Strykers. Conn now saw it a different way. The department had missed it, because you couldn't compile statistics on arrests that never happened. Someone in the gang unit was at the very least taking money not to go after the Strykers. At the very least. Worst-case scenario, they were actively distributing, insinuating themselves into the management structure. No, it wasn't the kind of racket a big city gang was running, but as he'd just spent the last two weeks telling Cady, people did all kinds of crazy, illegal shit for not very much money at all. They seized the opportunity in front of them. When Lyle Jenkins died, someone smart stepped in.

Someone connected to, or very possibly inside, the Lancaster Police Department. And Conn knew who, because he had something in common with the gang officers too. The majority of the members of the gang unit were trained by Kenny Wilcox, his training officer.

* * *

Cady switched off the mic, set her guitar in its stand, stood up and put her palms to the small of her back, and stretched until her spine popped. "Ow," she said, twisting from one side to the other to generate another series of cracks from her hips to her neck. She'd been sitting still for far too long, which was fine when she came out with a melody or a chorus or an idea to show for her work. That kind of soreness was like the way she felt after good sex, a pleasantly lingering ache the reminded her she'd done something awesome. Today she had nothing to show for hours of work except the frustrating sense that the song still wasn't right, the solution just out of reach.

She opened the drawer where she stashed her phone so it wouldn't distract her while she worked, and automatically swiped through her social media apps. The posts getting the most attention were the pictures Conn took at the Christmas tree farm. She paused to answer a few of the more recent replies, extolling the coats' cool features—a phone pocket, a loop for your ear bud cord, the gorgeous wool, the silk lining, the neat way the coat swung as she moved—and texted Em.

Have you seen the chatter about the coats? So cool!

The reply came almost instantly. *OMG so not what I was expecting. They weren't supposed to get this much attention.*

It's nice to have options. Cady slid her phone into her pocket as she climbed the stairs to the main floor in search of Conn.

Conn.

As much as she'd tried to put him out of her mind, he kept drifting into her awareness at the least opportune times. Most men played their cards close to their chests, but Conn had made an art of stuffing everything inside, just like he shoved his hands into his pockets. He all but vibrated with tightly leashed energy that danced between the demands of his job and the very real possibility it would consume him. He walked a fine line between light and darkness, between the good he did and the bad he was capable of doing.

That was the song she wanted write, about struggling with frustration, that sense of being trapped, wishing you could change that, not knowing how, feeling called to more. A song about her, about him, about everyone. Everyone struggled with that, in her experience. In their depths, everyone wanted meaning, connection, more than another song about love, lust, and everything in between. Maybe that's what her song was missing, the turn from falling in love to finding the love that led you through the deep waters everyone feared.

The idea held some promise. She set it on the back burner of her brain to let her muse chew it over, and headed upstairs for something to eat.

Conn was sitting on the couch in front of the fireplace, his laptop in front of him but dark and quiet. Arms folded across his chest, he stared into the low, flickering flames. Outside the big windows the twilight clung to the last rays of the setting sun, the bare branches of the trees not much darker than the sky.

He looked up when she cleared the landing. His face was impassive, and his eyes reminded her of the night sky, infused with color yet bleak, cold, empty. She longed to walk up to him, give him a kiss, rub his shoulder and tell him that together they'd face whatever was bothering him, but were they at that point?

If you have to ask, the answer's no.

He didn't move as she crossed the hardwood floor to the kitchen and ran water into her steamer. "I can't help but notice that there's a really big Christmas tree in my living room," she said.

"Shane brought it over while you were working. I hope that's okay. I didn't want to disturb you."

"I wish you had, but only because my session was pretty crap, and I wanted to tell him thanks. You look like your afternoon was about as productive as mine."

"That bad?" he asked, but she could tell his heart wasn't in it.

"That bad," she replied, tossing the towel over her head and breathing deep. The steam gathered on her face and made her flush as she remembered their erotic encounter in the bathroom. Lightning skittered down her nerves to pool hot and damp low in her belly.

She was going to be in a lot of trouble when she left town if using her steamer made her think of Conn. Still under the towel, she could hear him walking around. Sure enough, when she tossed back the towel and switched off the steamer, Conn was standing by the island, hands jammed in his pockets. His laptop and notebook were gone from the coffee table.

"What's wrong?"

"If I knew that, I'd fix it," she said, but with a smile to take the sting out of her words. "I'd ask if you wanted to hear it, but it's not even close to ready." It wasn't working, and worse, it was starting to take on the dense, over-kneaded feeling that meant she'd have to trash the whole thing.

"What about you?" she asked. "What were you doing all day?"

"Research," he said, like he'd spent the day handling spiders or digging through the trash. "It's not my thing."

She smiled at him. "What is your thing?

"The street," he said.

"I could see that," she agreed, openly looking him over. Even without his favorite watch cap on his head he'd blend right in with the guys on the corners. "But that option isn't available to you right now, because you're stuck here with me."

"I'm here with you," he agreed, subtly changing her words. "So I'm adapting. I'm an adaptable kind of guy."

"The computer?" she hazarded.

"Metrics," he said, lumping the word in with *research*. "Statistics. Analyzing trends."

"I've sat through meetings like that," she said, remembering hours of conversation about market penetration and crossover appeal, how soul-deadening if you just wanted to do, to be. "Do-be-do-be-doooo," she sang, then, when he looked at her like she'd lost her mind, said, "Sounds like an absolute blast."

"It's not my favorite thing."

She waited. She'd spent enough time around men, long hours on tour buses, and in the studio, and across tables and bars to know that sometimes the best thing you could do was keep quiet. Conn looked like he was being ground between two steel plates dusted with shards of glass. She offered him what she knew he needed. "Let's get out of here."

His lips twitched up in a ghost of a smile, but his eyes lightened. "Where do you want to go?"

Their options were so limited. Her house wasn't yet her home, much less the safe haven she longed for, and Lancaster itself was filled with threats. "For a drive," she said. "Let's just drive."

"I can do better than that," he said. "Want to take your car out for a few test runs at the airfield?"

Her brow furrowed. "Can I do that?"

"We run occasional rookie nights, where people can get the hang of the process so they're comfortable on race nights. Tonight is one of those nights."

"Yes," she said, and ran water into the kettle to make her Cady juice. "Or more specifically, *hell yes*."

"Bundle up," he said, already heading for his room. "Temps are in the twenties."

"Wind?"

"No wind."

She darted into her bedroom and scrambled into long underwear, wool socks, a pair of jeans, and several layers of sweaters. By the time she was dressed, the water was boiling. A hefty squirt of honey into the insulated cup, boiling hot water, and she was set. She jammed her feet into her hiking boots, pulled on the coat Emily made for her, and tugged Conn's watch cap over her hair.

"Oh, sorry," she said, and pulled it off to hand to him. Sparks flew as static crackled in her hair. "Ow."

"Keep it," he said. "It's not windy. I'll be fine."

Feeling a little like he'd just loaned her his letter jacket and not the least bit ashamed of it, she put it back on, wrapped a blanket scarf around her throat, and followed Conn down the hall into the garage. He walked to the driver's door, then looked down at her when she came up beside him and held her hand out for the keys.

"If I can drive it at the track, where chances are good I'll be recognized, I can drive it *to* the track," she said.

He wavered for a second, then dropped the keys in her palm. "Do *not* get us pulled over," he said.

"This time, I'll drive like my mother," she promised.

"How does your mother drive?" he asked, a wicked glint in his eyes.

"Very carefully," Cady said, indignant. "Really? You think my mom's a speed demon?"

"You never know," Conn said as he walked around the hood to the passenger door. "I once busted a mom in a Volvo station wagon for doing sixty-five in a thirty. She was running late for her daughter's ballet class."

Cady backed out of the driveway, stopping every few feet to adjust her position so she didn't take out a tree.

"Someday I want you to teach me to do that backing thing where you zip down the driveway at thirty miles an hour."

Conn looked up from his cell phone, obviously startled. "Any time," he said easily.

Were they not supposed to talk about the future? Because Cady was having a very hard time imagining a future that didn't include Conn by her side, day and night. *Don't be ridiculous,* she thought. He's got a job. Roots. He's not some aimless adrenaline junkie who can pick up and leave at the drop of a hat. As she drove through the gates and onto the main highway leading into Lancaster, she ratcheted back her expectations and tried to imagine herself in a hotel in London, maybe even Paris, after a show or an interview, checking her watch to calculate what time it was back in Lancaster. Shows ended around midnight. That would be right when Conn would be finishing his shift.

"Do you work nights or days?" she asked.

He slipped his phone in his pocket. "Three to eleven on patrol. Whenever when I'm needed for undercover work."

"Oh," she said, trying to think through the time difference. This was ridiculous. She'd text him like she'd text any other friend. Except Conn didn't feel like just her friend, and the sinking feeling in the pit of her stomach told her texting wouldn't be enough. "What were you doing?"

"Texting Shane to see if he was at the track with Finn."

"And?"

"He is. He brought my car, too. He's got the timing issue worked out. I told him Finn could give it a couple of trial runs before the next race night."

"That's nice of you to let Finn drive it," Cady said.

"I remember what it was like to be sixteen," Conn said,

then went quiet. He loosely gripped the handle over the door, but in way that suggested it was a reflex, not an indication that her driving frightened him. His hand flexed, the knuckles going white for a moment, then he relaxed.

"How long have you been drag racing?" she asked.

He huffed. "All my life. I started going to the races with my dad when I was six or seven."

"That's neat. He passed it on to you," she said, expecting that his father had given him the car when he had grown too old to race, or as a rite of passage.

"He left it behind when he left town. Eventually I forged his signature to a title transfer."

"Oh," Cady said, wishing she'd kept her mouth shut. "I'm sorry."

"Don't be," he said. "It happened a long time ago."

That was the thing, she reflected as she took the on-ramp to the highway leading south of town, that made writing songs so easy, and so difficult. Things happened. Their dad left when Emily was a baby, and yet Emily was still dealing with it. Conn's dad also left, and he never even mentioned his mother, so Cady assumed she hadn't been in the picture any longer than his father had. You could put something like that out of your mind, but never out of your soul.

She was home, but she wasn't home. Home used to be her mom's house. For the last eight months it had been a tour bus, a series of hotel rooms in which Queen Maud slowly took over more of Cady. Her roots felt shallow, dry, exposed.

Was this how Conn always felt?

Silence reigned on the rest of the drive. Conn was lost in thought about something, and Cady used the quiet to let the melody and lyrics for a new song burble through her head like a stream over rocks. Normally she had confidence in her process, but the last few months had been so abnormal, and the last few weeks had been like being tipsy and tossed in a blanket. The narrative arc she'd weave from notes and lyrics, carrying chords and bridges from beginning to end, weren't coming together.

Let it go, she thought. Let it all go, the song and the stalker, the sex and the secrets. Set it all aside and be here now.

The gates to the airfield were open, the lights on. Fewer trailers and trucks lined the taxi strip, and Cady heard nothing except the roar of engines and tires revving. She found Shane's trailer and pulled in beside it.

"No announcer?" she asked.

"The guys on the track run the show. Cars go one at a time, not in tandem, in case a rookie loses control," Conn said. "The point isn't to get your best time. It's to learn how the process works."

He did a fist-and-shoulder-bump thing with Shane, then Finn. "Hi, Cady," Finn said, his cheeks pink. He alternated between staring and looking away, then his gaze snagged on Conn's hat. He glanced at Conn's bare head, then Cady's covered one, then a crestfallen look crept over his face.

"Hi, Finn," she said, bumping him a little with her shoulder. "How's it going?"

"Good. Really good."

"I hear you want to race," Shane said.

"Well, not race, but drive fast. I've had a very difficult day and I would like to drive fast."

"Nice car," Shane said. "Three hundred horse?"

"Thereabouts. Hits sixty in under five seconds," Conn said. "How's the track?"

Shane wiped his hands on a rag and tossed it into a bucket on the trailer. "Dry as a bone. Great conditions, if you don't mind freezing your nuts off."

"Let's get you in the line," Conn said.

"Could Finn take me?" Cady asked. "That way you can talk to Shane about whatever he's fixed with your car."

Finn turned tomato red. Conn and Shane kindly ignored that, but Conn did shoot Finn a sharp look that made Finn straighten up. They got into Cady's Audi, and she drove carefully to the main runway, where a short line of cars waited to take a turn at the warming strip.

"You're going to do more harm than good warming up street tires," Finn said. "You want something slicker if you're going to race regularly. For tonight, just give it a quick rev to knock off any rocks you've picked up on the way here. Watch the guys in the reflective vests. They'll tell you when to move forward."

"Got it," Cady said.

"Uncle Conn's a good guy," Finn said.

"He is," Cady agreed, her attention focused on the drivers in front of her. Another car rolled forward, leaving her two spots from the warming strip.

"I'd hate to see him get hurt."

"Me, too," Cady said absently. "Wait, what?"

"You're wearing his hat."

Maybe it looked more like a girl wearing her boyfriend's class ring than she'd thought. "I am," Cady said somewhat stupidly. "I borrowed it when we were at the Christmas tree farm."

"I know," Finn said. "I saw the pictures on Instagram. Look, Conn's not like other guys, okay? He's not a player. He's never brought a girl to the track before. I can remember meeting, like, one girlfriend ever, and even then he brought her to a holiday dinner at my aunt Susan's house, not the track. Roll up."

So . . . the track matters more than a dinner with family? Of course it did. Family didn't last. In Conn's

mind, the track was forever. The track was the place he
did battle with his demons. It was like her studio. Cady
shut her gaping mouth and tapped the accelerator. "I'm
only here because he's my bodyguard while I'm home,"
Cady said. "He can't leave me alone. This is just work
for him."

Finn shot her a disbelieving look only a disgusted teenager could pull off. She'd seen the expression on Emily's
face many times. "You're up."

Cady rolled down her window to better hear the official's instructions. He beckoned her forward, positioning
her tires on the strip. "Foot on the brake?"

Terrified of running over a track official, she jammed
the brake to the floor, put the car in first, and tapped the
accelerator. The wheels spun for a second. The official
gave her a thumbs-up. Cady rolled the window back up just
in time to see Conn jog behind her car and open Finn's
door. "Out," he said with a jerk of his thumb.

Finn shot Cady a look then scrambled out of the car.
Conn slid in and slammed the door. "Passengers add weight
to your car," he said, reaching over his shoulder for the seat
belt. "Normally you make it as light as you can, but you're
stuck with me tonight."

She'd like to be stuck with him forever, but between
Finn's protective warning and the adrenaline rush of the
drag racing, her heart was pounding. The starting line official beckoned her forward. "Aren't you driving?"

"I'll go after you've had a couple of rounds. Eyes on the
lights."

The lights counted down to green. Cady gripped the
steering wheel with her left hand and the gearshift with
her right, and floored the accelerator. The car leapt forward, the RPMs revving up as she shifted through second, into third, barely pausing between shifts because she

still had the accelerator floored. The car shot past the red lights indicating the end of the quarter mile, and Cady let up on the gas pedal.

"Breathe," Conn advised.

"Wow," Cady said, then gasped in air. "Just . . . wow."

"Nice job."

"My shifting was weak," Cady said.

"You'll get the hang of it, newb."

"I should give you your hat back," Cady said as she crept around the turn to taxi back to the starting pole.

"You got a hood on that coat?" Conn said.

"No," she admitted. She was wearing Emily's design, and the longer she wore it, the more she liked it. She was both warm and looking very, very fine.

"Keep it, or Chris will have my ass."

"He's not going to . . . it's already on Instagram, isn't it?"

"Yup," Conn said.

"Great. Just great." She reached in her pocket and checked for texts. Two from Chris.

Goddammit Cady. Followed by a string of frowning emojis.

"Go again," Conn said.

She ran once more, already getting the hang of the test strip, improving her shifting and her time by half a second. Then she drove off the track and parked by Shane's trailer, where Conn's car was running. Finn was sitting half in and half out the driver's seat, listening to the rumbling engine with an attentive ear. He gave Shane a questioning thumbs-up, one Shane returned with a definitive thumbs-up.

"Why is it so loud?" Cady shouted.

"The exhaust stops right after the manifold," Conn said, his voice also raised. "Mufflers are great for making cars run quietly, but every inch of exhaust pipe reduces performance."

"Oh."

Finn hoisted his lean frame out of the car, then leaned through the open window after Conn got in, explaining something Cady caught only in snatches and didn't understand anyway. Conn tossed her a vague salute as the car rolled toward the waiting line.

Cady wandered toward the chain-link fence. The stands, normally full on a Saturday night, were all but empty. The canteen was open, one bored-looking girl alternately serving up the occasional coffee or hot cocoa and flirting with the various crew members. Finn was among the guys at the counter, nursing a cup of coffee. Shane walked to the canteen, hands shoved deep in his pockets. Cady wondered if he'd picked up the habit from Conn, or vice versa. He ordered a cup of coffee, then walked over to stand beside her.

"Conn asked you to keep an eye on me, didn't he?"

Shane just smiled at her. "I don't usually get to watch the races," he said in answer. "Usually I've got two or three cars I'm tuning up between runs."

"You don't want to drive?"

"Sometimes I do. But I don't feel about it the way Conn does."

She turned back to the track. Conn was second in line for the warming strip, staring straight ahead. She took the opportunity to watch him. His eyes resolutely turned forward, his jaw set. Something struck Cady.

"He doesn't look like he's having fun," she commented before she could fully think through the stupidity of that statement. Of course it wasn't fun for him. Maybe it was a different kind of fun, the kind that comes from a depth and breadth of experience, a total immersion in a hobby or sport. Conn knew cars and racing inside and out. She'd had a couple of moments of exhilaration. He had two decades of racing in his brain and body.

"This isn't much fun for Conn anymore," Shane agreed, to her utter shock.

She looked at him. "Why not? Why is he still doing it?"

"You'll have to ask him that," Shane said.

Cady thought about this. In her experience, doing something after the fun was gone meant you were either in something for a profound love and fulfillment or you were stuck in a rut you needed to hop out of. Based on the expression on Conn's face, she was leaning toward the latter.

He rolled up to the starting lights. They counted down from red through amber to green. The Camaro shot off the starting line.

"Good shifting," Shane commented. "It's trickier than you'd think."

"I figured that out after one run," Cady said. Conn had some serious driving skills.

They watched the car rocket down the runway, then turned in unison to see the time flash up on the LED display: 10.00.

"Damn," Shane muttered. He blew out his breath. "All we need is two hundredths of a second. I've *got* to figure that out."

"Figure what out?" Cady said. She felt like she'd been dropped into act three, maybe four, of a family drama. "I thought the point was consistency."

"You'll have to ask him that," she and Shane said in unison. "Got it. Good thing I like a mystery."

"It's not much of a mystery," Shane said easily. She liked the way he smiled at her, despite the serious look in his eyes. "Pretty common story, truth be told. But it's Conn's to tell, and I'm betting you're the right person to hear it."

Cady wasn't so sure about that. She and Conn were involved in a freakish, spur-of-the-moment relationship that was about sex and a total absence of privacy. They'd been thrown together because Chris thought she was in danger and Conn needed to be shuffled aside while Hawthorn tried to find out who'd beaten a man to a pulp and was trying to frame Conn for it. It was hardly something to write a song about. "What makes you think that?" she said, absently. Conn's car had crawled up the return runway and angled into the back of the line for another run.

"He's never brought another woman to the track," Shane said.

"He has to bring me to the track," she said, exasperated. Shane and Finn were acting like Emily and her BFFs, parsing every situation for meaning where there was none. "It's work."

"No, he doesn't," Shane replied. "You could be back at your house, or in a safe house, or in your car driving the back roads if you needed some variety. He's protected this place for as long as I've known him."

Trying to ignore the flicker of pleasure that the thought of being special to Conn brought her, because one hormonal teenage girl in her family was plenty, thanks very much, she thought back to their earlier conversation. She suggested a drive. Conn suggested the track. One glance at his face told her the second run held no more appeal for him than the first.

"Okay. I'll ask him," she said. Now the whole situation felt like a dare, except it looked like Conn's soul was on the line.

Conn's second run came in at exactly the same time as the first, which matched the runs she'd seen the last time she was at the track. "He's consistent," she said.

"Yup," Shane answered without humor.

Conn pulled through the gap in the chain link, the car growling like a junkyard dog. Finn wandered back from the canteen while Conn parked by Shane's trailer, slung himself out of the Camaro, and slammed the door hard enough to rock the car on its frame. Apparently the pull of male bonding and the car trumped the pretty girl behind the counter. "Hey, Conn," he said.

"I'll take a look at the timing," Shane said. Finn already had the hood up, the smell of oil and gas dense and acrid in the cold air. "Maybe it's off. You might need a new—"

"It's not the car," Conn interrupted. He shrugged out of the fire-retardant jacket and tossed it through the open window. His hair and shirt were plastered to his body with sweat, and the sight of steam rising from his shoulders sent a hot zing through Cady's body. "We both know it's not the car. Just forget about it for a while."

Anger and frustration radiated off Conn like the heat off the car. Finn dropped the Camaro's hood and took a step back. "Sure," Shane said. "You guys done?"

One eyebrow lifted, Cady looked at Conn. "We're done," Conn said. "Let's get out of here."

Cady waved goodbye to Shane and Finn, then got into the passenger seat of her Audi. "I think you need to drive more than I do," she said.

The fact that Conn didn't argue about it spoke volumes to his state of mind. He turned over the engine and whipped the car in a tight semicircle, then squealed out of the lot.

Cady waited until they were on the highway before starting the conversation. "That didn't look like much fun for you."

"It wasn't."

"Then why are you doing it? Loyalty to Shane?"

A muscle popped in his jaw. "He's got a waiting list a dozen names long for guys who want to drive with McCool's Garage sponsorships. He keeps me out of loyalty to me, not the other way around."

"Conn. Why?"

"When my dad ran that car, his best time was nine point

nine-nine. He ran that multiple times. I'm trying to beat his time."

Cady digested this for a second.

"I know it's stupid," Conn started.

"It's not stupid," she said tartly. "I was just trying to think of the right thing to say."

"Give up." Conn huffed out a bitter laugh. "That's the right thing to say. Just give up and accept that my reflexes aren't as fast as my dad's. The car is the same weight. I'm the same weight. His was more beer gut than muscle, but pounds are pounds. The weather is nearly identical. It's down to me. To my reflexes."

"Why are you trying to beat his time? Not that I discourage people from having goals," she added hastily. "Goals are good. But . . . why?"

The sharp white light from the dash cast Conn's face in planes and shadows. "He skipped town when I was in the fifth grade. My mom died a couple of years before then. He kind of fell apart when she died. Started drinking. It's nothing earth-shattering. It's not even that uncommon."

"That doesn't make it any less difficult. I'm so sorry," she said. "How old were you?"

"Ten."

"Who raised you?"

"I bounced around," he said, eyes firmly fixed on the road in a way that told her he wasn't seeing it, but rather an endless round of new rooms, packed bags, and different schools. "Extended family mostly, although I stayed a couple of times with a friend of Dad's when I got older and my aunt and I had a fight. I learned to make myself at home in other people's houses way earlier than the search module at the academy."

Cady all but gaped at him. He was so calm about it. "Conn, I can't even imagine. When Dad walked out on us,

Emily was devastated. She alternated between screaming fights with Mom and sleeping in her bed. She's still suspicious of people."

"Why aren't you?"

She thought about that for a moment. "I was a little older, able to understand Mom when she promised she'd never, ever leave like Dad did. And I had music. That's when I set my goal of being a singer-songwriter. If I lose that . . ." Her voice trailed off. Right now, losing music was a real possibility. She'd heard of dry spells lasting for months. Years. "Mom keeps what's hers," she finished.

"Maybe that's why you can be the way you are. You know she won't ever give you up." He smiled at her, rakish and so heartbreakingly vulnerable all at once.

She wanted to look away, but couldn't. She knew how he felt. In some ways, an unreliable parent was worse than one who cut out on you. Abandonment gave you something to push against. Unreliability kept your hopes up until you refused to hope anymore.

She and Emily couldn't trust their father, but at least they had their mother, who was the picture of reliability. Conn had no one. His mother died. His father treated fatherhood like something he could walk in and out of like a revolving door. But Conn didn't behave the same way. He did a job that at its most basic was a commitment to show up when called at the worst time in people's lives, day after day, year after year. He looked after Shane's nieces and nephews like they were his own. Conn expected people to duck out on him, with a glance, with their lives. So she met his gaze without flinching, and found that meant letting him see deep inside her, too. She wanted to look away, but couldn't.

Because she was falling in love with Conn.

"Why aren't you afraid of me?" he said, out of the blue.

She laughed, shifted her weight, rested her elbow on the

door panel and her temple on her bent fingers, the better to look at him. "Because you're not that scary."

He looked at her, one hand on the wheel, the other loose on his thigh, eyes heartbreakingly dark and vulnerable. "Most people are."

"Then they don't really see you."

"And you do?"

"I think so," she said, well aware that the dark cocoon of the car, the night, their unreal circumstances all contributed to an intimacy that might not stand the bright light of day, much less real life.

"I'm terrified of me."

"Why?"

"I'm capable of what you saw in that picture."

She considered this. "We all are. Pushed the right way, by the right person, we all are. But you don't act on it."

"No," he said quietly. "I don't. But I have that temper."

"And a fairly long fuse," she replied. "You've got people in your face all day, every day."

"Don't try to make me a better man," Conn said. "Don't idealize me."

That stopped her. She thought carefully before she spoke. "I'm not," she said at last. "All I can speak to is what I see. You have a shadow side. That doesn't make you bad. It makes you human."

They were on the long, straight highway out of town, heading for Whispering Pines. "How do you do that?"

"Do what?"

"See the shades of gray."

She shrugged. "I've been thinking about this lately. Love songs are easy. Songs about hooking up and dancing in clubs and broken hearts, all easy. Ramp up the beat and no one pays much attention to the lyrics. I've got an album ready to drop that's nine songs about all of those things, with nothing new or different or unique about it.

It's got all the right collaborators and all the right beats. It's slick and shiny and about as human as slick, shiny things are."

He cut her a glance. "It wasn't that bad."

"It's not bad. It's just not what I want to be doing. We get one life, you know? One human life. I don't know what to do. One thing lights me up inside. The other makes the most sense, capitalizing on momentum, fame, more money. All the big voices in my life are telling me to drop the studio's album."

He aimed the clicker at the gate. "Who are the small voices?"

"Mom. The voice inside me." The road to her house was dark, silent, only a few porch lights dotting the darkness, far fewer of them than the stars overhead.

"Add me to that list," Conn said.

She parked the car inside her garage, leaned over the console and kissed him. It was the least practiced kiss she'd given since high school, landing awkwardly on the corner of his mouth and obviously startling him. But then he turned to her, pressing his lips to hers and returning the kiss. His lips urged hers open, his tongue sliding in to rub against hers. She tightened her grip on his rough, flattened sheepskin collar and added the strength of her right hand, fisting her fingers in the front of his coat.

His hand grazed the top of her head, sliding his hat from her hair in a shower of staticky sparks visible in the car's dim interior. His hand cupped the back of her head, holding her mouth to his like she might get away. But she wasn't going anywhere. She couldn't get enough of Conn's lush mouth, his deft tongue sliding against hers, the soft, rough noise that escaped his throat when she nipped his lower lip, then licked the spot to soothe it.

The hand not in her hair snaked between her waist and the seat to haul her over the console, into his lap. She twisted as she moved, her bottom cradled against his warm thighs, her feet still in the passenger seat. It was awkward, but now she could cup his face as she kissed him, sliding her fingers through his hair. More importantly, he now had access to her body, his palms seeking out her breasts.

"I can barely feel that," she moaned when he squeezed the tender flesh. "Too many clothes."

He jerked up her sweater, only to find another sweater underneath, then a thermal undershirt under that. "How many layers are you wearing?" he grumbled.

"Four, I think," she said, twisting on his lap. She needed more, the hot visceral glow of skin-to-skin contact. "Keep going, there's one more—oh, God," she gasped.

He'd found her silk undershirt, the bottom layer except for her bra—barely any defense against the rough heat of his palm. She arched, desperate as he fumbled with her bra cup, then solved that problem by shoving her bra up. It was the least elegant look ever, three sweaters and a bra bunched around her collarbone, but the sensation when he pinched her nipple made her arch so strongly she banged her head on the driver's side window.

"Ow . . . no, don't stop, don't stop," she said.

"I can think of better places to do this than the front seat of your car," Conn said, but his hand didn't stop moving, squeezing and pinching, then gathering the silk to graze her nipples into a hyperaware state. "Or the backseat. You should have bought the bigger sedan."

She clamped her hand around the back of his neck and pulled his mouth to hers. The light in the garage door opener flicked off, leaving them in total darkness. "Shit," Conn said, and slapped his hand against the dash until he found the push button start and activated the interior lights. A soft pinging filled the air.

Cady looked into his eyes and saw nothing but a thin ring of iris around his pupils. Her brain said *standard*

response to dim lighting. Her body said *aroused male*
and triggered the desire to writhe against him, something
she wanted to do naked and horizontal. "Inside," she said.

He opened the door and caught her in one bulky arm
before she fell backward to the cement floor. In a move
worthy of any of the Dukes of Hazzard she gripped the
doorframe and lifted herself out and up until she could get
a foot on the floor, kicking Conn soundly in the thigh in
the process. He grunted, but followed her out, waiting
with the car door open until she'd opened the door leading to the mudroom. Light spilled from the kitchen into
the garage.

As soon as the door to the garage closed, they stumbled
down the hallway to the kitchen. The whole first floor
smelled of fresh evergreen, clean, enticing. Conn stripped
off her top two layers, turning her hair into a wild, static-
filled halo around her face. "Wait, wait," he muttered,
cupping both hands around her head to hold her for his
kiss. She took advantage of the lingering moment to slide
her hands under the hem of his Henley, then up his ribcage,
pulling his shirt off as she went. He broke away long
enough to let her strip him, then wrapped one arm around
her waist and hoisted her onto the kitchen island, stepped
into her spread thighs, and kissed her again.

His kisses were deep, raw, out of character for him. Before he'd been controlled, careful of the differences between
his strength and hers, but now he vibrated with a desire so
passionate it was almost desperate. Cady left off running
her hands over his shoulders and chest to grab the hem of her
turtleneck and silk undershirt and pull them off. Conn's
hands made short work of her twisted bra, and then they
were skin to skin. She wrapped her legs around his hips
and her arms around his neck, and pulled him close,
pressing her breasts against his chest, her belly to his.

His breath left him with a barely audible groan, then

he relaxed against her. She felt his abs lifting against hers as he inhaled, the hot, hard length of his cock pressing against his zipper, but mostly she felt the way the tension eased from him. His big hands stroked up and down her back, his thumbs bumping over every notch in her spine, from her nape to the waistband of her jeans.

He leaned back just enough to look into her eyes, asking a question, watching for a response. The first few times they'd done this, Cady was looking for nothing more than to release months' worth of tension built up on the road with a man she was attracted to. She didn't fool herself into thinking Conn wanted anything more than that . . . then.

Now? Now she knew him, knew his past and his fears; from there it was a short step to hopes and dreams. Now she could give him something she knew he'd gotten from so few people in his life: herself, freely offered.

"Hey," she whispered. Over his shoulder she could see his back reflected in the big glass windows overlooking the backyard, the breadth of his shoulders, his muscled spine, the twin dimples just above the waistband of his jeans. She reached around and trailed her fingers up the valley of his spine, and watched him shiver, felt his cock pulse in the notch of her thighs.

His next kiss was hot, possessive, and slow enough to seduce Cady into a state of total limp surrender. He cupped her breasts, gently squeezing her nipples; it was her turn to shiver and lift against him.

"Bed? Or here?" he asked, rough, like she had to make a decision now.

"Bed," she said, remembering the bruises on her lower back, his knees. The energy in the room had shifted from the frantic heat in the car to a tidal pull ebbing and flowing between his body and hers. "Definitely bed. Go slow. I want this to last."

He groaned, but visibly gathered his control, testing

himself as he popped open the button on her jeans and un-zipped them. She wriggled from one hip to the other to get them off. They'd just hit the floor when Conn wrapped both of his big pushy arms around her waist. She clung to him as he carried her into the bedroom. Still in his jeans, Conn paused by her nightstand to unclip his holster, cuffs, and badge. He took off her panties; she worked down the zipper on his jeans and stripped him to his beautiful skin. They climbed into bed together, Conn pulling the covers over them both to trap the heat roiling between them.

Braced on one arm above her, he locked eyes with her, trailed his fingers down her sternum, over her belly, and into the folds between her legs. She shuddered, both at the possessive look in his eyes and at the slick heat he found. She reached for his shoulders, then his hips, then wrapped her hands around his wrists, gripping tighter and tighter as his fingertips slid along either side of her clit. She was sensitive, juicy from the teasing friction of rubbing herself against him, and he knew her so well now. In a moment she was digging her fingernails into his wrists and sobbing out her release.

When she relaxed enough to remove her nails from his skin, he was fumbling in her nightstand for a condom. "That wasn't slow," she said.

He shot her a quick Conn-grin as he ripped open the packet and sat back on his heels. "If you're complaining about it, I must have done something wrong," he said.

"I'm not complaining," she said. Her hands were trembling as she slid her palms up his hair-rough thighs. "I'm just saying . . . it wasn't slow."

He aligned their bodies and nudged the tip of his cock into her soft, wet entrance. She gasped as the pressure stimulated nerve endings already strung to hypersensitiv-ity. He kissed her, his swollen lips brushing over hers making her aware of yet another place on her body attuned to him. "Again?" he asked, his voice nothing more than a low rumble in the heated cocoon of covers.

She couldn't think. He was no more than an inch or so inside her, stretching her swollen folds, encouraging her body to open to him and fold around him all at once. She hitched her heels high up on the backs of his thighs and lifted just a little.

"With me, Cady?"

"Yes," she gasped. The multiple-orgasm thing usually eluded her, and she considered it a courtesy if her partner didn't pound away for fifteen or twenty minutes afterward. Maybe she just hadn't waited long enough. Maybe she'd been with the wrong man. "Oh, yes?"

He gave her a little more, just enough for her body to take notice. His thrusts were shallow, slow, in rhythm to the hot way his tongue slid against hers. Gold wires of sensation tendriled through her body, then, as he slid all the way inside, drew taut. He was careful not to grind against her sensitive clit, instead taking his weight on his elbows and kissing her, again and again, so possessively and thoroughly she forgot what it was like to not touch him.

Hot honey poured along her nerves with each thrust, sweet and sticky and just rough enough to make her tremble. Sensation swamped her from all sides, but mostly from the energy pouring from Conn's body over hers. She opened to it, became the reservoir for it, offered it back to him with each lift of her hips, each welcoming lick or nip along his jaw.

He tore his mouth from hers and let his head roll against the pillow. "Fuck. Cady. Just . . . fuck."

"I know," she gasped. He was so hard inside her, sweat slicking the contact between their bodies. "I can . . . I think I can . . ."

"Yeah," he said. "Fuck, yeah. Do it."

She couldn't stop herself if she tried. Her release tipped

over the edge from possible to certain, and she froze, hips straining for contact with his, her entire sheath rippling against his hard length as he stroked in with a rhythm that must have cost him dearly to sustain. Then the tight, clenching fist inside her flung open and she cried out, sharp, short, unmistakable sounds of release.

Conn wrapped his arm around her shoulders and gripped her hip with the other hand, then plunged deep one last time. Cady trembled again from the sheer pleasure of feeling him come buried deep inside her.

Conn lifted himself off her and went into the bathroom. Cady lay in the blanket cocoon heated by their bodies, phrases and bits of what felt like might be a refrain drifting through the haze in her mind. When Conn emerged, he didn't get dressed or head straight for the shower. Instead, he came back and clambered over her to snuggle back into the warm bed. His arm locked around her waist, pulling her close.

"I could get used to this," she murmured, already half asleep.

His arm tightened around her waist. "Yeah," he said. "Me, too."

When she woke up the next morning, she had it. Overnight her brain had done that mysterious, magical thing, and the jumbled pieces of lyrics and melody and meaning were now at least a couple of verses, well on the way to a song.

"That's it," she said.

"What's it?" Conn asked.

She pushed at his shoulder. "I've got it," she said, which probably wasn't any more helpful. "Let me up. I need to write this down."

He obligingly lay flat so she could scramble over him. "That's a first for me," he said, clearly amused.

"What is?" she asked, distracted by the rhythm and

words in her head. She followed the trail of her clothes out of the bedroom and into the kitchen.

"Having a woman jump out of bed. Usually there's morning cuddling."

"I've got an idea for the song," she said, then did a double take. He was standing in the doorway, one shoulder braced against the frame, magnificently naked. "Do you want to cuddle?" she asked, torn.

"I'm good," he said, still smiling. "Go do your thing."

Thank God. She bolted for the stairs, desperate to get to the studio where her notebook and guitar waited. Noncreative types didn't understand the way a song, a melody, a lyric could well up inside you, suddenly fully formed where before there was only a muddled mess, or worse, nothing at all. She hauled open the door and thumped down on her chair, already reaching for her guitar. She had the strap over her head and the body balanced on her thigh, her hand patting for the notebook that held the lines she'd written down back in August, the ones she thought were going nowhere.

No notebook.

She came up short. When she'd heard Conn come back inside after chopping wood, she'd been so desperate to get out of the mental rut she'd left it on the little table, open to the last page full of scribbles and doodles.

Maybe not. Maybe she'd taken it with her, automatically tucking it into her pocket. She leaned her guitar back in the stand, trotted back up the stairs. Water was running in her bathroom, so Conn was taking a shower. Down the hall, into the garage to search her car. Not there. Then she went through her coat pockets. No notebook.

A creeping sensation prickled the skin on the back of her neck. Convinced she was being watched, she whirled around, but there was no one behind her. The light was bright enough that she could see the outlines of the trees sloping up the hill. A flash of movement caught her eye and she startled, her hand flying to her mouth.

Forget looking strong and unafraid. She bolted for the bathroom. Conn stood under the steam shower, both arms wrapped around his waist, turning his amazing shoulders back and forth under the pressure. He looked up when she hurtled into the bathroom.

"What?" he said, already reaching for the handle to shut off the water.

"My notebook is missing," she said.

CHAPTER SEVENTEEN

Conn hastily toweled himself dry enough that his clothes wouldn't freeze to his body, then yanked on his underwear and jeans. "Stay here," he said to Cady, unholstering his gun. Safety off, round in the chamber. "Lock the door behind me."

Her eyes were huge. "Why?"

"If someone was here, we don't know that he's not still here," Conn said. Cady's eyes widened. Even he could hear the deadly menace in his voice.

"I probably just forgot it—"

"Do you really think that?"

"No," she whispered. "I don't."

The one place he knew an intruder wasn't was the bathroom, so he pushed Cady back into the steamy room, cursing the total lack of safety in this situation. Then he cleared the closets, under the bed, then pushed the button to lock the bedroom door and closed it behind him. Not much protection, but the best he could do.

He searched the rest of the house like he was searching a drug den, methodical, every sense on high alert. On the main floor he looked behind the big tree waiting to be decorated, and downstairs he shifted all of Cady's boxes from home, peered into spaces you wouldn't think a human being could cram into, even pulled down the attic ladder to check up there.

They were the only two people in the house.

Gun still in his hand, he walked back to the master suite. "We're clear, Cady," he called.

A sharp snick as the bathroom door unlocked, then the bedroom door. She peered around the doorframe. "There's no one here?"

"No," he said. "From here on out, you stay in the garage while I clear the house. When did you last have the notebook?"

She was opening and closing the drawers, then the cabinet doors. "In my studio," she said, gathering her hair into a coil to keep it out of her face as she searched. "I think. I don't know. Most of the time I take my notebook with me when I go out, but I don't think I did this time. I just don't know. Maybe it fell out last night at the airfield? Oh, God. What if someone found it?"

"Hey," he said, catching her by the wrist. "I don't remember you having it in the car, so it's in the house."

"How can you be so sure?"

The catch in her voice meant she was near tears. "That's my job, to observe. We'll find it."

They didn't find it. They reached the crazy search point, where they were looking in drawers she'd never opened, in cabinets that held a collection of vases and a turkey pan used once a year. Finally they met up in the kitchen.

"Wait here while I search the yard."

"For my notebook?" she gave a laugh that was probably supposed to be lighthearted but reached into hysterical territory. "I'd remember if I took it outside."

"For footprints," he said.

He snagged the Maglite from his duffle and went out the sliding glass doors to the deck. The beam was bright and powerful, but in the end gave him nothing. The snow had melted, then frozen again, giving him nothing more than a surface to slip on as he walked the perimeter. No new footprints, no conveniently dropped wallet with ID and an incriminating note. Even the possum stayed inside, where it was warm.

He stopped and looked back at the house. Cady was in the kitchen staring at the spot on the counter where her kettle lived, probably waiting for it to boil. The house looked so homey, warm light spilling onto the snow, big comfy chairs snuggled around the fireplace, the tree stretching its branches to the ceiling, all ready to be decorated by Cady's family.

Maybe he'd be there for that. If he didn't catch the sick bastard fucking with Cady's mind, he'd be in the family room, listening to Christmas carols and drinking hot cocoa or mulled wine, watching Cady, her volatile sister, and her tough-love mother decorate a tree. It was a familiar scene, standing on the perimeter watching a family celebrate a holiday or a family event. He'd gotten used to feeling like an outsider. As close as he was to all the McCools, as narrow as the gap was between close friend and member of the family, he couldn't quite bridge the gap.

There was a holy, profound power to someone pointing at him and saying not, *Yeah, sure, you can come and stay for a while* but rather *You. I want you. You get to stay forever.*

There was no point in longing for what wouldn't happen. Eventually Cady would either go back on the road, or they'd catch this bastard, and she wouldn't need protection anymore. Either way, once she found out he'd put security cameras on her house without her permission, he was back where he started, where he'd been almost happy for most of his life.

Before he'd seen what he could have, and never knew he wanted.

Resolve shot down his spine. He was going to get some fucking answers for Cady, and for himself. Enough of this hiding-out, stay-out-of-everyone's-grill bullshit. He was going back to what he knew worked, getting in people's faces and being a scary motherfucker until somebody talked to him. Because maybe, just maybe, if he did that, he wouldn't have to tell Cady he'd violated her trust.

He climbed the stairs to the deck and let himself back into the house. Cady was on the phone. "He just came back inside," she said, and put the phone on the island. "It's Chris," she said, muting the conversation. "He's got details for the album's promotional tour."

An idea hit him. Let's start with Chris. "Do you have the Find My Friends app?"

Puzzled, Cady frowned. "Yes."

"Are you and Chris friends?"

She rolled her eyes. "I have no idea how to characterize my relationship with Chris," she said.

Chris was listing off cities. ". . . Baltimore, not ideal but I think we can pick up a pretty good–sized crowd from D.C., where you've got that big fan community, then New Jersey, then Philly, then State College, then Pittsburgh, I know, I know, Pittsburgh, but you have to do it . . ."

Conn picked up her phone and handed it to her. "Pull up the app."

"He's in Brooklyn," she said. "He said something about going out for sushi and the only place he'll eat sushi is at this crazy dive down the street from his apartment. He's had too much bad sushi—"

Conn peered over the top of her head to look at the phone. Chris's dot sat right in the middle of the block housing Eye Candy.

"He said he was in Brooklyn," Cady said. "He's lying to me."

Relief poured through Conn, profound and exhilarating. "Keep him talking. Get your coat," he said. "And text Eve and have her meet us at Eye Candy."

"I'm sorry, Chris," she said, juggling the phone from ear to ear as she slid her arms into Emily's coat. "I didn't get the part in the middle. After Baltimore. Can you go over the part in the middle again?"

Conn held her coat so she could find the arm hole, then took her hand and pulled her down the hallway to the garage. His heart was pounding. Maybe, just maybe, he was about to get really fucking lucky and catch Chris red-handed, with Cady's notebook and her grandmother's bracelet, and maybe a voodoo doll he was sticking pins into to make her hair go berserk.

Cady's hand closed reflexively on the armrest when he shot backward down the driveway. "Wait a minute," she said to Chris. "You promised me I'd never have to do another show in Poughkeepsie again. You promised. That hotel had cockroaches the size of rats! I can't even imagine how big the rats were!"

Chris's voice came placatingly through the phone.

"Good," Conn said. "Ten minutes. That's all I need."

Cady flicked a glance at the speedometer. Conn slowed down. Getting pulled over meant lost time, and possibly some guy deciding to be a hero in front of Cady, which meant publicity drawing attention to a problem that was, for now, a total secret.

"Eve's on her way." She checked the phone again, clicking between the Find My Friends app and the call, to make sure she was still muted. "I can't believe he lied to me. I can't believe he's still in town. I trusted him. I've trusted him with every part of my career. I can't believe this is happening."

Conn didn't say anything. He knew how hard it was to

trust and be let down, again and again. Cady's face was pale, her eyes wide with shock and fear. "What else is he lying about? Is he really planning to talk to Eric about a different album? The way he presents that will make all the difference. What if he's going behind my back and telling Eric I'm just being a diva, or that I don't have the material, or that I can't come up with it in time?"

"Hey," Conn said. He put his hand on her thigh. "One thing at a time. Confront him, and see what happens."

"How can I trust anything that's happened up to now?" she said. "How do I trust what he's said to the label, to anyone he's in contact with about appearances, or the future? This changes everything."

The tires screeched as they roared into Eye Candy's parking lot, startling Eve, who was getting out of a zippy-looking Altima. "What's going on?" she asked, then caught Cady's eye. "Cady, what's wrong?"

"I need to get into the bar," Conn said.

Eve didn't question him, just unlocked the door. "Take Cady and stay in your car," he said.

"The hell you say," Cady said indignantly. Chris's voice was still coming through her phone, but now that the door was open, Conn could hear him in real time. He was upstairs, in Eve's office. "

"Who's living in the apartment?" Conn asked, his hand on his weapon.

"Natalie," Eve said. "She moved in a couple of months ago. She was rooming with a passive-aggressive train wreck. My last tenant skipped without paying two months' rent."

"That bites," Cady said.

"Matt tracked him down," Eve replied with a steely glint in her eye.

Conn didn't doubt it. He held out his hand palm down to urge her to silence, and started across the dance floor.

He'd spent plenty of time in this club, both before Dorchester walked in as a bartender, and during the investigation, but never when it was as silent as a predawn stakeout. He moved carefully, crossing the floor at a stealthy pace, and nearly jumped out of his skin when he turned to see Cady right behind him.

"Jesus fuck," he growled.

"What? I snuck out all the time as a kid."

Eve was standing behind the bar, watching this play out.

"That you, sweetie?" Natalie's voice called out from the office.

"Yeah," Eve replied. "I need to do inventory."

"I'll be down in a few."

"Take your time," she called back.

Conn gave her a little nod of thanks, and turned to find Cady tiptoeing up the wrought-iron staircase circling up to the office, eyes down and focused on not missing a step and cracking her knee on the metal risers. Conn used his hands to haul himself up the stairs two at a time. He caught her by the waist just as she reached the landing.

"What the hell are you thinking?" he hissed.

"He's in there," she whispered back. "He's in there and he's been lying to me, and scaring the ever-loving crap out of me!"

"I know he's in there," he said stepping between her and the door, using his body to chivvy her against the railing. "I'm going in first."

"Stop doing that," she said, shoving at his shoulders.

In any other situation, he'd move, give ground, be respectful of her personal space, her body. But when they'd seen Chris's dot in Lancaster, every instinct in his body shut down except one. Protect Cady at all costs. "Be quiet," he said, low and dangerous, as he reached for his gun.

At the quiet snap of his holster releasing his Glock Cady went utterly still and lifted her hands from his back, respecting, if nothing else, the fact that there was now a loaded gun in play. He took a second to call up the office layout from his previous visits to Eye Candy. Another door on the opposite wall opened into the tiny apartment Eve lived in before moving in with Matt earlier in the fall. Behind Eve's office door came Chris's voice like Conn had never heard it, soft, quiet, without his usual hint of arrogance and posturing. It didn't sound like a guy talking during sex, thank God. It sounded intimate. Kind of sweet. Conn almost hated to interrupt, except Chris was probably a serial killer, using his itinerant profession as a cover for multiple murders around the world, and was now murmuring endearments in Natalie's ear while he carved her up like a chicken.

He took a single step across the landing and thudded his fist against the door. "Police. Open up!" he called, weight shifting to his left so he could kick the door in if Chris made a run for it.

"Conn?" Natalie said. "Is that you?"

It was really hard to be taken seriously when the individuals knew you by voice. "Open the door, Natalie," he said.

Silence, then the door flung open to reveal Natalie in 80s punk/goth mode. Black leather everywhere, black Joan Jett hair, and blue eyeliner. She cracked her gum at Conn. "Hello, Shoulders," she said.

Conn used his shoulders to barge into the office and look around. Chris was sitting on the sofa, one arm stretched along the back, the other on the arm, glaring daggers at Conn. "Nice to see you again, Officer McCormick," he said blandly. "I assume Cady's with you?"

Cady pushed past him, into the office, and glared at Chris. "What are you *doing here*?" she said, exasperated, annoyed, afraid.

"Having a delightful conversation with Natalie," he said promptly. "What are *you* doing here?"

"Trying to figure out what you're doing here!" Cady took a deep breath. "You said you were going home."

"I did. Then I came back."

"To *Lancaster*?"

"As you see," Chris said. "Is that really necessary?" he added, glancing meaningfully at Conn's weapon.

Conn could handle drunks, drug dealers, thugs, pimps, and prostitutes. While chasing down suspects he'd tripped over cracks in the concrete, racked himself climbing over fences, and on one memorable occasion, knocked himself out cold falling down a flight of stairs in an abandoned warehouse. He'd been kicked, hit, spit on, and sworn at so much he all but sat up and looked around when someone yelled *Hey motherfucker* in his vicinity. None of it, not a single second in the academy, or his follow-up training, or his real-world experience that prepared him for dealing with Chris Wellendorf.

Lacking the presence of either a threat or a fleeing suspect, Conn holstered his weapon, folded his arms across his chest, and squared up. Chris all but rolled his eyes.

Cady took over. "I'm serious, Chris. You hate this town. You called Lancaster a one-horse shit-kicking ghost town in the middle of fucking nowhere and swore the only time you'd set foot here was when I gave a concert."

"It's growing on me," Chris said. He was talking to Cady but looking at Natalie as he spoke. She gave him a little finger wave. "There's a great music scene here. The people are nice. Friendly."

Conn had never heard Chris use that soft, endearing tone of voice; based on the way Cady stared at him like he'd grown a second head, she'd never heard it, either. "You were right," she said to Conn. "He's acting really, really weird. Are you on crack? You've got to stop being on crack."

"Not even remotely," Chris said, smiling like an idiot. He dragged his attention away from Natalie, and focused on Conn. He could see the moment the wheels in Chris's brain gained some traction. "May I presume from Officer Tall, Dark, and Brooding's heavily armed presence that you attribute a more nefarious purpose to my vacation in Lancaster?"

His tone of voice was incredulous until his gaze met Conn's. "Start taking this seriously or we're going to step outside."

Everyone stared at him. After a few seconds of really tense silence, Chris got to his feet. "You have my full attention," he said, uncharacteristically solemn. "What's going on?"

Cady tugged Conn's watch cap off her head and jammed it into her pocket. Her hair crackled into a crazy halo. "*You're* what's going on," she all but shouted. "Conn knew you were hiding something. You lied to me about where you were!"

"Cady, your throat," Chris said, looking pained.

Natalie looked around, then said, "Excellent point. I'll make you some hot water with honey. Requests, you two?"

"I'll take a vodka rocks," Cady said.

"Cady," Chris started.

"Shut up. My nerves have been run through a shredder. I want a vodka rocks. Raspberry Absolut, if you have it. Which you two better not give me shit about. *And* the Cady juice."

"Queen Maud wants a vodka rocks, she shall have a vodka rocks," Natalie said soothingly. "Conn?"

"I'm on duty," Conn said.

"Water," Natalie said decisively. "Chris?"

"Whiskey. A double. If Cady's drinking, so am I."

Natalie sashayed out, closing the door behind her. "What. Are. You. Doing. Here," Cady said.

"I came back for what I thought was a booty call. It was a spur of the moment thing I didn't expect to last all week, but did, because life is unpredictable and glorious and I think I'm in love. Why?"

Conn's brain got stuck on the idea of flying somewhere for sex, and ground to a halt completely at the idea of Chris in love. He wrenched it back to the task at hand. "When did you come back?"

"Early last week." That matched with Conn's timeline of when Chris started acting strangely.

"The next day someone broke into Cady's house," Conn said. "The attacks on her website are coming from Lancaster. You're here . . ."

"You think I'd come back to Lancaster to drive Cady crazy?" Chris said, switching from serious to seriously pissed off in a split second.

Conn didn't move. "You fit the profile, and you have the most to lose."

"The most to lose?"

"If Cady goes her own way and doesn't drop the pop album."

Chris blinked. "For someone who knew nothing about the music business a couple of weeks ago, you've certainly picked up the lingo," he said. "Yes, there's a possibility she'll make less money if she chooses to work on a more personal album, but I'm in this for the long haul. I believe in Cady, in her voice, her vision, the way she connects with her fans. While I'm very happy to make money managing her career, I'm working with you because you're an artist I believe in, and am honored to work with," he said, turning to Cady. He wasn't pleading his case, just stating fact in simple, clear terms. So that's what Chris sounded like when he was being sincere, not a manipulative smart ass.

"But you've been pushing the label's album so hard," she said uncertainly.

"Because that's what I thought you wanted," he said patiently. "Remember your career plan? When you started having second thoughts, I casually mentioned to Eric that you might want to go a different direction."

"Oh God. What did he say?"

"What do you think he said? He fucking ripped my fucking head off," Chris said. "But that's my job, to take that flack for you so that when you and Eric actually talk, he's had a chance to settle down."

Cady looked abashed. "I know you run interference for me," she started.

Chris overrode her, his voice escalating. "Yes, we probably won't make as much money if you go with this album. But stranger things have happened, the label's willing to take a listen, and to me, the money's just a way of keeping score. Did you really think I was gaslighting you?"

"You were obviously hiding something," Cady objected.

"I wanted to keep her for myself, just for a while," Chris said, sharp and defensive. "I spend my professional life, which is my entire life, looking after other people's careers, interests, futures, happiness. I'm not complaining. Trust me, I'm not complaining, but . . . I just . . . I've never met anyone like her before. I wanted to keep it for myself for a while."

Conn had to agree that Natalie was one of a kind. He relaxed his stance, watching Chris. "I'm sorry, Chris," Cady said.

"A little privacy. That's all I wanted. I'm sorry I didn't tell you the truth." He cut Cady a glance. "You really thought I was gaslighting you," he said, and this time it wasn't a question.

"Chris, you're not exactly Mr. Sensitive, and lately

you've talked an awful lot about marketing, cross promotion, and measures of success."

"Doing my job, Cady," Chris said.

"And I was doing mine," Conn said. "You want to blame someone for this situation, blame me."

"I do," Chris said. He cut Conn a look that was both assessing and speculative in a way that put Conn on high alert. He'd seen that look before, and it was usually followed up with a shrieking phone call to his lieutenant and Conn getting his ass reamed. In this case, he deserved it. In the space of a week he'd managed to wreck years of trust between Cady and Chris. The relationship might never recover. "But let's put a pin in that for the moment, shall we? I'm not trying to drive Cady insane. Who is?"

Conn opened his mouth to reply, but shut it again when Natalie knocked on the door, then opened it without waiting for a response. "One Raspberry Absolut, one Macallan, and two waters with lemon, because it tastes better and makes it kinda fancy, for the working folk." She distributed the drinks. Cady perched on the edge of a chair and swallowed a third of her vodka; Chris knocked back the Macallan in one go. Conn sipped his water and made a mental note to buy some lemons. Finally Cady looked from Chris to Conn. "We can talk about it later, Chris."

He looked at her, obviously startled. "Okay."

"After all, you're on vacation. Conn's got this."

Chris held out his hand to Natalie, who took it, slid onto his lap, teased his nearly full glass from his hand, and sipped the Macallans.

Conn looked away, almost uncomfortable with the delight in Chris's eyes.

"We're out," she said, and suited actions to words.

She didn't look at him as they walked through the nightclub and outside to the car. Conn waited until they were back in the Audi before saying, "I was wrong about that."

"You were half right," Cady said. "He was lying about where he was. What now?"

Her voice was cooler, distant, lacking the casual intimacy they'd shared on the way over. A sense of foreboding filled Conn's chest. The cameras would be the ultimate betrayal now. He'd been hoping and praying it was Chris, because the next alternative up for consideration, without telling Cady he'd put surveillance on the house, was door number two: Kenny.

"I need to go see someone," he said as he pulled out of Eye Candy's parking lot. He squinted out the window; the sky had clouded over to the kind of gray that looked dismal but held enough light to need sunglasses.

"Okay," she said. "Who?"

"I can't tell you." At her look, he added, "It's better for you if you don't know."

"Is it dangerous?"

Maybe. He hesitated, and in that silence she got her answer. "You figured out who framed you for that assault. And now you're going to see him."

"Yeah," he said quietly.

A few silent minutes later they pulled into an empty space on the street across from the Eastern Precinct. Conn put the car in park, then he took her phone from her hand and added Dorchester to her contacts. "Get in the driver's seat. If I'm not out in twenty minutes, you leave and call Dorchester. He'll make sure you're safe."

"We're at the police station," she said. "Why not just go . . . oh. No. No way am I letting you go in there by yourself."

"Cady, if this is as bad as I think it is, you're being targeted, too. For me. Please. Get in the driver's seat and keep the car running. If I don't come out, you call Matt Dorchester and tell him I'm down and you need help."

"Not Lieutenant Hawthorn?"

Conn shook his head.

"You don't know if he's involved." It wasn't a question, and based on the way her brows drew down, he was re-ordering her entire world.

"I want him not to be involved," Conn said. But the last nagging puzzle piece had fallen into place. Hawthorn's dad, the former chief of police and current mayor, had trained Kenny.

How long had this been going on? How deep was the corruption? Did it spread from the gang unit to the chief's office to the mayor's office?

Cady pulled his watch cap lower on her head and tucked her braid down the back of her jacket. She hurried in front of the Audi and slid behind the wheel. One arm on the frame, the other on the door, Conn hunkered down on his heels.

"Twenty minutes," he repeated. "If I'm not out by then, you bolt. If you see someone coming toward you, you put it in gear and head for the back roads. Try to lose him in the alleys."

"That sounds like a good strategy, except this car stands out like a pink elephant." Cady flexed her hands on the wheel. "I should have bought a tan Accord. Something that blended in."

"It's not safe." Conn looked at the ground, tried to think of another strategy, and came up empty. "It's the best I can do for you right now."

"Go." She leaned over and kissed him, hard and fierce and possessive, then handed him the folder. "I'll be here when you get back."

Conn walked into the precinct he'd been assigned to for the entirety of his career as a Lancaster police officer. The two cops smoking outside the back door nodded in greeting. He walked down the hall past interview rooms and offices. Nothing was different, except there were more presents under the tree. The noise from the bullpen reached his ears, faint but familiar—ringing phones doubling up on each other, uniformed and plainclothes officers coming and going, televisions scrolling their black lines of closed captioned text in all four corners of the squad room.

The gang unit worked out of here because the highest volume of gang violence flowed through this precinct. They had a small conference room to use as a war room, laptops crowded on the oval table, whiteboards covered with assignments, filing cabinets containing older records. Conn walked up to the war room, opened the door, and took half a step inside.

Everyone looked up. He caught Kenny's eye. "Got a minute?"

Kenny's face betrayed no hint of knowledge at why Conn would be coming to visit him, other than the standard visit from a cop in trouble to his mentor. Kenny finished issuing orders to two undercover officers about the day's buy-and-busts, then met Conn at the door. They ended up in the same vacant, slightly more upscale conference room where he'd met with Hawthorn, then Cady and Chris, a couple of weeks earlier.

Was it really only such a short time ago? He was so different. Everything in his world had changed.

"What's up?" Kenny asked.

Conn tossed the file on the table. The picture of Jordy's most gruesome bruises and swollen eye slid halfway out of the manila folder. "How did I do?"

"With what?"

"Fastest time? Slowest time? Somewhere in the middle?"

Kenny cracked a grin. "You always did have to know where you stood."

"I'm fucking serious, Kenny." Conn thumped his finger on the folder. "You set me up to take the fall for this."

Conn shook his head. Kenny picked up the folder, shuffled the picture back inside. "It was a little test. Just to see
whose bed you got into."

Beating another human being wasn't a "little test."
"What, like being jumped into a gang? Except you beat
the shit out of someone else, blame me, and then leave me
twisting in wind? What the fuck, Kenny?"

"You weren't supposed to be shuffled off on some private security detail," Kenny said, waving his hand. "I was
going to get in touch with you on shift one night. Explain
everything. Then you disappeared."

Lightning fast, Conn said, "Why didn't you come out
to Maud's?"

"Who the fuck knows where she lives?" Kenny said indignantly, like Conn purposefully kept Cady's address a
secret from him. "I drove past her mother's place a couple
of times but your car was never there. Tried to burrow into
the paperwork trail on her house, and got nowhere, thanks
to Caleb fucking Webber. Every year he wins the pool for
Most Hated Lawyer. I couldn't get it out of Eve, because
she'd tell Dorchester and then he'd tell Hawthorn. I gave
up. I figured you'd either figure it out and come to me, or
you'd get desperate and come to me to solve your problem. Which I would have done."

Conn's brain, already whirring away at a high gear,
shifted into overdrive. It wasn't Kenny. But if it wasn't
Kenny threatening Cady, that meant he had to watch
the recordings from the cameras. The ones he'd installed
behind Cady's back.

"It's a big risk," Conn said. "What if the media got hold
of that?"

Kenny just arched an eyebrow at Conn. It took him a
minute. He was getting better at this thinking-rather-than-
reacting thing. "Jordy was in on it. That's why this is still
on the down-low. You paid him to take the beating."

"Promoted him," Kenny corrected, smiling. He was watching Conn closely, studying his reactions.

Conn's stomach heaved, but he maintained his impassive face, folded his arms across his chest. The move made him look bigger than he was, and more belligerent. "I'm listening."

"A group of us who feel we've been comprehensively screwed by the latest bargaining agreements with the city started a side business of our own. Consider us a little family within a family. We're still doing good work for the city and her fine citizens, but we're also looking after our own brothers. And sisters," he added conscientiously. "Gotta be politically correct."

Something dinged at the back of Conn's mind, but he let it go. "With Lyle Jenkins gone, you're taking over the Strykers territory."

"This started long before Jenkins showed up." Kenny's voice was low, even, and made all the hairs stand up on the back of Conn's neck. "Originally it was just protection money. They got tipped off when raids were happening, where the heat was coming, who needed to get out of town for a while. Enough to keep them one step ahead of us."

Who was "us" and who was "them"? In Conn's mind, Kenny stepped over the line the day he took a penny from a drug dealer. "Why me? Why now?"

"I need someone out on the streets."

Conn thought fast. Needing someone on the streets meant one of the recently promoted sergeants was working for Kenny, too. "Doing what, exactly?"

"Lift up your shirt." Kenny's face didn't change.

"You think I'm wearing a wire?"

"I didn't last this long without taking some precautions."

He already knew what Kenny would want. The average raid crime scene contained three things: money, drugs, and illegal weapons. With the exception of the guns, it was easy enough to skim a little off the top before anyone else showed up, and even those could be managed if you got creative. It was the oldest story in the dirty cop's book. Without changing expressions, Conn lifted his shirt and turned in a circle. Kenny was too old school. Conn could just as easily be recording the conversation on his cell phone. But he hadn't thought that fast. Getting out his phone now would only tip Kenny off.

"It's going to vary. Keep an ear on dispatch. You're already usually first on a scene. You'll get some warning. Try not to be in the middle of a call when something's supposed to go down."

"What's in it for me?"

"A share. A bigger share as the business grows. We've attracted some outside interest from Chicago."

"Chicago." That meant the mob or a bigger gang.

Kenny shrugged. Just an average day for the average criminal hiding in plain sight. "Everyone needs a mentor. Or a training officer. You in or out?"

Saying yes would cost him the only job he ever wanted, with the only family he truly believed would last forever. Saying no would put Cady in more danger than she was. "Hell yes, I'm in."

He walked into the precinct a cop suspected of an assault and walked out knowing his days as a cop were numbered. If he went to Hawthorn, he'd be fucked. Kenny would make sure every cop knew he was a snitch, which shortened his life expectancy considerably. How long until he stopped getting backup, or until some other East Side banger was framed for his murder?

Cady was white-knuckling the wheel, peering through the windshield at him as he walked across the impound lot, scaled the chain-link fence, and dropped to the ground a few cars down from her position. He opened the driver's door, barely waiting as she clambered across the console and into the passenger seat. He had the car in first and moving before he shut the door.

"What happened?"

He didn't know how to respond. His guts were in knots. "Nothing."

Cady put her hand on his arm. "Conn," she said quietly. "Tell me."

They drove back to her house through SoMa, Christmas lights twinkling, bell ringers on the corners, a quartet in Victorian costume singing carols while development volunteers passed out cider and gingerbread. When they were back on the highway, he spoke.

"It wasn't him messing with you. I thought it might be."

"You thought a cop was targeting me to put pressure on you?" She spoke carefully, as if trying to make sense of the tangled web of paranoia her life had become.

"It was possible. But it's not him."

Which left him only one option: watch the videos.

They pulled into her garage. "Keep the car running and the garage door open until I tell you it's clear."

She waited in the car while he checked the house. It was empty, the scent of the Christmas tree lingering in the air. He'd powered up his laptop while he cleared the house. A file was waiting in the cloud storage folder. He blew out a hard breath. What a mess. If he'd looked at this first, he would have known who was threatening Cady. But he'd tried to save his relationship with her, and in the end, cost himself his career with the LPD.

Now he would lose both Cady and the department.

He walked back into the dark garage and opened the passenger door. "I need to show you something."

She followed him into the living room, shedding her coat, scarf, and his hat, stuffing it in her coat pocket as she walked. "You're scaring me."

Conn got out his laptop and opened the lid. The screen flickered to life. He called up the video streaming from the cameras. Cady watched over his shoulder. "That's my front door." She pointed at the second view. "That's my deck. You put cameras on my house."

"I did." He'd always owned up to what he'd done, even when it cost him.

"I asked you not to do that."

"I did it anyway."

"Why?"

"Because it was the surest way to keep you safe." He found the date in question when her notebook disappeared, scrolled back through the video on the front door, saw light sweep the garage doors in the lower corner of the screen, heard a car door slam. After that, nothing. He switched to the rear angle.

A shape moved out of the shadows on the house's north side, wearing a dark coat, a cap, dark clothes. Conn registered jeans, boots, and gloves. The light was too dim to make out much more than a pale face, heading purposefully under the deck until reaching the doors into the walkout basement, where Cady's studio was. A quick glance back toward the woods, then another to the south side, which framed the face perfectly in the moonlight falling on the yard.

Emily.

Cady's breathing went shallow. Her hand covered her mouth as she watched Emily slide a key into the lock and open the door. Conn sped up the playback, compressing several minutes to just a few seconds, slowing back to real time when Emily appeared again. Cady's notebook was in her hand.

Of all the people he suspected, Emily's name wasn't even on the list, but in hindsight, he saw everything he'd missed. None of the attacks were personal, not because the attacker was a diabolical evil genius intent on destroying Cady's peace of mind, but because Emily didn't really want to hurt her. The signs of a stealth attacker weren't anything more than ease of access, using the key Cady kept in Patty's house.

Cady's face looked like every abandoned house he'd ever seen—empty, forlorn, like it was about to collapse from the inside. She stared at the frozen frame of her sister, the person she loved more than anyone else in the world, leaving with her notebook. Emily had reached in to dig a knife into Cady when she was at her most fragile.

"I'm sorry," he said.

She looked at him, her shoulders tense, her jaw set, fury seething in her eyes. "Sorry?" she repeated. "*You're* sorry?"

She snatched up the car keys from the coffee table. "Where are you going?"

"Home." She stopped. Rubbed her forehead with her thumb. The single word was so drenched in meaning and confusion, making him ache inside. She couldn't, or wouldn't, look at him, just stood in the doorway. He could see her entire body trembling with rage. All she'd wanted was to come home, relax, rejuvenate, find her footing in the world again. Instead, in the space of one afternoon, he'd cost her what she valued most: relationships.

"I'm coming with you," he said.

"No. Just . . . no." She gripped her keys, her knuckles turning white from the strain. "We were wrong. There's no real threat. Just my sister. It's not a police thing. It's a family thing."

He'd known the hit was coming. The hit always came, but it hurt this time, more than it had ever hurt in his life. He nodded, closed the laptop, and watched her walk out of his life.

Conn stood inside by the big tree he'd cut down, the

scent of pine and sap strong in his nostrils, and listened to the silence left in Cady's absence. He tried to tell himself it didn't matter. He'd done his job. But it had cost him everything. His career.

His chance with Cady.

CHAPTER EIGHTEEN

The gates to Whispering Pines were barely open when Cady jammed the shifter into first and floored it. The tachometer leapt around the dial, the engine revving before she downshifted and pulled out onto the highway.

Twin streams of fury seared down her throat, into her stomach. Conn, who should have known better, installed security cameras on her property without her knowledge or permission. His high-handedness enraged her, but it was nothing compared to the hell she was about to rain on Emily's head.

Her sister was home, using the two days the school provided seniors to study for finals. Cady braked to a halt outside her mother's house, slammed the car door hard enough to rock the frame on the axles, and stormed up the walk. Her hands were shaking too much to get the key in the lock, so she banged on the door with her fist.

Emily opened the door, a lollipop in one hand. "Cady! What are you doing here?" She peered over Cady's head. "Where's your big lug of a shadow?"

She was going to brazen this out? No. *Hell,* no. "Give me my notebook."

The words flew out like a slap, freezing Emily's face midquestion. For a minute she thought about lying; Cady could see the deception cross her face, then crumple under the weight of Cady's fuming thundercloud of anger.

"I can—"

"Don't even." Cady pushed past Emily, into the house. The television was paused in the middle of a *Buffy the Vampire Slayer* rerun. "Don't you even start with me. Get me my notebook, and my bracelet. Now."

Emily whirled and ran for her bedroom. Cady heard her dresser drawer open and close. Then Emily returned, tugging the black, spiral-bound notebook and the bracelet from a tattered tote bag bearing the public library's logo. She all but shoved them at Cady, like they would burn her hands if she held them too long. Cady snatched them, slid the bracelet onto her wrist, then riffled through the pages, afraid Emily's insanity had extended to damaging them. But the journal was intact, untouched. Even the waxed paper she'd put over her watercolor pages was in place.

Cady closed the notebook and clutched it to her chest. "What about my website? Did you do that, too?"

Tears trickled down Emily's cheeks. She nodded.

"How?"

"A couple of guys in my programming class were messing around with DDoS attacks. They helped me set it up."

"Tell them to call it off. Now. Bryan's closing in on them, and if he finds them, he'll show no mercy."

Emily's laptop, the top-of-the-line MacBook Cady bought for her birthday because Em needed it for her design work, was open on the coffee table. She sat down, swiping at her cheeks as she opened iMessage and typed out a fast message. "Okay, they're shutting it down."

Clutching her notebook and bracelet to her chest, Cady

scrolled down to Bryan's name in her texts. *I figured out who's behind the DDoS attacks. They'll stop.*

Three dots appeared immediately, then *WTF? Who?*

I'll explain later.

She powered down her phone, shoved it in her back pocket, and stared at Emily. Was this how Conn felt all the time, this sick, seething betrayal by the people who were supposed to love you the most, protect you, keep you safe, that left him angry, powerless? For a soaring, heady moment she let the tumult roil inside her, the rage, the frustration, the fear that nearly derailed her professional life. It coursed under her skin until every nerve ending was lit up.

Then a detail registered. Emily's Hello Kitty flannel pajama bottoms, faded and pilled, way too short for her, even before she rolled them at the waist and turned them into capris. She'd bought those pajamas for Emily five years ago, before she made it and Hello Kitty was a treat, not a fashion icon to study, back when Emily was just beginning to transition from tween to teen.

Her sister. No longer a little girl, not yet a woman, but always, always family. Crying like her heart was broken.

Cady stalked into the kitchen and snagged the box of tissues from the little desk where her mother paid bills and organized her calendar. Back in the family room, she tossed the box on the sofa. "I'm so mad at you right now."

Emily plucked tissues from the box, buried her face in them, and sobbed.

"I had something. For a new song. I had *something*." Words, as always, failed her when trying to describe the ineffable creative process. "I went into my studio to work, to start playing with it, using a melody I'd written down months ago, and my notebook *wasn't there*! What the *hell*, Emily?"

Emily's tear-streaked face lifted from the soggy tissues.

"You don't understand what it's like to be me! I'm just Queen Maud's little sister, stuck in Lancaster while you go off and tour the world and pose on the red carpet and date famous guys. You don't know what it's like to be a nobody!"

"Emily, what the hell are you talking about? I do know what that's like," Cady said, bewildered. "You know I do. You were there when I was a nobody!"

"But we were nobodies together!" Emily wailed. "Now you're famous and I'm just a stupid high school kid who can't even get followers on Instagram. Every time Ella Bergstrom gets chosen for another fashion show or gets another profile, she tells me how great she's doing all on her own, without her famous big sister's help. *Why don't you go to premieres with Maud? Why isn't Maud wearing your designs?* I'm a failure. I'm not going to get into Parsons."

Forget about maintaining equanimity in the face of a rival's greater success; Cady would have cheerfully splashed bleach all over Ella Bergstrom's workshop. "But why did you steal Nana's bracelet, and my notebook?"

Emily blew her nose. "Because I thought if you got frightened, you'd move home again."

"Oh, Em," Cady said.

More sobs. "You're leaving again, so soon!"

Notebook still clutched protectively to her chest, Cady sat down on the wingback recliner and watched Emily's shoulders shudder like her heart was breaking. Cady raised her voice a little. "Emily, that's crazy. There's no room for me here. You need that space in my old room to work on your portfolio. You had to know that. You've been acting weird ever since the concert. What's really going on?"

She plucked another tissue from the box and handed it to Emily, who immediately twisted it around her finger. Her voice was small, when she spoke. "My portfolio is crap. I thought . . . it's stupid . . . but I thought if I had your ideas, your bracelet, I'd make something amazing. That's why I stole your things."

That made sense. That actually made a lot of sense. "It's not stupid," Cady said. "That's why I wear the bracelet. When I didn't have much faith in myself, I'd look at it and know I came from a line of smart, talented women who didn't give up."

"I know. I've heard you talk about it for so long. It was the most meaningful thing in your creative process."

"Why didn't you just ask if you could have it?"

Emily wouldn't meet her eyes. "I didn't want you to know I was scared. You seem so fearless now."

Cady recognized the fear, the shame that came with struggling to make something, wondering how the world would receive it, whether or not you had what it took to be successful. "I know how you feel, honey. Trust me, I know." She worked the bracelet off her wrist and held it out to Emily. "It's time to pass it on."

Emily started to cry again. "No. It's yours. I don't deserve it, after what I did."

"It's not a question of deserving it. You're a Ward. It's all of ours. It belonged to Nana. She gave it to Mom after Dad left. Mom gave it to me when I moved out. Now I'm giving it to you. For courage."

Emily swiped the heel of her hand over her cheekbones and stared at Cady's outstretched hand. Her watery eyes held a mixture of surprise, longing, hope. "Are you sure?"

Cady didn't move. "You're one of us, Em. You're a Ward. You come from strong women. You've got our blood in your veins. You can't fail, because you can't ever *not* be one of us."

Emily reached out and took the bracelet. "I feel bad, getting it like this."

"Don't," Cady said. "Mom practically threw it at me when she dropped me off at the bus station because I was going to need all the luck I could get. Now it's a family tradition."

Emily gave a watery giggle. "I miss you. I'm scared when you're not here."

She leaned forward and gripped Emily's hand. "I know, honey. I miss you, too. All the time."

Tears rolled down Emily's face. "It's Christmas. You're supposed to be hanging out with me, but you were with Conn, all the time. I could tell you didn't want me at the sleepover. And I see all the pictures of you at the drag races when you're not supposed to be outside, looking up at him, and he's at sushi brunch, and picking out a tree with us . . . I hate that he's around so much."

Cady's eyes widened in shock. She'd known Emily wavered between pride and envy over Cady's career, but complications from a man in her life never occurred to her. "Conn? You never minded my bodyguards before."

"Because they annoyed you. He doesn't annoy you. You like him." She cut Cady a teary glare.

Cady grabbed her hair and coiled it to get it out of her face. "Emily, you're not the only person who gets scared. The last few months have been so hard. I've felt so alone, so uncertain about whether to drop the album or ditch it for something that might bellyflop. Conn was there for me. Not because I'm Queen Maud and I could introduce him to someone who might give him an acting job. He was there for me. People hang around all the time when things are easy, but when they're hard? Stressful? Uncertain? They fade away. Conn didn't disappear."

She wouldn't disappear for him. No matter what happened with the investigation, or with her album. He was hers.

That's what the song is about, being there for someone when things aren't easy. The words and the melody and the bridge fell into place. She opened the notebook and scrabbled around in the mess of chip bags and soda cans and tissues on the coffee table for a pen.

"What are you doing?" Emily asked, bewildered.

"I need a pen."

Em dug in the sofa cushions and came up with one. "You know, if you kept everything online like a normal human being, I wouldn't have been able to steal your notebook."

"Not funny, Em." She was barely aware of what she was saying, just getting down the notes, fragments of lyrics, yes, that's how the verse should turn, leading to the bridge. Yes. It all came back to her, what she'd lost when she couldn't find her notebook, as well as the new material. As she scribbled, drawing arcs from thoughts, folding corners of months-old pages, gathering the song together, knowledge bloomed sure and certain in her soul. This was coming together because she'd fallen in love with Conn.

When she sat back and blew out her breath, she felt weightless, as light as air, capable of soaring into the sky like a bunch of balloons. Her heart was pounding, exhilaration coursing through her veins. "Yes," she whispered. "Yes."

Emily watched her warily. "Did you get it?"

"I got it."

"Even the stuff you forgot?"

"Even that." She skimmed through a couple of pages in her notebook, felt a couple more puzzle pieces slot into place. The block was gone. It was all there, waiting for her to open to it.

"Good. I'm sorry." Emily's voice was small, her shoulders hunched inside the fleece sweatshirt. "I'm just really, really scared."

"Of what?"

Em huffed, then reached for a tissue to blow her nose. "Of sending in something that sucks. Just the application is intimidating. What if they laugh at it? What if I get in and I'm the worst student they've ever had and everyone laughs at me?"

"Sweetie, just do what you do. They're not going to laugh at your application. I'm getting texts from all my friends asking how they can get one of your coats."

"Really?"

"Yes, because they're fashion-savvy people who know when something's going to go big. You should stop watching *Buffy* reruns you've seen a dozen times and start figuring out who you want wearing one of your coats next fall, when you're in New York City, at Parsons."

"I'm afraid I'm always going to be in your shadow." She sniffed again, but the worst of the crying seemed to have passed. "You even got the cool stage name. Maud."

"I'm not sure how much longer Maud will exist. Even if she sticks around, I'm just your sister." Cady stroked her hair, gathering the strands away from Emily's face. "I'm just mom's daughter. That's what being Cady means to me. Being Maud is great, but my family defines who I am, not stage names or hit counts or chart rankings. That hasn't changed because I'm more famous than I was last year, and I hope it won't change when the inevitable happens and people move on to another sound, another musician. Maybe you'll be the famous one then."

"Ha." Emily tossed the tissue on the floor and reached for another. "Like I'll ever be more famous than you."

"You could be. If I don't drop the label's record, I could fade away into obscurity. I'll be a thirty-second cut on some *Where Are They Now?* show, working at Ruby Tuesdays and singing on street corners again."

"That will never happen," Emily said with the assurance of a teenage girl.

"It could." Cady spoke with the assurance of a woman who'd lain awake nights, worrying about it. "Em, everyone's got me on the up-and-coming superstar pedestal right now. Please don't put me up there, too. It's a long way down when I fall, and I need somewhere soft to land."

Emily toyed with the bracelet. "You're working on new material. I'm working on my application. We both need this right now."

"We can trade it back and forth. But I really think I'm going to be fine without it."

Emily's face crumpled, and her chin quivered before collapsing into tears again. Cady sighed. "Stop crying. Put your Uggs on. We're going back to the house for my guitar, and then we're getting hot fudge sundaes at DQ. How about if I spend the night, and we can work on your application and my song?"

Emily smiled. "Sounds great."

Cady sent her into the bathroom to wash her face. Emily sat quietly in the passenger seat during the drive, her phone in her hand as she stared out the window. Cady didn't push things. It would take time to repair the damage she'd caused, but sisters were forever.

The driveway was empty when they arrived, the sound of their car doors closing echoing in the garage. "Hello?" Cady called.

She toed out of her boots in the mudroom, ears cocked for a response. The house was suspiciously quiet as she padded past the dining room table to the kitchen. The only light on was the stove light. "Conn?"

"I don't think he's here," Emily said.

Cady peered into his bedroom. His duffle bag was gone from the floor, the bed neatly made, the drawers closed, the hangers in the closet pushed to the side.

"There's a note taped to your steamer," Em yelled from the kitchen. She held it out to Cady as she approached.

I took down the cameras. Sorry. Conn

Cady's jaw dropped open.

"What cameras?" Emily said.

"He installed security cameras. That's how I knew it was you."

Emily's brow wrinkled. "You said you didn't want security cameras. That's why we didn't have the contractor install them when the house was being built."

"I know. Conn did it anyway." Because it was the right thing to do. The safe thing to do. He would protect her from anything, even from her sister's anger. And because he'd done that, she'd had her breakthrough. Of all the people around her saying they'd do whatever it took to support her creatively, Conn was the only one who did what had to be done. Even though he thought it would cost him her friendship. Her love.

"He left?" Emily's voice was small, her shoulders hunched as she tallied up the damage she'd caused. "Or did you send him away?"

"Of course I didn't send him away." But Conn hadn't waited around for her to kick him to the curb. He'd done what he'd been taught to do: move on when he made a mistake, angered someone, hurt their feelings. He'd gotten into the habit of living light, making it easy to leave before someone else could hurt him. "But I didn't tell him to stay, either."

Remembering the way she'd slammed out of the house, she rubbed her forehead with regret. She knew how Conn felt about making mistakes with people he cared about. She should have taken the time to reassure him, but she'd been so blindingly angry with him, and with Emily, she'd just bolted for the Audi.

"You should go after him," Emily said. "I have to study anyway."

She looked at Emily. "I said I'd stay the night tonight, and I will." But finals started on Monday, and then Cady would tell Connor McCormick exactly how she felt. She was her mother's daughter. She didn't give up what was hers, and Conn was hers, now and forever.

Late on Monday afternoon, Cady parked in a visitor spot in front of Conn's apartment building, relieved to see the flicker of a television in his apartment. It wasn't quite five o'clock yet, but already the skies were dark, a few stars twinkling through the light pollution. Conn wouldn't leave lights on when he went out, so he must be home. Maybe he'd gotten a few days off after guarding Cady around the clock.

Several of his neighbors were feeling festive, their little balconies sporting Christmas lights, a flashing Rudolph, even a small inflatable Santa, but Conn's balcony was empty. Snow had drifted onto the lawn chair folded up against the railing, giving it a rather bereft look. But she knew how to fix that.

She opened her door and popped the trunk, then hauled out a moving box. It wasn't heavy, just awkward, so the climb to the third floor didn't take long. A young couple clattered down the stairs, flashing her a smile as they passed her, but neither one recognized her. She was grateful for the anonymity as she made her way down the hall to Conn's door and knocked.

"Hi," she said when the door opened. "I hope you don't mind me coming by unannounced."

He was dressed in a soft gray T-shirt and faded jeans, looking even more like a granite mountain with bleak eyes. His feet were bare. Surprise, perhaps even hope flickered on his face before he schooled his expression to nod at the box. "I know I didn't leave anything behind. What are you doing here?"

This wasn't going like she'd thought it would go, but she was tough. "Can I come in?"

After a second he stepped to the side to make way for

her. She walked in. The apartment had been cleaned since her last visit; there was room on the dinette set for the box. She set it down, pushed back her hood, and pulled off her gloves. The Monday night game was on the television, a pizza box and a beer on the coffee table. She perched on the arm of the sofa and glanced at the TV. "Who's winning?"

"Pittsburgh. What do you want, Cady?"

"Two things," she said. "First, I want to offer you a job."

He laughed. "A job. What kind of job?"

"Chief of security."

"I'm not interested in being your kept man."

"You are seriously the most obtuse human being on the planet," she said. "After the last couple of weeks, you think you'd be a kept man? Imagine doing all of that, plus my tour security. A different city, night after night, different venues, different publicity stops, different hotels. I need someone who can handle all of that so I don't have to. It's the most important thing someone can to do support me creatively. Kept man," she muttered.

"You want me to come work for you."

"Well. Not exactly. I want you to be with me forever, but that's kind of a big, scary thing to lead with, and I figured you'd get bored in about four seconds without something productive to do, so I thought a job would sweeten the pot a little."

Conn stared at her, obviously flattened by this offer.

"You want me with you forever."

"Yes." Her heart was pounding as she gave a shrug far more casual than she actually felt. "I know it's fast. I know it's crazy. I know it means leaving Lancaster and the McCools, and your job. If it's too much, I understand. But I'm asking, because I want you. Now. Forever."

"Even though I installed the cameras when you asked me not to. Even though I threw a hand grenade into your family and your relationship with your manager."

"I wish that hadn't gone down the way it did. But blaming you for finding out what Emily and Chris were doing is just blaming the messenger. Emily is responsible for her actions, not you. So is Chris. And you were right to install the cameras."

His eyes widened ever so slightly. "I was."

"I was stuck," she said. "I couldn't figure out how to move forward, whether or not to drop the pop album. I kept avoiding the things I knew would hurt but help, so things kept happening to me. I was angry with you when I saw the cameras and the footage, but when I settled down, I remembered that whether I make the right decision or the wrong one, I'm happiest when I'm in control of my life and my career. The cameras gave me that control."

Something odd happened to his eyes. Cady realized they'd filled with hope. "You're not mad at me," he said.

"Maybe a little." She smiled at him. "I try to be reasonable. Mostly I'm putting it behind me, because I'm writing again, thanks to you. Two new songs in the last couple of days. It's hard to think straight with Emily bursting in every five minutes to show me a new sketch, but they're coming." She decided not to tell him she'd written about him. About them.

"Are you staying at your mom's now?"

"I was, while Emily and I worked out some things. I'm on my way home now. Em and Mom are coming over on Sunday to decorate the tree and make cookies. Emily still needs me, but I need my own space," she said. "For my own life. With the man I love. I hope."

At the word "love," his face went utterly still. Then he shook his head, a hard, firm rejection. "No. Not a good idea. Families and me don't work so well together. Look what just happened—"

She cut him off, words tumbling from her mouth, her voice rising. "Yes, look at what just happened. My sister

acted out, my mom didn't see it, and neither did I," she
said. "We all made mistakes there, but not you. We'll for-
give her, because she was just a kid, trying to figure out
how to be an adult. That's what your family didn't do. They
pushed you away, blamed you for their failures and your
honest mistakes, taught you to take things away from yourself, to not let yourself have the things you want. I'm not
pushing you away. You can have me, Conn. All you have
to do is let me in."

"Cady—" he started.

"No, listen to me. I really want you to come with me. I
want you by my side all the time. It's immature—I mean,
I'm perfectly able to be on my own but I don't want to be—
and . . . and it's a shitty, shitty life on a big bus, staying in
hotels, which is not all it's cracked up to be, let me tell you.
Promo appearances, sound checks, concerts, I've got no
time to myself when I'm on tour. Days off are rare, scheduled weeks in advance, and I spend most of them sleeping. I'm asking you to—"

"Yes."

"—give up everything you know, leave the McCools . . .
what?"

He crossed the room to stand in front of her, close
enough that she could see his pulse thumping away in his
neck, the quick inhales and exhales, the way his eyes darkened. He raised his hand to her cheek and stroked his
thumb along the curve of her ear, then bent his head and
kissed her. "Yes, I'll be your body man."

"Okay. Good," she said, a little disoriented. He kissed
her again, hot and fierce and sweet. Her brain shut down,
all systems offline, leaving only the flashing light that said,
*Yes, this, this is what you were looking for and didn't know
you wanted. Him. This man. Forever.*

He lifted his mouth, then bent his forehead to rest on
hers. "Have you told Chris about this?"

"Not yet. I thought we could tell him together. It'll be fun." Her voice grew serious. "You'll quit the police department for me? I mean, you can think about it over the next few months. If I get my way, I'm not going to be traveling for a while. I'll totally understand if—"

"I may not have a job after tomorrow anyway," he said.

"Why not?"

"I agreed to work with Kenny. Hawthorn might think I'm playing both sides. He might want to go after him with someone who wasn't trained by Kenny."

"You haven't told Lieutenant Hawthorn yet?"

"He's been out of town at some conference." He shrugged. "Oh, well."

Where was the cop who'd been so furious to be saddled with her just a few short weeks ago? "I guess we'll deal with it tomorrow tomorrow," she said nonsensically.

"What the second reason you're here?"

She walked over to the box and parted the flaps to reveal chintzy eighties Christmas decorations scavenged from the boxes in her basement. "I brought over some of Nana's Christmas decorations. I thought . . . they'd remind you of Christmas with your grandma. Gold garland, the ornaments with the thread wrapped around them, colorful lights, tinsel, and a tabletop tree. You're invited to come decorate with me and Em and Mom. In fact, Mom says no excuses, or she'll track you down, but I wanted you to have a little bit of Christmas here, too."

"Thank you." He nodded at a battered bit of greenery in her hand. "What's that?"

"Mistletoe." She held it over her head, and beckoned him to her with one crooked finger. This time, when he laughed, his whole body relaxed.

Lieutenant Hawthorn returned from his conference on Tuesday morning. Conn was waiting by his office when he walked in just before eight o'clock. "Officer McCormick," Hawthorn said. "Come in."

The Block hummed around them, a little hive of activity as the holidays approached. Conn stood in Hawthorn's office, hands shoved in his pockets. The weight of his badge and gun registered more than they normally did, because he wasn't sure if this was the last time he'd wear them.

"I read your final report," Hawthorn said as he set his coffee on his pristine desk. "It's a little unclear as to how the mystery-stalker situation resolved itself."

"It was her sister," Conn said. "I saw a threat when it was just a teenage girl acting out."

Hawthorn gave him a sharp look, then an odd, raw laugh. "Don't underestimate the power of a teenage girl to ruin someone's peace of mind." He sounded like he was speaking from experience, but Conn knew better than to ask. "I assume she doesn't want to press charges and would prefer to keep this out of the media."

"Got it in one," Conn said.

"Good. Jordy's refusing to cooperate with us. All charges have been dropped. Abracadabra, you're back on your regular shift." He opened his laptop, then looked back at Conn while he waited for it to power up. "Anything else?"

"I'm putting in my papers," Conn said. He took his badge and his gun off his belt and set them on Hawthorn's desk. Only because Cady came back for him could he do this. Her love, her presence, made it possible for him to see a future without the police department.

"Explain yourself, McCormick."

"Cady offered me a job as her bodyguard. I took it."

One of Hawthorn's eyebrows shot skyward. "That was fast."

"I won't actually be leaving town for a few months,"

Conn said. "But after I tell you what I learned in my own investigation, I'll need to put in my papers anyway. I know who set me up."

"You do."

"It's Kenny. He's running the Strykers from the gang unit."

A slight widening of the eyes was Hawthorn's only reaction to this bomb. "And you know this how?"

"I put it together," Conn said. He set a file folder on Hawthorn's desk, and a memory stick. Hawthorn would want an electronic version, but not one sent through the department's email. "I went into the records and started looking at the arrests, the trends, which cases stuck and which ones went away. I couldn't make the data, which said the Strykers were fading away, work with my experience on the street, which was that the Strykers had the entire East Side in a stranglehold. So I started looking at the officers on the gang unit. The one thing they had in common was that Kenny trained them."

"He's not part of the gang unit."

"No, but until last year, he worked out of this precinct. Remember when he transferred into administration and everyone was so surprised?"

"He was distancing himself." Hawthorn had no nervous habits. You had to really pay attention to notice the most minute changes in facial expression. "What happened?"

"I confronted him about the assault. He said it was an initiation rite. He was going to track me down on shift one night and tell me what was going on. I wasn't supposed to be assigned to a special duty that basically made me drop off the face of the earth."

"Why you?"

"Because I had no one but the department. I was a loner, volatile. Kenny thought I'd be easy to turn."

"And now you're not alone."

Now he had Cady, but Conn could be mysterious and silent, too. "When he couldn't find me, he figured either I'd figure out what happened and go to him, in which case I could join them, or I'd go to him crying to make it go away, in which case he'd fix it and act like he knew nothing."

"What did you do?"

"I told him I was in."

Hawthorn's gaze flickered to the gun and badge on the table. "But you're obviously not in."

Police departments had factions that rivaled the tribal warfare tearing apart most of the world's hot spots. Conn had been singled out for one of those factions, which usually meant, in the us-versus-them world, that he was tainted to all the others. "Even if Cady hadn't offered me a job, I can't be that kind of cop. If that's what it means to be a part of this department, and Kenny turned it into an us-against-them proposition, I won't do it."

Hawthorn's gaze sharpened. "So if you didn't think you have to resign, you'd stick around until she went on tour?"

"I can't. I agreed to participate in illegal activities," Conn said. "That's grounds for termination."

Hawthorn shook his head. "Pick up your weapon and your badge, Officer McCormick."

Conn stared at him.

"You're right. That is grounds for termination, except when you can use your newfound detective skills and your experience as an undercover officer to get inside the ring and help us take it apart from the inside. Unless what you're really saying is you won't be a bad cop, but you also won't be a snitch."

The option of working to bring down the bad cops hadn't occurred to him; he'd seen only the chance to be in or to be out. "You want me to work for him?"

"Right now I don't have a case," Hawthorn said. "We've got suspicions, a paper trail, trends. But I don't have hard and fast evidence. You can get me the evidence we need to shut this down . . . if you agree to investigate your fellow officers. I know what they say. Don't betray a brother or sister in blue. But when your brother or sister in blue betrays everything the department stands for, betrays the trust of the community he or she is sworn to protect and serve, then you call upon a different loyalty: the loyalty to the cops who stand against corruption."

Like Kenny, Hawthorn made playing on his team sound cool, like being chosen, one of the elite in the worst possible way. Everyone rotated through Internal Affairs; it helped reduce the stigma of being the snitch who investigated and prosecuted other cops. But that didn't change the "us against them mentality" most cops had for Internal Affairs. Kenny's club was the cool kids smoking pot and ditching school. But unlike Kenny, Hawthorn's invitation was a more refined, more elite version of being a cop. It was being one of the best cops, the ones who held themselves to a higher standard every single day, in every single encounter with the public or with their fellow officers.

He didn't have to give up the only family he'd ever known.

Conn picked up his gun, then his badge from Hawthorn's desk. He secured the holster on his right hip, then pinned his badge to his belt pocket. Despite the added weight of the gun he felt lighter, freer.

Hawthorn's gaze sharpened. "You're taking a big risk. There's no guarantee they won't kill a cop to protect themselves."

Conn shrugged. "If I can take him down, I will. Leave this house a little cleaner than it was when I got here."

Hawthorn nodded. "By the way, McCormick. As Ms.

Ward's body man you were isolated, alone, and off-balance," Hawthorn mused. "And you handled it like a pro."

Conn blinked.

"All those things your superior officers write you up for? The inability to control your impulses, your hotheaded approach, your total disregard for protocol and safety? It's one thing to keep your head when bullets are flying. It's another to do it when it's the constant strain of a psychological threat. Nice job, Officer McCormick."

"Thanks," Conn said. The tips of his ears were turning red. He resisted the urge to shove his hands in his pockets of his utility pants.

"You're welcome," Hawthorn said genially. "Now go back to work, pretend I just reamed your ass, and help us take down these bastards."

CHAPTER NINETEEN

A few days later, Cady stood on the corner of the busiest intersection in SoMa, Cady juice in one hand, her guitar case in the other. She'd had dinner with Chris while Conn had another in a series of mysterious meetings he'd been involved in lately; she didn't ask, and he didn't tell. Chris had wandered off in search of a gift for Natalie. With Conn's watch cap tugged low over her eyebrows and ears, and her hair caught in a scarf, Cady had so far managed to avoid being recognized. A familiar energy pumped through her veins—anticipation, excitement, fear, and the thrill of doing something that left her both intensely vulnerable and intensely happy. It was, she realized, a throwback to the girl she'd been, singing anywhere, anytime, for anyone just for the sheer joy of it.

The group of kids playing Christmas carols on the opposite corner finished up and packed up their instruments and stands. She waited until they'd piled into their mom's minivan before heading over to claim the corner, then took a picture of the street sign, Christmas lights dangling in the enormous potted tree behind it, and sent it to social media. *Christmas carol sing-along, SoMa . . . come on down.*

Twenty seconds later a girl across the street looked up from her phone, scanned the street corners, and saw Cady. She waved. Cady waved back as she lifted her guitar strap over her shoulder and started tuning it. Out of the corner of her eye she saw Conn settle against the hood of the LPD patrol car parked by the corner. He was in street clothes—jeans, boots, Henley, denim jacket—but the way he exchanged a few words, then a laugh with the officer also leaning against the car sent the message loud and clear: also a cop.

The crowd gathered quickly as she started with holiday standards, then segued into popular carols. Just her voice, her guitar; no amps, no lights, nothing but her and the crowds. She tuned out the lifted phones and serenaded her hometown crowd the way she wanted to, not with a big concert, but just her, close enough to touch, back where it all began, on a corner in SoMa.

A bigger crowd was starting to form, spilling onto the brick-paved street and blocking traffic. The cop leaned on his cruiser, keeping the peace, but keeping an eye on the crowd in case he needed to shut them down. Conn was just keeping an eye on her.

"Move closer, folks," she called. "Get comfy with your neighbor. If we stay out of the street, I can keep singing."

She ran through all the standards, "Rudolph," and "Silent Night," and "God Rest Ye Merry Gentleman," even launching into "Grandma Got Run Over by a Reindeer" when a little boy shouted out the request. When she finished Dave Matthews' "A Christmas Song," she opened her eyes to find Conn standing next to the cop. She caught his eye, smiled. He smiled back.

"Okay," she said, then cleared her throat. "Okay. Thanks for coming down. One more. It's something new."

A whoop went up.

"Really new. So it might change," she warned. "It's kind of a love song, and it's kind of a work in progress."

She sang with her eyes closed, her head tilted back, her guitar dangling from her back, keeping time with her palm against her thigh, snapping on the opposite beat. Her voice, when it emerged from her throat, started in a conspiratorial croon, rising in volume, throaty and raspy, singing the song of defiant proclamation.

It wasn't a love song. It was real. It was the song that came to her like a gift from the gods, nearly fully formed, melody and harmony and words all at once, flowing from her in one short session. She didn't hide behind the easy, the power ballad, the sweetness. She held up guaranteed loss, time passing, the inevitable struggle and tears and pain, then wove the most quintessential truth of all, that only love redeemed the pain. She sang a promise, that she'd stand by him forever, not just when it was easy, but when it was hard.

In the back of her mind she knew the cafés and stores were emptying, customers gathering in doorways and windows, standing on the balconies of apartments over the shops and restaurants. The crowd went quiet, so quiet she could hear the bells jingle on the carriage horse's harness, the soft rush of tires on bricks as cars drove carefully through the intersection.

She could put this song on the label's album. It would fit the theme. But it belonged on the album she was making now, pouring from her, songs coming almost whole. Sharing this one was the biggest risk she'd ever taken, but she'd never felt so powerful, so vulnerable, and so whole. She stopped keeping time, lifted her hand as if calling for a witness, head back, throat bared to the sky, the last notes ringing clarion clear in the cold winter air.

Silence.

She stared at them, so she wouldn't look at Conn. They stared back, and then the corner exploded with applause and whoops, nearly lifting the bricks out of the street. She ducked her head, smiled, said thank you until she thought the words were meaningless. Then, because she couldn't stand it anymore, she slanted a look at Conn.

Tears stood in his eyes. He hadn't moved, looked like he wouldn't ever move. The cop beside him had tactfully moved to the intersection and was helping a couple of tourists find a restaurant. The crowd clapped and clapped and clapped, calling for an encore, but Cady barely heard them.

She put her hand to her heart. *I'm yours.*

He nodded. Blinked. Looked up at the sky. When he looked back at her, he withdrew his hand from his pocket and patted his own heart. *And I'm yours.*

The moment broke when someone surged forward and asked for a selfie, an autograph. She said yes to everyone, until the last person walked away smiling.

Conn straightened and strolled onto the sidewalk. "Sure you're ready to sing that for the rest of your life? Because based on that reaction, I think you're stuck with it."

"Every single day." His face was relaxed, casual, a smile twitching at the corner of his mouth. Conn McCormick, easy and happy and holding her close. "Forever and ever, amen."

He swooped her up in one arm and set her on a low wall surrounding the planter. With the added height they were face to face, which made it so much easier for him to kiss her.

"Well, isn't this cozy?" Chris said. He wore a hat with reindeer antlers on it, and carried a cup of what smelled like spiced cider.

"What are you doing here?"

"You gave a concert. I came to hear it," he said serenely. "And Natalie's working tonight. So am I, for that matter.

This town has a pretty astonishing music scene. I'm going to some clubs." He turned to Conn. "I hear you'll be joining Cady's entourage."

She'd sprung that on him over dinner. "We haven't talked about pay or anything," Cady said. "Conn's got some things to finish up here, too."

Chris's gaze flicked over Conn, clearly assessing what a beat cop in Lancaster would make. Then he pulled out his phone. "Do you know what we paid Evan?"

"No," Cady said. "That's what I pay you for, and I know what I pay you."

Without looking up from his phone, Chris named a figure that made Conn's jaw drop.

"More than the City of Lancaster offers, I assume?"

"It works for me," Conn said.

"You suck at this. You always, always negotiate. I just lowballed you, and Evan did mediocre work," Chris added. "Cady routinely told Evan to fuck off because he was annoying her."

"Well. He did annoy me and he fucked off and here you are. I don't eat tongue," Cady said. "Do not ever mention beef tongue, or any animal's tongue to me in the context of food."

"Okay," Conn said, obviously letting it go.

"I'm not going anywhere for a few months," Cady said, shooting Chris a stubborn look. "So we can finalize salary then. For now, Conn's staying with the police department."

Conn turned to Chris. "Are you okay with this?"

Chris sighed. "You've proved you're a paranoid, suspicious control freak who will stop at nothing to keep Cady safe. I can't believe you accused me of trying to terrorize her!"

"Like you don't eat kittens for breakfast," Conn shot back.

"Oh, I do," Chris said with an evil smile. "I do. But I

use their delicate bones to pick out the tufts of fur left in my fangs so it's not obvious."

"I give up," Cady said, throwing her hands in the air. "The two of you will drive me insane. Just don't mention tongue."

Chris smoothed the front of his jacket. "As I was saying, a paranoid control freak who will stop at nothing to make sure Cady's safe, which is the only thing I care about when it comes to the individual in your role with the Maud Squad."

"Cady. I'm Cady, from here on out."

Chris raised an eyebrow, but acquiesced. "With Cady."

"So we're good," he said to Chris, obviously wanting to hear him say it.

"What do you want, to exchange heart-shaped necklaces and pinkie swear?" At Cady's glare, Chris relented. "We're good. Remember I said that when someone with deeper pockets tries to hire you away from us. Which will happen. Oh, and that song you just sang? The one that didn't sound anything like 'Love-Crossed Stars'? Already on YouTube and already racking up the views. Twenty bucks says I hear from Eric before the night's over."

"This was the stupidest idea ever," Cady said. "Whose idea was it to wait until Christmas Eve to finish shopping?"

Conn wrapped his arm around her waist and pulled her out of the flow of harried last-minute shoppers jostling for space on SoMa's narrow sidewalks. Instantly Cady relaxed into his heat and strength and wrapped her arm around his waist.

"I'm not the one who waited until the last minute to do her shopping." He kissed her ear, then let her go.

"Rub it in." She looked through the shopping bags in her hands and checked the contents against the list in her phone. "You ordered everything online. That's cheating."

"When it comes to buying toys for kids, that's the only smart thing to do."

"True." She looked him up and down. "I doubt you'd be crushed at Toys 'R' Us."

"I wasn't worried about getting crushed. I was worried about having to break up a mob fighting over the last Nintendo DS. Then I'd have to do paperwork."

She laughed, her heart as bright as the lights strung along the overhang. "No paperwork on Christmas Eve."

He reached for her hand, and they strolled down the sidewalk. The crowds were too harried to recognize her, and if they did, they gave her the gift of a quiet night. "What time are the McCools expecting you tomorrow?"

"I said I'd come over for the game."

They were loading their bags into the trunk of the Audi when Cady leaned her hip on the taillight and looked at him. "Is the track open tonight?"

He laughed. "Hell yes. It gives guys an excuse to get out of the house. The weather's turning next week. Between extreme cold and bad weather, we don't run much in January and February."

"How about a couple of runs tonight?"

He thought about it for a moment. Something felt different. Everything felt different since Cady showed up at his door, strong and courageous. For the first time, he would go to the track without an expectation for a particular outcome. Somehow, one one-hundredth of a second didn't feel like the weight of all eternity on his shoulders. "Yeah," he said. "It's a good night for a run."

They drove out to the airfield, and turned into the pit. A rectangle of light shone through the open doorway to the hangar, and some joker had put a light-up Santa and reindeer on the hangar's roof, with Rudolph's nose flashing like a warning beacon. Shane and Finn were there, tinkering with one of the other McCool racer's cars.

"Hey," Shane said warmly, exchanging the now familiar fist clasp and shoulder bump. "Didn't expect to see you here."

Conn shrugged out of his denim jacket and into his racing coat. "I'm feeling good tonight. And I'm too stubborn to quit."

Shane tossed him the keys. "The weather's perfect. Go get 'em, tiger."

He couldn't really explain what was different. The answer was nothing and everything. The car was exactly the same as the last time he drove it, the night Cady sent her Audi flying down the track, a maniacal grin on her face. The weather was nearly identical. But at the same time, everything was different inside him. No matter the time on the board, tonight was his last run.

He rolled up to the warming strip, shifted into first, set the parking brake, and revved the engine. Roiling, oily smoke rose above the rear end. He got a thumbs-up, released the brake, and rolled forward.

Aside from a few heated hours with Cady, he'd never been so present in his body, so comfortable in his own mind. It was, he realized, because he was alone in his mind. All the shame he'd been carrying around, the voices of his family members saying it was time to go, time to pack up and move to the next sofa or partially furnished spare room or, worse, a room crammed with hoarder's crap were gone.

For the first time, he was racing for himself.

When the lights ticked down to green, he floored the accelerator and shot down the runway. A black watch cap over honey-colored hair caught his eye as he whipped past the bleachers. It was another detail, another stream coursing into the river of time carrying him along. The seconds felt elastic, like he had all the time in the world, could hear every revolution of the motor and drive shaft. Each shift felt magical, crisp and clean. Flow. Perfect, perfect flow.

Nine point nine-nine flashed up on the clock. When he rounded the corner to crawl back to the line of cars waiting for their run, Shane and Finn were going berserk, jumping and shouting, fists pumping in the air. People on their way to and from the concession stand made a wide circle around the two of them, turning from spots in the stands to stare, because Shane put the cool in McCool. It wasn't a great time, but they knew what it meant to him. He'd tied his dad.

Shane jogged up to meet him at the back of the line. "Yeah!" he shouted as he leaned into the window. "Nine point nine-fucking-nine!"

"Nailed it!" Finn shouted from behind him.

"You going again?" Shane asked.

He looked over at Cady. Tears stood in her eyes, but she lifted her fists over her head and pumped them twice. "Go again!"

"Yeah."

"Good." Shane swatted affectionately at Conn's helmeted head. "You own this tonight. Watch second. You still rush out of second."

It didn't matter if he did or didn't have it. This was his last run. Nine point nine eight or not, he was setting down this burden and moving on. The only way to prove he was a better man than his father wasn't to beat his time, but to be that man. With Cady, with her family, within the department.

Wait. Warm the tires. Wait some more. Watch the lights tick from red to orange to green, slowly, so slowly. Time had stretched and doubled back on itself. He had all the time in the world to step on the gas, shift through the Camaro's range of gears. The engine purred like a kitten, a soft, sweet rumble in his chest.

He knew. Deep in his bones, in his heart, he knew. He didn't even have to look at the clock, or turn to see Shane's and Finn's reactions. He could feel their energy all the way across the track. 9.97. He'd broken out. Disqualified.

Free.

He'd beaten his father's time. The extra weight he'd been carrying was his shame, his loneliness, his fear of never belonging anywhere. He'd put down his demons and picked up Cady's hand, trading the existential weight for a connection both weightless and stronger than steel.

He parked by Shane's truck and got out of the car only to get rammed back into it from the force of Shane's hug. Finn was applauding wildly, the sound muffled by the thick gloves covering his hands. Was this how Cady felt at a concert, this kind of exuberant, wild energy coming at her from the audience? Incredible.

"Damn," Shane finished. "Just . . . goddamn. You did it."

"I did." Conn bounced the keys gently in his palm. Then he caught Finn's eye and tossed them to him.

Finn caught them, then looked at Conn, as wide-eyed as a little kid on Christmas. "I can drive her the rest of the night? Thanks, man!"

"You can drive her the rest of your life, or hers, which will probably be shorter." Conn reached into the glove box and pulled out the title. "She's yours."

Finn's eyes got impossibly wider. "No way."

"Way," Conn and Shane said in unison.

"You should keep her." Shaking his head, Finn held out the keys. "She was your dad's car. Your dad gave her to you."

She was his dad's car, his pride and joy, but to Conn an anvil dragging him down like Wile E. Coyote after he ran off a cliff. His father never gave him the car. Conn just took it on, because he wanted to be close to his dad, to cling to all he had left of him. "Now I'm giving her to you."

"What's Mom going to say?" Finn said, looking at Shane.

"Conn and I talked to her a couple of hours ago. She says no street racing or she'll drive the car to the salvage yard herself, but okay."

"I've got a couple hundred bucks saved," Finn said. "I'll get you the cash as soon as I get to the bank. Or I can transfer the money with my phone. What email address—?"

Conn held up his hand, stopping Finn midsentence. "You're going to need that money. The head gasket's going to blow any run."

Finn seemed about to protest again, but shut his mouth when Conn gave him his stare. "Thanks," he saw awkwardly. He looked to be somewhere between tears and total joy. Conn remembered what that was like, to want wheels, cool wheels, that thing that defined you to your peers.

"I catch you street racing her and I'll have your ass in jail so fast you'll think you were caught in a time warp. And then I'll call your mom. Got a pen?"

"I won't. Just the track." He launched himself at Conn, thumping him on the back, all gangly teenage puppy energy. Conn took the pen Shane extracted from his jacket pocket and scrawled his signature on the title. Finn's hands were shaking when he took it. "Thank you. I mean it. She's the coolest car out here. Do you care if I tinker with the gear ratio?"

"She's not my car anymore," Conn said gently, feeling an unutterable sense of relief. "Turn her into a clown car like the Shriners drive. Go to town. She's all yours."

"Come back and race her any time," Finn said.

"Thanks," Conn said, genuinely surprised. "I'll do that."

Just like that, he turned and walked away from the fight he'd been fighting his entire life, whether to be like his dad or to leave him behind. His dad had taught him to go down fighting, locked in a cage match, but Cady taught him that sometimes the only way to win was to walk away. Before he'd had nothing to walk to.

Now he did. He had Cady.

She was waiting a few feet away, smiling. "That was a nice thing to do," she said when he joined her.

"Looks like I'm going to be traveling a lot in the future." He shrugged. "He loves that car."

"Win-win." She snuggled under his arm.

"Getting cold?"

"A little," she said. "I'm dressed for shopping, not the track."

"Let's get you home, then."

She looked up at him. "Good. A fire and some hot cocoa sound perfect right now." She lifted her chin for a kiss, hummed when his lips brushed hers. "But I already am home, Conn. I'm with you."

It all came together, the song and the season, Cady's body against his, the feeling of love and belonging transformed into a sense of weightlessness that carried him off the airfield. It was true. She belonged to him, and he belonged to her.

He was home.

Read on for a sneak preview of Anne Calhoun's next book

TURN ME LOOSE

Coming soon from St. Martin's Paperbacks

"Okay, team, huddle up."

The evening birdsong trilled through the screen door as servers, chefs, sous chefs, and the night's hostess gathered around Riva. She leaned against the prep table and scanned their faces, checking in with each kid, all of them involved in the East Side Community Center's after-school and weekend programs. The servers wore identical uniforms of black pants with black shirts tucked in, and a knee-length white apron. Kiara, the night's hostess, came in last, pen and paper poised to write down the night's menu before transferring it to the chalkboard intended for the front porch.

"Run it down for me, Chef Isaiah," Riva said.

Aware of his lead role in the kitchen, Isaiah straightened. "We have three mains today, the usual rib eye and chicken, and the special, salmon seared in a sauce of shallots and grapefruit, accompanied by asparagus and potatoes roasted in garlic, rosemary, and olive oil. Appetizers are bruschetta, mussels, and we have Brussels sprouts roasted in olive oil with bacon and onions."

Riva nodded approvingly. He'd come a long way from the kid who couldn't tell a Brussels sprout from a stalk of asparagus. "Anyone have any questions about preparation? All of the greens are from the early plantings at the farm, so they're nice and tender."

Her dream was to eventually quadruple her greenhouse space, but her mantra was to take it slow, grow organically, and most importantly, without drawing any attention to herself.

"Where's the salmon from?" Amber asked.

"Alaska. Flown in yesterday," Isaiah said without prompting. Amber made a note on her server's pad. "It's as fresh as you're gonna get in landlocked Lancaster."

"What do you recommend?" Kiara asked.

"It's all good," Isaiah said, "but if anyone asks, go with the salmon."

"What are we gonna eighty-six first?"

"The salmon," Isaiah said. He extended his hand over the large, cast-iron pan heating on the eight-burner stove, the movement automatic, practiced.

"Thanks, Isaiah," Riva said. "I'll come around one last time to check your stations. I'm working the front tonight, so you guys are on your own."

Subtle signs of tension rippled through the group. "You've got this. It's a Tuesday night, so we won't be very busy, but even if we were, even if we got slammed by Maud Ward and her entire entourage, you'd still have this," Riva said. "Work your station, and work together."

Kimmy-Jean, a newer addition to the program, worried at her lower lip. "What if no one comes?"

In the spring Oasis operated on a pop-up basis, opening on selected evenings and promoted through social media only. "They'll come," Isaiah said. "You just worry about getting your mise done, yo."

She walked through the kitchen, swiping up a bit of

spilled parmesan, adding extra bowls to Carlos's station, making sure the busboy/dishwasher, Blake, had his trays lined up and ready to go. Out front, the tables were all neatly set, silverware wrapped in linen, bud vases with a single bloom and small votive candles centered between the settings. "Let's not light the candles just yet," she said to Kiara.

The front was designed to look like a large, screened-in porch, the glass windows folded back to open the room to the breezes drifting in from the eastern fields, carrying a scent of warm earth and tender, growing things. The walls were covered in weathered barn boards, the tables made from smaller pieces reclaimed when she tore down the outbuildings that were ruined beyond repair. The server's station was just outside the kitchen, making it easy for the staff to grab a pitcher of water or a damp rag as they passed through.

Looking around, Riva couldn't believe she'd made this herself: supervised the renovation, done most of the interior work and decorating herself, scavenged and bargain shopped, painted walls and built tables. She'd come a long way in the last eight years, and the farm and restaurant were only stage one of her business plan.

Their first customers were a couple who chose the twilit section. Riva lit their candle and offered them the menu. "Do you want the windows shut?" the man asked his date. He was obviously anxious, taking out his phone and silencing the ringer, setting it on the table, then putting it in a pocket.

"I'm good," she said, giving him a pleased smile. "The air's still pretty warm. Maybe later."

"I'll be back in a minute with your drinks," Riva said, then looked up as the door opened again.

The evening progressed smoothly, just as Riva predicted. The program was a simple one, developed in conjunction with the East Side Community Center run by Pastor Webber. Get kids who'd grown up in impoverished, blighted neighborhoods so common to food deserts access to fresh air, sunshine, and the earth. Teach them to grow their own food, and cook it, which enabled Riva to teach them about healthy eating. It also meant Riva could give back, pay for the mistakes she'd made, and help other kids avoid the same mistakes.

Working in the front let things develop organically, for better or worse, in the kitchen. She liked waiting tables. Most of the recipes were her own, and getting feedback directly from customers enabled her to fine-tune accordingly. It meant she was close if the kids really needed her, but not watching like one of the hawks circling over a field, ready to pounce on every single mistake like a field mouse.

She automatically looked up when the front door opened and saw a single man standing there, his face hidden by the shadows. Tall and lean, he was nothing but a silhouette of a male figure in a suit, nothing that should have made her heart thunk hard against her chest and adrenaline dump into her nervous system. All her muscles screamed at her to drop the box of matches and bolt.

Don't be ridiculous, her brain told her body.

Then he took another step forward, far enough into the light for Riva to see his face. She knew she should have trusted her body, but by then it was too late.

Officer Hawthorn stood in her restaurant.

Kiara wore her most practiced smile as she approached him, menu in hand. Riva couldn't hear their conversation over her blood thrumming in her ears, but she could decipher it well enough based on the way he looked around, then the way Kiara extended her arm.

She'd seated him in Riva's section. A two-top, in the corner. He always sat with his back to the wall. Riva remembered that well enough from six years earlier. The table gave him a view of all entrances and doors, and the parking lot.

"Blaze on table fourteen," Kiara said to Riva, using the kitchen's slang for a hot customer.

Riva stifled a hysterical laugh. Ian Hawthorn was a blaze in every sense of the word, hot, and so dangerous she should turn and run. She could ask someone else to take the table. It wasn't a practice she encouraged, as it led to confusion in the restaurant, and there was no advantage to it for the kids. All tips were pooled and split among the kitchen staff and servers at the end of the night. They worked for each other, not just for themselves.

Worse, if she asked another server to take the table, the kids would wonder why. In milliseconds, they'd peg Hawthorn for a cop and start asking questions that would lead them to her past, to the mistakes she'd made, to the girl she'd left behind. Right now her goal was to serve him and get him out of the restaurant before anything happened to jeopardize the life she'd built.

Besides, it had to happen sometime, meeting him again. She'd been dreading this for the last six years. Might as well get it over with, so she could move on. He was her past; the Oasis was her future.

Shoulders squared, she took a deep breath and let it out slowly, then plucked her notebook from her apron as she walked to the table. "Welcome to the Oasis. My name's Riva and I'll be taking care of you tonight."

The look on his face when she started talking was priceless, almost worth what it cost her to walk across the floor and talk to him. Eight years earlier, Officer Ian Hawthorn had been all cop, lacking a sense of humor or a personality. His robotlike personality scared her, the implacability of it, the way he assessed situations, events, people, summed them up, then discarded them or used them, however best

suited him. But when he paused in the act of lifting open
the flap on his laptop bag and looked at her face, his jaw
literally dropped open.

Priceless.

Then his gaze skimmed her from her ponytail to the
tips of her clogs. She knew how it looked, wearing the
same uniform as the other servers, black pants and blouse
buttoned to her collarbone, her makeup subdued to the
point of pale and nondescript. In every way she was con-
scious of setting an example for the kids from the ESCC.
His reaction time, always quick, hadn't dulled. A split
second to look her over, the sharp flick of his gaze striking sparks she felt from her earlobes to her nipples to
deep in her belly. That's what it had been like, his gaze
flint against the tinder of her young, impetuous desire.

Then he shut his mouth, and the laptop bag. "Hi, Riva."

She ignored that. "Can I get you something to drink
while you look at the menu? We have craft beers from
several of the local breweries."

He looked at the menu, then back at her. "Water.
Thanks."

Her skin crawled as she spun on her heel and walked
away. The look in his eyes before he adopted the all-too-
familiar expressionless demeanor had been shock, then
pity. When she'd met him she'd been a college student.
Now, to his eyes, she was a waitress. She felt nineteen
years old again, running through every single thing she
said to Ian, every look, every shift of her body, frantically
trying to reassure herself she hadn't given anything away.

I'll be taking care of you today. It sounded like an in-
nuendo. God knew she'd thrown enough of them at him,
desperate, angry, humiliated, pushing back the only way
she could. He'd held all the cards, and she'd hated him
for it.

"It was your fault," she muttered as she poured ice water into a glass. "You were the stupid one. He just did his job."

She snagged a warm bread basket from the kitchen. "We still have the salmon?"

"Got plenty," Isaiah called from the stove.

When she came back out, Hawthorn was staring at his laptop screen. She set the bread basket on the table. "Are you waiting for someone?" He had to be waiting for someone.

"No. Just me."

Her heart did a traitorous little skip in her chest. He was alone. Why was he alone? She gathered the silverware and bread plate from the spot across from him. "Do you have any questions about the menu? We're a farm to table restaurant," she started. "The origins for the ingredients are noted on the menu. With the exception of the salmon, they're all from Rolling Hill Farm, or other farms around Lancaster. The rib eye comes from a ranch up the road. We harvested the asparagus this afternoon, and the Brussels sprouts this morning."

His gaze was no less piercing, six years later. "What do you recommend, Riva?"

He used her first name like he always had, like he had a right. The only reason she knew his first name was Ian was because she'd heard other cops call him that.

Assuming his tastes hadn't changed in the last seven years, she knew what he liked well enough to answer that question. Nights sitting next to him in an unmarked police car often included a run through a drive-through window, so she knew he preferred grilled chicken to burgers, salads to fries. She'd spent enough time with cops to know their diets were frequently atrocious; the Eastern precinct smelled of sweat, gun oil, coffee, and fast food grease. "The steak is our specialty, and very good but to-night I'd recommend the salmon. Chef Isaiah developed the sauce. It's a grapefruit and shallot sauce, very light, and it's delicious."

"Does it come with the asparagus?"

"Yes."

"I'll have that."

"Wine with the meal? Beer?"

He scanned the wines listed on the back. "A glass of the Shale white," he said.

Dismissed. She hurried to the kitchen and put in the order, then poured a glass of wine. She left the glass with him, touched base with her other tables, and brought more bread and a second beer to the first-date couple, who had both set aside their phones and were leaning over the table, actively engaged in conversation. She watched them from the safety of the server's station. It was an experience she hadn't allowed herself in seven years, and the reason why was sitting at table fourteen. Any relationship more serious than a casual hookup would require her to either tell the truth about who she'd been, or found a relationship on lies. She couldn't bring herself to do either.

With no appetizer, his meal should be ready in under twelve minutes. At the ten-minute mark she ducked into the kitchen. Isaiah meticulously wiped a dab of sauce from the edge of the plate, then presented it to her with a flourish. She gave the kitchen staff a thumbs up, took the plate from him, and carried it through the door.

On the way to the table she ran through the ways she could tell him he was wrong about her, that she wasn't just a waitress—except there was nothing wrong with be-ing a waitress—that she owned this building, the farm it sat on, and the tiny house hidden in the folds of the valley, too, that she'd been able to get loans, pay them back on time, help others. But in the end, she couldn't change the past, and she knew perfectly well that of all people, Officer Ian Hawthorn had no reason to give her the benefit of the doubt.

She set the plate in front of him without comment. "Can I get you anything else?"

"No. Thanks." He picked up his knife and fork.

"I'll be back to check on you in a few minutes."

The first-date couple ordered two bowls of ice cream drizzled with hot, dark chocolate and topped with raspberries. Head held high, she walked to the first-date couple's table and set out their desserts. "Enjoy," she said with a smile.

A couple of short yelps from the kitchen, an *Oh fuck!* audible throughout the dining room. The swinging door to the kitchen slammed against the wall. Her nose knew first, the stench of acrid smoke already filtering into the room. Three strides and Riva was through the door. A grease fire roared on the stove, spattering everyone in the vicinity with burning oil. Isaiah was on his knees in front of the big stainless stove. Beside him, Jake swatted at the fire with his dish towel, the surest way to injure himself.

"Stop!" Riva barked.

Jake stopped.

"It's a grease fire," she said. A small one, at that, but fire was fire. Her voice was calm, only slightly louder than normal, but it got the attention of every kid in the room. "Work the plan. Step one."

Galvanized, Jake scrabbled at the knob controlling the gas heat and first turned it up. "Shit," he said when the flames spurted for the range hood. He twisted the knob the other direction and the gas died.

Kimmy-Jean had a big water pitcher filled. Arm extended, Riva stepped in front of her. "Step two."

"I'm on it." Isaiah came up with the lid matching the

cast-iron pan and slammed it down on the pan, effectively throttling the flames. Oily black smoke hung around the now-silenced stove.

"It was a small fire, so what else would have worked?" Riva said.

"Baking soda. Lots of it," Jake said.

"Right. Remember that only works for small fires. What don't you do?"

"Pick up the pot," three of the kids responded. She had them now, back in their brains and bodies, connected to themselves, each other, her. "You'll burn yourself," Kiara added.

"Good. What else don't you do?"

"Throw water on it."

"Why?"

"Because water won't put it out, and the splatter can spread the flames or burn someone."

"Sorry," Kimmy-Jean whispered, her pale face flaming almost as brightly as the fire had. "I didn't know."

"Now you do," Riva said gently. "This one didn't spread. What if it had?"

"Fire extinguisher," Kiara said.

As one, everyone in the kitchen turned to look at the brand-new extinguisher, hanging on the wall beside the door to the dining room.

Where Ian Hawthorn stood, just inside the door, his laptop clasped loosely in his hand.

All the air sucked back out of the room, like he was the still center of a black hole. "Po-po in the house," someone murmured.